THE DREAM CATCHER

Sarah, Roz and Janie all have a dream – for Sarah, it's finding a way through the struggle of bringing up her partially deaf son Rory; for Roz, it is overcoming the difficulty of keeping her farm afloat and for Janie, it is how to escape an ever-growing emptiness in her life. When Janie's brother, a top City analyst, suggests they pool their money and play the stock market, they begin to make serious money. The sort of money that makes dreams come true. Good dreams can easily turn bad and when the gains are high, so are the risks...

THE DREAM CATCHER

THE DREAM CATCHER

by

Maria Barrett

Magna Large Print Books
Long Preston, North Yorkshire,
BD23 4ND, England.

British Library Cataloguing in Publication Data.

Barrett, Maria
　　The dream catcher.

　　A catalogue record of this book is
　　available from the British Library

　　ISBN　0-7505-1853-7

First published in Great Britain in 2001 by Little, Brown & Co.

Copyright © Maria Barrett 2001

Cover illustration by arrangement with Little, Brown & Co. Ltd.

The moral right of the author has been asserted

Published in Large Print 2002 by arrangement with
Little, Brown & Company UK

Magna Large Print is an imprint of Library Magna Books Ltd.

Printed and bound in Great Britain by
T.J. (International) Ltd., Cornwall, PL28 8RW

Extract from *Lady Chatterley's Lover* by D. H. Lawrence reproduced by kind permission of Laurence Pollinger Ltd and the estate of Frieda Lawrence Ravagli.

For my parents,
with love.

ACKNOWLEDGEMENTS

The last part of the novel, the signing off – with relief. Not that I don't love my work, of course I do, but there is always a blissful feeling of having connected with the world again, of managing to finish my sentences once it's over. It will be a relief as well to Sarah Dominick – née Shoesmith – who has been amazing this last year at not only finishing my sentences for me, but also interpreting instructions half-given, thinking on her feet and organising our lives with huge energy and efficiency. Thank you, Sarah, for your kindness to us all and for helping to make this year such a happy one.

I have a long list of other thank you's to the friends I have pestered with questions for my research and the people on the end of a telephone line I have cold-called and who have been incredibly helpful. Sally Drummond, who gave me inspiration for Roz while lime-waxing my bannister, Sarah Foulkes, Richard Pyper, who amended the medical details, Wil and Tracey Rydon, who talked me through owning a cow, David Roblin for his help with investment research, Dinah Lamming for answering all my banal questions about the City, and Liz Lawrence for her help with town planning regulations. I would like to thank Lloyds TSB, Walton-on-Thames, for information on how to raise money, various people at the Financial Services Authority, several private investigations agencies who would not be named, and Neil Brazil at the Stock Exchange. As always I should like to thank my editor, Barbara Boote, especially this time for not making me rewrite the entire novel, Mic Cheetham, my agent, for her support, Helen Anderson for continuing the excellent editing and Joanne Coen for a superb copyediting job.

Finally, I would like to thank my children, William, Lily and Edward, and my husband, Jules, for making all this worthwhile.

APRIL

Chapter One

Sarah pulled her old and rather battered Mini Metro into a parking space between two new, shiny four-wheel-drive vehicles and yanked up the handbrake. It made a rough crunching sound as she did so and she had to hold it for a moment, then jerk it violently up into place. She switched the engine off and climbed out of the car, slamming the door hard because the lock was damaged and that was the only way to ensure that it closed properly. The car rattled in protest as she walked away.

Sarah was early today but, as usual, Janie Leighton was there already. Always the first: clean trousers, smart sweater, expensive handbag, hair brushed and lipstick on. She stood alone in the playground, ten minutes before anyone else had arrived.

'Hello, Janie.'

Sarah crossed to her. They had been friends since their children had started at Wynchcombe Primary.

'Hi, Sarah. Did you finish early today?'

'No, I've been promoted.' Sarah worked for the local supermarket. It wasn't exactly a career, but it helped pay the bills.

'Have you? Gosh, that's great. Well done.'

'Don't get too excited.' Sarah gave a small, embarrassed laugh. 'I've been moved from checkout

to customer services. It's more money, margin-
ally, so I've cut down to four hours instead of
five.'

'Good for you. So at least you can put your feet
up for an hour before you collect Rory.'

'I wish. No, I can get some shopping, load the
washing machine, empty it, load the dryer, shove
the Hoover round and prepare some supper, so
as to have a bit more time to spend on Rory's
homework – when we're not doing speech
therapy, special English or listening skills that is!'
Again Sarah laughed, but falsely, and Janie gently
patted her arm. Rory was partially deaf and
sometimes the effort of it all seemed overwhelming.

'Come for tea,' she said, 'on Wednesday, or
Thursday. Can you?'

'Yes, thanks, we'd like that.' Sarah looked
towards the school and at the line of children
waiting at the glass door, ready to come out.
Little Katie Leighton was at the front; a gleaming, smiling, perfect child. Janie, she thought –
and not without a tinge of resentment – had no
idea how hard life could be. Why should she? A
GP's wife with a comfortable existence, needing
nothing, never stressed, happily married with a
normal, healthy, charming little girl to nurture.
But then she would touch Sarah with an invitation or a comment just at the right moment,
just when it was needed most, and Sarah would
wonder how Janie could have such intuition for
sadness. 'Actually, we'd love to come for tea,'
Sarah said. 'It would be a nice break for both of
us.'

'Good. Ah, here they are.' Janie moved forward as Katie turned to shake hands with her teacher and then rushed out of the classroom door towards her. Sarah looked at Miss Meaney, who motioned for her to come over.

'I've been summoned,' she commented, walking past Janie. 'Again. See you tomorrow.' Janie waved, then took Katie's hand in her own, leading her towards the car. Sarah went on to the classroom.

'Mrs Greg, I wonder if I could have a word?'

Sarah smiled, her face heavy with the burden of having to do so, and waited. She watched Miss Meaney expertly dispatch the children to their parents and saw Rory at the back of the class, head in a book, oblivious to the fact that the classroom had emptied and he was almost alone.

'I just wanted to say,' Miss Meaney began, as the last child went out of earshot, 'that we had a bit of an incident today.' She lowered her voice. 'The batteries went on his hearing aids in the middle of story time and Mrs Perry thought he wasn't paying attention and told him off. I'm afraid that he got a bit upset because he said he couldn't hear and...' She broke off. 'Ah, hello, Rory. I'm just having a word with Mummy, saying how well you've been doing recently and telling her about your aids today in story time.'

Rory Greg smiled at his mother and Sarah's heart brimmed over with love. She held out her hand and he came and took it, then she bent, to put her face level with his, and spoke loudly and clearly, as she always did. 'Hello, love. Did you have a good day?' He nodded.

'I'm not sure we put his aids in properly,' Miss Meaney said. 'I'm not terribly good at it...'

Sarah tilted Rory's face to the right, then the left, checking his ears. She smiled and stood straight. 'They're a bit skewwhiff but I'll fix them in the car.'

'Can I go and play tag with Katie, Mummy?' Sarah looked across and saw Katie Leighton playing with another little girl while Janie stood deep in conversation with the mother. 'Of course.' Rory handed her his school bag and his coat and ran off. Miss Meaney smiled after him. 'I'm sorry about today,' she said. 'He's been doing so well this term that I was worried it might mar his confidence.'

'He'll be fine,' Sarah replied. 'We have these little hiccups every now and then. It's very hard to tell sometimes whether he really can't hear, or he doesn't want to hear.' She smiled. 'Selective deafness and all that.' They both turned for a moment to watch Rory and Katie playing tag in the playground.

'I'll let you get on,' Sarah said. 'Is that Justin Betts still here?'

Miss Meaney turned. 'Yes. It's the third time he's been late this week.'

'Shall I take him for you? I'll hang on until Roz gets here if you like.'

'Would you mind? That would be very helpful indeed. I've got a meeting in ten minutes. Are you sure you don't mind?'

'Of course not. Justin?' Sarah called out. 'D'you want to come and play with Rory until Mummy gets here?'

18

Justin Betts, a big child with a mop of unruly brown hair, nodded and was out of the classroom in seconds. The game got louder and faster almost immediately he joined in.

'Thanks, Mrs Greg,' Miss Meaney said. 'I'll see you tomorrow.'

'Yes.' Sarah turned and Janie waved at her. She glanced in Rory's bag to check for his homework, then went across to join her.

Roz Betts was driving down School Lane too fast. Twice she had pulled up sharply to let other cars pass where the road became narrow, as she yelled at Kitty and Oliver in the back to keep the noise down.

'I can't concentrate!' she shouted. 'We're late, Justin is waiting for us and I'm trying to get to school as quick as I can, so *please* will you both stop arguing!' She stopped for a third time and waved as one of the mothers from Justin's class drove past. 'And if I hear that you've taken that guinea pig out of the box there will be *big* trouble! Understood?' She revved and the car leapt forward. She had one eye on the clock and one eye on the children in the back. 'Bugger,' she muttered low under her breath. It was three forty-five, she had to collect Justin, drop the guinea pig off to the Walshes, deliver the eggs and then get back to feed the pigs and do the pony. '*Oliver!* Leave that guinea pig where it is!'

She turned into the drive of the school and slowed down. Pedestrians, children, their mothers and their dogs, along with cars parked all the way up the drive, were the external hazards to

19

negotiate; Oliver and Kitty, four and three respectively, in the back of the car were the internal ones. Roz wasn't concentrating as well as she should have been and as she swung round the corner of the drive, intending to pull up right outside the playground, Kitty let out a scream and she jerked round to see what the hell the matter was.

Rory was 'it'. He ran round the playground, a swift, neat sprinter, with Justin Betts in his sight, but Justin was too fast. He was nimble and adept on his feet and as he darted round the slide and ran to the gates, Sarah, one eye on the game, shouted for them all to mind the road. Justin ignored her and ran out of the gate and across the road towards the playing fields. Rory!' Sarah shouted, 'stay in the playground!' But Rory didn't hear her. Intent on the game, and with his hearing aids not quite fitted properly, he dashed out after Justin just as Roz rounded the bend. She turned to see why Kitty had screamed, a guinea pig flew across into the front seat and she slammed her foot down on to the accelerator instead of the brake.

'*Rory!*' Sarah's voice cut the air like the howl of an animal.

Roz felt the thud of a small body against the car. She froze for a split second, then hit the brake. She thought she was going to be sick.

Sarah ran. She sprinted out of the playground and fell to her knees by her child. 'Oh God,' she cried. 'Oh God, Rory, please, Rory, please be all right...'

Roz climbed out of the car. Her whole body

20

was shaking and she thought her legs were going to buckle from under her. She knelt down by Sarah and Rory. There was the most terrible silence and even the air seemed to stop moving, then Rory opened his eyes and said, 'It's OK, Mum, I think I'm OK,' and Roz started to cry.

Janie and Roz sat in silence in the A & E department of St Richards Hospital in Chichester. Roz had her head in her hands, while Janie watched Katie on a row of seats opposite read a book to Kitty and Oliver, and, although hating herself for it, thanked God it hadn't been her daughter. She had brought Roz and the children to the hospital in her car. They had driven in complete silence, following the ambulance, and all the way there she had been unable to escape the sick feeling of terror that it could have been Katie. She was ashamed of herself at such a terrible reaction, but Katie was her life: Katie was everything.

She glanced sidelong at Roz, who was now biting her already devastated nails and rubbing anxiously at the ingrained dirt on her hands. 'Are you OK?' Janie asked. But Roz didn't look up; she simply shook her head.

A minute or so later Roz said, 'I just keep thinking, how could I have been so stupid? Why didn't I just stop and take a breath and calm down? I honestly don't know what happened, Janie. It all happened so quickly and it was such a stupid mistake!'

Janie didn't answer. There was nothing she felt she could honestly say that would help.

'God, I was in such a rush,' Roz went on. 'I've

got so much on my plate, what with the small holding, the organic vegetables, the free range chickens, the pigs, the dogs, the cat, the pony, the kids and the eternal bloody struggle for money. I just don't know how to cope.' She stared down at her hands, picking at a torn cuticle on her nail. 'I'm on a constant treadmill; no wonder I make mistakes.'

'You do too much,' Janie said. She felt she had to say something, that Roz expected some sort of comment, but she was loath to say what she really felt – that Roz was going to kill herself, or someone else, if she didn't slow down. But, sensitive and upset, Roz misinterpreted the remark as criticism. 'What d'you mean I do too much? How the hell can I do anything less?'

Janie's mouth dried up. It was her nature to skirt issues, to disguise the truth if it was even the slightest bit unpleasant. 'I don't know,' she stammered, 'I just think that you need to slow down, that's all.'

'That's all! Jesus, Janie! Would you like to tell me how? How do I slow down and still manage to get everything done?' Roz's voice had risen and several people looked over. 'If you really think that's what I need to do then by all means tell me how to do it. Please.'

Janie flushed. 'It was just a suggestion,' she said quietly. 'I don't know how to do it.'

'Exactly!' Roz stood up. She wiped her sweating palms on already dirty jeans and stared at Janie. She was feeling distraught, guilt-stricken and afraid and she took it out on the person nearest to her. 'How *could* you?' she snapped, louder than she should have. 'When the most stressful thing in your week is fitting in a hair appointment.'

The children stopped reading and stared at her. Roz knew immediately that she had gone too far. 'Oh God, I'm sorry,' she mumbled. 'I'm sorry, Janie, I'm upset, I...'

Janie looked down. The bloody awful truth of it was that, upset or not, Roz was right. 'It's OK...' she looked across at Katie. 'Don't stop reading sweetheart,' she said gently, 'Oliver and Kitty are really enjoying the story.' Katie nodded, but didn't resume reading. She stared at Janie for some sort of reassurance and so Janie smiled at her to cover her distress.

'I think I'll try and find Sarah,' Roz said. 'See what's happening. D'you want a coffee?'

Janie nodded.

'Milk, no sugar, right?'

'Yes.'

There was a moment of awkward silence, then Roz dug her hands in the pockets of her jeans and walked off.

'You'll need some change,' Janie called after her, holding out her purse.

'Oh God, yes, of course.' Roz shook her head and took the purse. Another mistake they both thought but, naturally, neither of them said it.

Sarah sat in a plastic chair by the side of Rory's bed in a curtained-off bay in A & E. They were waiting for the results of Rory's X-rays. He had, she'd been told, mild concussion and probably two broken ribs, but the X-ray would confirm this diagnosis and show up anything more serious. He was, the nurse emphasised, extremely lucky; she couldn't stress enough the importance of road sense.

Sarah had replied that road sense was far easier if you could actually hear the cars coming, and she'd wanted to add that if Rory had had the digital hearing aids that he needed then he might have been able to do just that. But she hadn't said it. She was talking to a nurse who had been sent to comfort, not to take an ear-bashing about NHS funding.

She looked up as the curtain was drawn back and a houseman put his head round it. 'Mrs Greg?'

'Yes?'

He came in and sat on the edge of Rory's bed. 'Hi, I'm Dr Allen. I've been having a look at Rory's X-rays.' He turned to Rory and Sarah noticed how he made sure that Rory could see his face properly before he spoke: she immediately liked him for it. 'How are you doing, young man?' he asked.

'Fine.'

'You gave everyone a nasty scare getting yourself run over like that!' He smiled and Rory smiled back. 'Still, you seem to be in pretty good shape. Not too much damage done by the looks of things, although you're off games for a few weeks. You've cracked a rib and it'll be sore for a while. Know where your ribs are?'

Rory put his hand on his chest. 'Where it hurts?'

'Sharp answer.'

He turned to Sarah. 'How long has he been

without hearing?'

'Since birth. He's been aided since he was three.' Sarah wanted to add more; she had the sudden urge to unburden herself with the whole story, every fearful, painful, frustrating moment, but she held it down. He was just another face in a white coat and God knows she'd seen enough of them over the past six years.

Dr Allen leant forward and peered at Rory's ears. 'Cool aids. I bet they help, don't they?'

'Sometimes.'

'Perhaps you ought to use them along with these.' He pointed to Rory's eyes. 'Watch and listen, especially when crossing the road.' He flicked Rory's chin. 'You're dismissed.'

Dr Allen glanced back at Sarah. 'The X-rays showed up what we thought; he's got one cracked rib, which might need paracetamol if it gets too sore, but the skull x-ray was clear. I've got a head injury card here which gives you a list of the symptoms and signs to watch out for. He's had a crack to the head so just keep an eye on him for forty-eight hours.'

Sarah nodded.

'If you're worried about anything, pop him down and we'll take a look. OK?'

'Yes, thanks.' She stood.

'Right then, I'll leave you to get dressed and go home. Take care, Rory.'

Rory nodded.

'Say goodbye please, Rory, and thank you.'

'Goodbye please, Rory, and thank you,' he obliged.

Sarah smiled. 'I didn't mean that!'

'I know.' He looked across at the doctor and said, 'Thank you, Dr Allen.' The doctor smiled and left the cubicle.

Sarah reached forward to help him off the bed. 'Come here and let's get you dressed.'

'Ouch!'

'I'll give you ouch!' Sarah said, then she gently pulled him to her and hugged him. 'Oh Rory Greg,' she murmured, 'what are we going to do with you?'

An hour later, Janie swung her Land Rover into the space next to Sarah's car outside the school and stopped, yanking on the handbrake. She glanced over her shoulder at Roz in the back with Kitty on her lap, then she looked at Sarah in the front. 'Is everyone OK?' she asked. There was a murmur of assent but no one made any attempt to move. Janie opened the car door and in the harsh interior light she could see exhaustion etched on Sarah's face. They all sat for a few moments, then Roz opened the rear door and jumped down, sliding Kitty on to the ground. 'Oli and Justin out now please, we've got to get home.'

Justin unfastened his seat belt, then did his brother's for him. Both boys shuffled out of the car clutching their bags and the guinea pig, which was safely back in its box, and Roz leant back in for her bag. 'Thank you, Janie,' she said. 'I'm sorry, you know, for things earlier.'

Janie shrugged. 'Forget it.'

Roz straightened up as Sarah climbed out of the car.

'Are you all right?' Sarah asked.

'I should be asking you that.' Roz stared at the ground. 'Sarah, I don't know what to say, I'm so sorry, I...'

Sarah touched Roz's arm. 'It's OK, he's OK. It was an accident.'

Roz looked up. 'Will you be OK on your own? D'you want me to come over tonight with a bottle of wine?'

'I'll be fine. I'm always on my own; tonight's no different.'

'I know that, but what with all the trauma today, I just meant...'

'I know what you meant, Roz, and thanks, but Rory and I will be fine. I think we'll have a pizza in front of the TV and a can of coke each.'

'Right.' Roz walked across to her car and unlocked it. She hustled the children inside, strapped them in and started the engine to get the heaters going. It was cold and she realised that she had begun to shiver.

'Bye!' she called out before getting into the car. Sarah waved and Janie who was helping Katie and Rory out of the small seats in the boot of her Land Rover, glanced up and smiled. Roz reversed, very slowly, as the children sat exhausted in the back and the guinea pig, unaware of all the trauma it had caused, made small whining noises inside its box.

Janie carried Rory to Sarah's car as Sarah unlocked it, and then Janie carefully deposited him inside. 'All right?'

'Yes, thank you.'

As she straightened, Sarah said, 'Why was Roz apologising?'

Janie shrugged. 'It isn't important.'

'Yes, it is. She upset you, didn't she? I can tell by your face.'

'She spoke the truth, that's all.'

'Meaning?'

'She said that my life was empty and she's spot on. It did upset me, but only because she was right and I don't know what to do about it.'

'Your life isn't empty, Janie. You do lots of things, you're always busy. It probably seems empty to Roz because she's so snowed under.'

Sarah smiled to try and reassure her friend, thinking all the while, Here I am, the mediator between Roz and Janie the fixer, the one who holds us all together as friends, when just now I would really like a bit of support myself. But she didn't say that to Janie. Instead she simply said, 'Roz always speaks too rashly Take no notice.'

Sarah went round to the driver's side of her car and opened the door. She leant in, looked at Rory and asked, 'All right love?'

'Can we go home, Mummy? I'm tired.'

'Of course.'

She turned back to Janie 'I must go, he's had it. Thanks for bringing me home from the hospital.'

'If there's anything else I can do, just ring me, OK?' Janie said.

Sarah nodded, but she knew it was an offer she wouldn't take up. She had been a single parent for six years now and she had learnt to be independent. People offered, but the reality was that nobody really wanted to be asked. 'Thanks.'

She climbed into her car and started the engine, flicking the lights on and releasing the handbrake. She reversed and, glancing in the rear-view mirror at Janie waved, then drove off. It was a six-mile drive to get home and she was tired, cold and, not for the first time, more than a little depressed.

Chapter Two

Andrew Leighton was already home when Janie pulled into the drive of Bank Cottage. She parked her car next to his and climbed out, aware of a small, niggling resentment that he had denied her the solitary hour she enjoyed with the paper and a glass of wine before his usual arrival time home.

She ushered Katie inside, refusing her pleas to watch the television, and called out to Andrew. He appeared in the hall in his shirt sleeves, a glass of wine in his hand.

'Hello, you look tired,' he said.

'Thanks.' Janie dumped their stuff by the door and Katie went across to give her father a hug.

'I didn't mean it like that,' he said over the top of her head. 'How's Rory? And Sarah?'

Janie went past him into the kitchen, taking the wine out of his hand and gulping down a large mouthful on the way. 'Rory is fine,' she replied as Andrew followed her in. 'A cracked rib and mild concussion; he was bloody lucky. And Sarah is, well, I don't know really.' Janie looked at him. 'Sarah is finding it tough, and to be honest she looked pretty depressed when I dropped her off at school.'

'Poor Sarah. God, what an awful fright for all of you. I've been worried ever since you rang.'

Janie began taking things out of the fridge. 'I

into the kitchen. Janie glanced up from the frying pan and smiled at Katie – clear skin, fresh and gleaming, hair brushed and pale pink pyjamas on.

'Almost,' she said. 'Why don't you sit down at the table and I'll bring it over in a couple of minutes.'

Andrew pulled out a chair for Katie and she sat while he put her place mat in front of her, filled a glass with water and fetched her named cutlery from the drawer. She swung her legs backwards and forwards, watching him and waiting for her supper. Janie served the omelette, added some sticks of cucumber and took it across to Katie. She pulled out a chair and sat down; Andrew poured her a glass of wine and brought it across.

'If you really don't want a curry, I'll cancel it,' he said, sitting down opposite her. He offered knowing she wouldn't take him up on it.

Janie took a mouthful of wine and held it in her mouth for a few moments, letting the dark, blackberry fruit drench her taste buds. She forgot the argument about the curry and swallowed.

'No, a curry will make a nice change,' she said, knowing that this was the right answer. Andrew smiled. He reached out and took her hand across the table. 'It's been a long day,' he said. 'You must be shattered. Why don't you pop up and have a bath and I'll get Katie into bed.' Janie nodded. How could she not be happy with such care and consideration? She got to her feet and picked up her wine. 'I'll drink this in the bath.' She ruffled Katie's hair. 'And I'll come and say goodnight once daddy's read you a story OK?'

34

thought I'd make Spanish omelette tonight; Katie can have hers now and we can warm it up later with some crusty bread and a salad,' she continued. 'Katie, would you like a bit of salad?'

'I've ordered us a curry, Janie,' Andrew interrupted. 'It'll be ready about nine. I thought you might be in late and that the last thing you needed tonight was to cook. I...' His voice trailed off as Janie stared at him, then looked away. There was a silence, a tense, injured silence while she struggled to control her sudden anger and disappointment.

'But I like to cook,' she said, her voice tight. 'It's what I do – cook and look after you and Katie, or hadn't you noticed?' She picked up the knife, ready to chop. 'Anyway, I've got the ingredients, they'll go to waste!'

Andrew's face had creased into a worried frown as he looked across at her, but instead of taking pleasure from his concern she felt irritated by it. She took a red pepper and placed it on the chopping board, slicing it neatly down the middle. 'It would have been nice if you'd asked me whether I had anything planned for supper before rushing in and ordering a takeaway.'

Andrew held his hands up. 'OK, OK, I'm wrong, again. I'm sorry for taking the initiative but I really thought I was doing the best thing.'

Janie looked up. Andrew always thought he was doing the best thing – taking decisions, advising, making choices based on sense and reason, and more often than not he was right. But every now and then she wished that he wouldn't just take control, that he'd let her get on with it and if she

31

made a mistake, if she fouled up, then so be it, she would have to deal with it and might possibly be the better for it.

'I'll take Katie up for a bath,' Andrew said. 'She can eat in her pyjamas.' He and Katie turned towards the door. 'Janie?'

'Yes, yes, fine.' She had snapped again even though she hadn't meant to. He stared at her, then shook his head and walked out of the room. Janie looked at the pepper, realising that it was a waste of time making a Spanish omelette for just one person but continuing to chop it nevertheless. Katie loved Spanish omelette so Janie would cook it just for her. Everything Janie did was for other people; perhaps, she wondered briefly, that's why she had no life of her own.

Janie Leighton had once been Janie Todd. She had been independent, sure of herself, adventurous – in a provincial way – and full of potential. Then she'd met Andrew Leighton at a party, got drunk, smoked far too many cigarettes and ended up in bed with him. It had been good, satisfying casual sex, for her at least, but for Andrew it had been more. He'd fallen in love with Janie, with her carelessness, her bravado and the dimples that she had on her back, just above her buttocks. He had been married before, had two small children who lived with their mother, and as a result he was cautious, sensible and wanted no surprises. He wanted to take care of Janie, to make sure that her carelessness didn't become recklessness, that her bravado didn't lead her into danger and to see that she gave up

smoking and cut down on the drink. He particularly wanted to make sure that no one else saw the wonderful dimples and so he asked her to marry him. And Janie, bowled over by the handsome, older man, was equally in love and so agreed.

It had been a happy marriage in the beginning and to some extent – in comparison with a great many other couples – it still was. Andrew was a good, safe husband and they had a regular, predictable sex life, friends, ample income, conversation – albeit on the dull side – and Katie. Janie was a natural homemaker, a conscientiou~~s~~ and loving mother and a good partner, and s~~he~~ had decided long ago that the positives far o~~ut~~ weighed the negatives in her life and that ~~she~~ should concentrate on those and forget abo~~ut the~~ rest. But recently, in Katie's second y~~ear at~~ school, Janie had begun to feel a space in ~~her,~~ a space inside herself, and one that co~~uldn't be~~ filled with decorating or gardening o~~r cooking~~ and caring for her small family. She ~~had begun~~ to dwell on that space and it had got~~ten so she~~ wanted to fill it and she knew how t~~o do it. She~~ knew that Andrew would neve~~r agree, she~~ wanted another child; he already ~~had two, he~~ was thirty-nine with two misc~~arriages behind~~ her; he was a GP who knew an~~d understood the~~ dangers to mature mothers w~~ho insisted on~~ carrying a child. She had a ~~son, a family,~~ complete.

'Is that omelette ready? B~~ecause there's a~~ little girl who's starving

32

33

Katie nodded, mouth full, and Janie left the room. She climbed the stairs to her bedroom and bathroom, went in and clicked the door gently shut behind her. She glanced at herself in the mirror and the same image that she had always known stared back at her, only tonight, as had so often happened recently, she wasn't sure who it was.

Roz opened the front door to Chadwick farmhouse and two dogs came bounding out towards her. They jumped up, she greeted them and then reached for the light switch just inside the door and flicked it. The shabby hallway was flooded with light and as Roz glanced down at the carpet she made her daily resolution to get the Hoover out tonight – a resolution that was never fulfilled.

'What's for supper? I'm starving!' Justin said behind her.

'Who knows?' she answered, then turning to him said, 'Did you help Kitty and Oliver out of the car or have you just left them strapped in and crying in the dark?' She glanced over his head and saw the two little ones straggling up the path. 'Well done, thanks, Justin.' She went back out, picked up Oliver, carried him inside, then returned for Kitty 'Right,' she said, assuming more control than she actually felt, 'it's baked beans on toast for supper, but only after I've fed the pigs. Justin will put a video on for you and you can watch that until supper's ready OK?'

'Hooray! I want to watch *Peter Pan!*'

'No, I'm not watching that, that's a boy's film. I want to watch *Cinderella!*'

'No, I'm not watching *Cinderella*. Mummy? Kitty says we've got to watch *Cinderella*, I don't want to watch...'

'Either you agree or you don't watch anything! OK? Now, I've got to go out before the pigs riot and we've all read *Animal Farm*, haven't we?'

'What's *Animal Farm*, Mum?'

'Never mind, darling. Put a vid on for them will you, Justin, and then get your homework out? It should be warm in the kitchen, do it in there at the table.' Roz kicked her shoes off, headed back out of the door and shoved her feet into wellies. She looked over her shoulder at all three children watching her and smiled. Despite all the hard work, the stress, the struggle, it was all right knowing that she had the children.

'You lot inside, go on, *now!*'

She clapped her hands and Justin turned, leading the way She walked down towards the pig field with her torch illuminating the path, glancing back only momentarily to see the lights going on in the house.

'Well done, Justin,' she muttered. 'Now for the pigs!'

Roz and Graham Betts had bought Chadwick Farm, with its small holding of eleven acres, six years ago. It had been Roz's idea – a perfect way to bring up children she had said, and a wonderful opportunity to work for themselves. She'd convinced Graham and they'd raised the money through a combination of Graham's redundancy package and a small inheritance from Roz's maiden aunt. It had been their great white hope,

36

their move from the city, their self-employed dream. They'd planned organic vegetables, hand-reared, home-cured pork, handmade chutneys and jams, asparagus, and sheeps' milk yoghurt and cheese. They would sell all this in markets across London – Notting Hill and Chelsea, Camden and Kensington. It would be quality produce, expensive and for the food connoisseur only, and it would undoubtedly be a roaring success. But one year into the project they had found themselves bogged down by the rules from the soil association for organic produce, a steep drop in pork prices, impossibly strict EEC food and hygiene regulations and an unexpected pregnancy. To add to this they had problems marketing the goods and distribution was something that they just hadn't thought of. The great white hope became a great white elephant.

In the second year they managed to eke out a meagre living, Roz doing everything with a second baby in a sling and a toddler on reins. But it was frustrating and exhausting; a ceaseless slog.

In the third year Graham went into antiques in an attempt to supplement their income and by the time Oliver was born – after another unexpected pregnancy – the antiques business was making a small profit. The small holding, however, although giving them storage space for the furniture and paintings that Graham shipped out to the States and Japan, barely broke even. They juggled the two businesses, always in need of more cash, not able to sell due to negative equity and only just managing. They somehow got by. It wasn't easy, but as Graham often said, it was at least happy – well, for most of the time.

Roz trudged back from feeding the pigs feeling cold and tired and she still had supper to cook, children to bath, the pony to do, the chickens to feed and a whole ruddy great stack of ironing. She had no idea what time Graham would be home – he was off at some auction somewhere, which she knew very little about and cared for even less. She reached the house, pulled her wellies off and opened the front door. It was cold inside as always, grubby as usual but full of the noise of the dogs barking, the children, who seemed to be killing each other, and the television which was permanently tuned in to the video channel. As she walked into the kitchen, pushing two excited red setters down, she saw Justin at the table with his maths homework out. A trail of biscuit crumbs and spilt orange juice surrounded him, but his head was bent in concentration and she wondered how he managed to work amidst such noise and chaos. Perhaps it was a deep-seated fear not to end up like his parents.

'Right,' she said to no one in particular, 'baked beans on toast coming up!' She reached in the cupboard for two tins of Heinz baked beans and grabbed the can opener. Roz Betts, purveyor of fine handmade foods and organic produce, ignored the irony of opening a couple of cans for her children's tea and got on with the job in hand. She didn't have time to worry and if she had've done she would have chosen to worry about Rory Greg. She would have wondered how and why the burden of her life had caused her to make a mistake that could have cost more than all this was worth.

Sarah's neighbour was waiting for her when she arrived home. She had rung Lindsay from the hospital and asked her to turn on the storage heaters which weren't on automatic timer. As she parked the old Mini Metro in the drive Lindsay came out of the house and Sarah was relieved to see her, reluctant, despite what she had said to Roz, to be alone.

'Hi.' She climbed out of the car and Lindsay came across to her. Lindsay was a single woman twenty years older than Sarah, a retired teacher, and someone with a solitary, calm and ordered life. Lindsay was often there, helping and re-assuring quietly and without any fuss, and she did it because she wanted to. It was a trade off – Sarah accepted the help because she knew that Lindsay wanted to give it, and Lindsay enjoyed the company and the friendship that came as a result.

'Are you all right?' Lindsay asked.

'Yes, just.'

'Come on, let's get you inside. You look exhausted. Shall I carry Rory in?'

'No, it's OK, I'll do it.' Sarah slammed her door shut and went round the passenger side to get Rory. 'D'you want to walk, love, or shall I carry you?'

'No, it's OK thanks, Mum,' Rory said. 'I'm a bit big now for carrying. I can walk.'

'Six isn't too big for a carry if you want one,' Sarah replied. But Rory had climbed out of the car and, holding down the urge to insist, she let him walk with Lindsay into the house.

'It's nice and warm in here, Lindsay,' Sarah said. 'Thanks.'

'Not at all. I've got a lasagne next door if you fancy it. I made a bit extra this afternoon after you rang and thought I could freeze it if you didn't want it. You're very welcome to it, Sarah, it wouldn't take a minute to heat up, I...'

'Thank you,' Sarah interrupted, 'we'd love it, wouldn't we, Rory?'

Rory turned and said, 'Pardon?' Despite three years of being aware that she should always speak to his face, Sarah still made the mistake every now and then of talking behind him as if his hearing was normal. She took a breath, suddenly irrationally irritated at having to repeat herself, and said slowly, 'Lindsay has offered us a lasagne and I said we'd love it, wouldn't we?'

'Yummy! It's my favourite.'

Lindsay smiled. 'I'll go and get it. D'you fancy a glass of wine, Sarah? I've got a bottle open in the fridge.'

Sarah knew that Lindsay didn't have 'a bottle open' and that this was another gesture of friendship, another offer of help. She hesitated instinctively for a moment, but it was just a moment. This was Lindsay. Sarah didn't have to refuse her help because she was the only one who offered and really meant it. 'I'd love one. If you're sure?'

'Of course I'm sure,' Lindsay said and brushed

past Sarah to pop next door to her own house for the food and wine. Sarah turned the lamp on, then ushered Rory upstairs. 'Let's get you washed and into your pyjamas,' she said, 'and settled on the sofa with a book. You can have your supper on your lap.'

'Can I watch TV?' Rory asked.

'It's good to see that your brain is intact,' Sarah said, propelling him gently into the bathroom, 'but no, you can't. Children's TV has finished and there's nothing else suitable on.'

'A video then?'

Sarah suddenly laughed. 'Nice try.' She glanced at her watch. 'Well, it's six-thirty now and supper will be at least half an hour, and then we'll need half an hour to digest it, which takes us up to seven-thirty, which is quite late enough I think...' She narrowed her eyes. 'But if you can find a video that lasts just an hour and no more then ... OK.'

Rory threw a fist in the air, then winced. 'Ouch!'

'That'll teach you to be cocky. Now, if you have a video there'll be no time for a story afterwards, you do realise that, don't you?'

'Oh no!'

'Sorry, but you've had a serious bump to the head and you need to get to bed promptly to rest.' She flicked his chin. 'No pulling faces –come on, let's get moving, or there won't be time for anything at all.'

Time was the only thing that Sarah Greg knew a great deal about, as it was something that, since

41

Rory had been born, had dominated her life.

It had all begun with time spent waiting. Pregnant with her first baby, two weeks overdue, Sarah had been carted off to hospital to be induced. 'The baby is in distress,' the consultant had said calmly, almost carelessly. 'We've got a high foetal heartrate, but I think we'll wait and see, Mrs Greg, there's nothing like time in a situation like this.' He had been right. Time had made all the difference.

'Is she under yet?' the same consultant had shouted across the theatre twenty minutes later. Sarah remembered that; she didn't remember much else but she remembered that and what had immediately followed. 'Nearly,' the anaesthetist had replied, 'about five or six seconds...' Sarah opened her eyes. 'I haven't got six seconds,' the obstetrician shouted, 'I've got to go in now or that baby will be dead...'

And he must have gone in then because Rory wasn't dead. He had been limp and not breathing, he'd had no pulse and had had to be resuscitated, then intubated to try to clear his lungs and body of the thick tar-like meconium that had almost suffocated him, but he was just barely alive.

'Time,' the consultant had said twenty-four hours later as Sarah lay stunned and stitched, bleeding inside and out. 'We don't know the extent of the damage and won't do for some time. There is a strong chance, however, that it could be severe.' Sarah had turned her face away as her tears wet the starched white pillow case.

'What does severe mean?' Nick, her husband,

42

had asked, but no one knew how to answer him. They took Rory home, once he could 'function' normally, and then began to understand the true meaning of time: watching and waiting, monitoring every stage of his development, week after week, month after month. In and out of hospitals for tests, diagnosis, physiotherapy and operations, and finally, having overcome all those hurdles and come out with a child who seemed normal, they'd found out that Rory was partially deaf. Time. It had taken three years. 'I'm afraid to tell you,' said the audiologist, 'that Rory's hearing is below what we would term normal. There is a thirty-five per cent hearing loss on the right and a forty per cent hearing loss on the left. Whether it stabilises or deteriorates at this moment, we have no idea.' Time. There it was again. And just three months after they had found out, Rory's father, Sarah's husband, Nick, had left them.

He needed time, he told her, to come to terms with what had happened; he needed time and space. 'And I don't?' Sarah had screamed at him. 'I'm supposed to just take it, get on with it, cope, am I?' Then Nick had said something that Sarah had never forgotten. He'd said, 'Don't shout, for God's sake, Sarah, Rory will hear you!' And Sarah had started to cry. She'd sunk to the floor and wept for a child who might never hear her scream, who would always be at a disadvantage, who would never quite fit in – a child who was deaf.

But she had coped. She had got on with it, taken it and coped. Nick had someone else, of course he did; he was a man, wasn't he? While Sarah had been reading up about hearing loss, speech patterns, lip reading and sign language night after night, Nick had been out with Melanie, finding comfort in warm arms and a soft breast. They divorced a year later, Sarah keeping everything amicable, calm and friendly when in truth she could have ripped the man's heart from his chest and served it up for supper.

And here she was, struggling for money because Nick had another family and keeping up with maintenance payments was hard for him – poor man. Here she was, working hard, saving diligently, caring for Rory who was, contrary to what she had worried most about in the beginning, immensely popular and bright into the bargain. Here she was, biding time. Time. In the end, it all came back to time.

'You all right up there?' Lindsay called from the hall. Sarah came out of the bathroom drying her hands on a towel and said, 'We're fine. Well, Rory is anyway I feel absolutely bloody awful to be honest with you.'

'I'll pour you a large glass of wine right now,' Lindsay said. 'I'll have it waiting for you. Shall I pop the lasagne into the oven too?'

'Thanks.' Sarah hung the towel over the banister, turned to Rory as he came out of the bathroom and bent to tie the cord of his dressing gown.

'Mum!'

'Sorry.' She ruffled his hair. 'I keep forgetting how grown up you are nowadays.'

'Pardon?'

'Get your hearing aids, please,' she said, slowly and clearly. He watched her lips. 'You can't watch a video unless you can hear it properly.'

Rory went back into the bathroom and Sarah waited. He handed the aids to her, she slipped them in and they went down the stairs.

'Here.' Lindsay handed Sarah a wine glass when she returned to the kitchen after settling Rory on the sofa.

'Thanks. Sorry about the background noise.' Rory was watching *Joseph and the Amazing Technicolour Dreamcoat.*

'Not at all, I might find myself singing along any minute. I know all the words. Forgive me if I suddenly burst into song.'

Sarah attempted a smile.

'Come on, it's not that bad. He's all right – it could have been much worse.'

'That's just the point!' Sarah swallowed a large mouthful of wine. 'He was all right this time, but what about the next time? He didn't hear the car! He just didn't hear it, he...' Sarah put her hands up to her face as Lindsay stood helpless.

'You have a good cry if you want to, God knows you deserve it!' Lindsay said. And that somehow made Sarah laugh.

'I deserve it, do I? That makes me feel a whole lot better, the fact that my life is so bloody awful that if anyone deserves a weep it's me!' She smiled. 'Thanks, Lindsay, I know where to come for comfort in future.'

Lindsay refilled their wine glasses and noticed

that Sarah's face had got a bit of colour back. 'I didn't mean it like that, I meant...'

Sarah reached out and touched her arm. 'It's OK, I know what you meant. But in some ways you're right; just when I thought it couldn't get any worse, it does.' She went to the cupboard and took a multi-pack of crisps down. 'The thing is that today just showed me how much more work I've got to do with Rory to get him to be aware, for him to be streetwise.' She pulled out two packets of plain crisps from the bag, emptied one into a small bowl and opened the other for Rory. Pouring a glass of orange juice, she took them through to him on the sofa, then came back to Lindsay

'Isn't there any way forward?' Lindsay asked. 'What about these cochlear implants? Haven't they had some success with those?'

'Not applicable to Rory; they're really only for the profoundly deaf. They have introduced digital hearing aids in some cases, which can apparently bring the quality of hearing right up to almost normal, but I've already asked about those and unless I'm prepared to buy them privately there's no hope of getting them.'

'And that's not an option, presumably?'

Sarah finished her second glass of wine and Lindsay poured a third. She could have made a joke about her circumstances; that's what she usually did, made some sort of witty, derogatory comment aimed at herself. But tonight she didn't have the heart. She simply said, 'I've got a bit saved up, Lin, but nowhere near enough.'

Lindsay glanced past Sarah to Rory on the sofa,

singing away to the tape. 'He's a lovely boy,' she said truthfully 'I'm sure he'll be OK. You know, lots of people don't even know he's deaf.'

'But I do, and he does.' Sarah followed Lindsay's gaze and smiled at Rory, who never quite got the words right, singing at the top of his voice. 'He does,' she said again, and the smile dimmed until it was barely a flicker of happiness that had passed across her face.

Chapter Three

Lucie opened her eyes the moment it was over and stared blankly up at the pale cream ceiling above her, its edges finished with faux-Victorian coving picked out in white, and its ceiling rose an ornate affair of stuccoed leaves and fruit of the vine. It was yet another characterless hotel – the name of which she couldn't for the life of her remember – hired for one night but used for just one illicit hour. She heard Alex sigh as he rolled off her, then he put out a hand and gently touched her face.

'That was wonderful. Did you...?'

She nodded and he nuzzled her neck, his breath hot against her skin. 'Good.' She reached for a tissue from the box beside the bed, stuffed it down between her legs and sat up. He watched her, puzzled. 'Are you all right, Lucie?'

'Yes, fine,' she said, a little more sharply than she had intended, then felt immediately guilty It wasn't his fault this wasn't working, he was doing everything he could to be nice. 'I'm fine, really.'

'OK. It's just that you seem a bit, well, distant, really.'

'Sorry.' Lucie dropped her legs over the side of the bed and stood up. She turned. 'I've got a lot on at work, that's all. I guess I'm a bit stressed.' It wasn't just an excuse, she *was* stressed; she was always stressed at work.

'Want to talk about it? I'm a good ear.'

Lucie shook her head. 'No, not really.' But she appreciated the offer; she couldn't remember the last time Marcus, her husband, had wanted to listen.

Alex sat up and held his arms out. 'Come here and give me a hug then, come on.' Lucie sat back down on the edge of the bed and he pulled her to him. 'For someone so in control you can look decidedly vulnerable at times.' He kissed her hair. 'Whatever it is at work, it won't last. You'll sort it out, Lucie, you always do, that's why you've got so far. You're good at your job, very good at it, so don't forget that, eh?'

Lucie let him embrace her and enjoyed the momentary comfort it allowed. Marcus rarely hugged her and almost never offered her any warmth or affection. 'I just feel under so much pressure at times,' she said, unable to stop herself confiding. She pulled back to look at him. 'At work I feel that if it wasn't for me the whole thing would collapse, and that's one hell of a responsibility.'

'Of course you do, you've got a lot on your plate,' he sympathised.

It was the fact that he understood, that and the sympathy. Suddenly the urge to talk to Alex, to unburden herself, was overwhelming. 'It's too much responsibility,' Lucie went on. 'I'm not sure I can cope.'

'Of course you can cope. What is it? A deal in the offing and you're the only one with the knowledge and experience to manage it, right?'

She nodded. 'A merger; potentially a very big

49

merger,' she said, then bit her lip. Alex was an investment manager, she headed up the corporate finance team at World Bank, and they both knew only too well the meaning of price-sensitive information.

But it seemed to go right over his head; he was interested in her, nothing else. 'So what?' he replied. 'You've done it before. You've pulled off some incredible deals, that's why you are where you are and earn what you do...'

'Yes, but this is so bloody complicated,' she interrupted. 'There are all sorts of problems looming with financing, rights issues and so on and I just don't have the people to back me up. For example, I desperately need someone with specialist knowledge of the communications market right now. I've got two of the biggest players on my hands and the bank keeps fobbing me off with our media analyst who, quite frankly, doesn't know diddley squat about the future of cable franchise...' She stopped abruptly and looked at Alex. She had said too much – it had slipped too quickly and easily off her tongue. They both knew it, but neither wanted to acknowledge that fact.

'It'll work out, Lucie,' Alex said. There was a moment of uncomfortable silence, then Lucie shrugged. 'I'm sure it will,' she replied. Getting to her feet, she picked up her underwear and turned towards the bathroom. 'I'd better have a shower and get going,' she said, but she was thinking, Oh God, I should have kept my mouth shut. What am I doing, spouting off about work? It's this affair, it's this whole stupid bloody thing; I don't know what I'm doing or what I'm saying.

Alex glanced at his watch. He hated doing so, but this was an affair conducted mostly at lunchtimes and they both had places to go afterwards, people to meet. He nodded and stood himself.

At the bathroom door, Lucie stopped and looked back at him. She felt very unsure of herself. 'I can trust you, can't I, Alex?' she asked. He crossed the room and kissed her. 'Of course,' he replied.

'Good.' She believed him, there was no reason not to. She smiled, then went into the bathroom and closed the door behind her.

Alex went across to his briefcase and took out his phone. He waited until he heard running water, then he dialled and made his call. Lucie, in the shower, didn't hear anything at all.

Lucie luxuriated in the powerful jet of hot water and the smell of hotel shower gel. She soaped her body and washed her hair in the conditioning shampoo supplied, holding her face up to the spray to wash away the lather. She felt anxious and confused but the subtle massage from the water jet helped to ease the feelings of guilt and self-doubt that she always had after sex with Alex.

Lucie Croft – she was still known by her maiden name – had been married for three years, but they hadn't been particularly happy years, marriage not being at all what she'd expected. She was a bright girl, strong-minded and not used to compromise, and she had found the

51

largely one-sided exchange of independence for domesticity difficult to take. She loved Marcus, her husband – she loved, admired and respected him, or at least she had in the beginning – but she didn't like being a 'wife'. She wondered briefly as she turned off the water and stepped out of the shower if that was where the problem had begun, with her reluctance to be what Marcus wanted her to be. But then you couldn't make a silk purse out of a sow's ear, could you?

Lucie had been head girl at school, had achieved her gold Duke of Edinburgh Award and had played netball for the county. She was a good, consistent tennis player, cunning at bridge and very ambitious. She came from a professional background – her mother was a barrister and her father headed up a management consultancy firm – so there was never any doubt that she would go through Oxbridge and then get herself a top job. Rising through the ranks of the corporate finance department – not a girly job – she'd worked bloody hard and played as hard as she'd worked. Then she'd met Marcus.

Marcus Todd was also a high flyer. A top analyst, he was younger than her but reputed to be well and truly on the ascent. They'd met on a business trip and had dinner in the hotel and Marcus had bought the most expensive wine in the restaurant at two hundred and fifty pounds a bottle, obviously to impress her. It had failed – anyone could take advantage of expenses – until he'd taken her to bed later on that evening and ordered another bottle of the same wine to pour over her breasts and lick off. Both, she realised as he signed, were on his own personal account. She had said, 'What an obscene waste of money,' and he'd replied, 'Who cares? The pleasure of tasting vintage 88 Clos de Vougeot Grand Cru on your skin is priceless.' Lucie had been torn then between thinking he was the most pretentious man she had ever met and the most attractive. The fact that the wine tasting had taken four hours and led to the best sex she had ever experienced tipped the balance. There was no looking back. Marcus was as energetic, dynamic and ambitious as she was. They had married within months and then realised within days that love was something that couldn't be manipulated like the price of a stock or share.

Lucie dried herself and sat on the edge of the bath. She didn't want to go back out and face Alex; if she was really honest with herself, she would rather that he simply dressed and left without another word, kiss or caress. Lucie had fallen into this affair. She had been seduced by the warmth and affection she found in Alex, warmth and affection that she didn't get from Marcus, and had fooled herself into thinking that a bit of love elsewhere would help the love at home. But she had been wrong and now she didn't know how to end it. She wasn't cut out for deceit, she hated herself for it and, besides, she *did* love Marcus. If only they could get it right and somehow both stop trying to take all the time and start giving instead. She sighed and thought, fat chance, then stood, put on her underwear and opened the bathroom door.

Alex was dressed when she came out. He had

straightened the bedclothes and was standing looking out of the window, waiting for her. 'Aren't you going to shower?' Lucie asked, taking her shirt off the back of a chair. Alex turned. He smiled and watched her dress for a few moments, enjoying the sight of it and thinking it almost as erotic as when she undressed.

'I think I'll go straight to the gym,' he said. 'I've not got much on this afternoon and frankly, well, I feel completely energised.' He came across to her and put his arms around her waist. 'You do that to me, Lucie. An hour with you and I feel amazing!'

Lucie tried to smile. She mumbled a reply and eased away from him to pull on her skirt. Why couldn't Marcus say things like this? Why couldn't Marcus feel amazing any more after an hour with her in bed? Turning to Alex, he spoke before she had a chance to open her mouth. 'When can I see you again?' He took hold of her hand. 'And don't tell me that it's going to be a couple of weeks, fobbing me off with work excuses. It has to be sooner; I need to see you.'

Lucie looked down at her hand and wished fervently that it was Marcus who was holding it. She liked Alex, she really did like him, but she no longer wanted to have an affair with him. She had never really wanted to, if she was honest.

'I'll ring you,' she said.

'Will you? You promise?'

Lucie hesitated but, despite her reticence and despite the guilt, it felt good to be wanted so much.

'I promise.'

'OK. As long as you promise.' Alex went back to the window where he'd left his briefcase, picked it up and said, 'I'll go first, shall I?'

Lucie nodded. He crossed the room, stopped to kiss her mouth as he passed her and opened the door. 'Bye, Lucie.'

'Goodbye.' A moment later he was gone.

Lucie pulled on her jacket, picked up her own briefcase, then sat down to wait. She gave him five minutes, stood again and collected the key to the room. They had already paid for it so it was just a case of dropping the key into reception on her way out. She glanced at her watch in the lift and thought about the afternoon ahead. Her only saving grace in all this emotional muddle was work, and with relief she pushed aside her problems and hurried back to it.

'Marcus? You coming, mate? There's an ice-cold bottle of Becks waiting in the pub and it's got your name on it.'

Marcus Todd turned from the window 'I'm right behind you, Johnno. I've got a couple of calls to make so I'll meet you there.'

John Daniels pulled on his jacket. 'Lighten up, man! You've just made this frigging bank two million quid in a morning. Leave the bloody calls!'

Marcus laughed. 'One's to the wife, mate. Can't be left, I'm afraid!'

'Don't be long! I need a bit of alcohol abuse and you're the perfect bloke to help me!'

'Yeah, yeah, yeah.' Marcus turned back to the window and let the noise of the dealing room

55

drown out any other thought in his brain. He had to ring Lucie, he knew he did, but he dreaded it. He dreaded hearing the tense, negative tone of her voice. He dreaded feeling the sinking disappointment and futile anger on hanging up that things weren't – couldn't be – right. He walked back to his desk and picked up the phone. There was a note from another trader, Jack, on his screen, a yellow post-it that said:

JAMMY BASTARD. YOU CAN BUY ME A BEER – NO, CORRECTION, A CASE OF BEER – SEEING AS YOU'VE JUST MADE A WAD LOAD. SEE YOU IN THE PUB.

It was a funny note and Jack was a good bloke – successful, made even more money than Marcus – but Marcus didn't smile. He tore the post-it off and screwed it up into a ball, aimed for the bin by the plant and lobbed it high in the air. It landed almost exactly in the centre of the bin. Everything Marcus did, every little thing Marcus had ever done, was a success. Except his marriage.

He picked up the phone and dialled Lucie's mobile. It rang twice, there was a three-second connection, then he heard the Vodaphone re-call service. Her phone was switched off, of course it was. He waited, then spoke to a computer.

'Lucie, hi, it's me. Just ringing to let you know that I'm going out tonight for a couple of drinks with a broker straight after work, so I'll be in around eight-thirty, nine o'clock. Hope that's OK and that you've not got anything planned.

Call me if you have. See you later.' He hung up and sat staring blankly at his screen for a few moments. She wouldn't have anything planned, she never did have, and it would definitely be OK. In fact, it would probably be preferable to him being in. He sighed, stood up and grabbed his jacket off the back of his chair, pulling it on as he left the office.

'Hey, Marco!' Someone from across the bank of screens called out as he crossed the room. 'There's a shift in the dot coms, they're on the up.'

'So?'

'You're not gonna leave this baby, are you? Marcus the invincible?'

Marcus held up his hands. Enough was enough. Without Lucie, what was the point anyway? He said, 'BillyBob, I've just made myself fifty grand this morning. You take the dot coms.' And he walked out of the office.

Lucie was on the phone when Marcus arrived home. He put his key in the lock, opened the door and heard her voice, with its familiar sharpness, its undertone of authority that left you in no doubt you were speaking to someone who knew exactly what they wanted and how to get it. He stood tensely, just inside the door, and listened. He heard Lucie sigh, let out a small gasp, then say, 'God, Janie, how absolutely terrible for all of you.' It was his sister. He relaxed and walked into the apartment.

Lucie waved as he came in. She was sprawled on the sleek, modern sofa – upholstered in slate-grey linen and piped with white – looking tired and not in the least bit comfortable. She had the portable phone clasped to her ear and Marcus heard her tutting as he went into the kitchen space to get a drink. He bent down to the fridge, took out a bottle of beer and flipped the lid off on the edge of the granite work top. He saw Lucie scowl at him but he ignored her. They had had the place – a warehouse conversion in Notting Hill – completely 'done' by some designer Lucie had read about in the *Sunday Times* style section and Marcus loathed it. He'd hated it right from the beginning, appalled by the fact that neither of them could be bothered to think for themselves and so had hired the latest hit man to do the job for them. He hated that it was someone else's choice, from the lighting right down to the knives and forks. And, deep down, if he'd been honest enough to recognise it, he hated the fact that Lucie was so far removed from any kind of domesticity that she could leave the furnishing of her home to someone who told her that the three square feet of brick out the back was a 'terrace' – and believe him.

He took off his shoes and left them abandoned by the fridge, walking around the 'work station' and into the main living area which was a huge expanse of window and tiled floor with the odd piece of very expensive and extremely uncomfortable designer furniture placed, to the exact inch, here and there for the right effect. He slipped off his jacket and chucked it on a low table – chrome and marbled melamine – knowing that it irritated Lucie, and heard her say,

'Marcus has just come in, Janie, I'll put you on, shall I? Yes, OK, love to Katie. Bye for now.'

He took the phone and walked across to the window with it. 'Hello, Janie,' he said, 'how's things?' He felt Lucie get up behind him and watched her reflection in the plate glass. She stretched, walked across to the kitchen area and switched the kettle on. He wanted her; at that moment he wanted her so much that he could have just thrown down the phone and taken her right there, in the glare of the lights on the hard, cold tiled floor. But it was impossible. He listened to his sister and the moment passed. He wanted Lucie, but he couldn't bear to touch her. He turned and looked at her. She mouthed the word 'bath' to him and he nodded. Then he said, 'You sound really down, Janie, that accident has knocked you for six. Is the little boy all right?' Again he listened to his sister while he watched Lucie, just visible in the bedroom. She took off her clothes, laying her suit neatly on the bed and dropping her underwear and silk shirt on the floor. Tomorrow it would be sent to the laundry for washing and dry cleaning. She threw her tights in the bin and Marcus said on the phone, 'Janie, why don't you come up for a couple of nights ... all right, just one night then, if you don't want to leave Katie. Come on Friday and stay till Saturday. Do a bit of shopping, have supper with us, stay here and potter back on Saturday morning. Andrew can have Katie, can't he? He's not on duty, is he?' In the bedroom Lucie disappeared and Marcus longed to get off the phone to see where she was. 'You will? Oh good. Yes, ring me tomorrow to confirm, ring me at work. Listen, Janie, I've got to go and get something to eat, I'm starving. I'll talk to you tomorrow then. Yup, it will do you good, it'll really cheer you up. OK, see you Friday. Bye.' He disconnected the line and dropped the phone on to the sofa on his way to the bedroom. Loosening his tie he walked through the bedroom, pristine in its shades of white, to the bathroom, to Lucie, wrapped in a towel ready for her bath.

'Poor Janie,' she said as he came in. She was sitting on the edge of the bath with a small mirror in her hand, plucking her eyebrows. 'Her friend's little boy is going to be all right though, thank goodness...'

'Not that you really care,' Marcus said.

Lucie looked up. She stopped plucking. 'No, I don't *really* care, you're quite right. How could I? I don't even know the people involved. But I am concerned – it's a pretty horrible thing to happen and Janie has my sympathy. OK? Does that clarify things for you?'

Marcus shrugged. 'Sorry, I didn't mean to be sarcastic.'

'Didn't you?' Lucie looked at her face again, but she had lost heart in the plucking; she was too wound up to be bothered with it now.

Marcus walked out of the bathroom. From just outside the door he said, 'I'll come in and we can start again, OK?'

Lucie stood and turned off the taps of the bath. She sighed. 'OK.'

He walked into the bathroom for a second time and sat down on a chair as she climbed into the

60

bath. 'So, how was your day?'

Lucie closed her eyes. She didn't want to think about her day and she certainly didn't want to tell Marcus about it. What could she say? Oh, it was all right; a couple of meetings, this merger isn't going too well and oh, by the way, I'm having an affair but the sex wasn't that good today 'It wasn't brilliant,' was all she said in the end. 'The merger is sinking and I'm supposed to be holding the whole thing afloat.' She looked at him. 'How was yours?'

'Good. I made a stack of money on one of the technology stocks, had a few beers to celebrate at lunchtime and met a mate after work. On the whole, not bad.' He smiled. 'More investment into my pension plan.'

Lucie smiled back. 'You'll never retire,' she said. 'You'll die with a headpiece on shouting sell, sell, sell!'

Marcus laughed. 'It's not only the money, you know.'

'Yeah, yeah, yeah.'

'It isn't, honestly It used to be, but now...' He reached for the soap. 'Shall I wash your back?'

'Hmmm, please.' Lucie leant forward and rested her head on her knees. 'So what is it then, if it isn't the money that drives you?'

Marcus stopped soaping for a moment. He had an overwhelming desire to tell her everything he'd ever thought, everything he knew, to un-burden himself suddenly and completely. But he didn't. He said, 'I don't know, I haven't worked it out yet.' Lucie laughed and Marcus handed her the soap. She had hoped that he might not stop, but she didn't say anything. She took the soap and relaxed back in the bath.

'Did I hear you ask Janie to stay?'

Marcus stood and dried his hands. 'Yes, she's coming on Friday I thought we could have supper here, cook something maybe?'

Lucie pulled a face. 'Let's go out.'

'No, let's stay in.'

Lucie looked at him. His voice had changed and she heard an edge to it. 'Why?'

'Because this is our home and I'd like to entertain in it.'

'OK, let's have a takeaway then. We can have a few drinks in the West End, go somewhere smart after work, then get a takeaway on the way home.'

'No, we'll have a few drinks here. And we'll cook.'

Lucie sat up. 'What is this, Marcus? You may want to cook, but I certainly don't. I'll have had a bloody tough week at work and the last thing I'll want to do is come home and stand over the bloody hob on Friday night while you pour cocktails.'

Marcus said nothing. He was thinking that for once she might have offered, might have just said, OK, I'll chuck some garlic and bacon in a pan, add some cream and wine and toss some pasta in it. All it would have taken was that and a bag of salad with readymade dressing. He stood up. 'We'll get a caterer in, I'll ask the girls in the dining room at work to recommend someone.'

'Oh.' Lucie finished washing and she too stood up. Of course, it never occurred to him that he could cook just as easily as she, but she didn't mention that. Why should she, if he couldn't think it out for himself? She reached for a towel and caught her arm on the heated rail. 'Ouch.'

Marcus turned. 'Are you all right?'

'Yes, but I've burnt my arm.'

'Run it under cold water. Stupid sodding place for a hot rail anyway, I've always said so.' He ran the cold tap in the sink for her as Lucie climbed out of the bath, wrapped the towel round her and held her arm under the cold water. 'I don't see why we have to go to so much fuss on Friday,' she said. 'It's only your sister.'

Marcus walked out of the bathroom and took off his tie, dropping it on the floor. That too would go for dry cleaning in the morning. 'No, it's not only Janie for supper,' he called out. 'I asked the chap I had drinks with tonight. He's a broker for White Lowen. I've just met him through work and I think you'd really like him. I thought we'd make up a party.'

Lucie came into the bedroom. 'So who is he, this mystery friend? You've not mentioned him before.'

'We only met a few weeks ago, at a brokers' lunch. His name is Alex,' Marcus said. He headed for the door. 'Alex Stanton.'

As he disappeared into the living area, Lucie sank down on to the bed. Her first feeling was panic, her second fear and her third terrible, suffocating guilt. She lay down, curled on to her side and closed her eyes. Alex Stanton. Marcus was right, she did like him; she liked him so much she went to bed with him.

63

Chapter Four

Janie had decided on black to wear to London; a simple, well-cut black trouser suit, with a white, long-sleeved, fitted silk tee-shirt underneath. She chose high-heeled black ankle boots and her expensive black handbag as accessories, and although it was spring and she would not need her coat she packed her pashmina in case she was chilly. She would drive, she decided, rather than get the train, and park outside the place in Notting Hill, leave her overnight bag in the boot and get a cab from there up to Oxford Street. She was looking forward to the trip. It made her feel that she had something constructive to do; it made her feel – though she would never admit this to anyone else – important.

She was ready by five to eight, her overnight bag by the front door, her handbag on the hall table, breakfast neatly laid out in the kitchen. The plan was to drop Katie off at school, come back for a quick coffee with Andrew, check that she'd left everything in order and then get on her way.

Katie was upstairs with Andrew getting dressed. She sounded happy, from the noise and laughter, but once again Janie found herself torn between the fear of leaving her daughter and the need for this rare moment of independence. She walked into the hall and listened to the banter for a few minutes from the bottom of the stairs. Katie, of course, wasn't in the least bit stressed by her departure, so she went back to the kitchen, reasonably content, to put two eggs on to boil.

Sarah always waited in the playground until the bell had been rung and the children had all lined up for school. She did this more for her own benefit than for Rory's. She felt better going to work knowing that he had gone in happy and content.

As she stood by the gate, she saw Janie arrive and waved to her. The bell rang, Janie dropped Katie off, gave her a big hug and hurried across to say hello to Sarah.

'You look smart,' Sarah said. 'Nice suit. Giorgio Armani?'

Janie laughed. 'Marks and Sparks. I'm off to London, to stay with my brother.'

'Marcus and the power woman. What's her name?'

'Lucie. Lucie – I can't chat now because I'm in the middle of a multi-million-dollar deal – Croft.'

Sarah smiled.

'She's not that bad really, just a bit high-powered and self-important. Makes me feel like the dull old housewife that I am.'

'You're not old,' Sarah said, 'dull, yes, but...'

Janie elbowed her and laughed. 'That's enough, thanks.'

They both turned as Roz drove into the car park, late, with her exhaust pipe making one hell of a racket. She climbed out, leaving Kitty and Oliver in the car, and ran Justin towards the school.

'Bloody exhaust fell off this morning!' she called across to them. 'More expense! Can you keep an eye on the little ones for me?'

'Of course!' Sarah called back. Roz disappeared into school and Janie made to leave.

'You have a great time,' Sarah said. She felt no envy, Janie deserved a break – didn't they all for that matter – but she did fleetingly wish that it might be her in the black trouser suit off to London for twenty-four hours. She leant forward and kissed Janie on the cheek. 'Send me a postcard,' she said.

'I'm only going for the night.'

'Send me one anyway, something rude and dead tacky.'

'OK.'

'And tell Andrew to ring me if there are any problems with Katie.'

Janie looked at her. Out of all the friends she had, Sarah probably had the worst deal and yet constantly remained the warmest and most giving. So much for divine justice. 'You've got enough on your plate,' she said. 'But thank you for the offer. I appreciate it.' She took her car keys out of her bag just as Roz came up.

'My word,' Roz exclaimed. 'This is a bit much for the school run, isn't it?'

'Janie's off to London for a well-deserved break,' Sarah said, and Janie shot her a look to say thanks for the support.

'Have a good time,' Roz said. 'Don't spend too much money.'

Janie smiled, with little sincerity, and hurried off to her car.

'I wish,' said Roz, 'I wish with all my heart and soul that it was me going off to London for a jolly. Janie doesn't know how easy she has it, she...'

'Yes she does.' Sarah interrupted. 'And it's not always as easy as it seems.' She hooked her arm through Roz's and said, 'Come on, some of us have to earn a living and you never know, there's always the big win on the lottery to look forward to.'

They walked together to Roz's car. 'That would solve all my problems,' Roz said, bending to peer at the hole where the exhaust should have been. 'A couple of million would make me really happy.'

'Would it?'

Roz stood up. 'You bet!' She looked at Sarah. 'And don't tell me it wouldn't solve all your problems either because you'd be lying.'

'It would solve some and ease others but there are some things, Roz, that I just can't change.'

Roz flushed. She glanced away for a moment, swamped with embarrassment and fear that she had offended Sarah. 'I'm sorry,' she mumbled. 'Of course there's Rory, I didn't think...'

'It's OK, most people don't think.' Sarah smiled and patted Roz on the arm. 'Anyway, that's part of your charm; where angels fear to tread and all that.'

Roz suddenly laughed. 'Am I really that out-spoken?'

'Yes.'

'Oh dear.' She opened the car door and peered inside. 'It's amazing what a Chupa Chup lolly will do for my peace of mind,' she said. Sarah peered into the car after her and saw Kitty and Oliver silent for once, a lolly stuffed firmly in each of their mouths.

'Know any good dentists?' she said.

'Of course, my children were never going to have sweets,' Roz said. 'They were going to eat organic wholemeal food, wear towelling nappies and always look immaculate.'

'In your dreams!' Sarah laughed and started for her own car. 'Whatever it takes to keep you and them sane,' she called. 'See you later, Roz.' She waved, watched Roz climb into her car, heard the roar of the broken exhaust and got into her own equally beaten-up Mini Metro.

A new car would be nice if I won the lottery, she thought, starting the engine. Plus a nice little cottage, with three bedrooms and a big, old-fashioned garden, and perhaps a decent holiday, some new clothes and a really good PC – maybe even a new telly and video. She smiled as she made her way into the village to work. And perhaps a skiing trip, tennis lessons, a small sailing boat – I can't sail, of course, but I could have tuition, or someone to sail it for me, a handsome captain of the seas... The list went on and on and kept her in good spirits all the way to the supermarket.

Andrew was waiting for Janie when she got in from the school run. He had rearranged his day so that he could work during Katie's hours at school, and had gone to quite a good deal of effort – and at short notice – to accommodate this trip. He was snatching a glance at the newspaper when she came into the kitchen and he looked up as she crossed to the fridge.

'I've left a shepherd's pie in the fridge for tonight,' Janie said. 'All you have to do is heat it up on one-eighty degrees for forty minutes, but I've written that down on the list so you don't have to worry about that now. And I've chopped some fruit for Katie – she can have it with yoghurt and a bit of honey when she gets in from school. And then there's croissants from the freezer tomorrow as a treat seeing as I'm away, and some freshly squeezed orange juice. Oh, and there's a homemade pizza in the freezer, I thought you could have that for lunch with salad. I bought a bag of ready-washed salad, it's in the bottom of the fridge. I–'

'Janie, stop,' Andrew said sharply 'Calm down, have a coffee, then get in the car and go. Just go, OK?'

'You're cross that I'm going,' she said. 'I knew you would be.'

Andrew stood up and folded the paper. 'No, I am not cross that you're going away, it has at least put you in a more positive mood than you've been in for months, but I am cross about this constant fretting. I do know how to chop fruit and heat a shepherd's pie, Janie. I even know how to *make* a shepherd's pie. I am not a complete imbecile.'

'No, of course not, sorry, it's just that...' She broke off and ripped her list from the fridge. She wanted to say, it's just that I need to do it, I need to feel that there's some purpose to my life, some sense of use and value. This is my job and I'm good at it, I want you to know that. But she didn't say any of it. She didn't see the point, minutes before getting into the car to drive to London, of starting an argument that couldn't be resolved.

'I worry, that's all,' she said.

Andrew sighed and came across to her. He held out his arms and she stepped into his embrace, not really wanting to be held.

'Now you have a good time, Janie, don't worry about us and come back tomorrow feeling refreshed.' Andrew didn't understand the purpose of this trip, just as he didn't understand Janie at the moment either. He rarely went away on his own and when he did – to the odd medical convention here and there – he couldn't wait to return home to the comfort of his wife and child. Andrew was content with his life, he was satisfied. He wanted nothing more than perhaps a few extra luxuries; to buy a small sailing boat one day or to trek the Himalayas. He and Janie had everything they needed, they were comfortable. And he was perfectly happy with that. He kissed Janie on the forehead, then said, 'Come on, you'd better get going. The sooner you start, the sooner you get there.'

'Obviously.' Janie smiled briefly up at him, then moved from his embrace and walked out into the hall to get her handbag. Andrew always said things that were so eminently sensible, so predictable. With her bags in her hand, she stood in the doorway and said, 'Are you going to see me off?'

Andrew hurried across. 'Here, let me take that bag! I know how much you pack, remember? It probably weighs a ton.' He took it from her hand and opened the front door. 'It does!' Out on the drive, he placed it in the boot of the car and opened the driver's side for Janie to climb in. 'Will you be all right, in all that London traffic? It's not like the country, you know.'

Janie climbed into the car and put her handbag on to the passenger seat. 'I used to live in London once. I drove everywhere.'

'Of course you did.' Andrew leant in to kiss Janie on the mouth. 'Bye.' He touched her cheek for one brief moment, then stood back and slammed the door shut. 'Have a good trip,' he called. 'We'll see you tomorrow.'

Janie pressed the window down. 'I will, thanks.' Then she accelerated forward and pulled out of the drive. In the rear-view mirror she could see Andrew waving and she held her hand out of the window to wave back. She had expected to feel sad – nervous and excited but mainly sad – at leaving Katie and her home. She felt none of those things, at least not at the moment. All she felt as she set on her way was a wonderful, expanding feeling of relief.

Roz stopped at the corner shop on the way back home from school to get enough supplies for the day and the following morning. She had abandoned going to the supermarket on a weekly basis as she found she spent far too much money trying to shop for the week and inevitably bought things they didn't need and sometimes didn't

71

even eat. Now she shopped daily, buying only exactly what they needed, and had found that she'd cut their food bill by a third. Of course there was still the monthly trip to Tesco for all the bulk stuff like washing powder and toilet rolls, but Graham did that because he was more prudent and got less carried away

Opening up Chadwick farmhouse, Roz let the dogs bound out and race around for a few minutes before she got her carrier bag out of the car and took it into the kitchen, with Oliver and Kitty trailing behind. She unpacked the shopping, looked at the sausages, potatoes, cabbage, cooking apples and tin of custard powder and thought, how sad. Toad in the hole with cabbage and mash followed by baked apples with custard. 'Glamorous,' she said to Oliver, 'my life is not.' What she wouldn't do to be going up to London for a snazzy lunch and dinner out.

'Oh well, there's always the post to look forward to.' She picked up a small stack of letters bundled together with a rubber band and rifled through them. 'Bill, rubbish, rubbish, rubbish, bill and oh, more rubbish.' She gave the advertising post to Kitty and Oliver to open and left the bills on the side for Graham to look at later. 'Why they send me information on so many special offers,' she said to Kitty, 'when I haven't got two pennies to rub together, I just don't know.'

'Don't know,' Kitty repeated.

Roz glanced up as someone knocked on the kitchen window. She waved and shouted, 'Come on in, Cecil, the door's open.' Major Cecil

Gorden owned the house at the end of the lane and the three fields to the right of Roz and Graham. He often called in for coffee, more for want of something to do than for friendship, Roz thought, but she never refused him a cup anyway. She liked the company; it was nice to have someone to moan to and the old Major was all right, a bit military and set in his views, but all right.

'Hello, Cecil. How are you?' Roz turned from the sink where she was filling the kettle. 'We haven't seen you for a while, I'll get the kettle on, shall I?'

'No thank you, Roz, my dear, I've just had a coffee with Daphne. It was she who suggested I come straight up actually, after we got the letter this morning.'

'Oh?' The Major was all right but Mrs G was most definitely not. Roz and Daphne didn't quite see eye to eye and that was Graham's way of describing it; Roz would have put it another way altogether. 'What letter's that then, Cecil?'

Major Gorden stood just inside the doorway and thought of what his good lady would say about the state of the kitchen. It had never really bothered him, he was not one for domestic fiddle faddle, but even he could see the grime on the floor and the debris of several days' washing-up.

'Well, it's something I've been meaning to mention to you, my dear, but haven't really got round to. Only now that we've got the letter and things are a bit more, well, concrete, so to speak, I thought I'd better come on over and get it straight.'

Roz switched on the kettle and rinsed a dirty mug under the cold tap. She spooned coffee into it and sat down at the table.

'You've lost me I'm afraid, Cecil. Get what straight?'

Major Gorden came in and sat down opposite Roz. She moved the unwashed breakfast things to the end of the table.

'The paddock,' he said. 'The four acres that border your small holding here. We've had an offer...' He fiddled with the letter, tapping it against the palm of his hand. 'A very good offer as a matter of fact, Roz dear, from a developer who seems to have connections in planning and would like to, erm...'

Roz heard the kettle come to the boil and switch itself off, but she didn't move. 'Would like to buy the land,' she said. 'Is that right?'

Cecil nodded.

'You told him where to go, I presume.' It was a lame statement. Even as she said it she knew that was the last thing the Gordens had done. 'It would ruin me, Cecil, an estate of houses all round us. I'd go out of business, or be forced out by the "residents association". Plus there's the organic soil thing and the issue of contamination, and the very idea of houses either side of us, halfway down our land, is just awful. Executive homes, isn't that what they call them? Small brick boxes that...' She stopped, suddenly aware that she was wasting her breath. There was a few moments' silence, then she said, 'How much?'

Cecil glanced down at the letter. 'It's a great deal of money, Roz. Daphne feels, we both feel, that it's too good an offer to turn down.'

Roz stood up. She walked across to the sink and held on to it for a while, her back to the Major and her hands gripping the chipped white enamel. 'They'll never get planning,' she said. She meant it to come out strong and forceful, but even to her own ears her voice was very small.

'I think that they probably will,' Cecil said, 'hence the big offer.'

Roz closed her eyes. She never cried, she was as tough as old boots, Graham said, but at this moment she was the closest she had been to tears in a long time.

'I'm sorry, Roz dear. I know it's a bit of a shock for you, but you must see that Daphne and I can't really afford to let this sort of offer pass us by. It just wouldn't make sense...'

'Of course not,' Roz managed to say, turning round. She tore a piece of kitchen paper off the roll and blew her nose. 'You have to think of yourselves, of course you do, Cecil. I'm sure Graham and I would do the same if we were in your position.' They were platitudes uttered to ease Cecil's embarrassment. She knew that she would never sell to a developer, never. She felt too strongly about carving up the countryside to build small, square boxes for no reason other than profit.

Cecil Gorden got to his feet. 'I won't keep you then, Roz,' he said, 'I can see you're up to your eyes in it.'

She thought, that's true, but it's never stopped you before. She bit her tongue. Roz the outspoken held back, for once. Instead she said,

'That's very considerate of you, Cecil.' And he looked at her for a moment, not at all sure about the sincerity of her remark.

'Right, well, erm, I'll say goodbye then. Don't bother to see me out, my dear, I can find my own way.'

'Yes, good.' Roz watched him go. She glanced down and saw Oliver and Kitty playing with the water in the dog's bowl, but instead of shouting she simply bent and removed it, saying nothing. She filled an old ice cream container on the draining board with water and placed that on the floor for them to play with, then she walked across to the table and sat down. She supposed she should ring Graham, tidy the house, get on with things and then ring the council to find out who was in charge of planning and get an appointment to see them. She supposed she should ring the Gordens and ask for the name of the developer. She really ought to get a move on. But she didn't do any of that. She sat and stared at the table while the children soaked the floor and themselves with water, then she put her head in her hands and let a wave of self-pity wash over her. She would fight, of course she would. She'd fight, well, to the death, but for now, just for this moment, she couldn't for the life of her even raise the energy to cry.

Sarah was in the aisles this morning, checking deliveries. They were short-staffed so she had been moved from the customer services desk and was back to regular supermarket duties until further notice. The manager said it might be for a few days or the whole week, who could tell with this awful flu virus going around?

She had just finished checking the delivery of tea when she heard a discreet cough and glanced to her right. A man stood with an empty basket and smiled at her. She smiled back, naturally, and recognised him from the week before.

'Sorry,' he said, 'to interrupt, but could you tell me if you stock Orange Pekoe tea?'

He had a great voice, dark and warm – she remembered that from last week – and he looked right at her, not just beyond her as most people who saw her turquoise-checked overall did.

'No,' Sarah said, 'that's a specialist tea and Earl Grey is about as specialist as we get. You might get it in the shop on the high street.'

'Right. Thanks.' He smiled again. It was an open, relaxed smile and it settled easily on his face, like he smiled all the time. 'D'you only work here mornings?'

Sarah blinked rapidly; she was taken aback. Not many customers talked to her. The general consensus of opinion was that people who worked in supermarkets weren't clever enough to work anywhere else. 'Yes,' she relied. 'I, erm, I work until one. I have to pick my son up from school at three-thirty.'

'Of course. I've seen you up at school, at Wynchcombe Primary. How old is he, your son?'

Sarah glanced behind her. A few odd pleasantries were OK, a full-blown chat was not. 'He's six,' she said, glancing down at her list. 'Sorry, but I've got to get on.'

'Oh yes, right, of course you have.' He nodded.

'Thanks for the tip.'

'Tip?'

'About the tea.'

'Right. That's OK.'

He walked away and Sarah bent her head immediately to her list. It was a small, local supermarket and nothing went unnoticed; she didn't want to get into trouble.

Ten minutes later, having moved on to the bread section, Sarah noticed the man again. He had put a packet of rolls into his basket and was searching – or at least he seemed to be searching – the bread shelves for something he couldn't find.

'Excuse me,' he said, 'I'm sorry to interrupt, but would you know if you have a part-baked ciabatta bread?' He stared up at the display of loaves.

Sarah reached up, handed him the loaf he wanted, then got on with her list. 'Thanks,' he said. 'You wouldn't know how long I bake it for, would you?'

Irritated, Sarah turned and he smiled at her again. It registered that he was an attractive man and she made a brief mental acknowledgement of his features, but that was all. Sarah had no time for men, attractive or not. 'It's on the packet,' she said. 'Just read the instructions.'

'Right, thanks.'

She went back to her list and ignored him. He waited a few moments more, as if he wanted to add something, but Sarah didn't give him the opportunity to. She ticked the last delivery on her sheet and walked away

78

Ten minutes later, as she finished taking a call on the customer services desk, he was there again and Sarah sighed as she saw him.

'I'm sorry,' he began.

'To interrupt,' she finished sharply for him. 'But...?'

This time he didn't smile. He bit his lip, looked over her shoulder, then said, 'It's OK, I've just spotted it.' He strode away and Sarah was embarrassed. It wasn't in her nature to be unnecessarily rude and she had been just then. She turned and saw him in the aisle behind her, and was wondering if she should apologise when the assistant manager appeared and said, 'You couldn't go on to till four could you, Sarah? Jean hasn't had her coffee yet.'

'Yes, no problem. Now?'

'Please.'

Sarah stepped out from behind the counter and glanced over her shoulder. Perhaps, she thought, she could catch him on the way to the till, but the aisle was empty and as she looked she saw his basket abandoned by the bread. Too late. He had gone and Sarah, who wasn't really sure why, felt disappointed.

Lucie sat in a meeting and tried hard not to drum her fingers on the table in front of her. Meetings were always too long and the men in them always said everything they needed to say at least twice. Women didn't. Maybe that was sexist, but it seemed to Lucie that the sort of women she dealt with really didn't have time to spare. They did their jobs and they also had homes to run, husbands to look after and children to nurture. They couldn't afford the extra hour it took to turn full circle in a discussion again. She glanced at her watch. It was three o'clock and surely Alex was back in the office by now. She had to get hold of him before tonight, she absolutely had to. He would have to cancel; have an illness, be indisposed, anything except come for dinner with his new friend Marcus Todd, who, unbeknown to him, was married to Lucie Croft, the woman he was having an affair with. She looked up at the men round the table, glanced at the clock on the wall and, in a moment of panic, suddenly said, 'Will you excuse me please? I have to make a call just after three, it's very important.'

Her client frowned, but she pretended not to notice. Lucie was the consummate professional; she had never interrupted a meeting before, but she was in a state and had to make her call. There was a murmur of assent round the table and she stood, reaching for her bag. 'I'll be back in five minutes, Jeff,' she said. Her colleague nodded, then addressed the table. 'Lets take a five-minute break here, shall we? Can I get anyone coffee?'

Lucie hurried out of the room.

In the next-door meeting room, she checked the number in her diary then dialled Alex's phone and waited. The line connected and she heard his voice mail message. 'Alex,' she said quickly, 'it's Lucie. Call me urgently please, on my mobile. It's three p.m. on Friday.' She didn't say any more – she had no idea who picked up his messages. Cutting the line, she immediately re-dialled and rang the switchboard of his bank.

'Hello, could I have the UK Equities dealing room please?' She waited and was put through a few moments later.

'Hello? Oh, hi, yes, I hope you can help. This is Lucie Croft from the corporate finance team at World Bank. I'm trying to get hold of Alex Stanton.' The male voice on the other end of the phone told her what she already knew, what she had found out yesterday morning, that Alex was away on a brokers' trip to one of the big industrial companies. She struggled with a momentary flare of irritation and said, as calmly as she could, 'Yes, I was told that yesterday, but the person I spoke to also said that he was expected back in the office this afternoon. Has he come in yet?' She waited while the person on the other end asked round the office and then informed her that Alex had come back to the office briefly but had just left again. 'Oh no, has he?' she said. 'What time did he come in? Half an hour ago? Blast! And he didn't say where he was going? No, of course not, I see.' She was at risk of making a fool of herself by sounding too personal. 'No, it's just that I needed some information from him on Tech Co. No, it's fine, I'll get it Monday. Yes, I will, I'll try his mobile. Thanks very much. Bye.' She cut the line a second time and flicked the page in her address book. She dialled Alex's mobile, the message service answered and she left yet another voice mail, her third today.

'Fuck,' she said aloud. She didn't know what to do. Chances were, she thought, that Alex had returned to the office after his trip, picked up his messages – not including hers – and had then

81

buggered off for the rest of the afternoon to the gym or the pub or God knows where. Lucie put her head in her hands. He'd probably switched off his mobile or even left it in his desk – he hated the thing anyway – and was happy and relaxed, looking forward to the weekend and especially the dinner with his new mate Marcus. She swore again and didn't hear the door open.

'Lucie?' She started and looked up. 'God, sorry, Jeff, I was miles away'

'I can see that. Have you finished your calls, because we'd like to get on?'

'Yes, yes, of course. I'll be right with you.'

Jeff looked pointedly at his watch. 'Thank you,' he said. Then he walked out of the room and a few moments later Lucie followed him.

Janie handed over the items she had chosen in Gap Kids and took her purse out of her handbag ready to pay. She had been shopping all afternoon, had a couple of bags for herself and a whole armful of clothes for Katie. She was pleased; she'd had a good time, with lunch and a glass of wine on her own in an Italian café and a good wander round the shops, not looking for anything in particular but buying what she fancied. She signed the credit card slip that the sales assistant handed her, took her bag and walked out of the shop. It had been an indulgent afternoon, but as she glanced at her watch she saw that it was only just five and so decided on a quick restorative coffee before she took a cab over to Marcus's office. The time, she thought, hadn't exactly flown by. Shopping was OK but it wasn't sustaining, not something she could do more than once every now and then.

Janie sat in the window of the coffee-house and people-watched for half an hour. It was a good pastime, but it only served to emphasise the fact that everyone in the world seemed to have somewhere to go and something to do except her. Of course she had the dinner with Marcus to go to and she'd done a good deal of shopping, things that Katie needed, new clothes to replace the ones she'd grown out of, but that was only today. The rest of the time she did nothing, or certainly very little, that she considered of any value. I need a job, she thought, then immediately dismissed the idea. What could she do? She had been a freelance stylist on a women's magazine when she met Andrew, but it wasn't a career she wanted to go back to. It had been hard work, with long hours in sweaty studios, little recognition and low pay. The magazine industry was like that, all kudos and silk knickers, nothing substantial. And besides, she wouldn't have a clue where to start now. It had been fun though, she'd had a sense of adventure then, a sense of future.

Janie finished her iced coffee and stood up. What did she have now, except the feeling that it was all going to be over before she'd had a chance to get there? She gathered up her carrier bags, slung her handbag over her shoulder and left the cafe. Perhaps she should talk to Marcus about this ever-deepening sense of gloom, perhaps he would know what to do. She walked out on to Regent Street, spotted a cab across the road, put two fingers in her mouth and gave a shrill

whistle. She smiled when the cabbie acknow-
ledged her and swung the cab round to her side
of the road. I haven't lost my knack then, she
thought, and that fact cheered her all the way to
the City.

Chapter Five

It was Friday night, seven-thirty, and Alex Stanton had been to the gym. He went on average four or five times a week, either to Cannons in the City during his lunch hour or to the Riverside in Chiswick, a couple of miles from where he lived. He didn't consider himself a fanatic, but by most people's standards he was extremely fit. He played tennis in the summer and squash in the winter and he ran at weekends, sometimes five or six miles on a Sunday morning. And it showed. He carried no weight, had washboard abdominals, well-defined pecs and rock-solid biceps with a butterfly tattoo on the left one. He had a circle of mates with whom he worked out and a tennis four who met every Thursday night throughout the year. He was popular in the tennis league, well-liked at work and highly thought of amongst the friends he had made at university. He was easy-going, affectionate, warm-hearted and unambitious. Alex Stanton worked in order to play. He liked his job, was good enough at it to make the bank money but he saw no point in doing more than was absolutely necessary. He had no plans other than to enjoy life and in that itself, as in so many other things, he was the complete antithesis of Marcus Todd.

Alex thought about this as he sat in the bar at

Cannons with an Isotonic drink. He thought about Marcus and wondered what his wife was like – that possibly she might be as driven and as high-powered as Marcus himself. Certainly he'd been surprised by the invitation to dinner; Marcus gave the impression the few times that they'd met for drinks that he didn't go in for much socialising, that he and his wife were too busy. He also wondered about Lucie as he sat watching people coming and going; he wondered where she was and what she was doing. He knew very little about her home life; she rarely talked about it, or about herself. But he liked that aspect of her, the self-containment, the feeling that there was so much there that he had yet to find out.

His affair with Lucie had been going on for several months now, though where it was going he didn't know, or particularly care. They had met at a Christmas drinks party, liked each other and chatted all evening. The following week he had seen her again by chance at a lunch in the City and after that it just seemed to click. She was married, of course, but that didn't really bother him. She was unhappily married, it made all the difference in his mind. Besides, it wasn't that sort of affair, not the deep-meaning sort. It was a laugh, great sex, and he liked the way they went their separate ways, led their separate lives, had no hassle.

Alex finished his drink and looked at his watch. It was time to go. He would probably be fifteen minutes late for dinner – Marcus said eight o'clock – but that was polite, wasn't it? If he hadn't left his phone at work – something he did quite often at weekends, not wanting to be contactable at all times – he could have called them to let them know he was on his way Or was that a bit too conscientious? Alex wasn't familiar with dinner party etiquette; all the dinners he went to were hosted by old friends with whom he could get drunk and fall asleep on the sofa. He had never had to worry about doing the right thing before.

Getting to his feet, he took his glass to the bar and collected his sports bag from the rack. Outside he found a taxi, gave the address and sat back for the ride to Notting Hill. He was looking forward to tonight; he liked Marcus and meeting new people was an experience, even if it wasn't always a good one.

Lucie lay in the bath and turned the hot tap on with her big toe. She had been in there for forty minutes and just couldn't summon the energy to get out. She was dreading tonight. She had been torn for the hour between leaving work and arriving home between doing nothing or simply getting a cab to a mainline station and catching a train, any train, heading out of London. But Lucie wasn't an escapist. She was and always had been aware of the consequences of her actions, and if she hadn't turned up at home tonight it would have thrown the situation open to chaos.

So here she was, soaking in perfumed water, her stomach churning, her face hot and her mind in turmoil. She had no idea how Alex would react and she had no way of even speaking to him alone because the house was so open-plan that there wasn't a square inch of privacy in the whole place. At least Peter and Julie would be there, so there was some kind of antidote to Marcus's intensity and someone to divert the attention if things got difficult.

Julie was an old friend of Lucie's from university who had also ended up in the City, and Peter was her husband. Lucie and Julie had once been close, but she had gone the way of most of Lucie's friends since she'd married Marcus and, despite denying it, kept her distance. It was something to do with envy, Marcus always said, envy of the fact that he and Lucie had everything. But Lucie didn't think so. She had never asked Julie, had never asked any of her friends, but she thought it was probably more to do with them not liking Marcus, with finding him too difficult and the friendship – if you could call it that, with Marcus always cancelling arrangements and inciting arguments – not worth the effort.

She wondered if Julie would sense that things were askew, if she'd know something was going on. She was fiercely bright and very intuitive, but then Lucie was now a competent liar and they were no longer close. Perhaps, Lucie thought, standing and reaching for a towel, it might actually be a relief if she did notice, it might be a relief for someone to know. She wrapped herself in a towel and stepped out of the bath. Secrets, Lucie thought, ate away at the very core of a person, they destroyed integrity. She dried herself, dropped the towel on the bed and opened her wardrobe to look for something to wear. Secrets, she thought, destroyed everything in the end.

Janie tipped the prepared salad into a large, open blue glass bowl and tossed the leaves briefly with her fingers. She placed the blue glass salad servers on top and turned to mix her dressing. Reaching for the olive oil, she poured a generous measure into a screw-top jar and turned to Marcus.

'Balsamic vinegar? Lemon juice?' she asked.

Marcus looked up from the *Evening Standard* and shrugged. 'Your guess is as good as mine, Janie. Try the fridge or the cupboard next to the fridge.'

Janie tried the cupboard first and found a jar of Marmite, some sachets of Cup-A-Soup, three Pot Noodles and a couple of half-full packets of pasta. She went to the fridge. 'Do you and Lucie ever eat anything?' she asked, peering inside.

'Yes, but nothing that has been prepared by our own hands.' He took a sip of beer, drinking straight from the bottle, and said, 'If it comes wrapped in cardboard and plastic we'll eat it and if we don't have to bother with plates then all the better.'

Janie laughed; she thought he was joking. 'Ah,' she cried, 'half a lemon. It looks a bit dry but it'll do.' She took it across to the jar, stuck a fork in it and squeezed the juice into the olive oil.

'Thanks,' Marcus said, 'for doing all this.'

She looked up. 'For doing what? I've only put what the caterer delivered into the oven, set the table and made a salad dressing. It's hardly "all this".'

Marcus looked at his watch. 'It's enough,' he said. 'And we're supposed to be treating you. I think Lucie was right, she said there was no point having people here and that we should have gone out to dinner. Perhaps that's why she's taken so bloody long in the bath, out of protest.' He drained his bottle of Becks. 'Either that or she's waiting to see if I get it together. Fat chance!'

Janie looked at him. She had always thought that Marcus and Lucie made an ideal couple. They were so alike; both driven, ambitious, wanting the same things and in love. Now she wasn't so sure.

'What's a fat chance?' Lucie asked.

Both Janie and Marcus turned to look at her. She had changed from her work suit into wide-legged black cashmere trousers and a sleeveless cashmere top. She had her hair loose and it hung around her shoulders, shining under the small halogen spotlights set into the ceiling. Janie felt dowdy by comparison. She had never thought of Lucie as attractive, but she realised now that with time, effort and money Lucie had transformed herself. She looked sleek and expensive.

'Nothing,' Marcus said casually, throwing a look at Janie that warned her not to contradict him. 'Are you ready now? Can I use the bathroom?'

'Yes,' Lucie said coolly, picking up on Marcus's disgruntled tone. 'But if you were waiting for me, why didn't you use one of the other bathrooms?' Their conversion had three double bedrooms, each with a bathroom attached, one downstairs – theirs – and two upstairs, along with a work area.

'My stuff is in our bathroom, we share it,

90

remember?' Janie turned away. It wasn't bickering, more a restrained hostility. She began to peel a garlic clove for the salad dressing and Marcus said, 'Janie's been getting supper organised.'

'So I see,' Lucie replied. 'Thank you, Janie. The table looks lovely, where did you get the flower arrangement?'

Janie had bought Lucie a bunch of white lily of the valley and had arranged them as soon as she'd arrived in a square glass vase with a few blades of elephant grass and some grey pebbles. It looked good, even if she did say so herself; it was in the exact style of the house.

'Janie did them herself,' Marcus said. He stood, leaving his empty beer bottle where it was. 'You're not the only one with perfect taste around here.' He smiled to indicate that he was joking, but Janie could see that Lucie hadn't found it amusing, that she was wounded by such unwarranted criticism. Lucie rubbed her hands over her bare arms as if suddenly cold and Janie said, 'Shall I open some wine while you're in the shower, Marcus?'

'Yes, do.' Marcus headed towards the bedroom. 'Lucie will get it for you,' he called before disappearing inside and closing the door behind him. 'Thanks...' Janie murmured, then she shrugged her shoulders at Lucie.

'Sorry,' Lucie said, 'he's not in a very good mood.'

'Don't apologise,' Janie replied, 'he's my brother. I remember him as a spotty fifteen-year-old who didn't speak to my parents for six weeks once.'

Lucie smiled. 'Six weeks? You got off lightly He's been in a bad mood with me for quite a bit longer than that I'm afraid.' She walked into the kitchen area and opened the fridge. 'White or red?' she asked.

'White please.'

Lucie took a bottle of white wine out and placed it on the work surface while she looked for a corkscrew 'Did the caterer send a starter?'

'Yes, marinated buffalo mozzarella with some vine tomatoes.'

'Yum, that sounds nice. Bread?'

'Some sort of olive oil and rosemary bread. It looks nice.'

'Good.' Lucie found the corkscrew and peeled the wrapping off the cork with the sharp point of the screw 'What did they send for the main course?'

Janie frowned. 'Didn't you order it, Lucie?'

'Yes, but I just told them to deliver what they thought best. I didn't have time to discuss it with them.'

'I see.' Janie watched as Lucie poured the wine. She wondered how two women with one man in common could be at such opposite ends of the spectrum. Here she was, her life dominated by all things domestic, and here Lucie was not even knowing the word. Somewhere there had to be a balance, hadn't there?

Lucie handed Janie a glass of wine and said, 'You look well Janie, are you?'

'Yes, I am,' Janie replied.

'And Katie and Andrew?'

'Both fine. Katie's growing up so quickly, she's

quite independent at times.' Janie took a sip of wine. 'So independent in fact that I feel a bit redundant now.'

'You should get a job,' Lucie said, tossing the comment off carelessly. She had never been able to understand why Janie didn't work. She was bright and articulate and wasted, in Lucie's view, on children and domesticity; most women were.

'Yes, maybe.' Janie could sense Lucie's disapproval and the last thing they needed was to open up a well-worn discussion on feminism. In an attempt to change the subject, she said, 'Who's coming tonight?' She looked at Lucie, who immediately turned away, but not before Janie noticed her cheeks flood with colour. Janie screwed the lid on the jar of salad dressing and gave it her full attention, shaking it vigorously

Lucie said, 'An old friend of mine called Julie Granger and her husband, Peter, and some friend of Marcus's, someone I've not met before. Marcus invited him.'

'Really? That's unusual, isn't it, for Marcus to go inviting people over for supper?'

Lucie shrugged.

'Well, good for him,' Janie said, 'he could do with a friend.'

Lucie didn't answer. She was fiddling with the controls on the oven and Janie said, 'I put it on to one-eighty. It's a circotherm oven, isn't it?'

Lucie turned and Janie saw that her face was wretched. 'I haven't got a clue,' she said.

'Lucie?' Janie moved towards her, suddenly concerned that she was going to cry. 'Lucie, are you all right?'

The doorbell rang. Lucie started physically, then looked at her watch. 'God, it's twenty past eight! I had no idea it was so late.' She put her wine glass down and hurried over to the door, her heels clicking sharply on the tiled floor. I wish they'd get rugs, Janie thought, the whole atmosphere in this house is too cold.

Lucie put her hand on the latch of the door and hesitated for a moment. She took a deep breath, tried to move some moisture round her dry mouth and then released the lock, swinging the door open. She saw Alex, saw his face register shock then disbelief, and before he uttered a word she blurted, 'Hello, I'm married to Marcus.'

Janie frowned. She had busied herself with adding some grain mustard to the salad dressing but she could hear Lucie and it seemed to her that Lucie wasn't on form at all.

At the door there was a brief silence. Alex was stunned. His immediate reaction was to turn round and leave, but Lucie had the door open and her face was desperate. He managed to gather his wits sufficiently to realise that there must be other people close by and say, 'I'm Alex. Is this where Marcus Todd lives?'

'Yes,' Lucie replied, then again she said, 'I'm Lucie, I'm married to Marcus Todd.'

Janie looked across. What an odd scene, she thought, then Lucie said, 'Please, come on in, Marcus is just taking a shower. Come and meet his sister, Janie.'

Janie put down the jar and moved out of the kitchen area. Alex walked towards her but he

94

didn't really see her; his mind was still reeling from the shock and he wasn't taking anything in.

'Hello, I'm Janie Leighton. I'm Marcus's sister.'

Alex held out his hand and took Janie's. He forced himself to smile and say, 'Nice to meet you, Janie. D'you live locally?'

'Oh no, I'm up for the day from the country, on a bit of a jolly.'

'How nice.' Alex looked beyond Janie as Marcus came hurrying out of the bedroom and across to him. He was bewildered by this bizarre turn of events and only just managed to smile again.

'Alex! Sorry, mate, I was in the shower.' The two men shook hands and Alex struggled to recover himself. 'Glad you could come. You've met my wife, Lucie?'

Alex blinked, then said, 'Oh, yes, yes of course.'

'And she's getting you a drink?'

'I think so.'

Lucie was in the kitchen area. 'What would you like, Alex?' she called. 'Wine, beer, or there's gin and tonic?'

'A beer, please,' Alex replied. He was sweating and hoped to God it didn't show. The doorbell rang again and Lucie said, 'That'll be Julie and Peter.' She hurried across to the door and pulled it open.

'Hello, Julie!' The two women kissed. 'Peter, hi, how are you?' Lucie kissed Peter and noticed how cool his cheek felt against the burning skin of her own. 'Come on in. It's good to see you, it's been too long.' She led them inside to Marcus who kissed Julie, shook hands with Peter and

95

introduced his sister and Alex. He was smiling a great deal and called out to Lucie to get more drinks. At least, she thought, taking a bottle of beer out of the fridge and pouring more wine, Marcus is enjoying himself. And, studiously avoiding Alex's eye while plastering a smile on to her face, she took heart from this small mercy in an otherwise dire situation and handed round the drinks.

'So, Janie,' Peter said, turning to her on his left as Lucie handed him his starter, 'What do you do down in the country? Do you work at all?'

'No, no, I don't work. I've got a daughter of six and...'

'But you're thinking of working, aren't you, Janie?' Lucie said, handing her a plate of the marinated cheese. 'Didn't you say earlier that you wanted some sort of job?'

Janie shrugged. Actually it was Lucie who'd said that but she didn't want to disagree, there didn't seem any point.

Marcus leant over her shoulder and refilled her wine glass. 'It isn't a job you want, Janie, it's some sort of small business or project that you can do in your own time. Something you might earn a bit of money from.'

'I'm not really sure what I need,' Janie said, taking a gulp of wine.

Marcus finished pouring wine and sat down. Lucie joined him a few moments later bringing her own starter with her. 'Cheers,' Marcus said. Janie raised her glass.

'You need to use your brain,' Lucie went on.

96

'You need some sort of stimulation.'

'What about adult education?' Julie asked. 'A degree maybe?'

Janie laughed. She was beginning to feel a bit embarrassed, being the focus of conversation. 'I don't think so, I'm not clever enough.'

'Nonsense,' Marcus cut in. 'But, you know, I did hear something on the radio last week about investment clubs, and that sort of thing might be exactly what you need.'

'What a great idea!' Lucie said. 'You could start an investment club. It's not as if you'd be lacking for any expertise!'

'What's an investment club?' Janie, who had drunk three glasses of wine very quickly, was beginning to feel more at ease with the conversation. Lucie had dimmed the overhead spots and two church candles burnt at either end of the table, suffusing everything with their peculiar, intimate light. The effect was almost immediate as everyone seemed to sigh and relax into their chairs.

'It's a number of people,' Marcus explained, 'each with a sum to invest, who get together and invest it as a group. They research and discuss their investments and also get a much better deal from the broker by doing one large investment rather than five or six smaller ones.'

'They're springing up all over the place, aren't they?' Lucie asked.

'They're pretty popular,' Marcus replied.

Julie turned to Alex. 'Have you come across any, Alex?'

'A colleague of mine invests for one group.

They phone him every now and then for advice but do most of it themselves. They do a pretty good job on the whole, I think. He's quite impressed.'

'There you are!' Marcus said triumphantly 'You could do it standing on your head, Janie. Get a few friends together, use me or Lucie or even Alex here for advice, and you're off! Easy peasy lemon squeezy.'

Everyone laughed.

'I'll think about it,' Janie said, smiling.

'You should,' Julie advised. 'If you got in quick with some of these dot com companies you could make a killing. It's money for old rope, providing you keep a close eye on the market.'

'But they're dodgy stocks, Jules,' Peter said, 'very volatile.'

'In the long term yes, but in the short term they'd be perfect. They'd be brilliant for a small investment club, wouldn't they, Alex?'

Alex glanced up quickly. He had been surreptitiously looking at his watch under the table and wondering how early he could get away The situation was killing him. He hadn't been able to so much as look at Lucie and every time Marcus talked to him he wanted to cringe. 'Oh, um, yes. I've done quite a bit of work on the dot coms recently and I've made a colossal return. You have to watch the market bloody closely but yeah, they'd be a good place to start.'

'There you are,' Marcus cried, 'it's all sorted!'

Janie laughed. 'What's all sorted?'

'Tomorrow morning you go home, organise some friends, each with a thousand pounds to invest, then you get Alex to whack it into his favourite dot coms and you're away.' He saw that everyone had finished and stood to clear the plates. Lucie watched him. He seemed oddly animated tonight, drunk almost, but he'd hardly touched his wine. 'Alex is a great broker, you can't go wrong with him.'

Janie turned to Alex. There was something about investments that appealed to everyone and she was no exception. The whole idea of the City and stocks and shares was sexy. It excited her, it was like a safe sort of gambling. That and the fact that she was on her fourth glass of wine and Marcus always had been the most persuasive of people. 'Would you seriously mind getting involved?' she asked him. 'I mean, if I did manage to get some friends together with some money to invest?'

'Of course he wouldn't!' Marcus called from the kitchen area. He came back to the table carrying the salad. 'Providing all the friends were female and as attractive as you, Janie.'

Alex forced a smile and as Lucie got up to go to the kitchen she shot him a look that was narrowly missed by Marcus. He began to sweat again.

'Seriously?' Janie said again. 'Would you?'

Alex glanced round the table and all eyes were on him. What excuse could he possibly give without sounding rude and causing offence? 'Of course,' he mumbled. He heard Lucie bang down a dish in the kitchen and concentrated on looking at Janie. 'I'm not sure I could do it right now, I've got an awful lot on at work, but sometime in the future, certainly I'd assist you.'

Marcus patted him on the back. 'That's the boy! I'll give Janie your number, shall I?'

Alex nodded.

'If you're absolutely sure?' Janie said.

'I'll serve it in here,' Lucie shouted. 'Can someone give me a hand with the plates?'

Alex and Julie both stood at the same time. 'I'll go,' Alex said, 'please, let me do something to help.' Julie sat down again, not in the least bothered. She turned to Janie and asked if she'd ever invested in the market before and the conversation switched to general investment as Alex walked into the kitchen area.

He stood next to Lucie and she handed him a plate. She didn't look at him so he stood there holding it until she did. He raised his eyes as if to say 'it wasn't my fault' and she shook her head. What the hell was he playing at, agreeing to get involved with Marcus's sister? It was suicide, like a macabre game of happy families. 'Sorry,' he mouthed at her. She shook her head again. it wasn't him who should be sorry, it was her. This whole thing was a mess and she realised, standing there dishing out pollo in porchetta, that the only person she had to blame was herself.

Chapter Six

The following morning after the dinner party Janie slept in. It hadn't been a late night; Alex had left just after eleven which broke the evening up and Lucie had gone to bed almost immediately after everyone left. She said she felt tired, but Janie wondered if she might be sickening for something, she was so pale. Janie stayed up for half an hour or so talking to Marcus after that, but she was relieved to get to bed herself. There had been an odd atmosphere at dinner, a tension which she put down to a group of people who hardly knew each other and had very little in common, except their jobs. Besides, Marcus had got her thinking with his suggestion of an investment club and she wanted a bit of time alone to consider what he'd said.

It was after nine when she finally got up and, getting straight into the shower, Janie was surprised at how good she felt. She had drunk a great deal, had slept fitfully and deserved to be feeling terrible. Instead, as she soaped herself in the shower with the expensive Jo Malone soap that Lucie left for guests – an attempt to show off in Janie's opinion – she tried to identify the feeling she had. She ran through a list of words in her head and came to optimism. She smiled; yes, that was it. For the first time in a long while Janie felt optimistic that the future had possibilities.

She stepped out of the shower and reached for a towel, dried herself, dressed and applied a light makeup. Then she went down into the kitchen area to make herself a pot of tea. That is, of course, if she could find some tea bags.

'Morning,' Marcus said from his seat at the dining table. The living area was immaculate. There wasn't a trace of the six people who had had dinner ten hours earlier and Marcus sat at a polished table drinking coffee, a half-full cafetiere in front of him, the Saturday *FT* open and propped up against the pot.

'Hello. Have you cleared all this up this morning?'

'No, I did most of it last night, just unloaded and reloaded the dishwasher this morning. Coffee?'

'No thanks, I'll make myself some tea if you don't mind.'

'I don't think we've got any tea bags,' Marcus said.

'Oh. It'll have to be coffee then.' Janie went into the kitchen area and took a clean cup down from the cupboard. 'You should have waited for me to get up and help,' she said, bringing her cup across to him. He poured her some coffee and said, 'You did quite enough last night. Those lily of the valley smell wonderful, by the way. I've been sitting here thoroughly enjoying them.' Janie smiled and pulled out a chair. That was typical Marcus, she thought, to say something completely unexpected. He could be taciturn, morose even, at times and then he would make a comment that seemed so natural and charming that it took the person he made it to totally by surprise. Sometimes she wondered if it wasn't calculated to do so, but perhaps that was unfair.

Janie added milk and sugar to her coffee and took a sip. 'Good coffee,' she commented.

'Of course.' Marcus folded the paper and put it away 'So,' he said, looking at her, 'did we solve the problem last night?'

'What problem?'

He narrowed his eyes. 'You started to tell me on the way home that you were bored and unhappy, but changed your mind and kept quiet. Or at least that's what I think you were going to tell me.'

Janie said nothing. She and Marcus had what she supposed was a typical sibling relationship. They liked each other, they got on, but they had never been close, they were too competitive for that. They had very different lives and very different partners and it was rare that they really felt comfortable with each other.

'I think this investment club thing is a really good idea. I think it would suit you perfectly, Janie.'

'It is tempting,' she said, 'I have to admit.'

'Of course it is. It's something that would use your brain, take up some time – but only as much as you wanted it to – and earn you some good money to boot.' He finished his coffee. 'You could come up to London every now and then for meetings with Alex, have lunch with me, really enjoy it.' Then he stood. 'I'll make some more coffee, shall I?'

Janie nodded and thought about what he'd just

103

said. While he was in the kitchen area she pulled the Saturday *FT* towards her and unfolded it, glancing at the front page.

'You know, the more I think about it, Janie, the more I think you'd be insane to ignore it,' he called across. Janie continued to read the front page of the paper. When he came back with a fresh pot of coffee, she said, 'Do you really think I could manage something like this, Marcus? I mean, I'm not clever like you – I'm not really sure I could do it.'

Marcus shook his head. 'Hey! Where's your confidence?' He pushed the plunger down on the cafetiere and poured them both another cup. 'Janie, you could do it easily. You'd have Alex to help you as well as all my expertise, mine and Lucie's...'

'But I'm not sure that Alex was keen to get involved,' Janie interrupted. 'He might not want to be bothered. It's not as if he's going to earn much out of it, is it?'

'Of course he's keen. OK, it might start small, but if you get it right within six months you could be making quite a bit of money, which is all commission for him.'

'Really?'

'Yes, really!' Marcus smiled. 'Don't look so serious, Janie! What have you got to lose?'

Janie thought about it for a moment. 'Nothing, I suppose, except my original investment.'

'You won't lose that, not with a team like us behind you.'

'How much would I need? I mean to start with?'

'I don't know, whatever you want, I guess. How many friends were you thinking of involving?'

Roz and Sarah immediately sprung to mind. 'Two others, maybe three?' She had no idea if they had any money to spare, especially not Sarah, but if it was a good return and low risk then surely they could borrow some? At least to begin with.

'Well, you could start with a thousand pounds each, maybe two thousand.'

'I see.' That was what she'd been expecting. 'And how long would it take to set up?'

'You decide on the people in the club, the sum to invest, the stocks to buy, make your purchase and that's it. A day, a week? You might want to draw up some sort of legal agreement about who put up what and that would take some time, but it's entirely up to you. You don't have to do it.'

'You make it sound so easy.'

Marcus suddenly laughed. 'It is easy, Janie! That's why I told you about it.' He was still smiling when Lucie appeared, but the smile faded as she came towards them, then finally disappeared.

'You're dressed,' he said.

'Very observant,' Lucie quipped, but it didn't come out as a joke. Janie instantly got up and took the coffee pot over to the kitchen. 'I'll make more coffee,' she said quickly, embarrassed by the change in atmosphere.

'Not for me,' Lucie said, 'I'm off to the club for a work-out.'

Janie had her back to them but she could sense the tension.

'That's very zealous of you,' Marcus drawled. 'I had no idea you'd become such a fitness fanatic.'

Lucie tossed off a small laugh, but even she knew it didn't sound genuine. 'I'm not, but I feel crappy. I drank too much and ate too much and I need a good sweat. I thought I'd do a class then have a sauna.'

'Good idea,' Marcus said and Janie turned.

'I shan't be here when you get back,' she said. 'I think I'll get off in half an hour or so. It might take me a while to get across London and I'd like to be back for lunch.' Actually she hadn't planned to be back for lunch at all, but she didn't want to stay. She had realised over the past twelve hours that one night with her brother and his wife was enough.

'Right, well, I'd better say goodbye now then,' Lucie said. She crossed to Janie and offered her cheek to be kissed. It wasn't an embrace, more a social nicety. 'Thanks for your help last night, Janie.'

'Not at all. Thank you for having me to stay I've had a great time.' Janie said it to be kind and they all knew that she'd had an OK time, nothing more.

Lucie collected up her sports bag and slung her handbag over her shoulder.

'Are you taking the car?' Marcus asked. He hadn't moved from his seat. He made no attempt to get up and kiss Lucie and she didn't come across to him.

'No, I'll walk. The fresh air will do me good.' She headed towards the door. 'Bye then, bye, Janie, have a safe journey back to Sussex.'

'Thanks. Bye.' Janie waved. She watched Lucie glance behind her at Marcus as she left the flat. But he missed her look; he had gone back to the paper.

Out in the street Lucie took several gulps of air, then leant against the wall and closed her eyes. What a mess, what a bloody stupid mess. Moments later she stood straight, dug in her bag for her phone, took it out and checked for messages. Her hands shook as she pressed the buttons. She heard Alex's voice, listened to the message with his home number on, obviously left last night, and then pressed the re-dial button. She got through at once, the phone rang for what seemed like ages and finally he answered it.

'Alex, it's me, Lucie.' She walked on with the phone at her ear, stopped at the end of the road by a low wall and sat down. Alex was furious about the previous night.

'I tried to tell you,' she said, 'I've called you five times in the last twenty-four hours. I had no idea that you two knew each other.' She felt tearful, desperate almost as she listened to Alex describe his relatively new friendship with Marcus. 'No, no, of course not.' She bit her fingernail. 'Listen, Alex, you haven't ever mentioned me to Marcus, have you? Have you ever mentioned that you're having an affair?' She held her breath waiting for his answer. It came and she closed her eyes with relief. 'Are you absolutely sure? Thank God for that. No, no, I don't think he suspected anything. It was just an awful, terrible coincidence.' She stood up. 'Look, you've got to get out of that investment club thing. You can't get involved, Alex, not with Marcus's sister, it would be too awful. OK, yes, all right then, I'll leave it, if you're sure you can handle Marcus. He can be very persuasive.' She wished instantly that she hadn't said that. It was too disloyal talking about her husband to her lover. 'Look, I've got to go,' she said quickly and Alex immediately asked when he would see her again. 'I don't know,' she replied. 'I think it might be a good idea to break things off for a while...' He interrupted her and she wished he hadn't. 'No, it's not like that. It's just that I need a bit of space, that's all, just a break. Yes, I will call, I promise.' She was lying; there was an intention to call, but nothing more. It was an empty promise. She said goodbye guiltily and pressed end, replacing the phone in her bag. She had no desire to go for a workout and suddenly felt exhausted and depressed, but there was no get-out. That is where she had said she was going and that is where she would be, if – knowing his obsession with being in control of all the facts – Marcus should ring to check where she was.

Janie arrived home just before lunch. She parked in the drive, left her bag in the car and hurried into the house, looking forward to seeing Katie. She hadn't thought what to expect but she was surprised at what she got. The house was neat and tidy – polished, vacuumed, nothing out of place. She smelt pizza in the oven, saw two plates of salad laid on the table along with place mats – the best ones – cutlery, linen napkins and two glasses. It looked like an intimate lunch party to which she hadn't been invited.

The weather was unexpectedly warm and sunny, the mid-sixties, with high white clouds scudding across a pale blue sky. The French doors from the kitchen on to the small terrace were open and she wandered across, standing in the doorway to look out at Katie and Andrew weeding the border in the garden, both with their heads bent to their work, content in concentration. Her first feeling was guilt – how could she have left them, even for twenty-four hours – and her second, which followed almost immediately after it, was jealousy. How could they get on so well without her? How could they go on as if she just didn't exist, gardening, lunch organised, a neat and loving home behind them? It was ridiculous this feeling, she knew it, but it was real nevertheless. She stepped out, conscious of the stabbing ache in her chest, and called hello. Andrew looked round, shielded his eyes from the sun, saw her and stood.

'Katie, it's Mummy,' he said and Katie spun round, jumped up and ran across to her. Janie hugged her and some of the pain eased.

'We didn't expect you so early,' Andrew said, coming across. 'I thought you'd ring.'

'I tried,' Janie replied. 'There's a message on the answerphone.'

'I told you I heard the phone,' Katie piped up, 'but Daddy said to leave it, the answerphone would get it.'

Andrew smiled. 'Sorry,' he said to Janie; then to Katie, 'You will get me into trouble saying things like that.'

'But it's the truth, Daddy, it's what you said.'

'Never mind, there's plenty of pizza anyway,' Andrew said, 'enough for everyone.' He turned to Janie. 'Kiss?' Janie leant forward and he kissed her mouth. 'We missed you,' he said. 'Didn't we, Katie?'

'Yes.'

He took Janie's hand. 'It doesn't look like it,' Janie said as they went into the house. 'It looks as if you've managed perfectly well without me.'

Andrew looked at her. 'Do I detect a hint of pique in your voice, Janie?'

'No!' She dropped his hand abruptly and went across to switch the kettle on.

'Sure?'

She shrugged. How, she thought, would he feel if he went away and got back to find that the locum had done a better job than him and was more appreciated by the patients than he was? There was an element of satisfaction in knowing that things weren't as well-managed without you.

She reached up into the cupboard for the tea bags and said, 'There wasn't one tea bag at Marcus's place. Can you imagine not having tea bags? I thought everyone had tea bags.'

'Perhaps they ran out and hadn't had a chance to restock.' Andrew came over and peered into the oven. 'D'you think it's done yet?' he asked, opening the door to get a better look at the pizza.

'Didn't you put the timer on?' Janie countered. Her voice had an edge of superiority to it that wasn't lost on Andrew.

'No, I've no idea how it works.'

'Good,' Janie said, 'at least I'm not completely

110

redundant then!' And Andrew laughed. Only to Janie it hadn't been a joke.

'Oh, by the way,' he said, taking some juice out of the fridge, 'Sarah rang earlier. She said to ask you to ring her at Roz's house as soon as you got back. There's some kind of crisis apparently, only she wouldn't say what, except that it wasn't medical and that I needn't worry.'

'Oh?' Janie had made her tea and sipped it, liking as always to drink it piping hot. 'I'll ring as soon as I've got the lunch. I wonder what can have happened?'

'Ring now,' Andrew said, 'I can get lunch on the table.'

Janie didn't look at him. 'Right.'

'Are you eating with us?'

She moved towards the hall, carrying her mug. 'No,' she said icily, 'I'm not hungry.'

Puzzled by her attitude, he watched her go, then called Katie in to wash her hands. He really had no idea why she was so upset.

Sarah had started on the hall when Roz came down the stairs. She was on her hands and knees scrubbing the skirting board and walls with an unbeatable combination of scourer pad and Jif. It was one-thirty and she had been there since nine – cleaning, tidying, chucking months of accumulated rubbish away and keeping an eye on the children, who up until lunchtime had been agog in front of Saturday morning TV. She glanced up, saw Roz showered and changed and said, 'Hello. You look better. Did you sleep at all?'

'Yes. I slept for a couple of hours. God, Sarah,

111

you didn't need to do all that!'

'Yes, I did, look at the difference. Anyway, it's nearly finished so just thank me and forget it.'

Roz smiled. 'I'm the outspoken one, not you. Thank you, Sarah.'

'Not at all. Come on, I'll make you a cup of tea.'

Roz ran her hands through her hair, short and newly washed, and followed Sarah into the kitchen. 'I was furious when Graham rang you this morning, but I really don't know what I'd have done without you.' Graham had had to go up to Newcastle to collect a piece of furniture for a client. It was an arrangement that he just couldn't get out of so he'd rung Sarah to come and look after Roz. She had, he told Sarah on the phone, literally gone to pieces. It was as if all the stress of the last six years had suddenly erupted and left her helpless. She was constantly weeping, had been up all night unable to sleep and she hadn't eaten for twenty-four hours. Sarah had come immediately and sent her to bed with two paracetamol and a hot milky drink.

'Blimey!' They had reached the kitchen and Roz stood amazed. 'I never knew the floor tiles were this colour!' Sarah suddenly laughed. 'Seriously! I had no idea they were pale blue. I always thought they were grey it must have been the grime!' Roz went across to the kettle, filled it and put it on to boil. 'Tea?'

'Yes, please.'

'I'd better get the kids some lunch. Have they been all right? Is Rory all right? He didn't mind having to spend the morning over here, did he?'

'They've been fine and Rory was delighted to be able to watch three hours of uninterrupted TV. He's in seventh heaven actually. And they don't need lunch, I've fed them already. They had baked beans on toast.'

Roz found herself near to tears again and turned away.

'Oh, and I phoned Janie. She rang ten minutes ago and is on her way over.'

Roz turned back. 'Janie?'

'Yes.' Sarah looked at her. 'Janie is a good organiser, Roz, and she's a good thinker. Talking to Graham this morning before he left, he was keen to get things moving and Janie is the one to help. You need some sort of action group against the development, to get a petition going, and you need supporters. Janie would oversee all that, I'm sure she would, and she'd have more ideas...' Sarah broke off; Roz's face was stony.

'I'm not happy about Janie getting involved, Sarah.'

'Well, it's too late,' Sarah said sharply 'I've asked her and frankly you need all the help you can get.'

The kettle whistled and they both stood and looked at it for a moment. 'Janie is a good friend, Roz,' Sarah said gently, 'it's just that recently you've not been able to see it. She gets lonely and bored...'

'Ha! What I wouldn't give to be bored!'

'There you go again, you see?' Sarah went across to the kettle and took it off the boil. 'Janie has her own problems; she lacks confidence in herself and she's as vulnerable as the rest of us,

Roz. Don't let resentment ruin a good friendship. The three of us have been friends ever since the children started school.'

Roz looked away. Sarah took it as a good sign and took over making the tea. She brought the pot and two mugs over to the table, took a bottle of milk out of the fridge and said, 'Come on, don't brood. Let's drink our tea and see what Janie has to say when she arrives, all right?'

Roz nodded.

'Good.' Sarah sat, poured tea into the cups and handed one to Roz. Just as she did so there was a knock at the door, which was open, and someone shouted, 'Hello? Can I come in?' Sarah went to stand. 'It's Janie,' she said, 'she must have come straight over.'

Roz got up and moved towards the door. 'You stay there,' she said, 'I'll go.' She glanced over her shoulder at Sarah as she headed off towards the hall and said, 'Thanks, Sarah.' Then she disappeared and Sarah heard her say, 'Hi, Janie, thank you for coming over, I really do appreciate it.' Round one to me, Sarah thought, and she stood as Janie came into the kitchen.

The three women had lunch before they did anything else. Janie had picked up a couple of big bunches of asparagus on the way over which she steamed and served piled high on dinner plates with a huge knob of butter. It was the nicest meal Roz had had for a long time and it lifted her morale.

When they had finished eating, Sarah said, 'Right, let's clear this away and get down to business. Why don't we take our chairs out into the sunshine and let the children play in the garden?'

'Great, but I've got to do the pigs. I forgot them this morning and they need feeding.' Roz looked weary as she said this, burdened by the prospect of it, so Janie stood and said, 'I'll do the pigs, Roz, I mean if it's not too complicated.' Roz shook her head. 'No, no, it's fine. You won't...' She was about to say, you won't want to get your hands dirty, but stopped herself. Janie would have been offended. Instead, she said, 'You won't know what to do.'

'Then tell me. Come on, you look exhausted. Let me help for once.'

Roz shrugged. This wasn't a good idea. 'All right, if you're sure.'

Sarah glanced at Janie. 'Borrow Roz's wellies,' she said. 'You don't want to ruin your best Russell and Bromleys.'

'They're by the back door,' Roz said. 'Come on, I'll get them and explain about the pigs while you try them on.'

'I'll clear up,' Sarah said, 'then I'll take the chairs outside. It seems a shame to waste this wonderful sunshine...' She stopped and sighed. She was talking to herself. Roz and Janie were deep in conversation and hadn't even heard her. A few minutes later Roz came back in and said, 'It was nice of Janie to offer to do the pigs. She didn't have to do that.'

'She wanted to,' Sarah replied, 'to help out.'

Roz pulled out a chair. 'I didn't think she'd...'

'No,' Sarah said, cutting her short. Sarah didn't

like to talk about either friend to the other; she didn't feel it fair. 'Janie is far more proficient than she gets a chance to be.' She finished washing the plates, stacked them neatly on the draining board and dried her hands. 'Come on, let's get organised. I'll take these two chairs if you take the one you're sitting on. Shall we go out the back or the front?'

'The front, I think, by the wall, it cuts out the wind. I'll grab a pad and pen and see you out there. I'll gather the kids up too; they're all upstairs playing.'

Both Sarah and Roz set about their tasks and within minutes had everything set up. Roz stood, shielding her eyes from the sun, looking across the fields to see if Janie was OK with the pigs, and Sarah called to Justin and Rory not to be too boisterous with the little ones around. 'Here she comes,' Roz said. 'She looks...' She broke off and glanced worriedly at Sarah. 'Oh dear, she looks as if she's had a fall. She's covered in...' Sarah stood too and Janie saw them, extending her arm in a wave.

'I took a dive,' she called, coming towards them. She was grinning, despite the fact that her beige jeans and white tee-shirt were both filthy. 'They're bloody strong those pigs, aren't they? I emptied the slops into the trough like you said, Roz, and one of the sows nudged me from behind to get me out of the way. I jumped back, seeing the size of her, and fell through the gate, flat on my back!' She started to laugh. 'Luckily I managed to kick the gate shut with my foot and get up to lock it. You should have seen my face, I

116

was terrified! Eaten alive by free range pigs in West Sussex!'

Roz put her hand up to her mouth and stared at Janie. Hungry pigs were unpredictable and she said in a small voice, 'I should never have let you go, it could have been very dangerous.'

Janie looked at her for a few moments, then said, 'I'm not as wet and pathetic as you think I am, Roz.' It took all her courage to say it and she was bright red once the words were out. Roz looked down at the ground. There was a silence and Sarah thought, OK, this is it, we might as well abandon things now. Then Roz said, 'I'm sorry, Janie. I think I misjudge you,' and Janie nodded. There was another silence, this one more contemplative, then Sarah announced, 'It's three o'clock already! Come on, let's sit down and get going on ideas.' They had already explained everything to Janie over lunch. 'We can make a note of them and draw up an action sheet.'

She sat and took up the pen and paper. 'Janie,' she offered, 'why don't you start?' Janie sat as well, crossed her legs and leaned forward. 'I have had an idea,' she said. 'It's not directly related to the offer for the Gordens' land but it would help to raise money to fund any action.'

Roz folded her arms and looked straight at Janie. For some unexplainable reason she had an odd sense that something important was about to be said. 'It involves all three of us,' Janie began, 'and if we do it right, it could become very big.' She took a breath. 'Very big indeed...'

Chapter Seven

It was Monday morning, seven-thirty a.m., and Janie was up and dressed. The house was neat and tidy and breakfast was laid on the kitchen table, ready to be eaten. She sat, coffee at her elbow, in front of the PC in the small box room upstairs that they used as a study, printing out the last of the lists she had prepared the previous night and checking each one as it came off the machine. She heard the alarm clock go off in the bedroom, waited for the last sheet to go through the printer and finally collated the lists and slipped them into a plastic file.

She went downstairs, made a coffee for Andrew, a hot chocolate for Katie and took both up on a tray. Andrew was already awake as she entered the bedroom.

'Morning.' She placed his coffee on the bedside table and opened the curtains.

'Hmmm, coffee in bed.' Andrew sat up, reached for the pillow and stuffed it behind his back. 'What's all this in aid of?'

'Nothing. I was up first so I did the coffee. Simple.' Janie smiled. 'I'm off early by the way, I need to be at school for eight-thirty, not eight-forty-five.' She hadn't told him about the investment club yet, she didn't want the idea pulled apart before it had even got off the ground. She had told him about Roz and

Graham's plight though and he was as supportive as she'd expected him to be. Good causes were Andrew's thing. He said, 'You know, maybe you could put a notice up in the surgery, once you've got it designed and everything, with somewhere to sign underneath if people want to lend their support. What d'you think?'

Janie came across to the bed and bent to kiss him. 'I think that's a great idea. I'll mention it to Roz, thanks.'

Andrew caught her hand as she moved off and held it. 'That trip to London did you good,' he said. 'You look happier. Are you?'

'I'm fine,' Janie said. But that was half the problem really, the fact that she couldn't or wouldn't explain how she felt. Andrew looked at her, wanting more, but no more came so he said, 'Good.' As he climbed out of bed he asked, 'Is Katie up yet?'

'I'm just going to get her,' Janie replied. She freed her hand from his and walked out of the room.

At eight o'clock Janie made her calls. She rang Roz first, spoke to Graham and asked him if Roz could make it to school at half past eight and not a quarter to nine. He said he didn't know, he doubted it in fact, but he'd do his best to chivvy her along. Janie said, 'Tell her it's important, Graham, please.' Then she rang Sarah, who was ready and just putting some washing in the machine. 'I'll leave on the dot of quarter past,' she said, 'so hopefully I'll see you there at eight-thirty exactly.'

119

Janie hung up and went into the kitchen to hurry Katie up with her breakfast.

At eight-fifteen, Janie and Katie left the house. Janie had a suit on, she carried her briefcase, one she had resurrected from her last job, and a thermos flask. It took less than ten minutes to drive to school and Katie was delivered into the playground where a teacher was on duty at twenty-five past eight. Roz was already in her car waiting.

'Hello.' Janie knocked on the window and Roz opened the car door. She looked smarter than she usually did, wearing a freshly ironed shirt and floral summer skirt. She climbed out of the car and Janie said, 'Oh, where are Oliver and Kitty?'

'At home with Graham,' Roz said. 'He volunteered. I'm off to see the bank manager after this and then into Chichester to get myself something smart to wear for action group meetings and the like.'

'Good for you,' Janie said and she meant it. 'Come on, this morning's meeting is in my office.'

Roz smiled and Janie led the way across to her Land Rover. They waved to Sarah as she drove up and by the time they had climbed in and got settled Sarah had delivered Rory to school and was at the car.

'Jump in the back,' Janie said. Sarah did as she asked.

'I've made coffee. Shall I pour us a cup while Roz gives you a copy of what's in my file?'

'Hmm, please.'

Janie handed her briefcase across to Roz who

took out the plastic folder and started sorting through the sheets.

'There's three for the Action Against Development group, now known as the AAD, and four for the investment club,' Janie said, pouring coffee from the thermos into plastic cups. 'Here.' She handed one across to Sarah who took it and placed it in the drinks holder between the seats.

'I always thought this was terribly pretentious, having drinks holders in a Land Rover,' Sarah said. 'Now I think it's quite nifty.'

Janie smiled. 'Actually, it is pretentious.' She handed a second cup to Roz and finally poured her own. 'Right, let's get on. Firstly, I've drawn up a list of what needs to be done as far as the AAD is concerned. I thought what we could do was look at the list, think about it and then meet tomorrow to decide who's doing what. I have initialled each point with who I thought most appropriate, but they are only my suggestions. Secondly, I've done a draft of the letter to the local papers; read it later and tell me what you think. And finally there's a draft petition. I thought we could copy this to as many people as we can and get them to fill in the names.'

'God, Janie,' Roz said, 'this is brilliant!' She speed-read through the bits of paper. 'It really is! It must have taken you ages.'

Janie shrugged. 'Not really. Now,' she said, 'moving swiftly on.'

Sarah smiled. 'You've even got the terminology, Janie! Very professional.'

Roz laughed, then stopped suddenly, seeing Janie's face.

'The other stuff,' Janie went on, too excited to be bothered with humour, 'is on what we talked about on Saturday; the investment club. I don't know if you've given it much thought, but...' She glanced up and saw that Roz was nodding. 'I spoke to my brother last night and he assured me that if we want to go ahead and set it up this week he is certain that Alex Stanton, the broker I met at their house for dinner, will work with us.'

Sarah, who had been scanning the notes, suddenly looked up. 'Really? Does he do much of this sort of thing then?'

'Not at the moment, but Marcus seemed to think that it was quite a good opportunity for him and he's very good, apparently. He's quite a high flyer.'

Roz said, 'Is the thousand pounds you mention here the minimum or the maximum investment, Janie?'

'I think it should be both. I think we should agree on a sum that we can all raise so that no one feels intimidated by numbers.'

'I agree,' Sarah said. She had thought long and hard over the weekend about this idea of Janie's, indeed thought of almost nothing else, and on Sunday night had got out her finance file to check on her savings. She had problems to solve and she had dreams, all of which needed money. It wasn't the answer to everything, but boy would life be easier with a bit of cash to spend. And she could just manage one thousand pounds. She had more saved, but she wanted to be sure that the sum she invested – at a pinch – was money that she could afford to lose.

Roz read on and Janie sipped her coffee in silence, waiting for a reaction. In just forty-eight hours she had gone from feeling redundant and depressed to this – an ever-mounting sense of excitement and a life that suddenly had direction.

'So?' She couldn't help herself, her impatience boiled over and she had to ask. 'What do you think?'

Roz placed the notes on her lap and looked at Janie. Sarah slipped hers into her bag.

'I'm impressed,' Roz said, and she was. She had talked it over at the weekend with Graham and he was all for it. Janie's brother had made a packet and with him behind them surely they could make a success of a thousand quid? 'Janie, I think it's a great idea but my biggest worry is time. Will we really have the time to commit to this? What with everything else going on.'

'Good point. I can only do evenings,' Sarah said. 'And they'll have to be at mine because I haven't got anyone to babysit. Is that OK?'

'Evenings are fine,' Janie replied. 'I can come to you, bring the coffee and biscuits, or the wine when we make a profit.' She looked at them both. 'I'd thought that it might take us a couple of nights a week at first, to get set up, to get into some kind of routine comparing our notes on companies and sharing thoughts and so on. And I thought that at the start of each evening we could spend an hour or so on the AAD to kill two birds with one stone, so to speak.'

'Two nights a week sounds OK,' Roz said, 'except when Graham's away.' She turned to Sarah. 'Perhaps you could come and stay if

Graham's away and then we could meet at Chadwick Farm?'

Sarah saw the sudden possibility of company without feeling like a burden. To be able to get together with her friends, married friends, without feeling like she was encroaching on their time with their partners – which she often felt she did – would be a bonus. She liked the thought of it. 'That sounds fine,' she said. 'I think it would work.'

'Talking of work,' Roz said, 'how much would we have to do on the stock market? I don't know if I'm clever enough to be researching companies and stuff; I haven't a clue what I'm doing.'

'Don't worry about that. Just read the financial pages of the papers and keep your eyes open. What I thought I'd do was get a basic list of stocks to look at from Alex and put in a lot of the legwork myself to start with.'

'Oh Janie, are you sure?'

Janie smiled. 'I'd love it,' she answered honestly. 'I thought we could each of us take a sector of the market that we had an interest in. Off the top of my head last night I thought you, Roz, might like to look at food groups, seeing as that's the field you're involved in?'

'Great idea!'

'And Sarah, I wondered about supermarkets, seeing as you work in one, and I thought I'd do pharmaceuticals, getting a bit of help from Andrew. I thought we could all look at dot coms, seeing as they're on the up, and when I get a list from Alex or Marcus we can decide on the other sectors and split them up between us. I'd be more than happy to take on the bulk, seeing as I'm the one who doesn't work.'

Both Sarah and Roz were silent for a few moments.

'Well?' Janie asked. 'How does it sound?'

Sarah was the first to speak and she answered honestly. 'It sounds exciting, Janie.'

'Roz?'

Roz was more hesitant, partly because she still wasn't completely sure of Janie and partly because she was more wary of golden opportunities; she'd had one of those already in Chadwick Farm and look where that had got her. 'Yes, I agree, it does sound interesting,' she said.

Janie stared out of the window, trying not to lose her composure. She couldn't believe how much she suddenly wanted this and she didn't want to analyse why. Roz stared at Janie. A thousand pounds was a lot of money and wasn't to be easily parted with, but there was something in Janie's face, something compulsive, dynamic and committed. She seemed to pulse with the energy of the idea.

'Count me in,' Roz suddenly said. She wasn't going to stand on the side looking at the water, she was going to jump in. There was another silence, then Sarah added, 'Me too.'

Janie smiled. It was meant to be a modest parting of the lips but she couldn't help the wide grin that broke out. She was delighted; triumphant. 'Fantastic,' she said. There was a moment of conspiratorial silence, then all three women smiled.

Roz looked at her watch. 'Let's arrange the first

meeting now and then I'd better get going. I need to be at the bank at nine-thirty. I've got the first appointment.'

'Right,' Janie said, taking out her diary, more for show than use; she knew she was free all week. 'How does tomorrow night sound?'

'Sounds great,' Roz replied. 'Sarah?'

'Yes, tomorrow's fine. At my house?'

Roz and Janie nodded. 'We'll start with the AAD stuff, then go on to the investment club agenda. I'll draw one up today.'

Sarah handed her empty coffee cup across to Janie and said, 'When will I need the money by? I need to give notice at the bank if I'm making a withdrawal.'

Janie looked at Roz. 'I don't know, what do you think, Roz?'

'Why don't we look at what's out there and make a decision tomorrow night? I'd get the money out anyway, Sarah, so that you're ready if there's something good on the market.'

'OK.' Sarah glanced at the clock on the dashboard. 'I must go,' she announced, 'life at Duffields goes on.' She opened the car door and climbed out. Janie pressed the window down. 'At least until I make my first million on the stock market,' Sarah added. Janie laughed.

'Thanks, Janie,' Sarah said, rubbing her hands over her arms. 'I feel really quite optimistic about all this. I feel that life is about to change.'

Janie looked at her. 'It has already,' she said, 'for all of us.' Roz climbed out too. 'It will be nice,' she said, before closing the car door, 'to have something else in my life, something other than

126

that bloody farm and all its pressure. And, hopefully, it'll take my mind off the Gordens' land.'

'If we get it right you might be able to buy the Gordens' land,' Janie joked. Roz smiled. 'See you later, Janie.' She slammed the door shut, Janie waved and, shifting into gear, drove off. It was still early but she had an awful lot to get through today.

Sarah had been five minutes late for work this morning after the meeting with Janie and Roz. This meant that she kept her head down and steamed through her duties far faster than she really needed to, firstly to try and make up for it – she had always been one for fair play – and secondly not to antagonise the manager even further.

She had finished the stocklists in record time, had helped with deliveries and now was back on customer services, filling in time until she had to cover on the tills during coffee break. It was a quiet Monday morning with no queries and only one complaint so far, so she decided to sort out the file, putting everything in date order. She was halfway through this when she sensed a figure at the desk.

'Can I help you?' she asked pleasantly, while stapling two notices together. There was a discreet cough and she glanced up. Involuntarily she blushed.

'Oh,' she exclaimed, 'it's you...' She stopped, aware that once again she had been rude, then stammered, 'I mean, erm, can I help you?'

'I hope so.'

The man she had upset last Friday stood in front of her in the same worn but impeccably clean jeans, loose wool sweater with checked shirt underneath, and scuffed brown suede brogues. For all she knew he might have been there all weekend. 'I was wondering,' he began, not looking at her face but staring hard at something just above her right shoulder, 'if you'd like to have a quick lunch, a sandwich, or something at the pub, or pizza, curry, whatever you like really, with me, erm, today, or tomorrow even or Wednesday, Thursday or Friday or any day next week? It's just that...' he paused only to draw breath, 'you, erm, said that you only work mornings and I thought, seeing as we're both parents at Wynchcombe Primary, that it would nice, I mean better than a drink in the evening, which can be difficult, with baby sitters and stuff and I...'

His voice trailed off, as if he had suddenly run out of breath. He stared down at the counter. 'I can do any lunchtime really as I work just across the road...'He cleared his throat and looked up.

Sarah blushed again. Lunch, drinks, dinner, chats, anything at all to do with the opposite sex she just didn't entertain. She had no time for it. She had never really got over Nick's betrayal, and certainly wasn't going to open herself up to that sort of risk again. Besides, she was happy, of a sort, being alone. So normally she would have simply said no – if it had been an ordinary request for a date she would undoubtedly have refused. But it wasn't an ordinary request. It was a sort of plea, a desperate attempt to make a friend, and she knew looking at him that she hadn't the heart to turn it down. One quick sandwich, she thought, and that's it.

'OK,' she said. 'Today is fine. I finish at one, so how about a sandwich at Muffins across the road?'

He looked suddenly taken aback. 'Today? Really? A sandwich across the road?'

Sarah smiled. 'Yes. That's what I said.'

He smiled back and again she noticed, as she had last week, how it lit his whole face from inside. 'Great!' He cleared his throat again. 'I mean, yes, I mean great. I'll, what, come by at one to pick you up?'

'I'll meet you in Muffins,' Sarah said, 'at about ten past one.' She picked up the stapler and the sheets that she was stapling together to indicate that she had work to be getting on with.

He took the hint. 'Right, OK, ten past one in Muffins.' He dug his hands in his pockets and turned to go. 'Oh, erm, my name's Jack, by the way.'

'Sarah, Sarah Greg.'

'Jack Lowe.'

Sarah suddenly smiled; he was so wonderfully unassuming. 'Nice to meet you, Jack Lowe.'

He smiled back. 'See you later, Sarah Greg.'

Sarah was still smiling when he left the store, waving at her through the plate-glass automatic doors as he went, and had to check herself in case anyone thought she was a loon, standing alone at the customer services desk and grinning inanely. 'I'll look forward to it, Jack,' she said to herself, then stopped, completely amazed that for once

129

the prospect of a date – however low-key – didn't fill her with dread.

Jack walked into his office above Dean & May Solicitors – which was good for business – and picked up the post from the mat. He could smell coffee so he called out good morning to Dodi, his secretary, and went through to the little kitchenette that they used, sometimes more than the office.

'Hiya, Jack. How's things?' Dodi was an Australian, twenty-five, engaged to a local lad and saving wildly to get married by working for Jack during the day and for the pub, the wine bar and the bistro every available evening and weekend.

'Things, my dear Dodi, are great. How about you? Nice weekend? Lots of tinnies and a barbie?'

Dodi thumped him playfully on the arm, which she often did, and he winced. She was a big girl, well-built, and didn't know her own strength. She had been with him since he started up in West Sussex a year ago and they had what even he would have called a good working relationship. She was quick-witted and ambitious with a shed load of sense – her words, not his – and she kept his natural lack of motivation in check.

'So what's new?' he asked. 'Any messages?'

'Two. Both enquiries from local lawyers for divorce cases. I've got the numbers, please can you call back.'

He pulled a face. 'For a small provincial town, there's an awful lot of adultery going on.'

'Nothing else to do,' Dodi said. 'A multiplex cinema and a good health club would make all the difference.'

Jack burst out laughing. 'Dodi, you're a treasure!' He took the pot of coffee and poured some into the two mugs Dodi had got ready 'You call them back,' he said, 'get the details.'

Dodi took her mug from him. 'No, you call them, Jack. They want to hear from you, you're the one with all the knowledge.'

'Oh God.' He walked out of the kitchenette to his desk and sat down.

'I know you hate it but these cases pay the bills. You've got to do them, Jack, they're bread and butter money.'

'OK, OK.' He sighed and put his head in his hands, staring across at her. 'What would I do without you, Dodi?'

'You'd go out of business,' she replied sharply, 'and end up on the street selling the *Big Issue*.'

'Thanks. I didn't expect such a literal answer. It was more of a rhetorical question.'

Dodi sat down at her own desk. 'We don't need rhetoric, we need retribution,' she said.

Jack smiled and leant back in his chair. 'Nice play on words. Retribution of the spurned wives and cuckolded husbands type, you mean?'

'Yes, I do.'

'You know, Dodi, for an Australian you're really quite bright.' His reflexes were quick; they had to be. He ducked as a hole punch came flying through the air and hit the wall behind him. He had been expecting it. Not only was Dodi the most wonderful secretary, she was also very easy to wind up.

131

Jack Lowe was thirty-four, unhappily divorced and living alone in a small cottage with three acres of land on the outskirts of Wynchcombe. Three acres of land that he had been slowly and surely creating and changing, since the first moment he saw them, into gardens.

He had one son whom he adored and one ex-wife whom he didn't. She had left him two years ago, fed up with his inability to earn enough money to buy her all the things that she wanted, and moved in with a professional footballer. She now drove a Mercedes 80sl, wore designer clothes, had her tummy button pierced and spent more money in an afternoon than he earned from his small business in a week. He supposed she was happy, but he had never asked. They were light years apart.

Jack cared little for material things – he never had and probably never would do. He earned enough money from a business he didn't like, a business he had relocated in order to be near his son, to pay maintenance for Jamie and to be able to treat him when he came to stay on alternate weekends and the odd week night. He saved a little and spent the rest on his garden, for which his passion never faded. Indeed that was possibly the root of all his problems, what had started the whole split with Sandra. The gardening.

Jack had inherited a business from his father at the age of twenty-three, a small but very lucrative private investigation agency in south-east London that brought in a good income for very little work. At the time he had been doing an apprenticeship at the Royal Horticultural Gardens at Wisley and loving it; he had never imagined any other career than gardening. Then his father had had a massive heart attack and died in the ambulance on the way to St Thomas's hospital, leaving a business with four staff that needed running. Jack was the only one to do it, with a brother living in New Zealand and a mother who had been dead twelve years. He could have sold it, he realised later, but back then he had been young and inexperienced and grieving. It had been very hard to make the right decisions in the midst of all that mess.

So he took over the business and Sandra, who worked as his secretary, comforted him in the one way that she knew best. Within months they were an item and Jack could hardly believe his luck when he looked at the young woman who had once had a brief career as a glamour model. By the end of that year they were married, Sandra gave up work, Jack picked up the ropes of the business and they should have been happy But they weren't.

The trouble was that Jack loved his garden. They had bought a terraced house in Putney when they married and he had transformed the small bit of turf and shrub at the back of it into a modern courtyard garden. He had lit it and put in a square pool filled with water lilies. He had put down gravel and brick and terracotta and filled the spaces with exotic plants and pots brimming with staggering arrangements. He commissioned garden furniture that fitted the space exactly and created a hidden oasis of water and plants. It had taken a year to finish and in that year he had neglected his business, his

133

friends and, inevitably, his wife.

The business began to falter, Sandra began to stray and Jack found himself desperately trying to keep an ailing company afloat, people employed and his wife in Prada handbags. To compensate for this he gardened in his every spare moment, creating gardens for friends – only charging them for materials – as his life staggered unhappily on. They had a baby; it was, Sandra said, the only way they would stay together. But, of course, babies drive even good marriages apart and bad ones have no hope. When Jamie was two Sandra walked out, taking Jack's only real achievement with her. His son.

Sandra moved to Sussex with her boyfriend and married him a year later. Jack followed them down, closing the London branch of Lowe Investigations, which by then consisted only of him and a boy from the Youth Training Scheme, and opening in a very small way in Abbey Down, the nearest big town to his son's school. The reason he was there was Jamie. He cared very little for work, spent all his time outside on his three acres of burgeoning garden and he saw his son, who also, quite miraculously, had a love for the feel of the earth in his hands.

'Whatchya doing for lunch?' Dodi asked, coming across to Jack's desk mid-morning. She was checking that he was writing the quotations for the calls he had made that morning and her casual glance at the notepad in front of him didn't fool Jack for one second. He held it out to her. 'No, not a garden plan or a list of plants. I've charged the one from Dean and May downstairs three-fifty, giving them a fifty quid discount for the business, and the one from Sniff ya bum–'

'Smith Album,' Dodi corrected but she couldn't help smiling.

'Yes, them. I've charged them a nice round four hundred.' He looked at her. 'OK?'

She did the diver's OK sign and continued to glance over his notes. 'So, what are you doing for lunch?'

Jack fiddled with his pencil. 'Actually,' he said, 'I'm, erm, meeting someone.'

Dodi looked up. She narrowed her eyes and said, 'You mean, a date?'

He avoided her stare and flushed. Good Lord, he thought, I'm nearly ten years older than this young woman and I'm acting like she's my teacher. 'Sort of,' he replied.

Dodi started back for her desk. 'Good for you,' she said as she sat down. And she meant it. Jack Lowe was far too good a bloke and far too much of a dish to spend his life on his own with a bunch of plants. 'I'll just get one sarnie then,' she finished and went on with her work.

Jack was at Muffins at one p.m. exactly. It was busy with the lunchtime rush but he secured two seats at a table with a couple of elderly ladies and ordered himself a coffee. He wished he'd had the foresight to bring a paper or better still a literary novel. Nothing impressed women more than a man who read well. He sighed. Sadly, the only book on his beside table was an encyclopaedia of plant infestation and the life cycle of the lug-wort beetle was not exactly riveting conversation. The coffee came, he took a sip, burnt his tongue and was in the act of holding his tongue out of his mouth between his teeth to cool down when Sarah came into the bakers. Embarrassed that she might have seen him thus, he jumped up suddenly and knocked into the old lady on his right, who spilt her tea all over the table and on to the sleeve of her turquoise cardigan. Jack immediately began to mop the table and the old lady's arm furiously with his handkerchief.

Sarah came across and he said, 'Sorry, Sarah, I'll be with you in a moment...' Then, to the old lady, 'I'm so sorry, madam, I just wasn't looking where I was going. I hope this is OK, can I get you another tea, or a bun maybe, or one of those nice cream cakes – some more tea, yes? Something else?' He glanced up at Sarah and stopped for a moment. He thought she looked wonderful; fresh-faced, with brown hair cut short and unstyled and wearing jeans and a white tee-shirt. Natural and cool, like a short burst of breeze. The lady he was mopping pulled her arm away and said, 'I'm fine, thank you. Just watch what you're doing next time, young man.'

Jack nodded, blushed and glanced sidelong at Sarah. She caught his eye and smiled.

'Disastrous start,' he said, pulling out a chair for her. 'Sorry.'

The two ladies made to leave and Jack remained standing, helping them with their chairs and their coats. Sarah thought that kind, it was polite without being patronising. Finally he sat down, mopped the last bit of spilt tea from the table with a paper napkin and smiled at her.

'What would you like to eat?'

'A tuna and cucumber sandwich on brown bread, please,' Sarah replied, 'and a cup of tea.'

'Right. I'll have...' Jack looked up at the board but he hadn't brought his glasses, for reasons of vanity, and he couldn't read the writing. 'I'll, erm, have, erm...' He took a wild guess. 'Chicken and salad.'

Sarah said, 'They've run out, it's crossed off.'

'Oh, right.' Jack shrugged. 'I'll have the same as you then. I'll just go and order.' He went to the counter, gave their order across and waited for the girl to pour Sarah's tea from a huge stainless-steel tea pot.

'Milknsugar?'

'Sorry?'

'Milknsugar?'

Jack bent his ear towards the girl, who from her look obviously thought him subnormal. 'MILK AND SUGAR?' she said slowly and loudly.

'Oh, right. Milk please, and I'll take a couple of packets of sugar to the table.' She handed them over, along with a small plastic spoon, and Jack went back to Sarah.

'I wonder why they don't have cups and saucers for the eat-in trade?' he asked. This was his first experience of Muffins; Dodi usually grabbed a sandwich for them both and he ate his at his desk or on the job.

'To save on the washing-up I should think.'

'Good thinking, Batman,' Jack quipped, then he winced. It had just rolled off his tongue, something he always said to Jamie. He turned away and bit his lip. On a scale of one to ten he reckoned this lunch was scoring minus-three.

'So, Sarah,' he began, but the girl behind the counter called, 'Two tuna on brown!' before he had a chance to continue and he said, 'That's us. I'll just pop up and get them.' Pop up, he thought, taking the two sandwiches on paper plates – what am I, a bloody jack-in-the-box?

He placed the sandwiches on the table and asked Sarah if she wanted anything else.

'No, no thanks,' she replied. 'This is lovely.'

'Is it?' Jack sat and lifted the corner of his sandwich. He saw pale fawn sludge topped with thin, drooping cucumber. 'I think mine died in the fridge last night.'

'Mine is very nice,' Sarah said, shifting her eyes and pulling a face to indicate there was someone behind Jack.

'Good, at least that's someone satisfied then. Unlike the poor tuna, who, from the look and smell of its flesh in my sandwich, probably died from something rather gruesome.'

Sarah was still nodding her head frantically and rolling her eyes, but she couldn't speak because she had a mouthful of sandwich. Someone behind Jack tapped him on the shoulder.

'Do you wish to make a formal complaint about your sandwich?' the lady asked. She was wearing a brown-checked Muffins overall and Jack caught a glimpse of her badge which bore the word 'Manager'.

'Oh no, I, erm...' Jack blushed, deeply embarrassed.

'He's got the most awful sense of humour,'

Sarah chipped in, smiling at the lady 'He was trying, but failing...' she threw her eyes heavenward in exasperation, 'to be funny.'

The woman nodded, then smiled. 'I see,' she said, which clearly she didn't. She turned back to her table and Jack put his hands up to either side of his burning face. 'If there was a big, gaping hole in the floor right now I could cheerfully jump in it,' he said.

He had completely lost his appetite.

'Actually,' Sarah said, leaning forward to him and lowering her voice, 'it was quite funny.'

'Really?' Jack looked hopeful.

She shook her head and smiled. 'No, not really, but I was trying to make you feel better.'

Suddenly he laughed. 'Thank you.' He took a bite of his sandwich. 'Hmmm, delicious,' he remarked loudly for the benefit of the table behind him. Sarah took a sip of her tea and glanced at her watch.

'Jack,' she said, 'I'm really sorry, but I can't stop long. I've got to get home and get some supper ready because tonight Rory's got listening therapy and I like to have supper ready for when we get home or else it's too late to eat.'

Jack was silent for a moment. I've blown it, he thought, I've made a complete dick of myself and she can't wait to get away. She's even bolting her sandwich.

'That's fine,' he said, 'it was only a spur-of-the-moment thing anyway.' He was saying it to convince himself more than her. He felt let down and disappointed, not with Sarah but with himself. Why on earth, when he had been so bad at dating the first time round that he'd ended up marrying the only woman he had ever slept with, did he think he'd be any good at it ten years on?

'I'm glad I came,' Sarah said, finishing off her sandwich.

'Are you, or do you always eat this quickly?'

She blinked in surprise, then said, 'Actually I was being polite. I usually eat much quicker than this.'

Jack smiled. 'Touché.' He left his sandwich and dug his hands in his pockets. 'Right, erm, well, thanks for coming.'

Sarah stood. 'Thanks for lunch. My sandwich was really very good. And...' She broke off, braced herself, then said, 'Why don't we have a drink next time, in the evening? I can ask my neighbour to sit with Rory and, well, a glass of wine might relax us both.'

'OK,' Jack said, but he thought, and the rest. I think I'm going to need half a bottle of gin to feel relaxed after this fiasco. 'I mean, that would be nice, really nice.'

'When?'

He frowned. 'You mean, like, when? You want to set a date?'

She nodded.

'Tonight? Tomorrow, Wednesday, not Thursday because I have Jamie, but any night after that...'

'Wednesday then,' Sarah said. 'At the Anchor. I'll meet you there at eight-thirty and if there's a problem, I'll send word via Jamie at school.'

Jack stood up. He felt odd, light-headed; he could hardly believe his luck. 'On Wednesday, really?'

'Yes, on Wednesday.'

Jack grinned. He opened the door for Sarah and went to follow her out when the girl behind the counter shouted, 'Oi! That'll be four fifty-eight please!' He spun round. 'Oh goodness! I'm sorry, I wasn't trying to do a runner, really I wasn't, I, erm, I just forgot...'

Sarah glanced at her watch. 'I must dash,' she said.

'Yes, of course, you go, I'll stay and pay...'

She held out the three pound coins she had been clasping in her palm for the last ten minutes but he shook his head.

'My treat,' he said. 'Though not really much of one.'

'Thanks.' Sarah smiled. 'I've gotta go.'

'Sure. You get off. See you Wednesday then.'

'Yes. Bye, and thanks.'

Jack shrugged. He watched her go off down the street from his position in the doorway, blocking the entrance until she had disappeared from sight, then he turned back into Muffins and, ignoring stares from the mainly elderly clientèle, paid his bill.

Chapter Eight

It was Wednesday afternoon and Sarah was standing outside the school waiting until most of the other children had been collected before she went across to Miss Meaney. She caught sight of Janie hurrying across the playground towards the classroom and she waved. Janie called out, 'You OK?'

'Just waiting to see Miss Meaney. Again.' Sarah rolled her eyes and smiled but it did nothing to fool Janie, who stopped rushing and said, 'What's up?'

Sarah wished she could just brush over it, make light of it, but she couldn't; she had to talk to someone. 'Rory got his box today,' she said, 'you know, the radio aid? It's supposed to make life in the classroom easier but apparently he's thrown a wobbly about it. He's refusing to wear it and hasn't spoken to anyone all day.'

'Oh.' Janie looked at her. 'He'll get used to it, Sarah,' she offered. It was all she could think of to say.

'I suppose so.'

Janie patted her arm. 'Try not to worry Kids hate anything new but it won't be new for long. I'll have a word with Katie about it, shall I? See if she can't encourage him a bit?'

Sarah shook her head. 'Thanks, Janie, but don't worry. I'll see what Miss Meaney has to say first.'

'OK.' Janie glanced at her watch. 'I must go. I'll

see you in the morning, yes? At the station for nine?'

Sarah nodded and Janie carried on. Sarah watched her greet her daughter with a smile and a kiss and envied her the ease of such a relationship. When she got to the classroom herself Rory was sitting in the corner, withdrawn and sad.

'Mum's here, Rory.' said Miss Meaney

He looked up and Sarah forced a smile but he didn't move. Miss Meaney took her arm.

'I think it might be a good idea to let Rory lead the way with the radio aid,' she advised. 'It's quite a big transition from hearing aids to that and he needs to come to terms with it. Let him decide when he wants to wear it, Mrs Greg, and maybe a chat with him about it might be a good idea?'

Sarah nodded. A chat, she thought. As if I haven't already had a chat about it. I've talked and explained and gone over and over things until I'm blue in the face. But she didn't tell Miss Meaney this, she thought it might sound a bit hysterical. So she just nodded and said, 'OK, we'll talk tonight.' She went across to Rory and squatted down. 'Come on,' she said, clearly and loudly, 'what say you we get an ice cream on the way to Ali's lesson? You choose. Anything you like.'

Rory nodded and Sarah could tell that he was close to tears. She held out her hand and stood up. Rory took it and she gently pulled him to his feet. They said goodbye to Miss Meaney and headed for the car. Once inside it, Sarah said, 'Can I have a look at your radio aid then?'

Rory sat silent.

'Is it in your bag?'

He nodded and she reached in the back for his school bag, opening it up to take out his radio aid receiver and transmitter. 'Wow,' she said, 'this looks pretty high-tech.' Still Rory said nothing, so Sarah examined the box and ear phones, had a good look at the microphone, then asked, 'Shall we try it?' He shook his head and stared down at his feet which he had begun to kick against the glove compartment.

'You don't like it?' Sarah could see his eyes fill. 'Well, I think it's pretty cool,' she said, swallowing down the terrible hard lump that had come to the back of her throat. If she could have taken the shame and the embarrassment for him, taken his pain, she would have done so. 'I think that it's pretty special to have one of these, you know, and it's going to make a big difference to hearing things at school, things that you wouldn't be able to hear without it, like Mr MacIntyre's voice... Och de noo...' She smiled at her truly terrible Scottish accent but there wasn't even the faintest response on Rory's lips. 'I know it's a bit hard now, but you'll get used to it, love, I'm sure.'

'I hate it,' Rory said quietly 'I hate being different. Everyone looks at me and I've got that pratty box round my neck like a deaf person and everyone thinks I'm stupid because I can't hear...' He sniffed and wiped his nose on his bare wrist. It left a trail of mucus on the skin that normally Sarah would have reprimanded him for. It was odd, she thought briefly, how Rory had never really considered himself deaf. He just got on with it and that was one of the things –

and there were hundreds and hundreds more –
that she loved him for.

'It is not pratty,' she said. 'Where did you get
that word from, by the way?'

'At school.'

'Well, it's not a very nice word and your radio
aid certainly isn't pratty.'

'It is. It's pratty and stupid and I'm not wearing
it.' Rory looked at her defiantly and she
shrugged. 'OK,' she said, 'whatever you want.'

'I want,' said Rory, kicking the glove compartment, 'to smash it to pieces.' Sarah gently but
firmly put a hand on his leg to stop him kicking.
'Well, you can't,' she replied. 'It isn't ours, it
belongs to the Education Authority, and we
would have to pay for it if you did that.'

'So?' He stared at her, the challenge on his face.

'So it would mean no sweets for a year.' She
tried to smile, to lighten the situation. 'Or maybe
two years.'

Grudgingly, Rory smiled back and Sarah leant
across and put her arms round him. 'Come here,'
she said, 'because I need a huge hug.' She held
him for a minute or so, then pulled back and
looked at his face. 'OK?'

He shrugged and she released him. 'Come on,
let's get off to the sweet shop before we go to
speech therapy and buy the biggest and most
expensive ice cream they have.' She started the
engine, put Rory's radio aid back in his bag and
shifted into gear. As she reversed out of the
parking space, she glanced sidelong at him with
an aching heart. His expression, she thought, was
one of utter despondency.

145

It was five o'clock and Marcus was leaving the office early. He had arranged a game of tennis with Alex – not really his sort of thing, but he wanted Alex on board for Janie and her investment club and he thought tennis would go some way towards helping that along. Besides, it beat sitting in a dark bar on a warm sunny evening. So he left his desk as it was – he never tidied it – and made his way up to St Paul's to buy some kit.

In the sports shop he asked for advice. He chose a Prince racket, top of the range, some Nike cross-trainers and Reebok shorts and tee-shirt. Labels were important to Marcus. They gave him confidence and he never bought anything that didn't have a discreet but still-visible logo somewhere on it. He paid for his goods on his credit card without even looking at the total and asked the sales assistant to remove all the labels and stick everything in a sports bag, which he then paid for separately. After twenty minutes he had the complete tennis set, along with three tubes of expensive tennis balls. He was ready to play Alex.

Jumping in a cab, Marcus sat back to enjoy the ride to Chiswick. It was a hell of a way in mid-week rush-hour traffic and the meter clicked incessantly even when the cab was at a standstill. But, as with everything else Marcus did, the expense just didn't seem to register.

At six-fifteen he made it to the Riverside, booked in and waited for Alex. He drank a glass of water, watched the early evening activity and attracted several glances from the women to-ing and fro-ing from aerobic and step classes. Marcus was an interesting man. He was tall, well-built and gave off a sense of power that could be felt even from a distance. He had a brooding quality and an edge of secrecy that many people found alluring. It was as if the dynamism of his personality pervaded his nice but ordinary looks and lifted them to another level. If he had wanted to be unfaithful to Lucie, which he never had, he would not have had to look far for partners. But adultery wasn't on his mind, it never had been. Marcus wasn't that type; he wasn't interested enough in other people to want to get involved with anyone else.

Marcus Todd wasn't interested in much really, but at least he made no pretence about it. He could do most things without much effort; play a decent game of tennis, swim, make witty conversation, charm friends, look good, speak French. The list was endless, which was probably why he couldn't be bothered. What was the point if everything could be done at a wink? Where was the challenge? Except in the stock market, of course. Except in pitching his wits against the never-ending risk of fluctuating share prices and in winning the point in a game that was bound to beat him in the end.

Marcus was an analyst. Not just any old supplier of information about companies but a top-dollar spokesperson for *The Money Programme*, a million-pound-bonus-earning creator of wealth. Marcus was head of his team, regularly made hundreds of thousands of pounds in a single deal

147

and he loved it. He lived off the adrenaline, knowing that nothing else on earth gave him the same kind of buzz. He loved his job, he loved making money and he loved the fact that he could just walk into any shop he fancied and spend as much as he wanted to without even noticing the dent in his bank account. But it seemed, if not to him then to everyone else around him, that that was all he loved, and instead of being envied as he should have been he was sometimes rather pitied. Something in Marcus's life had gone awry. He had ceased working to live and begun living to work. He wanted money for the sake of money, not for what it could buy, and even if he was aware of it himself he didn't know how to change it.

'Marcus. Hi!'

Marcus looked round as Alex approached. He stood and the two men shook hands. Alex had a sports bag over his shoulder and said almost immediately, 'Shall we get on? I booked a court for six-thirty.'

'Great.' Marcus picked up his bag and followed Alex towards the male changing room.

'Have you played much yet this season, Marcus?' Alex said over his shoulder.

'I haven't played for years, Alex,' Marcus said, without a hint of embarrassment. 'I'm looking forward to it.'

That wasn't exactly true; he was approaching the game with the same nonchalance that he did everything else, other than work. He didn't really want to be here, but Alex had said Wednesday was his tennis night and Marcus was keen to speak to him. So what if he had to whack a few balls around to get what he wanted, it would be worth it in the end.

The two men changed and Alex led the way on to the court.

'This investment club thing,' Marcus said, pulling the top off the can of balls and waiting for the hiss of pressure. 'Janie is keen to get started and I've asked her and her two friends up to my office tomorrow I said I'd speak seriously to you about it and let her know if you're interested.'

Alex had put two balls into his pockets and said, 'I'm not sure, Marcus. I don't really think I've got the time to spare at the moment...' He started for the other end of the court, swinging his racket. Marcus bounced a ball on his racket in small even taps as he made his way to his end of the court.

He stood, waited for Alex to get into position and then hit the ball across. Alex whacked it back and Marcus returned it. Both men hit hard and the rally ended with Alex knocking the ball into the net. He swore.

'It wouldn't take much time,' Marcus called, waiting for the ball to come across, 'an hour or two a week, max.' Alex hit the ball and Marcus returned it with an excellent backhand that surprised even him.

'Why me?' Alex asked, pulling another ball out of his pocket. 'Isn't there someone you work with who could do it for you?'

'I trust you, Alex,' Marcus said. Alex thumped the ball across but hit it long, his embarrassment draining his concentration. 'You're an excellent broker,' Marcus continued, hitting another ball across, 'you'd do a good job for Janie, I...' He lunged forward and returned a low forehand. Alex missed it. 'I'd feel happy with you in on it.'

They continued to warm up and ten minutes and a few serves later they were ready to start. They came to the net and Alex held his racket up. 'M or W?' he asked, with reference to the Wilson logo on the end of his racket.

'M,' Marcus said, then he continued, 'I've got a couple of good tips, too, for Janie to get going with. I really think she could make a bit of money in the next few weeks, but I need a good broker, someone who can feel the market and buy and sell at exactly the right moment.'

Alex twirled the racket, dropped it and it fell on M. 'I'll serve,' Marcus said.

'Fine. What sort of tips?' Alex asked, unable to hide his curiosity.

Marcus bent to pick up a ball from the net and saw Alex watch him. He had Alex's attention.

'A couple of dot coms, a small industrial that's subject, I think, to a take-over.'

'I see.' And Alex did see too. He was an opportunist; he liked to make the most of every available chance that came his way and this, he had to admit, was beginning to look like a good one. Marcus was renowned for his skill and Alex saw a small opening to make a bit of extra cash himself.

'Which end?' Marcus asked, content that he'd got as far as he needed to for the moment.

'I'll stay here,' Alex answered. 'Let's get on, shall we?'

'Right.' Taking the balls to his end of the court, Marcus warmed up his shoulders, got into position and served. It wasn't a good serve, but for someone who hadn't played for six years it wasn't a bad one either.

At the end of the first set, Alex led six games to four. They were reasonably well-matched, although Marcus was probably a stronger player, which would have shown if he'd had a bit of practice. At the net both men drank some water and Marcus wiped his forehead on a towel. Alex said, 'How many people in this investment club of your sister's?'

'Three: three women.'

'And they're in London tomorrow?'

'Yup, at my office. Come for lunch if you like, come and meet them.'

Alex frowned. 'I don't know, I...'

Marcus shrugged. 'Shall we play on?' Alex nodded and they separated to opposite ends of the court.

In the second set Marcus took the lead and was winning three games to two when the next set of players turned up on the court. 'Bugger,' Alex said, glancing at his watch, 'we've run out of time.'

Marcus scooped up the balls with his racket and foot and headed towards the side of the court. 'Never mind,' he said, and he didn't. They collected up their things and made their way off court.

'So will you be giving any more advice?' Alex asked in the changing rooms as they stripped for a shower.

'I thought I'd keep my eye open for some good investment opportunities!'

Alex laughed and his brain went into overdrive. If Marcus gave his sister advice then what was there to stop Alex shifting a couple of grand on the back of that advice? He could do it through a trust, nobody even had to know he was doing it except himself. He stepped into a hot shower and took some time to consider the plan as the water gushed down over his body. He soaped himself, shampooed his hair and any concerns regarding Lucie went out of his mind. This was one hell of an opportunity, too good to turn down. If he agreed to broker for Janie's investment club then surely he should be entitled to a little bit for himself on the side? Only it wasn't really a little bit he was thinking of. He knew full well that if he could free up the cash there were likely to be several situations over the next few months where he could double, maybe even triple, his money. That was Marcus's reputation, that was why he was considered one of the best.

Alex was a reasonable broker but Marcus was flattering him when he said he was good. He knew what he was doing, he was competent but he was never going to make a fortune; he didn't have the instinct for it. Now if he was told what to watch, if he was pointed in the right direction, then who knows what he could achieve? He stepped out of the shower and saw Marcus already dressing.

'Where're you going for lunch tomorrow?' he asked.

'Soho, for dim sum. Are you going to join us?'

Alex hesitated, then glimpsed the label in Marcus's suit. I want one of those, he thought, I want to wear bespoke suits and hand-made shoes, and he said, 'Why not? I'm happy to give it a go.'

Marcus turned and smiled, a genuinely delighted smile, and Alex was instantly pleased with his decision. It never occurred to him to question why Marcus should be so delighted.

'We'll be at the New World Restaurant in China Town at one tomorrow. Meet us there.'

Marcus pulled on his jacket and bent to lace up his shoes.

'Time for a drink?' Alex asked, buttoning up his shirt.

'Sorry,' Marcus replied, 'I've got to dash.'

'Right.' This wasn't good form – a quick drink was obligatory after a game of tennis. Marcus threw his kit in his bag and zipped it up. 'Thanks for the game, Alex.' He slung his bag over his shoulder and Alex thought, he's not even going to wait for me to dress. His shock must have registered on his face because Marcus then said, 'You don't mind, do you? I've got a ton of work to do at home.'

'Oh, no, no, of course not.' Put on the spot Alex would never admit to being offended; that wasn't good form either.

'See you tomorrow then,' Marcus called.

Alex pulled on his trousers. 'Yup, see you then.' And Marcus had gone before he had even had a chance to zip them up.

Sarah opened her front door and glanced at her watch. It was seven-fifteen, they were over an hour late home and she was tense and upset. The speech therapy lesson had been terrible, a waste of time, and she had ended up getting cross; she couldn't help it. She spent a good deal of her hard-earned money on these extra lessons, she had told Rory on the way home, to make sure that he didn't ever feel behind, that he got all the advantages there were on offer to him. But if he couldn't even be bothered to answer Ali, if he couldn't even be bothered to look either her or Ali in the face, then there was no point; there was no point in any of it.

Looking over her shoulder, she saw Rory sitting sulking in the car with the door open and had a good mind to leave him there. But they both needed some food and she had arranged to go out and he needed a bath and to get to bed before Lindsay came in to sit with him.

'Come on,' she called, 'we both need some food. Supper will be ready in five minutes.' Walking inside, she smelt the slow cooker and felt a rush of relief. There was nothing more comforting than the smell of dinner ready and waiting to be eaten. In the kitchen she slipped off her jacket and lifted the lid of the slow cooker to check on supper. It was a monstrous earthenware pot in an electric cauldron, circa 1984, and it had been her mother's before hers. Sarah loved it. She would chop and throw all sorts of things into it with a pint of stock and it would always come out smelling delicious, a medley of flavours and textures that somehow miraculously seemed to work together. Tonight it was neck of lamb with discount red peppers from the market, tomatoes and chickpeas. She was lucky that Rory ate anything, but then perhaps it was that he simply didn't have any choice. There had always been just the two of them for as long as he could remember so he ate whatever she ate, there was no question about it.

Switching on the kettle, Sarah reached for a packet of cous cous and measured a cupful into a bowl. The kettle boiled, she covered the cous cous with water and went outside.

'Rory,' she said, opening the passenger door, 'come in now. Supper is ready and I'm not waiting for you.' He kept looking straight ahead and made no acknowledgement of her comment. Irritated, she said, 'I mean it, I am going to serve it up now and I won't wait for you.' She went back to the kitchen and had started to serve the food when she heard the front door slam.

'Rory?' He was on his way up the stairs and ignored her. 'Rory, supper's on the table,' she said, loud enough for him to hear. She took a deep breath and hung on to her patience by a thread. 'Please, you need some food. Come down and eat it.' Again he ignored her and carried on up the stairs. Sarah went to the kitchen window and stood looking out at their tiny garden for a minute or so, thinking about what to do. She had half a mind to insist that he came down and half a mind to ignore him and get on with her own supper, but in the end her maternal instinct won out and she went upstairs to see if he was all right.

'Rory?' She knocked on his open door and walked into his room. He was lying in bed, his school shoes kicked off, the duvet pulled in tight around him. 'Rory, we can't have this sort of nonsense,' she said, clearly and loudly, the effort of which was exhausting in itself. 'I can't deal with it. Either tell me what's wrong or get up and start acting like a normal human...' Her voice trailed away as she saw his shoulders shake under the duvet. She stepped across the room and knelt down beside his bed. Touching him, she felt the shudder of his weeping and her whole body ached. 'Rory?' She eased him round to her but he kept his face hidden as he sobbed. 'I hate it...' he managed to say, 'I ... hate ... being deaf...' And for all the world Sarah wished that it was she who was deaf instead of him.

Later, after he had sobbed himself quiet and they had talked in the fading light from the window, Sarah took him downstairs and gave him some supper warmed up in the microwave. He ate heartlessly, toying with the food and pushing it round his plate, and as he kept his head down Sarah glimpsed Lindsay at the back door and motioned to her through the glass that tonight was off. 'Come back in half an hour,' she mouthed and Lindsay disappeared before Rory saw her.

When he was finally in bed, Sarah sat with him until he went to sleep and stroked the side of his face. She had done that when he was a baby, it had been the only thing at times that soothed him, and still now she could see that it somehow eased the pressure in his brain.

At eight-thirty she went downstairs and poured herself a large gin, drinking it neat. It wasn't very nice but it was all she had in the house, and boy did she need a drink.

Lindsay knocked on the back door. Sarah opened it and Lindsay said, 'God, you look ghastly! What on earth has happened?' Then she said, 'That's not neat gin, is it?' Sarah nodded. 'Hang on, I'll get you some tonic for it,' and she disappeared next door, returning just a few minutes later with an unopened bottle of tonic water. She splashed some into Sarah's glass and propelled Sarah into a chair. 'What happened?' she asked again. 'Why aren't you going out?'

Sarah shook her head. 'Rory,' she began, 'Rory can't cope and nor...' Her voice faltered and she took a slug of gin. 'Sometimes, Lindsay, nor can I...'

Lindsay went to the cupboard, took down a glass and sat at the table, reaching across for the gin bottle to pour herself a drink. She added tonic and swilled it round in the glass to mix it, giving Sarah a chance to compose herself. Then she said, 'Sarah, you cope wonderfully. You never panic, you keep your worries to yourself and you let Rory be. Don't underestimate the power of that. What's happened? Why the doubt?'

Sarah stood to turn on a lamp and when she came back to the table she was carrying Rory's radio aid. 'The root of the problem,' she said, laying it on the table. 'The reason he's so upset. I think it's just hit him that he's deaf.' Sarah pulled a face. 'Poor lad, a bit slow on the uptake.'

Lindsay smiled. 'That's better, the famous Greg sense of humour.' Sarah sat down. She picked up the black box with its wires and shoes for the hearing aids and said, 'It's bloody awful, isn't it? It says – whoa guys, I'm deaf...' Her voice cracked and Lindsay reached across and patted her arm. 'No wonder he's so upset.'

'Isn't there an alternative?'

'Not really, nothing with the same reliability Honestly, Lin, my heart could just break. He'll get lost at school – he's in a class of thirty-two and he's the odd one out. With that many kids no one needs to bother with him; if he starts to go under how can they spend time and resources on him when there's such demand from everyone else?' Sarah put the radio aid down. 'It's not really this, it's everything compounded, the whole deaf thing. Him getting knocked down in the playground and feeling alienated at school, me not being able to afford the best for him, always feeling that if only Nick was here then it might be different, we might be seeing this differently, more positively...' Sarah broke off and drained her glass. How often had she taken solace in alcohol? She had lost count. There had been evenings in the beginning when she could hardly get up from the sofa she had drunk so much cheap plonk from Duffields.

'Another?' Lindsay said.

Sarah shook her head. 'I've no doubt Rory will have me up in the night and I don't want to be knocked out with gin.' She turned the bottle towards her to look at the label. 'Mother's ruin. Too damn right!'

Lindsay suddenly laughed. 'Sarah,' she said, 'you always have something funny to say. You are a wonder.'

Sarah smiled. 'Thank you, Lindsay, and while we're on the admiration thing we might as well make it mutual. You're a good friend. I appreciate all the tonic water and food and wine and company.' Sarah looked up. 'I'm not going to go tomorrow,' she said. 'It's not fair to leave you with a distressed Rory.'

'Of course it is,' Lindsay said sharply, 'and you are going, full stop. Your friend Janie has prepaid for your train ticket and it's a good opportunity, Sarah. You are not going to cancel! I was a teacher, remember? I've seen more truculent six-year-old boys than you've had hot dinners and if I don't know how to handle them by now then I've wasted thirty years of my career.'

Sarah smiled. 'D'you really think it's a good opportunity?'

'I wish I'd had it.' Lindsay sipped her drink. 'If you make a bit of money, Sarah, you never know what that might allow you to do for Rory. If you make a lot of money, then those opportunities increase.' Lindsay looked at her squarely 'You are going and Rory and I will be fine.'

'Thank you.'

'Which reminds me, what about that chap you were supposed to meet tonight? Have you sent word to him?'

Sarah suddenly jumped up. 'Oh my God! I'd completely forgotten about Jack! I mean, I hadn't forgotten that I was meeting him, but I've forgotten to let him know that I couldn't make it

159

and of course he'll just think that I've stood him up and...' She put her hand up to her mouth. 'Oh Lin, how awful. I feel absolutely awful, I...'

'Phone the Anchor,' Lindsay said. 'Now.'

Sarah looked at her watch. 'He might have gone,' she said, 'I doubt he'll still be there, it's nearly nine o'clock. He wouldn't have waited half an hour.'

'Of course he would. You would, wouldn't you?'

'Yes, but...'

'Then so would he. Go on, phone now.'

Sarah went to the phone and looked up the pub number in the phone book. 'It'll probably be a waste of time,' she said, dialling. 'I'm sure he wouldn't have waited...'

But Jack was still there. He was sitting in a dark corner with a pint on the table in front of him and was getting slowly but surely more and more depressed. He felt miserable, stupid and embarrassed for himself. Of course she wasn't here, why should she be? She'd just said it to make a quick getaway at Muffins; she'd said it to humour him, to ease the situation. She'd had no intention of turning up for a drink with an idiot who couldn't even manage a decent sandwich lunch in the local bakers. And who could blame her? Jack took a sip of his pint. The bar was packed, three deep, but he had a good view of the door from where he was sitting and no one even remotely like Sarah had come in. He replaced the glass on the table and looked at his watch. It was just after nine and she was half an hour late. He sighed. Be optimistic, he told himself, have some confidence. To some people, he thought, half an hour late is polite and she did have to see to Rory and maybe the babysitter had been late or the traffic was keeping her. He took yet another gulp of beer, not enjoying it at all, and thought he'd give it till quarter past, or maybe even half past to make sure. If she hadn't arrived or rung by then, well, she'd obviously had no intention of coming in the first place. It had just been an excuse to get rid of him at Muffins, he'd made a fool of himself, it had all been a big mistake... Jack's mind went off on another full circle as he sat with his pint and because of the noise and his half-hidden position, when the phone rang behind the bar he had no chance of hearing it.

A young girl – only her second night and already she wasn't sure she could cope with the stress of the mid-week darts night – took the call and, unable to raise the energy to shout over the din of the bar, said to the nearest few people, 'Jack Lowe? Does anyone know Jack Lowe?'

Several of the people right at the front heard her but no one looked even remotely interested. She gave it a couple of minutes, served someone with two pints and a gin and tonic, then went back on the line.

'Sorry,' she said, 'there's no Jack Lowe in the bar. I've asked around, but he's not here. OK?' She caught the eye of the pub manager and abruptly hung up. 'Call for some bloke called Jack Lowe,' she said, passing him on the way to serve another customer. The manager nodded. Should get himself a mobile, was what he thought, and he went down to the cellar to change a barrel.

Jack sat with his pint until nine-fifteen, then he went up to the bar to get another one. He was out now, he might as well get plastered – it was better than sitting at home on his own.

He ordered a pint of ale and a whisky chaser and said to the pub manager, 'Has anyone phoned here for me tonight? My name's Jack Lowe.'

The manager pulled the pint and grabbed a glass for the whisky. The darts were about to start, the bar had gone crazy and he really didn't have the time or the staff to be acting as a message service. He shrugged. 'Sorry, mate,' he said, 'not that I know of. That's three fifty-five please.'

Jack handed over the money and took his drinks back to his seat. The manager didn't give it another thought. Why should he? He had a pub to run.

Chapter Nine

Janie had always been very organised. In every aspect of her domestic life she executed things with detailed precision and so it followed that in her new business life she would do the same. It was eight o'clock on Thursday morning and she was dressed and ready to go to London. She had breakfast laid, her handbag with all the right things in it on the hall table and three second-class rail tickets in her jacket pocket. She had an itinerary typed up in a file in her briefcase and a list of possible investments to talk about on the train up to London, and she had made three copies of each of these things. She was just replacing them in her case having checked them as Andrew came into the kitchen with Katie and he said, 'All set then?'

Janie smiled. It was a genuine smile, not the sort she had been used to offering him recently as a forced attempt at happiness. 'Yes,' she said; then to Katie, 'Remember that you're going to tea with Alice tonight, won't you? Alice's mum will pick you up from school, OK?'

Katie nodded and sat down at the table. She picked up the cornflakes and began to pour them into her bowl. Both Janie and Andrew said simultaneously, 'Careful...' But it was too late as the cereal came rushing out with the force of gravity and spilled all over the table.

'Uh-oh, sorry.' Katie uttered it like a little sing-song and usually Janie felt a surge of irritation at the insincerity of it; it never sounded the least bit sorry at all. But this morning she shrugged and came across to the table saying, 'If you didn't tip the box like that none of this would happen. Why don't you ask Daddy or me to pour it for you?' Katie didn't answer, she was too engrossed in reading the back of the cereal packet aloud with her stilted, newly acquired reading skills. Janie glanced up at Andrew and shook her head, but she didn't hold down a sigh or tut or roll her eyes as she normally did and he said, 'You seem much happier lately, Janie.'

'Do I?'

'Yes.'

She smiled a second time – a rarity for Janie – and replied, 'Actually, you know, I think I am.'

Graham stood in the kitchen with Kitty on his hip and Oliver hanging on to his leg. Both were crying: they'd had some sort of falling out. Justin was trying to read aloud to him and Graham could hardly hear above the din, so he told him to speak up a bit. It was into this furore of noise that Roz came, wearing a suit that she'd had in the cupboard for ten years and which she'd had to fasten at the back with a safety pin.

'You look nice, love,' Graham said.

'What?' Roz shouted.

'I said you look nice,' he yelled.

'Thanks,' she shouted back. 'Not bad after three kids and a ton of egg and chips.'

Graham smiled and she took a roll out of the

164

bread bin and bit into it. Kitty began reaching for her whilst howling so Roz took her out of Graham's arms and he bent to pick up Oliver. The din suddenly stopped, except for Justin's loud, laboured reading and Roz said, 'Justin, put a sock in it for a minute will you, love?'

'That's his homework,' Graham remarked, 'let him finish it, Roz.'

'He can finish it in the car with me.' She turned to her oldest son. 'Justin, can you get your sweater and shoes on please? We're off in five minutes after I've fed the chickens.'

'Is that all you're having?' Graham asked, looking at the half-eaten, discarded bread roll.

'I'll have a good lunch, I expect,' Roz said, 'which, knowing Janie, will cost me an arm and a leg. Or rather one of the pigs' legs!'

Graham laughed. 'Come on, love, you'd better get going or you'll miss your train.' He lowered Oliver on to his feet, handed him a drink which took his mind off things and Roz lifted Kitty across to Graham, making for the door. Kitty started wailing. 'I think it's teeth,' she called as she got to the door. She blew them both a kiss, waved and left the howling behind her.

Justin joined her out by the car as she scattered seed around for the chickens. 'The cat left a huge rat in my room this morning,' he said.

'Oh great!' Roz answered. 'Nice alarm call.' She turned to him. 'How big was huge? Does Daddy need to get the Jack Russells in?'

He held up his hands to measure about three feet. 'You mean a giant rat?' Roz said. She laughed. 'Come on, really how big?'

'I don't know, about the size of a kitten.'

Roz narrowed her eyes. 'Are you telling the truth, Justin Betts? Because if you are...' She turned to see Graham in the doorway

'Roz! It's eight-thirty! You'll be late for the train! Come on, leave the bloody chickens, I'll do them later!'

'Oh God, right, erm, right. Thanks, I will.' She hurried back to the door, put the bowl of seed just inside it and slipped off her wellies. 'Justin says there's rats again. We'll need Mike's dogs in if they're as big as he says they are.'

Graham shook his head. 'Rats in the house, rats in the planning office, debts, ruin. Not a very happy future, is it?'

Roz had bent over and was pulling the strap of her navy slingbacks over her heel when she said, 'Oh, I don't know...' She stood up once more. 'Actually, I feel that I'm doing something quite positive for a change. Something that goes beyond the drudgery and the chores and the constant cycle of earning in order to spend on this place.'

Graham looked at her. This business with the stock market was not to his liking. He had never gambled, had only taken one risk in his life – Chadwick Farm – and look where that had got him. It wasn't that he disapproved, more that he was sceptical. He'd given Roz three months to make a profit on one thousand pounds and if she couldn't do it by then, she was out of it.

'This could really be something good for us,' Roz said. Graham nodded. He could hear Kitty wailing in the kitchen where he'd left her with a

166

drink and some biscuits and glanced behind him. 'It won't be good for anyone if you miss the train,' he said. 'Go on, go!'

Roz reached up and kissed his cheek. It was something she rarely did, not being given to shows of affection. 'Bye, love,' she said, then, 'Come on, Justin, let's go!' And climbing into the car, she started it up and winced as the engine missed twice, then finally caught. Moments later she was gone and Graham turned back inside to face the drudgery that Roz was so confident she could leave behind.

Sarah said, 'And if there's a problem, then I've asked Miss Meaney to ring...'

Lindsay stopped her by placing a firm hand on her arm. 'You told me,' she said, 'just a few minutes ago.'

'Right, of course I did. Sorry.'

Lindsay picked up Sarah's jacket and held it out for her. 'I will take Rory to school. You get to the station in good time, buy yourself a coffee, a paper and forget about us. You've taken the day off work, Sarah, go and enjoy it for God's sake.'

Sarah managed to look a bit more enthusiastic. 'OK,' she said, 'thanks, I will.'

Rory came into the hall. He was eating a piece of toast and looked at her. He took in the blazer and cream trousers, her smart shoes and ear-rings. 'You look nice,' he mumbled through a mouthful. Sarah said, 'Kiss?' And he came across to put his arms round her waist. She knew that some boys of six and seven didn't do the kissing thing any more – they were too old for it – but as

167

she kissed the top of his head she was so relieved that it hadn't hit Rory yet. 'I'm off,' she said.

'See you tonight?'

Sarah looked down at his upturned face and was struck again, as she so often was, by the intensity of maternal love.

'See you tonight,' she said. He dropped his arms and she opened the front door. She hesitated. What had seemed so easy a few days ago when the arrangements had been made now seemed suddenly alarming and Sarah felt a surge of panic at leaving. Lindsay came to the door, putting her hand on the latch, and said, 'Off you go or you'll miss the train.' Sarah nodded and stepped forward. Don't glance back, she thought, or you'll never go. She climbed into her car, threw her handbag on the passenger seat and started the engine. She drove off and she didn't glance back. Bother London, she thought when she'd done it, leaving without tears was achievement enough.

Lucie sat waiting for Alex in a Costa coffee bar in the West End, far enough away from where they both worked not to cause any rumours. She actually had a meeting at the head office of a big company she was working for just off Oxford Street so it was much more convenient for her than for him, although she wouldn't have given that fact a second thought. She used the time spent waiting to look through some papers in her case on the forthcoming deal, but she had to make a conscious effort to quell her irritation. Not only was Alex acting like a complete prat but he was also ten minutes late and punctuality was something that Lucie put great store by

'Hi, Lucie. Have you been here long?' Alex appeared at the table but Lucie made no attempt to stand up to be kissed by him. She glanced up from her papers and said, 'Since eight-fifteen. That was the time we arranged to meet.'

'God, is it later than that?' He lifted his arm and made a show of looking at his watch. 'Blimey, it's almost eight-thirty! Sorry!' He sat, perching on the edge of a chair, and looked at Lucie's coffee. 'D'you want another one? What was it? Cafe latte?'

'Yes. I'll have another one.'

Alex stood and crossed to the coffee bar. He ordered one cafe latte and one espresso, waited for them, then came back to where she was. Lucie put her papers away and he placed the coffees on the table. He looked at her. 'It's good to see you, Lucie,' he said.

'I'm surprised you weren't on time then,' she replied. Alex looked momentarily startled, then he frowned. He stirred some sugar into his coffee and sat down. 'What's all this about?' he asked. 'It's obviously not us, is it?'

'No, it's not about us, it's about you. Marcus told me last night that you'd agreed to go in on this investment club thing. He told me that you'd had a great game of tennis and that you were having lunch with him today to set it up.' She stared at him, her face pale with anger. 'I can't believe you'd do it, Alex? Why? Why are you hanging out with my husband? Do you like the risk? Does it make you feel good, knowing that

169

you've slept with his wife? What is your thing, Alex, tell me please, because I just don't get it, I...'

'Whoa! Hang on a minute.' Alex held his hands up to stop her. 'I am not hanging around with your husband as you put it. It wasn't my idea for the tennis, but Marcus is very difficult to say no to. I can't just drop him, he's a mate, or at least he was until last Friday!'

Lucie shook her head. 'Not good enough,' she said. 'You make excuses if he wants to see you. It's not as if you're old friends, you've only just met. You make excuses and you get out of arrangements and you don't get involved with anything that Marcus does, you...'

'Stop telling me what to do!' Alex suddenly snapped. 'I'm not your puppet. Actually, I'll do what I think is right, OK?'

Lucie glared at him. 'No, it's not OK. This is my marriage you're talking about.'

'Well "your marriage" didn't seem to bother you that much in a hotel room last week, did it?'

'That was before...'

'What? Before you thought you might get caught?' Alex was angry too now.

'Yes, all right then, before I thought we might get caught. Do you want to break up my marriage, Alex?'

Alex looked at her for some time, then he said, 'I think your marriage was broken before you met me, Lucie. If it had been whole you wouldn't have slept with me, would you?'

Lucie's face changed. He saw that it registered hurt, as if he had slapped her, then understanding and finally sadness. She bit her lip and looked away. Alex took a sip of his coffee but it was stone cold.

'I've got to go,' Lucie said a few moments later. 'I've got a meeting.' Her voice wavered and he heard the catch in it. It surprised him; he had never imagined that Lucie Croft was the sort of woman to cry 'I'll just go to the loo. Wait here for me, will you?' She stood and Alex nodded. When she'd disappeared inside he stood as well, but he knocked her folder off the table as he did so and the papers scattered all over the floor. Alex bent to pick them up, read the title of the first page and, unable to help himself, flipped through the remaining sheets. They were back in the folder and on the table when Lucie returned from the toilet.

'Alex, look, I'm sorry if I sounded high-handed, it's just that I don't want either of us to ... well, to get hurt.'

Alex dug his hands in his pockets; he knew what was coming.

'I honestly think that if you get involved with this investment club thing then you'll be getting in over your head. It's not a good idea, Alex, it really isn't.'

Alex had the immediate urge to ask: for whom? But he said nothing. As far as he was concerned, if he made money out of it then it couldn't be a bad idea.

'Alex?' She didn't have his attention. She could sense that he wasn't thinking in the same way as she was and it made her very uneasy.

'Lucie,' Alex said, placing his hand on her arm,

'relax, please. I know what I'm doing and it'll be fine. Trust me.'

Lucie shrugged. It was laughable; how could she trust him, when she couldn't even trust herself? 'It won't be fine, Alex,' she said. 'It will end in tears.'

'Nonsense,' Alex replied.

Lucie didn't press her point. What was the use of saying any more? She took up her folder and tucked it under her arm. 'Bye, Alex,' she said.

'Can I see you again? Can we meet up next week?'

She shrugged and turned to go. 'Lucie?'

'I don't know,' she finally answered over her shoulder. She began to walk away. 'I really just don't know.'

The train pulled into Victoria Station and Janie stood first, pulling on her jacket and bending to pick up her briefcase. She looked at Roz who was reading the back of the paper that belonged to the man on her right. Sarah stood too. She checked her handbag was zipped up and slung it across her shoulder. The train slowed, the man next to Roz folded his paper away and she too got to her feet.

'I didn't finish the article,' she whispered to Janie.

'Here,' the man said behind her, 'take it with you and finish it at your leisure.' Roz turned, Janie blushed and Sarah held down a smile. 'Oh, right, thanks.' She took it and the man went past her. The train stopped, he opened the door and stepped out on to the platform. 'That was nice of him,' Roz said, stepping down after Janie. They waited for Sarah and all moved off together into the crowd.

'I don't think he meant it to be nice,' Janie said. 'I think he was being sarcastic.'

'Oh.' Roz looked disappointed. 'And I thought I'd scored.'

Marcus was waiting for them when they arrived at his office. He asked reception to send them up and came to the lift to meet them.

'Hello.' The women stepped out and, with the exception of his sister who always wore what was exactly right for whatever occasion, they looked like tourists. He noticed that Roz's suit was much too tight and that her shoes were scuffed and the heels muddy, and he wondered why Sarah, who was by far the most attractive of the three, didn't do more with herself and get some decent clothes. Janie at least had dressed well. She wore a long, fitted skirt that hung beautifully and a short jacket with a white silk tee-shirt underneath. To his mind she had never been a stunner, but she knew how to make the most of herself and he was pleased now. To Marcus looking the part was just as important as playing it.

'How was your journey, ladies?'

'Fine,' Janie said, 'typical Connex South East, what more can we say?' She turned to her friends. 'Marcus, let me introduce you to Roz Betts and Sarah Greg.'

Roz shook hands first and saw how Marcus looked at her, barely concealing his distaste for her suit. She felt the smoothness of his fingers

173

and thought, poof. Never done a hard day's work in his life. She had taken a slight dislike to him, but that wasn't unusual; Roz was quick to judge.

Sarah smiled as Marcus took her hand and she too briefly registered how silky his skin was. They shook hands and he had a firm grip. Sarah liked that; she couldn't bear wet handshakes.

'Come on down to my office. I want to have a quick chat about a stock I've caught sight of this morning before we do anything else. I've just bought a load and I thought you might be interested.'

'What is it?' Janie asked. 'We've been discussing what we might buy on the way up.' They followed him down the corridor.

'It's a small dot com company launched this morning.' He opened a door in a glass wall and the women walked into a huge open-plan office space banked with screens, keyboards, phones and long work stations. The noise was incredible.

'Institutional sales are on the right there and the analysts down there to the left. Here, look...' Marcus reached up and pulled one of the screens on the work station round to face them. 'Rightbuy dot com. There, the one in yellow. It's up two pence since I left the office.' Marcus held his finger under a line on the screen which showed the name of the company, its current price and its opening price in the market that day. 'It's risen, what, eight pence since opening this morning, Peter?' One of the sales team glanced over his shoulder. 'Yup. Started at twenty and it's now at twenty-eight. What d'you reckon, Marcus, far to go?'

Marcus grinned. 'It'll rise another forty or fifty pence over the next few days is my educated guess. There's a lot of hype about this one.'

'Really?' Roz peered forward to see the screen. 'D'you really think that it'll rise that much?' She glanced at Janie and could see that Janie was thinking exactly the same as she was.

'D'you think we should buy it, Marcus?' Janie hadn't taken her eyes off the screen and saw the price move up another point. Her stomach started to churn with excitement. 'I mean, is it a good risk?'

Marcus looked at her. 'It's a risk, Janie, you've got to understand that. These dot com companies are really moving, but it's all paper money based on future earnings, they've got very little else to recommend them.'

'So you're saying that it's too much of a risk?' Sarah asked. Marcus shrugged. 'That's up to you.' That was the way Marcus worked and everyone knew it. He highlighted a stock, gave the facts and left it at that; it was as far as his recommendation went. It wasn't conventional, but it worked; not one of the stocks he'd ever highlighted had been a downer.

'Meeting,' Janie said. The three women moved together and Marcus stood back a pace.

'What d'you think? I hadn't expected to have to make a decision so quickly, but it looks like we've wandered into something pretty good.'

Roz was hooked on the whole atmosphere of the place. She loved the buzz, she loved watching the numbers move knowing that they represented real money 'I'm in,' she said quickly, knowing that if she thought about it she might change her mind.

'Sarah?' Janie was expecting Sarah to be cautious and was almost hoping she would be. She felt herself being swept away on a wave of investment fever and needed Sarah to anchor her. 'Let's do it,' Sarah said.

'Really?' Both women turned to look at her.

'How much?' Janie asked.

'All of it,' Sarah said and surprised even herself. Janie stepped towards Marcus and said, 'We want to buy into Rightbuy dot com.'

'Right, I'll get Alex on the line.' He picked up a phone and dialled. 'Alex, hi, it's Marcus. Yeah, good, thanks, you? Great. Alex, can you buy...' He put his hand over the mouthpiece. 'How much?'

'Three thousand pounds' worth,' Janie said. He went back on the line to Alex. 'Three thousand pounds' worth of Rightbuy dot com. What? Yes, USM, launched this morning. You haven't? Oh, right, yeah, look at it. Opened at twenty, now at twenty-eight. Great, yeah, OK. Thanks, Alex. Speak to you in five.' Marcus hung up. 'He'll ring back,' he said, 'when he's bought the stock. Names for the certs?'

Janie glanced at Sarah and Roz and they all smiled. 'The Housewife Trust please, Marcus.' Marcus smiled as well.

'Up-market and professional then?'

'Yes, something like that,' Janie said, still smiling.

Marcus's phone bleeped and he picked it up. 'Alex, hi. Yup, you did, great. Has it?' He pulled the screen round to face him. 'Top man, Alex! Yes, I do, it's the Housewife Trust please. Yup, thanks.' He disconnected the line, then to the women he said, 'Alex got in at twenty-nine and it's just gone up to thirty-one.'

'Great! We've made...' Janie got out her calculator and began to work it out.

'You've made two pence a share, on ten thousand, three hundred and forty-four shares, which gives you a profit at the moment of two hundred and six quid, roughly.'

'Bloody hell.'

'There'll be more to come, I think,' Marcus said.

Roz shook her head. 'No, I mean bloody hell that's impressive what you just did with the numbers, not the amount of profit.'

'Thank you. It's all part of the job.'

'Marcus is being modest,' Janie said, 'he was always a whizz at maths.' All three women stood looking at Marcus for a moment, all somewhat stunned by the past few minutes. It had taken less than a quarter of an hour to put them in business and less than two minutes to put them in profit. It was all rather incredible. 'Shall we move on for the tour?' Marcus asked. The deal was done and dusted and he gave it not another thought.

'Oh, yes, erm, great.' Janie almost had to shake herself to move from the spot she was standing on, looking at that one line on the screen. 'Sarah, Roz?'

Both women nodded, but Janie could tell they were having as much difficulty tearing them-

177

selves away from the magic numbers as she was.

'Great,' Marcus said, 'let's go.' And not really wanting to at all, the three women followed him down the office while he explained who did what and how things worked. But they were all so preoccupied that none of them heard a single word he said.

Lunch was dim sum at a Chinese restaurant in Soho. Alex arrived half an hour late – as was his habit – but he arrived with the news that Rightbuy dot com was up to forty-four pence and was forgiven instantly. It set the lunch off to a good start. They ate small parcels of oriental food – prawn with ginger wrapped in a slippery white skin and fried seaweed and chilli pork deep-fried in a won ton. While Sarah worried, even as she ate, about how much it was all going to cost, Roz struggled with her chopsticks, twice dropping something on to her lap and privately thinking, I'm glad I wore an old suit; I wonder if soy sauce stains? Janie, however, ate with perfect ease but didn't really enjoy the food as she was trying hard to commit to memory every word that Alex was saying. She was a businesswoman now, a professional, and she took it, like everything she did, extremely seriously

Marcus was on great form; on better form, in fact, than Janie had known him for a long time. He seemed to have rediscovered an energy that she hadn't seen in him for years and it surprised her. Something else that surprised Janie was both men's reaction to Sarah. It wasn't that she had never thought of Sarah as attractive, of course she had. It was just that out of the dull, ordinary context of school and Duffields she was unexpectedly taken by how uniquely lovely her friend was. Sarah had a manner that charmed; she was warm and soft and spoke with a wicked sense of humour. It seemed to draw Alex to her in such a way that Janie felt excluded, even though she sat between them, and Marcus was almost flirtatious.

At the end of the lunch Marcus offered to pay, but they all stood their ground, insisting that each pay their way. Sarah felt a moment of panic when the bill arrived, mentally calculating how much they had eaten, realising that the trolleys had come round in an unending procession. She held her breath while Janie looked at it, then Janie burst out, 'Marcus, you toad! No wonder you wanted to pay – the bill is the princely sum of five pounds each.'

Everyone laughed. They paid, stood, made their way to the exit and blinked as they walked out into the sunlight after the darkened restaurant interior.

'Thank you, Marcus,' Janie said, reaching up to kiss his cheek. 'For organising this. It's been a good day.' They may not have been close but she cared for Marcus even though she didn't understand him. She wished that they had done something like this investment club a while ago and then maybe they'd have had more in common.

'It's been a pleasure,' he said. Sarah looked at him and teased, 'Are you sure? Three country bumpkins plodding through your office, picking

179

straw out of their teeth. You've been very patient with us, Marcus.'

Marcus leant forward and kissed Sarah, something he rarely did to people outside his own family, and she coloured. She was surprised and a little unnerved. 'Of course I'm sure. It was fun,' he said. Sarah smiled and turned away. You old fool, she thought, it doesn't take much to flatter you.

Janie turned to Alex. 'So we'll hear from you, Alex, when you think it's time to sell Rightbuy dot com?' They had been discussing over lunch how long they should hold on to the stock for. Marcus had advised not more than a week. It was a quick, high-profit deal.

'Yup. Probably in the next few days or so I'd have said. Right, Marcus?'

'Definitely. As we discussed, this is a short-term buy. Alex will keep a sharp eye on the price for you and as soon as it starts shifting he'll get out.'

Janie looked at Sarah and Roz and the expression 'hanging on to every word' sprang to mind. She nudged Sarah, who started, then said, 'Right, we should let you two go.' She slung her bag across her body 'Roz?'

Roz fastened her jacket, having to pull it in tight to get the buttons done up. She shook hands with both men and said goodbye. Marcus and Alex watched them walk off and disappear into China Town, then Alex said, 'Are you heading back into the City?'

Marcus dug his hands in his pockets. 'No, I've got to see someone in the West End first.'

'OK.' Alex had been hoping to get a ride with

Marcus; now he'd have to get the tube. He held out his hand. 'Thanks for organising lunch, Marcus. Great place.'

'Yes, it is, isn't it?' They shook hands. 'I'll leave the Housewife Trust up to you then, Alex, and I'll be in touch the next time I think there's something good coming up.'

'Great.' Alex felt vindicated. He had invested four thousand pounds into Rightbuy dot com himself this morning and was already pleased with the decision to get involved with the investment club, despite the row with Lucie earlier. 'Bye, Marcus,' Alex said and the two men parted, both taking different directions.

On Shaftesbury Avenue Marcus hailed a cab. He had no meeting in the West End, he just didn't see why he had to share his cab with Alex.

The train was hot and stuffed to the last square inch with bodies when they got to Victoria. It was tourist season in the great metropolis and it was also peak commuter time. Sarah, Roz and Janie, after a couple of hours of window-shopping, squeezed themselves in amongst the office workers and the French exchange students, pressed closer together than they would have liked, and waited for the train to move off. Janie's phone rang. The sharp, high-pitched musical bleeping went unnoticed by all three of them at first, then Sarah said, 'Janie, that's not you, is it?' and Janie bent to get her briefcase, bumping her bottom on the lady behind and apologising whilst still trying to get the phone out. She finally managed it, answered it and said, 'It's Alex.' She

181

listened for a few moments, then said, 'That's fine, Alex, whatever you think. Yes, OK, I'll speak to you tomorrow.' She ended the call, dropped the phone into her handbag and turned to Sarah and Roz.

'Alex thinks we should probably move out of Rightbuy dot com tomorrow. He's going to keep an eye on things, but he thinks it might have gone as far as it's going to go.'

Sarah nodded and Roz chewed her lip. They both looked disappointed. 'So how far has it gone in total?' Sarah asked, holding her breath; two hundred pounds, she told herself, was better than nothing.

Suddenly Janie burst out, 'It's gone up to ninety-five pence a share!'

Roz let out a screech. 'Ninety-five pence!'

Sarah shook her head. 'My God, I can't believe it ... we've made sixty-odd pence a share, that's almost...' She began to try to add it up in her head, but Janie got there before her. 'It's doubled our money in five hours,' she said. All three women looked at each other. There was a moment's stunned silence, then – quite out of character – Janie threw her fist in the air and said, 'Yes!'

Chapter Ten

Dodi had been in the office since eight a.m. trying to catch up on the work that was left over from yesterday. She didn't mind working over-time, Jack was very good at time off in lieu or extra cash, but she did mind having to cover for him for his own stupidity He had rung in yesterday morning with the worst-sounding hangover she had ever heard. He could barely speak and she wondered if he might have had alcohol poisoning. Silly bugger, she thought, ruining his chances of romance by getting sozzled. It was probably nerves, but that didn't excuse it, or the fact that she was left holding the fort on what had turned out to be one of their busiest days yet.

She finished the filing, stood up to make herself a coffee and heard the door downstairs go. Mug in hand, she went to the landing and looked down.

'Jack?'

He came up the stairs two at a time. 'Morning, Dodi. What's the matter? You look shocked.'

'Just gobsmacked to see you in before nine-thirty, that's all.'

'Well, miracles do happen,' he snapped, 'so don't just stand there gawping, go and make me a coffee if you're making yourself one.' He went past her into the office, threw his case down on the desk and took off his jacket. He sat, pulled the in-tray towards him and started looking through his post.

'Jack?' Dodi stood watching him, unsure of what to do. In all the time she had worked for him he had never come in and got straight on with work and he had never ever been in early. 'Jack, are you all right?'

He didn't look up. 'I'm fine thank you, Dodi, and I'd be even better with a coffee.' He started to make notes on his pad about the first letter so Dodi took herself off to make the drinks. When she came back five minutes later Jack had worked his way through the post and was filing it away.

'You've left some notes here on my pad. Can you explain them?'

'Yes, one is a missing persons case. I'm not sure you'll want it because it's out of area, that's why I didn't just take the booking. I said you'd ring back and talk it through. It's a Mrs Trevvy; the number is there, below her name. And the second note is about a surveillance case. It's a Mr Betts, he's made an appointment to see you on Monday morning.'

'Right. I'll ring Mrs Trevvy now. What else is in the diary for next week?'

'Tuesday and Thursday are busy, you've got a phone tap installation...'

'You checked that it's a private line didn't you, Dodi? And that the bills are paid by Mrs Barnet?'

'Yes.' Dodi bristled; Jack rarely bothered to check the details, he always assumed – quite rightly – that she knew how to work within the confines of the law. 'And you've got a hotel

184

watch, you know, in Brighton,' she finished.

The muscle in Jack's jaw twitched. He hated hotel watches; the seedy end of the market, catching people in the sorry act of betrayal.

'OK, I'll pencil her in for Monday afternoon and Wednesday then. I can travel if that's what she wants, they're not my days for Jamie.'

Dodi stood where she was. She must have been staring at him because he said, 'Dodi, whatever is the matter with you?'

She shook herself. 'Nothing.'

'Good. Look, I want you to get on to the local paper and place an ad. I'd like a big one and I've written what I want to say down here.' He passed across a piece of paper that he'd taken out of his briefcase. 'It's for neighbourhood surveillance.'

'For what?'

'Neighbourhood surveillance – it's watching houses.' Dodi looked blank. 'You're going to buy a house, right?' Jack said. 'But you only ever go to that house in the afternoon to view it, or when the current owner tells you to. Yes? Well, all the other times there could be things going on in that street that you know nothing about. I mean, the road could be used in rush hour as a short cut by literally hundreds of cars, you could have ravers down the road who have late-night parties or, get this one, you could have someone living next door who breeds Alsatians and is always out walking the dogs every time you view the house, so you know nothing about it until you move in. Then, wham! You're woken every morning rain or shine at six-thirty by fifteen howling puppies, who bark all day long and all night, except when

185

they're out for their walk. I reckoned that if someone is going to spend a hundred thousand pounds on a house, then what's a couple of hundred quid more to make sure they're not making a massive mistake?'

'Jack, that's a brilliant idea!' Dodi was stunned. 'I can't believe it won't take off.'

'It has,' he said. 'I'm jumping on the bandwagon. I heard a couple of firms are doing it in London and it's going down a treat.'

'Bloody hell!'

'What's that? Bloody hell, you're a thief, or bloody hell, I can't believe you'd stoop so low, or...'

'Bloody hell, it's amazing. I've never seen you so ... so...' Dodi searched for the right word. 'So determined,' she finished.

'Yeah, well,' Jack frowned, 'it's about time I pulled my finger out and stopped being such a failure.'

'You know what, Jack?' Dodi replied in her broad Australian twang. 'I don't know what happened on that date but this is the most sense you've made since we first met.'

'Thanks, over a year of crap then.'

'Yeah,' Dodi replied. She never held back the truth. 'More than a year, actually.' And she went back to her desk to make the calls she had been asked to.

Janie was in the garden when the phone rang. She was replanting a bit of the border that had been getting her down for years. Hurrying to the house, she dropped her gloves on the terrace and

186

slipped her boots off. She answered the phone breathless and Alex on the other end said, 'Is that Janie Leighton?'

'Yes, hello, Alex.'

'You recognised my voice, Janie, I'm impressed.'

Janie wanted to say, don't be, because I don't know a single other well-spoken man who would ring me in the middle of the day, but she didn't. She said, 'I never forget a voice, or a face,' which was in fact true.

'Janie, good news. I sold ten thousand, three hundred and forty-four shares in Rightbuy this morning at ninety-five pence a share. I hope that's OK?'

Janie sat down. Usually she would have worried about her muddy gardening trousers on the chair cushions, but at this moment that didn't even enter her head. 'That means,' she said, 'we've made...' She was trying hard to work it out.

'You've made a total gross profit of six thousand, eight hundred and twenty-seven pounds.'

'Good Lord.'

'I will need to take my commission out of that, of course, which on the first twelve thousand pounds is almost two per cent.'

'Of course...' The numbers made very little sense to Janie; she was too overwhelmed with the words thousand and profit in the same sentence.

'And I've done something quite useful,' Alex went on. 'I've bought the stock for T plus five and sold for T plus four which means that there's no hanging around.'

Janie was lost. 'Hanging around? What's T plus five?'

'Don't worry too much, Janie, all you really have to know is that we'll issue your cheque minus our commission on Friday.'

'What about share certificates and all that?'

'There aren't any. I bought your shares in the name of your nominee company, the Housewife Trust, so there's no paperwork. The shares go straight on to the Crest Register – that's the new stock exchange settlement system.'

'Oh, right.' Janie was thinking, settlements, stock exchange, nominees. Her head was beginning to swim and she was the one who thought she knew what she was doing.

'You all right, Janie?'

She looked down at her muddy trousers and suddenly jumped up off the chair. 'Oh, yes, of course, I'm fine. It all sounds, erm...' She began sweeping the soil off the cushion cover. 'Wonderful. Thank you, Alex.'

'Not at all, Janie.' He meant it too. He'd just made himself a gross profit of nine thousand pounds on the small personal investment of four thousand he'd made. Not bad for one deal. 'I'll be in touch,' he said. 'Bye for now.' And whilst Janie was mid-sweep, he hung up. She stood motionless for a moment, her hand poised above the chair, then she let out a hoot and abandoned the dirty cushion cover. Sod it, she thought, with two thousand pounds I can buy six new chairs.

Sarah was stacking shelves when her name was called out over the tannoy. 'Sarah Greg to the supervisor please.' She felt instant panic; this number was only for emergencies. She put down the packet of tea she had in her hand and hurried over to the supervisor's counter.

'There's a phone call for you, Sarah,' the supervisor said. 'It's personal.' The supervisor was a large, grey-haired woman of fifty with a frizzy perm, who rarely smiled and felt it her duty to run Duffields like a regimental sergeant major on her shift. She didn't approve of Sarah, she'd said so several times in the staff coffee room. She didn't approve of single mothers, they were a drain on society. She looked at Sarah when she handed the phone over and tapped her watch. 'Company time,' she said. 'Please be brief.'

Sarah nodded and took the receiver.

'Hello?'

'Sarah, it's Janie. Sorry to ring you at work, I'll be quick. Alex sold our shares this morning at ninety-five pence a share.'

'Wow!' Sarah burst out, then she caught the supervisor's eye and blushed. She turned to the right to avoid the woman's stare. 'Janie, that's fantastic!' she whispered. 'I can't believe it.'

'Me neither. Meeting,' Janie went on, 'Monday night. Can you do it?'

'At mine?'

'Yes.'

'No problem. Rory's listening therapy shouldn't go on too late. I'll have the drinks ready. I think this calls for a celebration,' Sarah said.

'Me too. Thanks, Sarah. See you later at school.'

'Bye.' Sarah replaced the receiver under the

189

watchful eye of the supervisor and turned to go. 'I hope it was important, Sarah,' the woman said. Sarah grinned; she couldn't help herself. 'Not really,' she replied. She walked away and went back to stacking tea, knowing that the supervisor watched her every step with resentment and, for once, not caring in the least.

Roz was up to her eyes in it. Kitty hadn't left her side since Roz's return from London, Oliver had a temperature and was asleep on the sofa in the playroom and Justin had found another rat, only this one had been very much alive. She had been trying to contact Mike with the Jack Russells all morning to see if he could come over to clear them out. Graham had locked himself away in the box room they used as an office, working on something he darkly called 'the mission', and the house looked as if the kids and Graham had had a fantastic day while she had been in London; the remains of a good time were littered all over the place.

Standing at the sink washing the breakfast things with one hand, the other holding Kitty on her hip, Roz, remarkably, was humming. Normally, with this much on and at this point in the day, she would have been tearing round the house in a fury, chucking things into drawers, kicking rubbish under beds, worrying, ringing Mike every ten minutes and shouting at Graham to get himself downstairs and pull his weight. This morning, however, she was singing; humming at first, then voicing a few lines of the original Italian. She trilled an aria from *La*

190

Boheme, one of her old favourites, and surprised herself with her memory. She hadn't been to the opera for years, she hadn't even heard the music, but it all came back to her this morning.

She was just rinsing the last mug when the phone rang. She stopped singing, Kitty grizzled and rubbed her eyes and for once, before answering the phone, Roz had the foresight to put her in the pushchair by the back door, tuck a rug round her and wheel her inside over to the phone. She pushed her up and down and reached for the receiver.

'Hello?'

'Roz? It's Janie.'

'Hi, Janie. I had a lovely time yesterday, thanks for organising it.'

Janie, on the other end, was momentarily taken aback. Roz wasn't given to compliments; it wasn't her manner to enthuse.

'That's all right, I, erm, I enjoyed it.'

'Good. What can I do for you, Janie?'

This was more typical Roz, blunt and to the point. She didn't chat on the phone, she simply didn't have the time.

'I rang to tell you that Alex sold Rightbuy dot com this morning at ninety-five pence a share.'

'My God!' Roz stopped pushing Kitty and stood still for a moment. 'That's over two thousand pounds profit each, isn't it?'

'Six thousand, eight hundred and twenty-seven pounds, split three ways, minus the commission.'

'Bloody hell, that's more profit than I make in several months from this place.' Roz was almost speechless; almost. 'So what's next then?' she went on. 'When shall we meet up to discuss the next investment? Has Marcus got any ideas?'

'Monday,' Janie said, 'at Sarah's. Eight-ish?'

'Perfect,' Roz said. 'Graham isn't off to Glasgow till Tuesday afternoon so he'll be around to babysit Monday I'll be there.'

'Great. See you later at school then, Roz.'

'Yes, see you later. Oh and, erm, thanks, Janie.'

Janie smiled. 'Bye, Roz.'

Roz hung up and said to the top of Kitty's head, 'You know, Kitty darling, sometimes life really does take an odd turn and before you know it you've embarked on something that you never expected you would do and...' She peered down into the pushchair – not that she expected an answer from her daughter – and saw Kitty fast asleep. 'All of my great wisdom wasted,' she murmured, then she wheeled Kitty into the hall, left her by the bottom of the stairs, quickly checked on Oliver, and then went up to tell Graham what had happened.

Roz tapped on the door of the box room and heard Graham mutter something she took to mean come in. She gently pushed the door, felt some resistance and shoved harder. Graham let out a shout but it was too late as she crumpled three piles of paper laid out on the floor with the bottom of the door.

'I said hang on,' Graham snapped.

Roz stepped into the room and immediately bent to straighten the mess. 'Sorry, how was I supposed to know that you'd have half the rainforest scattered all over the floor?' She picked up one of the pieces of paper to look at it.

'What's this? Local government corruption in town planning?' She read the print-out of the news article, then looked up and said, 'It costs a fortune to surf the net in the middle of the morning, Graham. I hope you know what you're doing.'

Graham looked up from where he knelt. 'Not exactly,' he replied, 'but I'm starting to get more of an idea as I go along.'

Roz flicked through the other articles in her pile. 'Do I get the impression that you think there's something fishy going on with the Gordens' land deal, Graham? There's a lot of stuff here on corruption in local town planning. It's a bit far-fetched, isn't it?'

Graham knelt back. 'Not when you see this it isn't.' He held up his pile of papers and read, "Designated green belt countryside areas in East and West Sussex." An article dated spring last year on stringent building regulations on green belt sites. "Local villages to be kept local." An article on keeping development out of small villages which can't sustain the growth and restricting it to the brown-field sites nearer to larger towns where the infrastructure can adapt. How about this one, December last year? "Local town planning rejects scheme for redevelopment of rural area." And so it goes on. Up until February this year there are seven references I found on the net to planning and they all reject the sort of development proposed for the Gordens' land. So I started to look a bit harder and I came across certain rules and regulations

193

for house building issued by the local town planning department.'

'Graham! This must have taken hours. How much time have you spent on the ISDN line for God's sake?' Roz wasn't the slightest bit interested in what he was saying, she had spent the last few minutes mentally totting up how many minutes he'd been on-line at three pence a minute.

'Roz, listen to me. Forget the ISDN line for a moment, please.' He stood up and went to his desk. 'I went to the town hall yesterday in Hersley to look up some things on building regulations and I found these...' He held up a clear plastic folder filled with photocopies. 'These are the regulations for building in the region. We are considered a green belt country-side area, the whole village is, along with a ten-mile radius up to the Wested Estate and the South Downs. Building here is extremely difficult, almost impossible. That's why we got Chadwick Farm so cheaply. The land can't be developed on, or at least it couldn't be, so the value is lower.'

Roz was losing patience. 'So?'

'So how come the Gordens got an offer on their land if building here is so impossible?'

'I don't know, Graham. Perhaps the regulations have been relaxed recently, perhaps there's a get-out clause in the rules that the developers know about. There could be any number of reasons. Whatever they are you can be sure that we won't know about them.'

'Exactly!' Graham looked at her smugly

'What do you mean, exactly?'

'We won't get to know about them because you can bet your life that they're not above-board and legal. There's something going down at that office, Roz, and I'm going to find out what.'

Roz stood up. She had lost her patience. For once in her life she had done something successful; she had stopped farting about and got on with it and she now had two thousand pounds to show for it in twenty-four hours. Yet here Graham was, head in the sky, making ridiculous suggestions about corruption in local government and she was supposed to be impressed. 'Get a life, Graham,' she said cuttingly 'This is nonsense, you're wasting your time.'

'No, I'm not. There's something going on, Roz, I'm convinced of it.' He took a breath. He had to tell her, the money had to come from somewhere and that somewhere was the joint account. She'd find out soon enough anyway 'I'm so convinced in fact that I'm going to see a private investigator on Monday morning. I want him to sniff around for me, find out what he can...'

Graham stopped short; Roz had started to laugh. She looked at Graham in his faded jeans and worn socks with a hole at the big toe, with his worried frown and receding hairline, and tried to imagine him at the centre of espionage. Antiques dealer and small holder, yes; ace spy, definitely not.

'What's so funny?' Graham was affronted. This was important to him, he really believed in what he was saying.

Roz's laughter faded. 'Nothing, I...' she continued to smile at him, 'I just don't see you in the role of detective, that's all.'

'It's hardly that,' he said coldly

'No? It seems a bit far-fetched to me, a bit boys' own adventure. Is it really worth it, Graham? Wouldn't you, we, be better off focusing on rallying support and getting up petitions, causing a stir?'

'We'll do that as well,' he replied. 'We've got to do everything and anything that we can, Roz, if we want to save Chadwick Farm. If they build opposite us we'll be ruined. You know that as well as I do. Don't ridicule me for making a effort.'

Roz looked down. 'I'm not ridiculing you,' she said, 'I'm simply questioning the viability of your idea.'

'It's worth a try,' Graham said finally and Roz, even though it was against her better judgement, had to agree with that. She crossed the room and reached up to hug him. 'All right,' she said. He held her close and kissed her hair which smelt of hairspray, something she hardly ever wore.

'Did you come up here for a reason?' he asked.

Roz held her breath. She hadn't planned it, she hadn't even known she would do it until that moment when she said, 'Just to see if you wanted a coffee.' She didn't tell him. The profit and the success of the investment club was her secret. And as she turned to go, with his order for white coffee with two sugars, she realised that she didn't regret keeping it that way in the least.

Janie was at the PC in the upstairs study when Andrew came home. He was so rarely in for lunch that he felt quite illicit opening the front door to a silent house and a couple of stolen hours with his wife.

'Janie?'

Janie came to the top of the stairs in her gardening sweater, socks and her knickers.

'Is that an invitation?' he asked, looking up.

Janie frowned. 'No, I had to take my gardening trousers off because they were muddy and I couldn't be bothered to change.'

'I'll come up, shall I?' Andrew started for the stairs, but Janie said quickly, 'No, Andrew, don't. I mean, I've, erm, I've got to finish this list. I've just spoken to Marcus and he's given me a list of stocks to look at and I wanted to get it done before I go off to school this afternoon.'

'Oh.' Andrew was used to this kind of rejection; their sex life had long since stopped being spontaneous. 'How about a pub lunch then? I've got a couple of hours off from the surgery; we're trying out a new locum and I'm not needed. Shall we pop up to the Cricketers for a ploughman's?'

Janie twisted the pen she held in her fingers and her frown deepened. Why couldn't he take her seriously? When she said she had work to do, that's what she meant; she wasn't just saying it for the sake of it. 'I really do want to get this list finished,' she said, 'then I can give it to the girls to look at over the weekend.'

Andrew looked at her for a moment, then said, 'OK, I'll go on my own and have a pint and a sandwich then.' He moved towards the front door and Janie called, 'You're not cross, are you,

Andrew? I mean, you do understand, don't you?'

Andrew turned. 'I understand, Janie,' he replied. 'I thought that perhaps you'd changed for the better this last week, but now I realise that I was mistaken. You've swapped one obsession for another.' He shrugged. 'Good luck with it.' And he walked out of the door.

Chapter Eleven

Lucie was standing in front of the mirror in the bathroom applying her makeup when Marcus came in. He was dressed ready for work, as immaculate as ever in pin-striped suit, handmade shoes, Egyptian cotton shirt and silk tie. She watched him in the mirror as he came to stand behind her and gently laid his hands on her shoulders. It was the first time he had touched her in weeks.

'You feel tense,' he said.

'Hardly surprising.' Lucie had worked most of the weekend on a forthcoming deal and had come home the previous night drained and exhausted. 'I don't feel as if I've done anything but work for the last ten days.'

Marcus said, 'You haven't.' He squeezed her shoulders and began to massage her neck.

'Hmmm, that's nice.'

His fingers were strong and he had a knack with massage. It was something they used to do a lot.

'Have you got much on today?'

'No, thank God. The document should go off this morning and after that I plan to take it easy for the rest of the day. I don't think I can slope off home just in case there's any last-minute panic, but I think I'll go to the gym at lunchtime or maybe even sit in Finsbury Park with a sandwich and a magazine.'

'The *Investor's Chronicle*, I hope.'

Lucie smiled. 'Definitely not the *Investor's Chronicle*.' She looked at his reflection. 'What about you? Have you got much on?' She thought, this is ridiculous, this impersonal chit-chat, but it was at least free of acrimony, which was a relief.

'Not a lot.'

'Maybe we could have a sandwich together?' As soon as she'd said it she knew she was going to be rejected and wished that she'd kept quiet. She hated his rejection, it was blunt and insensitive.

'I don't think so,' Marcus said. He gave no other reason and despite the silences that she had got used to, despite the lack of affection, the moods and the disharmony, all of which she lived with, his reply still cut her to the quick.

She looked away from him and he felt her shoulders tense. He dropped his hands away and said, 'I've been thinking of taking a holiday. In a month or so. What do you think?'

Lucie hesitated. She wasn't sure for a moment if he was asking her if she'd like to go or if she minded him going without her. She rummaged in her makeup bag for a lipstick to stall for time but when she looked up he had walked away. She applied her lipstick, then followed him into the bedroom.

'It's a good idea,' she said, 'a break would be good.' That left it open; that gave him an indication that she would like to go without inviting another rejection.

'That's what I thought.' Marcus combed his hair, then re-aligned his shirt cuffs with his jacket sleeves and said, 'I'll book my holiday then.' And, glancing at Lucie, he said a brief goodbye and left the house.

Graham had disappeared into his office upstairs the moment he'd got up. He left it briefly to shower and dress, then he went back and closed the door behind him. Roz got on with it. She washed and dressed the children, took Justin to school and collected Mel – a young girl who helped out with babysitting – from up the road on the way home. Then she too went upstairs to shower and dress. When Graham came down at half past ten she was waiting in the kitchen in a clean skirt and an ironed shirt.

'Hello. Where's Kitty and Oliver?'

'Mel's got them in the playroom. They're watching *Teletubbies*.'

Graham turned from the sink where he was filling the kettle. 'What's Mel doing here?'

'I collected her on the way back from school. I thought I'd come with you this morning to see this bloke. If that's OK?'

Graham shrugged. 'Of course it's OK, if that's what you want. But why the change of heart? I thought you didn't approve.'

'I was being unfair and I wasn't thinking. Frankly, anything that we can do to stop this deal is better than nothing.' That didn't mean she wasn't still sceptical. She had an underlying sense of doom, a feeling that it was all a big waste of time, but that was something she would keep to herself; her husband deserved her support.

Graham spooned instant coffee into two mugs

201

and then looked up at her. 'Is that an apology of sorts?'

Roz smiled. 'It's the closest you'll get to it, Graham Betts, so take it or leave it.'

The kettle boiled and he made the coffee. 'I'll take it,' he said. 'We're due to meet this chap at eleven, so we'll leave after this coffee, shall we?'

'Where's his office?'

'Abbey Down.'

'Right.' Roz took her coffee and held it between both hands. The thing that really worried her about all of this was the expense. She said tentatively, 'Will it be expensive d'you think, Graham? I mean, we won't be letting ourselves in for all sorts of escalating bills, will we?'

'This Lowe chap...'

'Lowe?'

'Jack Lowe Investigations Limited. Mr Lowe said – and I quote – "We have a set fee scale and I don't surprise anyone with extra expenses." What he quotes is the total cost.'

'I see.'

'So, we listen to what he has to offer, ask him to quote and then consider whether or not we can afford it. OK?'

'OK.' Roz glanced at her watch. 'We'd better go,' she said, 'if we want to get there by eleven.' She stood, had a couple of mouthfuls of coffee and poured the remainder down the sink.

Graham scowled at her and she said, 'Sorry, I couldn't drink it all.' He finished his and picked the car keys up off the dresser. 'Bye, Mel!' he shouted into the hall. Roz went past him to kiss the children and he was waiting in the car with the engine running when she stepped out of the back door. She climbed in, slammed the door shut after her and a bit of the inside panel dropped off. It was then that she finally voiced something that had occurred to her right from the beginning.

'If the developers offered us as much money as the Gordens, even if it was a dodgy deal, would you want to sell up, Graham?' She turned to him in the rusty falling-to-bits old car and he hesitated. She held her breath. Roz had put every spare ounce of her energy, determination and love left over from the children into Chadwick Farm. It was hard work, badly paid and sometimes depressing, but it was their life, a life they had chosen – not been given or stumbled into, but chosen.

Graham said, 'This is our home, Roz. Ours. Mine, yours, Justin, Oliver and Kitty's. And the Bettses don't sell out.'

Roz smiled. 'Thanks, Graham.'

He shifted gear, swung the car round and they drove off.

Dodi laid three coffee mugs out on a tray with a small bowl of sugar and a couple of teaspoons. She had even been out to Duffields and bought some chocolate biscuits; anything to cheer Jack up. She arranged these on a plate and carried the tray through to the office. On the way she caught sight of a full wastepaper bin and decided to empty it, liking the place to look tidy when they had clients in. Bending, she pulled a pile of discarded magazines from the bin and looked at them. Seed catalogues, plant brochures and a gardening magazine. She was flicking through the latter when Jack came back to his desk.

'Why you throwing these out, Jack?' she said, without looking up.

'Because I've wasted enough time on gardens,' he replied. 'Time to move on.'

Dodi looked at him. 'I'll put them aside,' she said. 'You might change your mind.'

'No, chuck them please, Dodi.'

'Really?'

'Yes, really.'

Dodi tutted to show her disapproval and decided privately to keep them no matter what Jack said. He might think he knew what he was doing, but in her experience people with passions rarely lost them.

'Okey doke,' she said and carried them into the kitchen at the back to put them in her bag.

'Dodi? Door please,' Jack called and she went immediately out on to the landing and pressed the buzzer for the door downstairs. She stood there, listening to the voices below, and finally stepped forward to look down over the banister.

'Mr and Mrs Betts?'

'Yes, hello?' Graham, in front of Roz, stared up at a well-built, tanned young woman, whose open smile wasn't at all what he'd expected.

'Hi, I'm Dodi, Jack Lowe's gofer. Come on up.'

Roz and Graham exchanged glances at the word gofer and began the steep climb up to the office. At the top Dodi held out her hand, smiled at them both again, then took them through to Jack.

'Would ya like coffee? I've got it all ready?'

Roz said, 'Yes, please, we both would; both white with no sugar, thanks.' She glanced round the shabby, dim office as Dodi went off and wondered what on earth they were doing there. If this turned out to be a colossal waste of money, then... She tuned into Jack's conversation with Graham.

'I've got it here,' Jack was saying. 'I made a few photocopies for your information.' He leant across to the desk and took up a clear plastic folder. 'Have a look through those and you'll see what I mean.

Roz looked quizzically at Graham, who began to explain.

'Mr Lowe–'

'Call me Jack, please,' Jack interrupted.

'Jack was just saying that after we spoke the other day he went along to the planning department to check on plans for buildings in our area and found that the regulations for West Waltham are incredibly stringent, not only because it is a green belt countryside area but because it is also a flood plain area.'

'Flood plain? What, because of the River Arun? What does that mean?'

'It means,' Jack said, 'that a flood plain area is regulated by all sorts of restrictions from the environment agency, who basically want no building on it at all. Planning is not, or shall we say shouldn't be, an option.'

'So they won't be able to build?' Roz was finding this all a bit tricky to follow.

'Not in theory, no. That doesn't mean they

won't though. Look, at the planning department I copied two house plans on houses that have been built in the last six months and you'll be able to see how strict the regulations are. Any houses that have been approved have a minimum garden size of fifteen metres' depth and a front drive area of six metres before the garage. You can't have window to window interlocking, the minimum distance for back-to-back gardens is twenty metres and all plans have to comply with current daylight, sunlight and overlooking guidelines as advocated by the department of environment and transport. You'll be able to see from that house there what I'm talking about.'

'Yes, I do see...' Graham opened out the plan so that Roz could have a look. 'See there, love, the frontage is seven metres.'

'And here I have some other plans. These are for a development by Glover Homes that was built last year. It was in a green belt countryside area and the houses don't comply at all with regulations. See? Here, look at the size of that garden. There are five big houses crammed on to tiny spaces. Houses that size should have parking for at least three cars and the drive area is tiny...' Jack handed the plans across.

'Hmmm, I see.' Roz glanced up. 'Erm, how much has your time cost so far, Mr Lowe, I mean, Jack?'

'Nothing. I just wanted to check for myself that there was some kind of case to answer. I didn't want to take it on and waste your money, Mrs Betts.'

'Do you think there's a case?' Graham asked.

'Am I right, is something going on?'

'Please, sit down.' Jack waited for his clients to sit, then went round the desk and sat down opposite them. Dodi brought coffee in, handed it round, then she too pulled up a chair.

'Dodi has been making a list of all planning applications over the last two years for the whole Hersley area. She's only halfway through it, but already she's found three instances where one particular builder, Glover Homes, has been successful when others have failed. Now that may just be because they're a good building company with very skilled land buyers – certainly they're a national builder – or it may be something else. At the moment it's too early on and it would be dangerous to speculate. People have reputations.'

'So, how do we find out which one it is?'

'Well, the first thing to do is work through the rest of the list. Then we need to find out which developer has made the offer on the land adjacent to your property. If it is this particular builder, and I have a feeling that it is, then we need to track their planning application. Firstly, there should be objections because of it being a green belt and flood plain area, and secondly, if they want to put six or seven big homes on to the site then it won't fit with regulations. I would take an educated guess that their application is being reviewed at this moment, or at least they're working on it. If they've put in an offer, they must be pretty confident of getting planning. So...' Jack took a slug of coffee, swallowed, then went on. 'Firstly, I'd want to track the land buyer for the developer, keep my eye on him and find out if he's spending time with anyone from planning. Secondly, I'd want to track the planning application officer or officers at Hersley planning department, and thirdly, I'd need to check on each member of the council committee. It's the committee that pass the applications and if there is corruption then it's my guess that it's probably one or several members of the committee. I need to find out who's doing what and who's spending time with who. I'd look at things like who has a new car, or who's been on an exotic holiday, that kind of thing. I might even do some credit cheeks; there's lots of things I can access if I need to.'

Roz was taken aback. 'Is it all legal?'

Jack smiled. 'Yes. There are lots of data protection laws and privacy laws but I work well within them. I'm not a bandit, Mrs Betts. Some things may be covert, but they're not illegal.' He drank some more coffee. 'The thing is that anything of this nature, fraud, corruption and so on, is very difficult to prove. I'm not going to catch anyone red-handed, people aren't stupid. They cover their tracks, they are careful, but they do make mistakes and it would be my job to keep watch for mistakes.'

Roz glanced at Graham and he said, 'You didn't answer my question earlier. Do you think there's something going on?'

Jack held up his hands. 'At the moment, I don't know. There is something that needs to be looked at, but that's as much of an answer as I can give you, I'm afraid.'

'I see.'

'You don't have to make up your mind now you know,' Jack said. 'Take some time to think about whether you want to go ahead with this kind of investigation. It's expensive and I wouldn't want you to go ahead unless you were absolutely sure.'

'What does expensive mean?' Roz asked. 'How much are we talking about here?'

'I've done a quote for you, Mrs Betts.' Jack took out an invoice and handed it across to Roz. Dodi caught a glimpse of it and was impressed. He had done it himself on the PC and it looked very professional, far better than the cheap slips she used to write out for him. From his performance this morning no one would ever have known that less than a week ago he could hardly drag himself up the stairs to work.

Roz looked at the quote and handed it across to Graham. 'What if it takes longer than the time you've quoted for here?'

'That's my problem. I quote for the job – if I run over then that's my bad management.' He smiled. 'I don't usually run over.'

Liar, Dodi thought, you've never finished a job on time yet.

'And what do we do with the information once you've found it?'

Roz asked. 'I mean, if you find out that the planning office is corrupt then what do we do about it?'

'You blow the whistle on them. I'll have put together enough of a case to be convincing, hopefully with photos, witness statements, financial evidence, that sort of thing, so there

209

should be enough corroborative evidence to report them. It will certainly put an end to the land deal with your neighbours at least, and it might even stop the whole thing completely.'

Graham, holding the quote in his hand, said, 'Right, well, that all sounds fine and this looks quite acceptable but I've one last question. What's your personal opinion on development in rural areas, Jack?'

Jack took a few moments to think before he answered. 'I haven't really given it much thought to be honest, Mr Betts. I'm not against development but I am against greed. If there are rules regarding where you can and where you can't build then those rules should be adhered to by everyone. If they are being broken for nothing more than profit and personal gain, then I'd be the first person to speak up against it.'

Graham looked at Roz but he didn't have to say anything. He could tell just by the look in her eyes that they were in agreement on this one. He said, 'We'd like to accept the quote, Jack. How soon can you start?'

Jack smiled. 'This morning.'

Dodi stood up and went round to Jack's side of the desk. This was a good job and she wasn't going to waste a moment. 'I've got some papers to sign here, if you don't mind; a disclaimer and an acceptance copy of the quote.' She handed two sheets across to Graham. Then she looked up and smiled at him. Strike while the iron's hot, she thought. 'And would you mind paying a deposit up front of, say, a hundred pounds?' she asked.

After they had gone, Dodi put the cheque into the business paying-in book and took it over to Jack's desk. 'Is there anything else to pay in from last week?'

Jack reached into the drawer in his desk and took out an envelope. 'Here.' He handed it across and Dodi took out two more cheques. 'That was good work this morning, Jack,' she said, leaning on his desk to fill in the paying-in slip. 'I liked the spiel about development.'

'It wasn't spiel,' Jack said, 'I meant it.'

Dodi looked up. She stared at his face for a moment as he looked out of the window and said, 'You did too, didn't you?' She closed the paying-in book and stood up straight. 'I don't know what that lady did to you on your date the other night, Jack, but you can tell her from me that you've–'

'Nothing,' Jack cut in.

'Sorry?' Dodi frowned.

'She did nothing, she didn't show up. I got as pissed as a fart and drowned my sorrows in seven pints and three shorts, or that's as many as I remember anyway.'

Dodi's expression was hard to read. Jack thought it was a mixture of distaste and pity; stupid old bugger, he could almost hear her thinking. But it was in fact shock and hurt on his behalf that she felt. He didn't deserve that, was what she actually thought.

'I'm sorry,' was all she could manage to say.

He shrugged, suddenly embarrassed. 'Well, I'm not. It made me realise what a pathetic figure I must be.' He switched on his PC, ready to continue work. 'Not any more though.'

Dodi took the hint and stepped back. 'I'll run these down to the bank,' she said.

Jack didn't look up, he was too busy accessing his software. 'You do that,' he said distractedly and Dodi turned to go. She liked the new Jack, she liked him a lot, but it didn't stop her lamenting the passing of the old one and hoping that, maybe, some part of him still remained.

Lucie glanced at her watch on the way up to Joe Allen's and realised that she was on time, which of course was a waste with Alex because he was always at least ten minutes late. So she stepped into Penhaligans and tried on several of their perfumes with the assistance of a well-spoken young lady, but with no intention to buy whatsoever. When she had wasted fifteen minutes she thanked the girl, told her she would return – which she wouldn't – and left, making her way along to the restaurant. Alex was waiting for her.

He stood as she came to the table and kissed her. Lucie let him kiss her cheek, but made no effort to return his affection. She hadn't wanted to come, had in fact only done so because he had rung her that morning and almost insisted that she join him for lunch and, without snapping or being very rude in an office full of people, she could do nothing but agree.

'What would you like to drink? Wine, beer?'

'I'll have a glass of wine please; white, dry.'

Alex ordered for her and passed her across a menu. 'They have good salads,' he said. 'You like salad, don't you?'

Lucie put her menu down on the table and looked at him. 'What's this all about, Alex? I thought you understood that things were over between us.'

'Are they? I understood that you wanted some cooling-off time and I understood that you didn't approve of me getting involved with your sister-in-law's investment club, but I didn't think it, we, had finished.' He reached across the table for her hand and she let him have it. She couldn't be bothered to resist. 'When I asked you if I could still see you,' Alex went on, 'you said you didn't know. That didn't sound to me like our relationship was over.' He wove his fingers between hers. 'It's not, is it?'

Lucie shrugged. How the hell did she know? She knew what she was doing was wrong for her, that betrayal left her weak with guilt. She didn't want to get caught, she didn't want to lose her marriage, but what sort of a marriage did she have? She co-habited with Marcus, they lived in the same house but they had separate lives. He didn't touch her – she couldn't remember the last time he had held her hand across a table. She loved him, but where was all that love going? Nowhere. It needed an outlet, her sexual energy needed an outlet, and her need for affection – the basic need that every human being has – had to be satisfied. She looked back at Alex.

'I don't know what I want, Alex,' she said. He kissed her hand and it felt good. So good that she experienced a rush of warmth between her legs.

'Do any of us know what we want, Lucie? I don't really know what I want, so I take what's

213

there and enjoy it. I love to lie with you, Lucie, you make me feel good. That's enough for now, isn't it?'

Lucie shook her head. 'I don't know,' she said again and Alex continued, 'Marcus doesn't know about us and he isn't likely to ever find out. You're unhappy; you're sad and stressed and lonely and I can ease all that. You like being with me, don't you?' He smiled and kissed her hand again. 'Come on, admit it?'

Grudgingly Lucie smiled back.

'You like sex with me, don't you?' He was still smiling. 'Come on, admit it? And you like salads, which is why I've brought you here for lunch...' He moved his fingers up her hand and stroked the soft, smooth skin on the inside of her wrist. 'You do like salads, don't you?'

'Yes!' Lucie replied. Suddenly she laughed. 'God, Alex, you're such a salesman.' She pulled her hand away and held the menu up over her face. 'And what about you? What do you like? Why are you so persistent with me when you could have a nice, uncomplicated single girl in your bed?'

'Who wants nice and uncomplicated? I like complex. I like the way that you meet me in a hotel bedroom in a suit, holding your briefcase, and I know that you've been kicking ass in that bank of yours.' He lowered the menu down so that he could see her face. 'I like the way that ten minutes later you're lying underneath me, naked, all sense abandoned. I like the way you moan and move your hips and really get into me and then shower and dress and leave as if nothing had ever

214

happened between us. And I like this; I like the secrecy and the intimacy of knowing that it's only us, no one else knows, no one else matters...'

'You're a thrill-seeker,' Lucie said. 'You get off on risk, don't you?'

Alex reached under the table and placed his hand on her thigh under her skirt. He moved it up between her legs and looked at her. 'I don't know what you mean,' he said.

Lucie smiled, then gently moved his hand away.

'Come back to my flat after work tonight?' he asked.

She sighed. 'I don't think so, I...'

'Please?'

She thought, he really wants me. 'Alex, I–'

He didn't let her finish. 'Please,' he said quickly, 'come back and let's get things on a level again. Let's move past that dreadful night at your place and the investment club thing. Please?'

Lucie hesitated. She looked at her hands on the white tablecloth, hands that needed to touch, that needed to be held and kissed, and she said, 'OK.' She looked at him. 'I should finish around seven. I'll come then.' She didn't know what she'd tell Marcus, what excuse she'd make for being late, but she did know that in the end it wouldn't really matter because he wouldn't really care. In fact, she thought, taking a sip of her wine, he probably wouldn't even notice that she wasn't there.

Marcus finished on the phone and looked at his watch. It was twelve-thirty and he was irritated that the last call had taken so long. He stood, stretched and went over to the water tank. He poured himself a glass and someone asked him what he was doing for lunch. 'I'm out,' he said. He rarely gave out details of his private life in the office.

Back at his desk he called the Pavilion in Finsbury Square and booked a table for one o'clock, then he dialled Lucie's office. He wasn't sure what he was going to say to her; it probably needed an apology but he wasn't very good at saying he was sorry. He hadn't behaved well that morning – he'd been insensitive and he'd hurt Lucie, he knew that much. Though how to get past it, how to get on to a secure footing with her again, he had no idea. Things recently had begun to go very wrong. He was at fault, he realised that, but he didn't know how to stop being at fault. He had somehow become closed off from her, from life itself really, and he didn't seem able to open himself up again, or indeed decide if that was what he really wanted to do.

The line connected and he heard it ring. Maybe lunch would help, and if it didn't then at least it might be a start.

Lucie's secretary answered and told him Lucie was out. Did he want to leave a message? Marcus gave a curt no and rang off. He pulled his jacket on, took his car keys out of his desk drawer and left the office. On the way out he told reception to switch his phone to voice mail as he didn't know how long he'd be away from the office.

In the street, Marcus made his way along to his car. He didn't usually drive to work but the morning had been bright and sunny and he

216

hadn't been able to resist the lure of an open-topped car. He had parked on a meter, then offered one of the boys from settlements twenty quid in cash to pop down every hour and feed the meter for him with pound coins. He pressed the alarm pad, the car bleeped and he opened the driver's door and slipped inside. That's all you could do with a car like that, slip into it; the seats were low and upholstered in black leather and the interior space was minimal.

Once inside, Marcus started the engine, revved it, enjoying the throaty roar, and pressed the button for the roof. Overhead the system whirred into action and the roof peeled back to reveal a bright blue sky. He put on his sunglasses, put a CD in the player and pulled out of the space. Lucie would be at the gym. He would go there, interrupt whatever she was doing and take her out for lunch. If she didn't have much on they could even go up to the West End. He turned down Threadneedle Street and accelerated. He attracted attention – a good-looking, well-dressed man in an expensive car – and he enjoyed it. Marcus wasn't vain but he did have an inflated ego. Most men in his position did.

At the gym, Marcus pulled up outside, double-parked and went into reception. He asked the girl if Lucie had signed in and she checked on the computer.

'No,' she said, 'there's no card gone through for Lucie Croft.'

Instantly irritated, Marcus said, 'Are you sure?'

'Yes.' She wasn't the most helpful of the gym staff; she was working her notice and off to

217

Australia at the end of the month. She actually couldn't give a damn.

'Could you just tannoy her, to make quite sure she didn't slip through without signing in?'

'She couldn't have got past me. There's no way she could have–'

'Could you just tannoy her, please?' Marcus asked, as calmly as he could.

The girl rolled her eyes and sighed. 'It's a waste of time,' she said. 'I told you, I'd know if she–'

'Do it, please,' Marcus suddenly snapped, 'and we'll see.'

The girl switched on the tannoy and called out Lucie's name. She then sat back and folded her arms. Marcus walked across to the seating area and picked up a copy of the *FT*. He flicked through it, watching the desk out of the corner of his eye.

'Excuse me?' the girl from the desk called. 'Hello?'

Marcus turned. 'I wouldn't bother to wait,' she called across to him, 'she's not here. I just checked with the manager and he said she wouldn't have got in without us swiping her card.'

Marcus said nothing. He dropped the *FT* back on to the coffee table, turned on his heel and walked out. As he left, the girl on the desk said, 'Arrogant prat.' He didn't hear it and if he had he wouldn't have cared.

Back in his car, Marcus thought for a moment about what to do. He felt stranded, irritated and disappointed. He'd left the office and had no desire to go back. It had been a shitty morning anyway and he was owed weeks of holiday that he hadn't taken over the past two years. He might as well call it a day; no one would bother him if he didn't go back in. So he dialled the office on his mobile, left a message on his assistant's voice mail, then started the engine. The truth was that he didn't really have anywhere to go, or anywhere that he wanted to go. He sat in the car for a few minutes, the CD blaring and the engine ticking over, the people coming to and from Cannons gym staring at him as they went past, then finally he made a decision. He would drive down to Sussex, go and see Janie. Why not? She would be glad to see him and might even cook him dinner. He could have a pint in the local with Andrew Cheered by this idea, Marcus pulled out into the traffic. Perhaps not a pint with Andrew, it wasn't that kind of relationship, and maybe not dinner there, it would be too much, but the drive would be good. He was closing himself off again, shutting himself down and leaving not even half an inch for anyone to get anywhere near.

Janie was in the kitchen when Marcus arrived at Bank Cottage. She was making a cake in a direct refutation of Andrew's comment on Friday about her exchanging obsessions. They hadn't spoken about it at all over the weekend, but she had made damn sure that he had had every thing he could possibly have wanted or needed and that the house and the social activities had been run with clockwork precision. She wasn't going to let him get away with it. She was doing something at last that made her feel valued and she wasn't going to let Andrew walk all over it.

The doorbell rang just as the timer for the oven bleeped, so she quickly took the cake out, put it on a cooling wire and hurried to the door. The bell rang again. She was flustered and opened the door with her apron on and flour on her cheek.

'Marcus! My God!' She was momentarily lost for words. What the hell was he doing here? Her first thought was that he had lost his job, but she dismissed that as ridiculous as she glanced behind him at a bright red sports car. 'Gosh, erm, what a nice surprise!'

Marcus had bought a huge bunch of expensive flowers from a stall on the King's Road on the way to the A3 and handed them over now saying, 'Is it? You don't mind me crashing in like this, do you?'

'Of course not, it's...' Janie held the flowers, embarrassed by their extravagance. 'It's wonderful. Come on in, please.'

Marcus stepped inside and smelt cake. He instantly pictured Lucie and thought that that was a smell their house would never possess. 'Are you baking?'

'Yes, to prove to Andrew that I *can* do two things at once.' She laughed and led the way through to the kitchen. 'These flowers are beautiful.' She bent her head to the blooms and breathed in their scent. 'They smell divine.' She went to the sink, ran the tap and said over her shoulder, 'I'll pop them in some water and then I've got to go and get Katie. Will you come with me? She'd be delighted to see you at school.'

220

'Does she know who I am?'

Janie turned, but saw that Marcus was smiling and smiled with him. 'It's been a long time, Marcus,' she remarked, 'and it's not for want of asking.'

'I know. Sorry. Shall we go in my car? Katie could just about squeeze in the back of the Porsche 911. It's a convertible.'

Janie took her apron off. 'That would be lovely,' she said, as she thought, where will it end? Will he ever spend enough?

'Come on then.'

Janie turned the tap off, put the flowers in the sink and joined Marcus by the front door. She took her house keys off the hall table and they went outside.

'Very nice,' she said, looking at the car, not knowing what other comment to make. This sort of thing was out of her league.

'Glad you like it. Hop in.'

Janie managed to squeeze herself into the space and plopped into the passenger seat, unsure of the car's height and not judging it quite right. 'It's hardly hopping in,' she said and Marcus laughed. He started the engine and revved it. Janie raised an eyebrow. 'What is it about younger brothers?' she asked. Marcus pulled out of the drive, sped off down the road and Janie's head hit the back of the seat with the force of the acceleration.

Sarah was waiting in the playground at school when the Porsche pulled up. She turned, along with several of the other mothers, and was stunned to see Janie climb out. Then she thought, if anyone was going to climb out of a sports car, it was more than likely to be Janie. She waved and Janie brought Marcus across.

'Hello, Marcus.'

'Sarah. Nice to see you. How are you?' He leant forward and kissed Sarah's cheek. 'Have you been playing tennis?'

'Oh no, nothing nearly so civilised. It's my warm weather kit – shorts, tee-shirt and trainers. Scruffy and comfy.'

Marcus glanced down at his suit. 'Quite right too, far better than this straight-jacket,' he said.

'Sarah, I'll leave Marcus with you if that's OK? I just want to pop in and have a chat with Miss Meaney,' Janie said.

'Yes, that's fine.'

'Of course it is,' Marcus went on. 'Sarah can give me all the lowdown about the investment club while you're gone.' Then to Sarah he said, 'So? How's it all going? I heard about the coup with Rightbuy dot com. Well done. What's next on the hit list?'

Sarah turned to him. 'I don't know. We're meeting tonight to discuss it.'

'Did you see the article in the *FT* at the week-end about media groups?'

Sarah shook her head.

'It was very interesting. Small media companies constantly falling prey to the giants. As soon as they go public they're snapped up. There's only a few left apparently.'

'What section was it in?' Sarah asked. 'I bought the Saturday *FT* and I didn't see it.'

'I'll fax it to you if you like?'

'No fax.'

'Oh well.' He shrugged and Sarah watched his face as he stared openly at the other mothers in the playground. He was out of place; there was an undercurrent of curiosity as all eyes at some point glanced at him, but it didn't seem to register. He dug his hands in his pockets and Sarah said, 'Is it worth looking at small media groups, d'you think?'

'Probably. There's been quite a bit of speculation recently on takeover bids and anything connected to cable or satellite communications is a good bet. Don't be fooled by the press though, journalists aren't always right and the biggest diamonds aren't always the easiest to spot.'

'So is that a yes?'

'You might think it is, but I couldn't possibly comment.'

Sarah laughed. 'God, what was that programme? About politics, wasn't it?'

'Yes, *House of Cards*, with...' Marcus looked at her. 'You have a wonderful laugh, Sarah, it's very...' He stopped to search for the right word. 'Spontaneous.'

Sarah smiled. 'Spontaneous is a very kind way of putting it, Marcus. Others have described it as neighing, erm, loud and raucous and I think someone even said ridiculous once.'

Marcus chuckled. 'Well, I like it.'

'So, do you think it's worth looking at small media groups?' Sarah asked.

Marcus narrowed his eyes. 'Ah, haven't given up then? Why don't I give you that article and

223

you can have a look for yourself? I've got to see a client down this way at the end of the week. I could drop it in to you, along with some other stuff on the market, if you like.'

'Oh no, I wouldn't want to put you out.'

'Not at all. In fact, I'd enjoy it – far better than just coming down for a boring client meeting. Maybe we could have a sandwich at the pub and discuss it?'

Sarah hesitated for a moment, then thought, why not? 'I'd like that,' she said. 'It'd be nice.' It would be too; something to look forward to. Sarah liked Marcus. He was up front and easy to talk to; uncomplicated. It made a change.

Sarah saw Janie coming towards them with Rory and Katie. 'When did you have in mind?' she asked. 'I work every day until one but I might be able to get off early.'

'Friday? I think it's Friday I'm due down here. Is that OK?'

'Yes, that sounds fine.'

'It's a date then. Good.'

'What's good?' asked Janie.

'This whole investment thing,' Marcus replied before Sarah had a chance to explain.

'Really?' Janie looked at Marcus.

'It seems to be going very well,' he went on, 'it's just what you needed, Janie.'

'Well thank you, Marcus, nice of you to say so.' She turned to Sarah. 'He is quite nice some-times,' she said. Sarah smiled, and as Marcus bent to talk to Katie she watched him and puzzled at why he hadn't told Janie he was down in Sussex on Friday. Then she glanced up and saw Rory and whatever Marcus had said was forgotten. The sight of her son, alone and forlorn, walking across to her trailing the bag with his microphone aid in it behind him made her heart sink. Everything else simply went out of her mind.

The meeting at Sarah's that night started at eight-thirty. Each of the women had made a list of what they wanted to look at and, after speaking to Sarah on her way out of the playground, Roz had gone home and got Graham to run a print-out of all the articles in the financial press on small media groups over the past six months. She had it with her, along with the notes she'd made in the bathroom while the kids were in the bath.

'Preferred stocks,' Janie said, to kick off. 'Who wants to go first?'

Roz got out her notes. 'Small media groups,' she said. 'I've done some homework and I think Marcus could be right, there's one or two that look very interesting.'

Janie made a note on her pad. 'Actually, I narrowed it down to one,' Roz went on. 'I think Prestwick Communications is a good bet. There's lots of stuff in the press about them. Quite a bit of speculation about a bid from the Searson Group, the media giant. Here, I copied the articles for you both.' She handed a couple of photocopies over to Janie and Sarah.

'Was there anything else?' Sarah asked.

'There was Sarasota, an advertising and marketing group, but they're not very well reviewed.

No one has ever tipped them.'

'What do they do?'

'Advertising, obviously; they've got a big public relations arm, PRP, who do media research and marketing. Oh, and they run a couple of TV shopping channels.' Roz handed over the one article she'd found on Sarasota.

Sarah looked at her. 'Where? What network?'

'Sky.' She chewed the end of her pen and looked at Sarah as it began to make sense. 'They're very cheap at the moment, undervalued as far as I can see...'

In her head Sarah kept going over what Marcus had said about the best companies not necessarily being the ones that were favoured in the press. He had such a skill in this kind of thing. 'If they're cheap and undervalued, wouldn't they make a better bid proposition for Searson Group than Prestwick? I mean, there's a headline here that says Prestwick are overvalued.' She shrugged. 'I don't know, what do you think?'

Janie, who had been reading through the news print-outs, said, 'Are you two saying that you want to take a risk on a company that might be subject to a take-over bid?'

Roz and Sarah looked at each other. The thought that they might be in with a chance of repeating the success of Rightbuy, but in bigger amounts, was highly tempting.

'I don't know,' Sarah said honestly

'Well I do, and the answer is yes, Janie. Marcus has told us to watch small media groups and I'm happy to go with that tip.'

Janie sighed. This wasn't a business, this wasn't

226

proper investment, it was tantamount to gambling. 'But was it a tip?' she asked. 'Did Marcus make a recommendation?'

Sarah, more cautious than Roz, shook her head. 'No, it wasn't a recommendation as such, it was more like a subtle hint.' She bit her fingernail while all three women looked at each other.

'How much would you want to invest?' Janie said at last.

Roz took a breath. 'All of my money; the original investment plus the profit from Rightbuy dot com.'

Sarah stared at her. 'Are you sure, Roz?'

'If we can pinpoint the right stock then yes, I'm sure.' She leant forward. 'The way I see it is that the market is moving up, right?'

They all agreed.

'So, we put our money into something that isn't as volatile as IT stocks but will more than likely grow with the market at worst and might be subject to a take-over at best. We could take a two-month view on it and then think again. According to what I've read, Searson Group are anxious to make a bid for something. We might not even have to wait that long. And, if they do make a bid and it's not for whatever we've invested in, then it'll still have a positive effect on the share price of our stock. Activity in the sector always does.'

Sarah blinked rapidly, then stared at Roz. It suddenly struck her that you could be friends, good friends, with someone for years and still not really know the depth of them. This was talent; this was clear thinking and strategy and it took

Sarah's breath away 'You're wasted on pigs and sheep, Roz,' she said.

Roz smiled.

'No, really, I mean it. I think that sounds really impressive. Janie? What d'you think?'

Janie couldn't say. What she actually thought was, terrific! It's all my idea, I do the legwork, get it all organised and then Roz comes along and starts taking the whole thing over with her bigger and better ideas. Great! Bloody Roz, wading in knee-deep, thinking she knows it all, showing off. But she didn't voice any of this. She hesitated, looked at Sarah, then said, 'Very impressive, yes, of course.'

Sarah thought again about what Marcus had said. 'This Sarasota stock, what's the share price?'

'Fifty-nine pence,' Roz replied. 'Why? D'you think that's a better bet than Prestwick?'

Janie felt excluded; she wanted to add her bit. So she said, 'If Prestwick *are* overvalued then, despite what the press say, any predator is going to think twice about them.'

Roz turned. 'You're right.'

'Was there any other company, Roz, that might be subject to a bid?' Sarah asked.

'Only the two that I could find.'

'Well,' Janie ventured, 'maybe we should have a closer look at the market over the next few days and then invest. There's no immediate hurry, is there?'

Both Sarah and Roz agreed that there wasn't. 'You are always so sensible, Janie,' Roz remarked. She saw the look on Janie's face and added quickly, 'I mean that as a compliment.'

'Yes, well...'

'So, we're all agreed,' said Sarah, changing the subject. 'If after a more careful look Sarasota seems like a good bet, then we want to invest in it in the hope of someone taking it over. Yes?'

There was a silence.

'For a two-month period,' Janie added. 'Then we think again.

'Yes,' Roz said.

'Yes,' Janie finally added.

Sarah looked at them. 'How much?'

Janie shrugged. 'In for a penny, in for a pound,' she said.

'All of it.'

'Roz?'

Roz smiled. 'If we're into metaphors, then we've got to speculate to accumulate...'

Sarah rolled her eyes. 'Right, it's agreed then.' She looked at both of them. 'And let's just hope that the early birds catch the worm.'

Roz and Janie groaned and then they all burst out laughing.

JULY

Chapter Twelve

The early birds did catch the worm.

The Housewife Trust, a nominee company, bought sixteen thousand, nine hundred and forty-nine shares in Sarasota plc on the twenty-fifth of April for fifty-nine pence a share. On the nineteenth of May an announcement was made that the Searson Group had put out an offer for Sarasota plc and the share price leapt to one pound seventy pence a share. That was a better valued stock, the analysts said; that was bloody good luck, Roz remarked. The trust sold their shares at one pound sixty-nine pence a share and then had a working capital of over twenty-seven thousand pounds.

Over the next few weeks they watched the market and made several quick deals in certain stocks, raising their capital to fifty thousand pounds. Then they started to track the dot com companies, which were now rocketing out of all proportion. The trust began to double its money on certain deals. They had a run of luck in buying shares in two more companies just before a take-over announcement was made regarding the company, and although Sarah spoke to Marcus on a regular basis the women put their success down to precision research and pure and simple luck. It was a spectacular result for Janie, Sarah and Roz, but it was small feed in comparison to the sort of profit that was being made in a market that just kept going up and up.

By the end of June they had amassed a staggering one hundred and ten thousand pounds from a three thousand pound initial investment. It was time, they all decided, to spend a little of it. Janie was on the phone to Marcus with her plans as soon as she had agreed with Roz and Sarah how much they should be taking out of the fund. It was Friday night, the first week in July

Marcus put the phone down and looked across at Lucie. She was curled up comfortably on the sofa – or as comfortably as one could be on a grey linen designer settee – her glasses on, watching the television. He was reading on the leather Bauhaus chair, a chrome reading lamp positioned over his right shoulder.

'You look tired,' he remarked. 'Why don't you get off to bed? It's only rubbish you're watching anyway, isn't it?' Lucie didn't answer; she barely even heard him. It had been the usual Friday night for them, or what had become usual over the past couple of months. She had come in late with an M&S ready meal in a carrier, which she then stuffed in the oven while she poured herself a large glass of wine and seethed with resentment that Marcus neither asked where she had been nor mentioned the possibility of getting some supper ready himself. She had begun to drink half a bottle of wine before dinner at weekends. It was the only time they were together and it was the only way she could unwind enough when she was with him to get the food down. And she needed to eat – she was losing too much weight.

Lucie was losing weight because she was unhappy. She was working very long hours, she had no marriage to speak of and she was locked in an affair with Alex that she just couldn't seem to drag herself away from. She liked it, no, loved it when she was with Alex and hated it, deplored herself for it when she was alone.

'Lucie? I said you ought to get to bed,' Marcus repeated. 'You look exhausted.'

Looking across at him, bleary-eyed, Lucie heaved herself into a sitting position and stretched. 'I am exhausted,' she said. She dropped her legs down and shuffled her feet into her slippers. She yawned and got to her feet. She was a bit unsteady; the combination of drink and tiredness. 'Where are you sleeping?' she asked. Marcus had taken to using the spare room on occasions recently, telling her that she needed the rest and didn't want him snoring and turning beside her. She was so tired most of the time that she didn't even notice if he was in the bed or not, but she couldn't be bothered to argue with him. She wanted to think that he was saying it to do the best for her, but she knew in her heart it was an excuse not to have to lie beside her.

'In the spare room,' Marcus replied. Lucie nodded and made her way to the bedroom. 'Goodnight,' she said. She didn't make any gesture or even turn to look at him. There was no point, doing so only invited more rejection.

In the bedroom she took off her clothes, went into the bathroom and wiped her face with a flannel. There was a time when every night she would shower before bed so that she would be

235

clean and scented for Marcus when he got in beside her. Now she flopped into bed with the sweat and grime of the day still on her body and having barely removed her makeup and brushed her teeth.

Lucie didn't bother with her teeth tonight. They had run out of toothpaste and she was too tired and depressed to search cupboards for a spare tube. So she climbed into bed, switched off the lamp and passed out within seconds. She never heard Marcus come into the bedroom to gaze at her in the semi-darkness while she slept. He did so for at least ten minutes, not touching her, then he turned and walked away

Back in the living area – as Lucie liked to call it – Marcus looked through the papers that Lucie had left on the table, then checked her diary. It was exactly as he had expected it to be. He went to his own briefcase, took out the travel brochures he had got from the agent that afternoon and turned to the pages he was interested in. He wanted to get away; in a few days' time he wanted to be out of the country and the destination wasn't really that important. He looked at a few places, marked the pages in the brochure and determined to ring the agent first thing in the morning. He didn't bother to check the prices; he wasn't interested in cost, only availability. He replaced the brochure back in his case, switched the lights off and made his way upstairs to the guest bedroom and bathroom. There he undressed, washed and slipped into bed. He didn't even entertain the idea of sleeping with Lucie. Nothing could have been further from his mind.

Janie woke up early on Saturday morning. She knew it was early because it was only just light outside and the birdsong was loud and vibrant. She stretched in the warmth next to Andrew and rolled over carefully so as not to disturb him, opening her eyes to peer at the alarm clock. It was five-thirty.

'Why are you awake?' Andrew murmured.

Janie rolled back and looked at him. 'Sorry, did I wake you?'

'No. It's those perishing birds. They sound like they're having a rave up there in the tree.' Janie smiled and he put his arm out. 'Come here and give me a hug,' he said. 'We might as well do something now we're both awake.' Janie moved towards him and snuggled down into his embrace. His body was warm and familiar and although she didn't feel particularly aroused she relaxed under the gentle pressure of his fingers.

'It's been too long,' Andrew whispered, moving above her, 'you've been a bit preoccupied.'

Janie returned his kiss. 'I'll have to reward you for your patience,' she murmured, reaching down to caress him. Andrew moaned softly and Janie moved down his body to take him in her mouth. As the birdsong died down and the light broke across the sky, Janie and Andrew took pleasure in each other and in celebrating the more confident and empowered woman she had become.

At eight, having both fallen asleep again, they woke when Katie came in and asked to go down to watch television.

'Where's your nightie, Mummy?' Katie asked. Janie reached over the side of the bed and lifted it off the floor, while Andrew grinned at her. 'Here, darling,' she said, 'I was so hot in the night that I had to take it off.'

Andrew sat up and reached for his dressing gown from the ottoman at the end of the bed. 'Come on, Kate, I'll take you down and get you some hot chocolate. Tea, Janie?'

'Please.' Andrew left the bedroom and Janie got up, went to the bathroom, then pulled her nightie back on. She opened the blinds, put some pillows up against the headboard and climbed back into bed. On her bedside table she had a stack of magazines and, reaching for the one off the top, she settled down to read it. Andrew came up a few minutes later with a tray of tea and the paper. 'Not *PC World* again,' he remarked, placing the tray on the ottoman.

'There's an article here on DVD drives,' she said. 'I definitely think that I should get one, don't you?'

Andrew shrugged.

'Many of the special offers around at the moment include them as part of the package,' she went on, 'and frankly, I'd rather have that than a digital camera. There's an ad here for a mail-order company and they're including a scanner and a colour printer, all for a thousand pounds.' She looked up. 'Not bad, eh? I reckon I could get a really good package for fifteen hundred, don't you?'

Andrew had poured the tea and was adding milk. He didn't answer and Janie said, 'Andrew?

Haven't you got any interest at all in updating our system?'

He came across with her tea, placed it on top of the stack of computer magazines and office furniture catalogues, then said, 'Actually, Janie, no I haven't. This is going to be your system, not ours. This is for your business. We already have a perfectly good PC for our family needs.'

Janie took her tea and looked at him. 'Do you mind me spending money on a PC?'

'No, I don't mind.' Actually that wasn't true. He did mind, he found the whole thing about Janie's investment club infuriating, but he would never have said. Janie had become obsessed; these last few weeks all she had talked about was share prices and the market and how much everything was worth and valued at and it had seemed at times that money dominated her every waking hour. He did mind because it had no bearing at all on what he did for a living – seeing sick people, trying to cure them and if he couldn't then trying to ease their slow or some-times rapid journey to death. They seemed to have disconnected as a couple. They had two separate worlds and whereas Janie used to long to hear about Andrew's day, used to need involve-ment in his life, almost as stimulation for her own life that didn't have much in it, now she could hardly be bothered to ask him what he did and who he saw. He got into bed next to her and took a sip of his tea. 'As long as it isn't a waste of money,' he said. 'You've always talked of this investment club as a short-term thing, so I just question whether buying a new computer will

239

really be value for money.'

'I used to think of it as short-term, but now I'm not so sure. I mean, we've been bloody successful, Andrew. Who knows what we might go on to achieve?'

'You've been lucky,' Andrew said. He climbed out of bed, leaving his tea, and went into the bathroom. He was irritated; talk of the investment club was beginning to really get up his nose. 'It's been a very good market,' he said, coming to the door with his hands full of shaving foam, 'you've had tips from one of the city's top analysts and the IT sector has rocketed. In other times you might not have been even one-tenth as successful.' He disappeared again and Janie heard him filling the sink. Why couldn't he, just for once, recognise what she had achieved and say well done? She too climbed out of bed and followed him into the bathroom. 'If you don't want me to do this, then you've only got to say,' she challenged.

He turned from the mirror above the sink. 'Of course I want you to do it,' he replied. It was true, he did want her to have an interest, he liked her happy and successful. 'I just...' He broke off, not able to put into words exactly what he wanted to say. He could see that there had been a void in her life and he could see that she had occupied a space that needed to be filled. He just hoped that the space wasn't a gap in their marriage, wasn't something lacking in their life together. He said, 'I just hope it doesn't take us over.'

Janie came in and stood behind him with her

hands on his back. He looked at her reflection over his shoulder in the mirror. 'It won't,' she said. But the odd thing was that as she said it she was already thinking about something else. She was thinking about something she had read in the *FT* yesterday.

Alex had owned a brand-new BMW six series with a soft top for less than twenty-four hours and he was delighted. He had taken the afternoon off work on Friday to wait for it to be driven over from the garage and as soon as it had arrived he'd put the roof down, got in it and taken to the road. He had driven all round town, cruised the King's Road with his stereo blaring, raced down the A3 to Guildford to test the speed and stopped off at a pub in Bramley where he'd parked outside and sat looking at the car through the window as he drank his orange juice. A short time later, he had driven at high speed back up the A3 into London and had gone round to visit at least five of his closest friends to show off.

Later that night, after a curry with some mates, Alex had driven the King's Road again with a friend and attracted a good deal of attention from a gaggle of girls outside the Goat in Boots. He'd stopped for a drink, he and the friend had picked up the two prettiest girls from the crowd – both on a night out from Essex – and taken them to a club. He'd fallen into bed, completely sober and without his companion, whom he'd just driven home – for the hell of it – at four a.m. He was up again at eight for an early game of tennis and was still high on excitement.

241

All his life Alex had wanted a fast car. He had wanted to be looked at and admired and thought to have wad loads of cash and now he had. It made him feel that, at last, he had arrived. He was where he wanted to be, even if he had got there on the back of someone else, and it felt good. It felt the best and he was determined to enjoy it.

At the Riverside, he arrived for his game of tennis in new Ellesse kit with a Prince racket worth a hundred and twenty pounds slung over his shoulder. He had revved the engine hard in the car park and noticed one of the young women getting into her car stare across at him. She smiled as he climbed out of the BMW and his ego swelled. Not that it needed to get any bigger; the last two months it has steadily grown to almost gigantic proportions. He was sleeping with a top investment banker – who was incredibly sexy and mercifully married – he was making the most money independent of work that he had ever made and he was doing both with very little effort or cost to himself. He had it made and he couldn't keep the smile off his face as he walked into the club and booked in for his tennis.

'Hello, Alex!' He turned from reception to see Aiden Thornton, a colleague from work. Aiden held out his hand and Alex took it. 'Aiden! Good to see you. What are you doing over in this neck of the woods? I thought you lived in W1.'

'The girlfriend. She's got a place in Barnes.'

'Ah.' Alex was slightly embarrassed to see someone from work in his leisure time. He suddenly felt conspicuous in his flash white kit.

'Nice car,' Aiden said. 'I saw you coming in. How long have you had it?'

'Some time,' Alex lied.

'Lucky bugger.'

'Yes, it's great.'

'I bet your girlfriend likes it. All women love fast cars, or so they say.'

'Girlfriend?' Alex was confused.

Aiden suddenly flushed. 'Oh, sorry, the person you were with the other night? I, erm, I thought it was your girlfriend.' He glanced over his shoulder as if looking for help. 'I, erm, we, Sophie and I, we saw you with her the other night, Friday, in the Rat and Ferret off Sloane Square. We just assumed it was your girlfriend.'

'No,' Alex said. That must have been Lucie, they'd met well out of area for a drink after work. Shit, he thought, shit, shit, shit. 'She was an old flame,' he went on. 'We met up by chance and had a drink together. I didn't see you, Aiden. Where were you hiding?'

'Oh, we didn't stop, it was too packed. We came in, I spotted you in the corner and was about to come over when Sophie dragged me out saying it was too crowded and too smoky.'

'Shame, we could have had a drink.' Nothing could have been further from the truth.

'Ah, Sophie.' Aiden looked relieved to see his girlfriend. He was embarrassed; he had obviously stumbled on to something indiscreet and couldn't wait to get away 'You ready to go then?' Sophie looked puzzled. 'Alex, this is Sophie, my girl-friend. We're off to have breakfast with some of her chums in Chiswick. Sophie, this is Alex Stanton. He's a fellow broker.'

Sophie nodded. She got the hint about breakfast. Whoever this smug person in the flash tennis kit with the flash car outside was, Aiden didn't want to spend any more time with him.

'We'd better go,' she said, thinking that she would make Aiden pay for her missing her usual cappuccino in the bar at the gym with an expensive coffee and pastry somewhere else. 'Nice to meet you, Alex.'

Aiden said, 'See you Monday then.'

'Yup. Have a good weekend.' Alex watched them go, then turned with relief towards the tennis courts. He was smug, it was true. He'd managed to get away with the Lucie situation with a bit of quick thinking and a clever lie. Aiden hadn't sussed a thing. He waved to his tennis partner who he'd just spotted across the indoor tennis arena and made his way over to their court. Sadly, his inflated ego had grown just a little too big. He had no idea that when they got outside Aiden said to his girlfriend, 'He's bonking someone he shouldn't. That's who he was with the other night. He got dead cagey when I asked if it was his girlfriend.'

'Looks like he's earning something he shouldn't as well,' Sophie replied, nodding towards the BMW. 'And don't try telling me that's his company car.' They walked over to Aiden's Golf GTi and climbed in. 'Because if it is, then why haven't you got one as well?'

'Good question, Sophie,' Aiden said, but he couldn't think of an answer.

Sarah was in her tracksuit when Lindsay arrived. It was ten-thirty but Rory was dressed and ready to go. He had his swimming bag and his packed lunch by the front door and was watching Saturday morning TV.

'Hi.' Sarah opened the door and Lindsay came in. 'You look great! Ready for action,' she said. Lindsay glanced down at her jeans and trainers, something she rarely wore – purchased, in fact, for today's outing with Rory – and shrugged. 'Not too much action, I hope.' She popped her head into the sitting room. 'Morning, Rory.'

'Hello.' Rory managed to wave, smile and say hello without taking his eyes off the television.

Back in the hall Sarah said, 'Thanks, Lin, for today I know it's short notice but I can't remember when I had a day out on my own. I'm really looking forward to it.'

Lindsay smiled. 'So you should. It'll do you the world of good, a day out with your friends. You were lucky to get tickets, they're very hard to get hold of.'

'Are they?' Sarah led the way into the kitchen and put the kettle on. 'It's a corporate day for entertaining clients, but apparently Marcus's guests dropped out so he's asked me and Janie instead.' Sarah turned. 'I don't suppose he could get anyone else at just a couple of days' notice.'

'Don't do yourself down, Sarah, I'm sure this Marcus is delighted to have you and his sister for company.' Sarah smiled over her shoulder. Nice, she thought, but naïve. 'I think his wife's coming too,' she went on. 'Coffee, Lin?'

'Please, I'd love one.' Lindsay picked up a glossy brochure on hearing aids from the kitchen table. 'What's this? New hearing aids?'

Sarah turned from the cupboard. 'Microlink. It's a miniature attachment to Rory's hearing aids that can pick up a microphone. I was wondering if they might be better than the box.'

Lindsay flicked through the brochure. 'They look amazing,' she said.

'Hmmm.' Sarah brought the coffees over and sat down at the table. 'They get a lot of interference, apparently, but they look wonderful. I'm thinking about it.'

'How much?'

Sarah smiled. 'Expensive, very expensive.' She took a sip of her coffee. 'We've all agreed to take some money out of the investment club and I thought I might spend mine on these. If they work properly, that is.'

Lindsay put the brochure down. 'Anyone else would have bought themselves a nice holiday or a new car.'

'We're not anyone else,' Sarah said. 'I wish we were.'

They finished their coffee in silence and Lindsay stood to go through to the living room.

'So, what's in store?' Sarah asked.

'*A Bug's Life* this morning, at the Port Solent Megaplex, then sandwiches watching the boats and an afternoon on the beach. I thought we might go to Wittering, build a few sandcastles, take a dip, fly the kite.'

'God, Lindsay, that's fantastic! I didn't expect you to do all that with him, I just thought the swings and McDonald's.' Sarah stood too. 'You are good.'

'Any excuse for an old bird to act like a young one,' Lindsay said. 'Actually, I'm thoroughly looking forward to it.' She glanced down at her feet. 'Providing these trainers don't rub.' Sarah smiled and they went through to round up Rory for his day of fun.

When Lindsay and Rory had gone, Sarah went upstairs to get herself ready for the day ahead. She had been planning this time alone ever since Marcus had rung on Thursday night and the first thing she did was to run herself a long bath, sprinkling some rosemary and sandalwood oils into it and drawing the blind so that she could relax. While the bath was filling, she laid the outfit she had just bought on the bed along with the shoes and smiled. It was cheap, a snip in fact, and she was thrilled with it. Sarah didn't often shop and when she did it was nearly always for new jeans because her old ones had worn through the knee, or for new boots because the heel had fallen off the ones she'd used to death. She was a great replacer of clothes, not a buyer for the luxury of having something new or different to wear. But this outfit was especially for today. It was a knee-length pink silk dress with shoe-string straps and cut on the bias. She had known as soon as she saw it that she would wear it once and probably never have the opportunity to do so again, but she couldn't resist. Hearing aids for Rory, something totally impractical for herself.

To go with it she had bought a pink rib-knit cardigan, which she would wear again, and pink high-heeled strappy sandals that she wouldn't. She had bought fake tan from Sainsbury's, plus a bottle of hot pink nail varnish for her toes and a pair of silver Indian earrings. It was extravagance in the extreme for Sarah, and the whole lot, all except the fake tan from New Look – even if she was the oldest person in there by at least twenty years – had cost her fifty pounds.

With the bath run, Sarah stripped off, washed her hair, then did her face. She cleansed it, exfoliated it, put on a mask and climbed into the bath. She slipped two pieces of cucumber over her eyes, closed them and lay back to relax. She felt pretty odd but she was determined to persevere; it had to be good for her, even if it did feel rather banal. A couple of minutes later she dropped the cucumber into the bath and reached for the soap. After nearly seven years of sprint showering, lying around with salad on her eyes just wasn't her thing. She gave herself a good scrub, washed the face mask off under the running tap and climbed out of the bath. She'd only been at it for five minutes but she was all pampered out.

Pulling on her dressing gown, Sarah blow-dried her hair, painted her toe nails and, with bits of tissue stuffed between her toes, went downstairs to get on with the ironing. By eleven she had whizzed through two baskets and it was time to get ready. This too was executed with maximum speed and minimum fuss and she was downstairs again and waiting at the sitting room window by eleven-fifteen, just as Marcus pulled up in a bright red Porsche.

Oh dear, thought Sarah as she saw his car, I hope the neighbours don't gossip. Then, as he climbed out alone, she felt a moment of panic. Where was his wife, Lucie, and Janie?

Marcus parked on the pavement outside Sarah's small, modern semi-detached house with two wheels on the grass of her pocket-sized front garden. He climbed out wearing a navy linen suit and brown suede brogues and carrying an enormous bunch of pink lilies, wrapped in hot pink tissue and tied with pink gingham ribbon. Sarah went out to meet him, having given up on the neighbours gossiping – it was inevitable – and he said, 'I knew you'd be wearing pink. Here, these are for you and they match your outfit.'

She took them, blinked rapidly from nerves and said, 'Where're the others?'

Marcus frowned. 'Others?' There was a short silence, then he said, 'Oh God, didn't I tell you? Lucie has had to work and I didn't have the heart to ask Janie in the end. When I rang she went on about doing the garden at the weekend and I sort of assumed that she wouldn't be interested. It's just us, I'm afraid.' He looked at her. 'You don't mind, do you?'

Mind? Sarah thought for a moment. It was a bit of a surprise, she had to admit, and she'd been looking forward to a day out with Janie, but no, she didn't really mind. If Marcus wasn't uptight about it then nor was she. Besides, she thought, looking at the flowers, I suppose I should really think of him as a friend now; I've seen enough of

249

him these past couple of months.

'No, of course I don't mind,' she said at last.

'Good. So aren't you going to ask me in for a drink? And those flowers might need some water.'

She led the way inside and into the kitchen. 'What would you like to drink?'

Marcus smiled. 'Actually nothing. It was just a ruse to get you off the pavement.' He glanced at his watch. 'If we get going straight away we can have a drink at the hotel.'

'Hotel?'

'Yes, I booked a table in the restaurant at the Goodwood Park hotel for one o'clock.' He laughed momentarily 'You look startled, Sarah, like a rabbit caught in the headlights. It's only lunch and everyone who goes to Goodwood racing has lunch or dinner at the Goodwood Park Hotel.'

Sarah felt foolish. 'Do they? Great, well, I'll put these in water and grab my bag and a scarf,' she said. Marcus stood in the hall and wondered what to say about the house, which was nice but incredibly ordinary. He decided to say nothing. Sarah appeared with a pink paisley headscarf and tied it in front of the mirror, Audrey Hepburn style. She slipped on a pair of sunglasses that Rory had insisted she buy last year, sleek and black and a bargain at only two pounds and fifty pence, then she turned.

'You look amazing,' Marcus said, and he meant it.

'Thank you...' Sarah faltered; she was so rarely complimented that it took her quite by surprise.

She glanced down at her outfit and brushed an imaginary thread from her dress. She didn't know what to say, but she couldn't deny that she was flattered. A compliment from an attractive man, no matter how platonic the relationship, was always good for morale. 'Erm, shall we go?' she said hurriedly and led the way out of the house.

Marcus followed her and as she locked up he took her hand. 'This is for the neighbours,' he said. 'I just saw the curtain twitch to our left so we might as well give them a good show.' He led her to the car, opened the passenger door for her and she slid inside, her face burning. He jumped over the driver's door in one athletic stride and into his seat.

'Oh my God...' Sarah clasped her hand to her mouth and Marcus laughed. He looked at her and said, 'Come on, Sarah, today will be fun, even without the others. I promise.'

Sarah nodded.

'I rarely go out on a jolly, so we might as well enjoy it,' Marcus added.

Sarah thought, nor do I. He's right, this is a day out to remember. She settled back in her seat and as Marcus started the engine and revved it, Sarah glanced up at the blue sky, then finally smiled. She was going to enjoy herself and why not? She had earned a bit of fun.

The entire Betts family was waiting for the lorry that chugged up the drive of Chadwick Farm at noon that Saturday. They received the call that it was on its way at eleven-thirty and Justin was the first to spot it from his bedroom window at five to twelve. It took the driver a full five minutes to manoeuvre round the gate, but once he was in, Roz, Graham and all three children went outside to watch him bring the lorry and its cargo up the drive.

The vehicle stopped with a hefty hiss just short of the front door and the driver climbed down, stretching as he did so.

'Mrs Betts?'

Roz stepped forward. 'That's me.'

'Delivery of one prize Jersey cow from the farm dispersal over at Dresdon Farm. All paid for, that right?'

'Yes, should be.' Graham shot Roz a glance which she studiously ignored, signing where the driver told her to.

'Where d'you want her?'

'We've got the stable ready. It's round the side,' Roz replied. The driver went round to the back of the lorry and unlocked it. The whole back panel came down and Roz saw the cow, heavily in calf, shuffling and straining against her rope.

'All right, Damson,' the driver called in, 'we're here now, no need to get yourself in a state.' He jumped up and carefully edged himself to the front of the cow to untie her. He did so, held on to her rope and eased her backwards. 'She's coming down,' he shouted, 'make sure she doesn't miss her footing, will you?'

Graham went to one side of the ramp, Roz to the other and, keeping their distance, they gently steered the cow down the centre of the ramp. On the ground she snorted and looked at them with weary brown eyes. Roz patted her nose. 'There's a good girl,' she said. 'Come on, we'll show you to your new home.'

Graham took the rope, the children walked alongside him and Roz followed behind.

'Mum, what's she called?' Justin asked. 'Mum? Mum?'

'Sorry,' Roz said. 'Damson. She's called Damson.'

'And how much did she cost?' Graham added.

Roz had been waiting for this. 'A thousand pounds,' she replied, 'and a bargain at that.'

'I see. We'd better talk about this later,' he said. Roz swallowed. Graham turned and looked at her over his shoulder. 'As soon as she's settled.'

Roz nodded. The driver of the lorry caught up with them and walked beside Graham. They took Damson into the stable yard and he took her rope, tying her to the gate post.

'She'll be fine in the field,' he said, 'but bring her in at night and make her comfortable. She's got about two weeks to go, so be gentle with her.' He stroked the cow's neck and patted it. 'I'll leave you to it then,' he said finally. 'Bye, Damson. You do a good job for this lovely family, won't you now?' He looked at Graham. 'Give us a hand to turn the truck round could you, mate? See me out?'

'Yup, sure.' Graham moved off and Roz and the children gathered round Damson. 'Don't crowd her, kids,' he heard her say as he strode away Then, 'Kitty, stay away from her back legs in case she kicks you. Oliver, don't do that... Kitty, no! Stay away from her back legs... That's right,

Justin as gently as you can...' He smiled, followed the driver to his lorry and guided him down the drive.

Back at the house, Roz was in the kitchen when Graham came in. 'I've put her out in the field,' he said. 'Do we keep the harness on or take it off when she's out?'

'Take it off.'

'Good, that's what I've done.'

Roz was standing behind the table, avoiding his eye as he spoke to her, and now, looking up, she said, 'Graham, there's something I need to tell you.'

He pulled out a chair, sat and looked straight at her. 'I thought there might be.'

Roz took a breath. Up to now she hadn't said much to Graham about the investment club; in fact, she'd hardly mentioned it at all. It had been her secret, her own precious piece of success and she hadn't wanted to share it. She had wanted to hug it to herself, to think about it privately and keep it safe. It was selfish, she knew that, but after so much failure with Chadwick, after such a struggle, she just wanted a bit of private glory before she opened up what she had done for criticism. She said, 'This investment club, it's, well ... we, all of us, we've made quite a bit of profit.'

'That's good to hear.' Graham folded his arms across his chest. 'At least we've got our capital intact.'

'Yes, we've got that, and a bit more.'

'How much more?' Suddenly curious, Graham unfolded his arms and leant forward. 'You've got a funny look on your face, Roz.'

'Have I?'

'Yes. How much more? Five grand?'

'More.'

He narrowed his eyes. 'Ten?'

'More.'

'Come on, spit it out. I'm not doing this for the next five minutes. Tell me how much.'

'We've made a net profit on three thousand pounds of original investment of about – and this is still a rough figure because we've got commission to pay and then there's–'

'How much?' Graham interrupted. Roz stopped. She took a deep breath and said, 'Over a hundred thousand pounds.'

Graham was stunned into silence. He sat for a few minutes staring into space, then he shook his head. 'You're not joking, are you?'

'No.'

'How? How did you make such a lot of money so quickly?'

'On the dot com stocks, which have gone bananas, and on three stocks that were subject to a take-over bid.'

Graham was still shaking his head. 'I can hardly believe it. How did you know all this? It can't have been just luck, surely not?'

'Marcus, Janie's brother, has given us a couple of tips and Sarah has been boning up on the market. She knows loads; she's always coming out with stuff that we'd never have thought of. And we discuss it all, read all the bumf – we get sent a lot of information from broking houses now – and there's quite a bit of luck as well in picking the stocks vulnerable to a takeover...' She broke off and shrugged. 'Actually, I don't really know how we've done it, not really I can hardly believe it myself.'

'So Damson's cheque came from your profit?'

'Yes. We all decided to take out two thousand pounds to spend.' Roz twisted her hands together. 'I had some work done on the stable and the house as well.'

'What work?'

'The plumber came and has put in a new boiler. Next winter the heating should work properly And I had the stable fixed up; new door, replaced a bit of the roof, replaced some of the timber where it had rotted...' She looked at him and they were silent for a few moments. 'I'm sorry I didn't tell you.'

'Why didn't you?'

'I wanted to keep it to myself for a while and I ... I didn't know what you'd say.'

'Great is what I say!' Graham stood and came round the table to her. 'Come here and give us a cuddle. Why would I say anything other than well done, love?'

Roz relaxed against his chest. 'Because you don't approve?'

He pulled back to look at her. 'No, you're right, I don't entirely approve, but you wanted to do it and you've made a success of it. Presumably that's the end of it now, you can take your money and retire. How could I not be pleased for you?' He eased a loose strand of hair off her face. 'Apart from which, we got a new boiler out of it. No more ice on the inside of the windows as well as the outside.' He kissed her and released her. 'Talking of the new boiler, let's have a look at it. I can't believe I haven't noticed it. When did you have it done?'

'Last week.' Roz smiled. 'And Graham?'

He turned on his way to the laundry room and looked over his shoulder at her. 'Yes?'

'You never notice anything.'

Jack Lowe had booked a table for lunch in the restaurant at the Goodwood Park Hotel. A table for one person at midday Not that this sort of place was usually his style – too far out of his price range – but after weeks of listening in to conversations in the pub, the wine bar or the café frequented by various junior staff at the planning department, he'd finally heard something more interesting than the ins and outs of a twenty-something's love life – mostly ins from what he could gather – and this was the result. Two junior members of the planning department had been invited to Goodwood Races on a corporate day out, which was business-speak for an all-paid-up jolly. Who it was with and why Jack had yet to find out, but his educated guess was that it had something to do with Glover Homes.

He sat in his car at five to twelve and opened his briefcase, quickly transferring the equipment he'd brought with him into his pocket. He had the latest micro-digital video camera and a powerful tiny microphone, the size of a small button, with its own miniature recording system, in his top blazer pocket. The stuff wasn't exactly legal but the tape he took was purely for his own private consumption. No one would ever know he'd done it and it would give him a foothold on the case – a foothold he badly needed. He had worked hard on this job; it had taken up far more of his time than he had anticipated and he wasn't really getting anywhere. There was something really dodgy going down here, but how he was going to prove it he still didn't know.

Jack walked into the hotel on the dot of midday. He went through reception to the restaurant and checked in with the maître d'.

'A table for one,' he said. 'The name is Lowe.'

'Ah yes, sir, table four. If you'd like to follow me?'

'Lovely, but, erm, could I ask you to check something in the kitchen for me before I sit down? I've got an allergy to garlic, quite a severe one actually, and I wondered if there was any dish that the chef could prepare for me that would be completely free of it? I swell up you see, have palpitations, get a rash, that sort of thing...'

The maître d' hesitated for a moment, not quite sure about this request, then said, 'Of course, sir. I'll check with the chef now, before we get busy.'

'Thank you so much.'

He hurried off and Jack glanced down at the lunchtime bookings. A table for eight was booked in the name of Redfern; they had table eleven. So far so good. Walking across the restaurant, Jack found table eleven and picked up the large floral display from the centre. Between a spray of tiny rosebuds and a chrysanthemum daisy, he hooked the miniature microphone from his jacket pocket on to the stem of some foliage. He turned as the maître d' came back into the restaurant. 'These flowers are spectacular,' Jack said, holding the bowl up. 'Are they the Goodwood colours?'

'No sir, we have them done locally to match the restaurant decor.'

'Very nice, very nice indeed.' Jack replaced the bowl and looked at the maître d'. 'Table four you said?'

'Yes, sir. It's this way.'

'And was there anything on the menu that I can eat without cause for alarm?'

'Yes, sir. The chef has said that he has an excellent fillet of wild Scottish salmon which he can grill for you and serve with Hollandaise sauce, or there's a rack of lamb which, without the sauce, is garlic-free, and only the wild mushroom tartlets from the entrées have garlic.'

'Wonderful.' Jack took his seat at table four, directly across the restaurant from table eleven, and was relieved that he wasn't going to have to make a fuss and ask to be reseated. He had a perfectly good view from there, which was lucky because he could tell that the maître d' already had him down as an oddball without any more strange requests.

He was handed a menu and a wine list and left alone. He felt in the right-hand pocket of his blazer for the recording system and patted it. He didn't like doing it, but where needs must...

The waiter came over to take his drinks order: a glass of orange juice and half a bottle of sparkling mineral water. He wrote it down, glanced over Jack's shoulder at the party of eight who had just come into the restaurant and stood aside to let them pass. The waiter could hardly keep his eyes off the three women who went first. Jack knew the type; all highlights and high-lift bra. He watched the group sit down, recognising Bill Redfern, the land buyer for Glover Homes, and Stan Gamley, chief planning officer for the local council. There were three others with them: the chairman of the council – nice one, Jack thought – and two junior members of the planning department, one of whom had discussed this event and what to wear to it with her girlfriend in the pub on Tuesday night – thanks very much. All eight were dressed for a day at the races and it was clear as they sat down that Redfern was their host. As Redfern called the waiter over to order champagne, Jack reached into his pocket to switch on the tape. He settled back with the menu strategically placed so that he could keep his eye on the party and wondered what to order. He didn't want to spend much money and from the look of the menu that meant asking for a bread roll and butter.

Sarah climbed out of the Porsche and wondered if that place for young ladies that taught them how to get gracefully out of sports cars was still in existence. She had always thought the idea of it particularly ridiculous, but as she heaved herself up with her legs sprawled apart and her pink thong on display, she wondered if a few lessons might not be a good idea. Marcus, thankfully, was looking towards the restaurant and so missed the main part of the spectacle, but as they walked towards the hotel he said, 'Nice knickers, Sarah,' and she determined to stick to trousers in future.

Inside the hotel, Sarah excused herself and went to the ladies' to brush her hair and touch-up her lipstick. She rarely bothered much with her appearance, she liked to look neat and that was as much thought as she generally gave it, but today was different. Today she didn't feel like Sarah Greg; she felt altogether more glamorous and exciting than the woman who was a single mum and who worked in Duffields. She smiled at herself in the mirror and, opening her bag, slipped the scarf away, ran a comb through her hair and then reapplied her pink lipstick. If she had been able to afford perfume she would have doused herself liberally with it to add to the effect, but perfume hadn't been on her Christmas list for years. She didn't have the money for luxuries like that.

Marcus was perched on the arm of the sofa in reception waiting for her and stood as she came out. 'Is everything pink today?' he asked, smiling at her. She blushed, but fired back, 'I like to be colour co-ordinated, but no, not everything is pink. The veins on my legs are blue.'

Marcus burst out laughing and, in the restaurant, Jack Lowe turned to see who was having such a good time.

'Shit,' he murmured. He recognised Sarah immediately, took in the dress and the makeup and the wonderful high-heeled strappy shoes and thought, shit, shit, shit.

'Sir?' The waiter materialised by his side and, lifting the menu over his face, Jack said, 'I'm not

261

ready to order yet.' The waiter walked away and Sarah and Marcus were shown to their table, just two away from Jack.

Jack didn't know what to do. His first feeling was panic. His hands began to sweat and his face felt hot but then he took several deep breaths and managed to calm himself. He was being absurd. She would never recognise him – they'd only met a couple of times, three at the most. This was madness, he had to calm down. But he couldn't stop the sick, sinking feeling of embarrassment that swamped him. He tried to focus on the menu and signalled to the waiter that he wanted to order.

'Sir?'

'Yes, hello, erm, I'd like to order the salmon please. No starter, just the grilled salmon for my main course.' Jack said all this with the menu lowered only sufficiently enough to see the waiter, who looked just above his head, unable to meet his eye.

'Vegetables, sir?'

'Sorry? Oh yes, erm, peas and carrots and chips please.' Jack lowered the menu a fraction more. 'And could I have today's paper please.'

'The paper, sir?'

'Yes, I'd like something to read with my lunch.'

'Right, sir.' The waiter reached for the menu, but Jack held firmly on to it. There was a moment's tussle, then the waiter realised that Jack wasn't going to relinquish it and backed off. Jack cringed, then lifted the menu once again to cover his face, but just as he did so he noticed Sarah glance in his direction. She looked at him for a moment, he could see from the corner of his eye that her face was turned in his direction, then she said something to her lunch partner and Jack heard him laugh. It was too much for him. He stood, still holding the menu, his head bent as if in deep contemplation of it, and left the restaurant. He retreated into the gents' where he leant against the wall and put his head in his hands. 'Shit,' he said aloud. 'I'm a bloody laughing stock, a pathetic figure. God, why Sarah? And why now? Why not when I've got some dolly on my arm who adores me? Why when I'm working and appear to all intents and purposes a sad, lonely bastard who can't find anyone to lunch with!' He banged his head against the wall. 'Shit, shit, shit.'

The door opened and he stood up straight. In the mirror he saw two men enter – Gamley was one of them – and go to the urinals. Jack headed for the cubicle, went in and locked the door. He sat in silence and listened.

'Jesus, I needed that slash...' Jack put his ear to the door. That wasn't Gamley, that was his companion. 'Redfern can't half put it away. He's had three pints and at least half a bottle of champagne.'

'He bought three pints in the pub, Del, but I didn't see him drink them. Watch yourself, son; don't get so pissed that you don't know what you're saying, all right? This is business.'

Jack lifted the miniature digital camcorder out of his pocket, climbed up on to the toilet seat, then the cistern, and aimed it over the top of the cubicle at the urinals.

'No chance, Stan. That Deb's been giving me the come-on all day. I don't want to waste an opportunity like that'

Gamley turned, Jack could see from the image on his camera. 'You listen to me, son. Redfern pays these girls to keep the likes of you and me sweet. They're professionals and they'll give you a good time, but you make sure that you watch your back, right? Don't get yourself in over your head because Redfern'll have you if you do. Understand?'

The younger man stood staring at Gamley as if Gamley had just bitten him. He had his flies open and his penis hung limply from the opening. Gamley turned back to the urinal and flushed it.

'Come on, do yourself up, son, and let's get back to the party. We've got what Redfern wants, but he's not getting it for free. Remember that and you'll go far in planning.'

The younger man fastened his trousers and both men crossed to the sink to wash their hands. They left the room a minute or so later and Jack climbed down from the cistern and sat on the toilet seat.

'Thank you, thank you, thank you,' he murmured. He turned off the camera and kissed it, dropping it into his pocket. 'Dear God, thank you.' He stood, flushed the chain just in case anyone else should come in, and left the cubicle. In the reception area he asked for his bill for lunch saying that he didn't feel well, paid for the salmon he wasn't going to eat and left the hotel. He went to his car in the car park, climbed in and sat back in the driver's seat. Finally he smiled; he had struck gold.

He turned the radio on and prepared to wait. All he had to do now was retrieve the microphone, by saying he had dropped his tie pin on their table when he'd been looking at the flowers, and he'd be home and dry. Not bad for a day's work. Despite Sarah, not bad at all.

It was after five when Marcus pulled into the car park of the Wayfold Inn and slung the car into a parking slot near the garden. He climbed out, went round to help Sarah and she said, 'Thanks, but one showing of my underwear is enough. I'll get myself out.' He smiled and turned towards the garden, looking at the views from it over the downs.

'It's my round,' Sarah said from behind him. 'I'll share my winnings.' Marcus pressed the alarm pad, the car bleeped and he followed her into the bar. It was dark and stuffy in there and they both blinked to try and adjust their eyes after the bright sun outside. 'Why don't you tell me what you want,' Sarah said, 'and get us a seat outside. I'll bring the drinks out.'

'OK. I'll have a coke please,' Marcus said, then he went through the back door of the pub into the garden and found a bench looking out at the view. A few minutes later Sarah came out carrying two glasses of coke and sat down next to him on the bench. 'Cheers!' she said. They clinked glasses and Marcus said, 'You seem to be on a bit of a winning streak. The investment club and now the races. I think I should bank my luck

265

with you.'

Sarah sipped. 'I do, don't I?' She smiled. 'I must say it makes a nice change.'

'You know, while you've got it you should make the most of it.'

Sarah looked at him. 'What?'

'Your luck.' He turned to her. 'You know, I wasn't sure about mentioning this, Sarah, but I think I've got a bit of a tip, picked up from Alex. It concerns a small organic food company that produces dairy products and has expanded into ready-prepared meals. They're doing incredibly well, they're undervalued and I'm pretty sure that any minute now, literally, they're going to be snapped up by one of the big food giants like Unilever or Grand Met.'

Sarah put her drink down on the grass, hesitating before she answered him. 'Pretty sure?'

Marcus smiled. 'You know what my pretty sure means by now, don't you, Sarah. We've been meeting and discussing this whole business for a couple of months. I don't mention anything unless I've done my homework.'

'So you think we should invest?'

Marcus paused. 'I think,' he said, 'that you should try to raise as much money as you can and buy heavily into this stock. It's currently at fifty-one pence and if it gets taken over that could rise to a couple of pounds at least. It's a really good opportunity and I don't often say that.'

Sarah was mentally calculating in her head how much stock they could buy with their current fund when Marcus continued, 'If you could raise seventy-five thousand pounds each then you

266

could make enough money to retire on, Sarah.'

She looked at him. 'There's no way I could raise seventy-five thousand pounds. No way.'

Marcus shrugged. 'No, perhaps not.'

'Anyway, who said I want to retire? I like Duffields.'

Marcus suddenly laughed as Sarah had meant him to. 'Of course you do. So, if you didn't retire you could send Rory to a really good school, a small prep school say, with lots of sport, small classes, the sort of quality teaching that he needs, extracurricular activities such as chess and IT skills, amazing art...'

Sarah held up her hands. 'Stop! What is this, an advert for independent education? I can't raise the money, Marcus, so there's no point in talking like this.'

'No, of course you can't.' He sipped his drink and Sarah bent to pick up hers. She stared out at the view but didn't really see it. Marcus had put the germ of an idea in her head and it was multiplying by the second as they sat there. 'You really think this stock is a dead cert?'

'Nothing on the stock market is a dead cert but, put it this way, it's the best tip from Alex I've had for a long time.'

Sarah's stomach turned over. She sat in silence for a few minutes more, then she said, 'I've got a couple of insurance policies; can I cash insurance policies in, d'you know?'

'I think it depends on the policies. Have you got an endowment on your mortgage? You could cash that I'd have thought.' Marcus finished his drink. 'D'you want another?'

Sarah shook her head. She couldn't get this thing out of her mind now. He had hit a raw nerve and all she could think of, all she could see, was the possibility of some sort of future opening up for Rory. From the moment Sarah had found out that her son was deaf she had determined that he would lead as normal a life as she could make for him. But school was such a struggle: the big classes, the noise, the lack of scope in his learning, the microphone aid, the teasing. He wasn't unhappy, but she didn't think he was achieving all that he could do and that was simply because of the lack of opportunities. He wasn't unhappy, but he was hardly happy either.

'Are you all right, Sarah?'

She turned. 'I was just thinking,' she replied, 'how wonderful it would be if Rory could go to Ledworth House. It's a small boys' prep school in acres of ground with wonderful sports facilities and classes only half the size of Wynchcombe Primary. We looked at it, Nick and I, when I was pregnant, but of course after Nick left there was never any possibility of...' She broke off and stared down at her hands. There had not been any possibility of much really, after Nick left. There had been years of emptiness and abandonment, years of feeling that she was as disabled as Rory, years of not having a future. 'It was just a dream then, just a dream...' She bit her lip and looked up at Marcus again. 'If we could raise the money,' she asked, 'when would be the best time to invest?'

'As soon as possible, while the share price is low and there's no bid speculation yet.'

'I must speak to Janie,' Sarah said, suddenly excited. 'I'll ring her as soon as I get in and tell her what you said. I'm sure she'll...'

Marcus had placed his hand on her arm and she looked down at it.

'Janie doesn't know about us, does she?'

Sarah was wary. 'What about us? What is there to know?'

'That we meet up quite a bit, enjoy each other's company...' He shrugged. 'No, you're right, what is there to know?'

He dropped his hand away and Sarah said, 'No, I've never told her anything, not that I think there's anything to hide...' She felt it was important to say that, to make it clear that she had never entertained any feelings for Marcus other than friendship and a quite casual friendship at that. 'It's more that I'm not sure how she'd feel about it, knowing Lucie as she does.'

'No, you're right. Thanks.' There was another silence, then he glanced at his watch and said, 'It's nearly six you know, we ought to get going.'

'My God, is it?' Sarah picked up her glass and finished the coke. 'I will have to talk to Janie,' she said, as they made their way back to the car. 'If we want to invest in this stock, that is.'

'Of course.' Marcus opened the door for her and she slipped inside the car. 'But it's your idea, OK?'

She smiled. Everything he had ever mentioned to her was 'her idea'. She supposed it was just his modesty.

'OK,' she said, then she strapped herself in and

269

Marcus started the car. They drove home in silence, Sarah with her dream and Marcus with the net to catch it in.

Chapter Thirteen

After a weekend of thought, the first thing Sarah did on Monday morning when she got to school was collar Roz and ask her to look at the organic food company on the internet. She said, 'I think this could be a really good tip, Roz. Let's meet tomorrow night at my house.'

'Right. I'll have to check with Graham but I think it's clear.' She had written down the name of the company on the back of her shopping list. 'I'll let you know what I've got and if I can make it this afternoon, OK?'

'Fine.' Sarah dropped Rory off in the classroom and made her way back to her car. She saw Janie arrive and stopped her briefly as she hurried towards the playground with Katie. 'My house, tomorrow night. Can you make it?'

'Yes, sure. What's up?'

Sarah, short of time, said, 'I'll tell you later. Just make sure you can come, that's all.' She smiled, waved and climbed into her car, going on her way to work.

As soon as she finished work, Sarah hurried home. She opened the front door, dumped her bag in the hall and went straight across to the phone. She took up her file, found Alex's mobile number and dialled. She got the message service; typical. Didn't anyone ever work at lunch time in the City? Leaving a message, she asked Alex to send her everything he had on Wye Valley Organic Foods and to give her a call later on. Then she hung up and got on with the daily chores that never ceased no matter how much money the investment club earned or what clever ideas they all had.

Having loaded the washing machine, emptied the dishwasher and finished the washing up from the Sunday roast that she had cooked last night for Rory and Lindsay, Sarah dashed round the house with a can of polish and a duster, hoovered downstairs then up and finally made Rory a Marmite sandwich on brown bread and packed it in a little box with an apple and a Penguin biscuit. Tonight was listening therapy and so they usually had a picnic in the car whilst practising listening to sounds from the audio tape that the teacher used. Sarah made sure that Rory always did the homework; she was pedantic about that.

Then she left the house, having forgotten to eat herself, and went to school to collect Rory. In the playground she saw Roz, who handed over a clear plastic folder filled with print-outs from the computer. 'Looks interesting,' she remarked. 'Can't wait to hear what it's all about.'

'It is and you will,' Sarah replied. Then she ran into Janie and said, 'I've had an idea, a hunch about an organic food company. I think it's a good one but we need to talk it through.'

'Great. See you tomorrow then. I checked with Andrew and it's fine. I'll bring the wine. What time d'you want us?'

'Eight? Eight-thirty?'

'See you then.' Janie went on to collect Katie who had invited another little girl for tea and Sarah watched her for a moment, feeling suddenly envious. She rarely did teas; what with homework and extra lessons and just keeping Rory's head above water, there didn't seem to be any time left for enjoying themselves. She sighed, took hold of Rory's hand and headed for the car. What she wouldn't have given for a normal night at home, with Rory playing outside with a friend and her cooking chicken nuggets and chips.

Alex got Sarah's message when he got in from lunch and went immediately to the files. He took out all the latest reports on Wye Valley Organic Foods, of which there were only two, and went along the corridor to photocopy them. Then he went back to his desk, put his phone on to messages and sat down to make notes. It didn't look like much of a stock, it was cheap and by the look of it undervalued, but then so many small stocks were. But Sarah had a nose for an investor opportunity. She had a gift for spotting the right stocks and who could tell, a bit of leg work might pay off on this one too. It certainly had on all the others.

Marcus rang the travel agent on Monday afternoon and booked himself a three-week holiday on Capri. He had seen a hotel that he liked the look of, but frankly he didn't care much where it was as long as he got away. He paid for the trip up-front and in full, and didn't even question the fact that he had to take a suite because all the deluxe rooms were already booked, or the fact that he was paying a whacking great single supplement for going alone. He asked that the tickets be couriered to his office and booked himself a cab to the airport for Friday lunchtime. He was ready, he had set everything up and now all he had to do was wait.

On Monday evening, Alex left work early. He slipped the photocopies of the information on Wye Valley into an envelope and sent it through the company, first class, along with a copy of his notes. He was tired, it hadn't been a very good day and he was still drained from a rather extravagant and wild weekend. The last thing he wanted to do was see Lucie, but she had requested the meeting. She was, he felt, getting steadily more depressed by the state of her marriage, but what he could do about it he really had no idea.

At the wine bar she was already waiting; he was late and she sat at a table for two in the corner working on some papers. When she saw him she waved and hurriedly stuffed her papers into her briefcase. 'Hi.'

He went across and smiled at her. 'Hello. Drink?'

'Thanks, a glass of wine please.'

'I'll get a bottle, shall I?'

Lucie glanced at her watch. 'Not for me. I'll only have one glass, I've got to work tonight.'

Alex felt thwarted; he had mentally prepared himself for a night with Lucie and had expected her to want to come back to his flat as she so often did now. 'Two glasses then,' he said and went across to the bar.

Bringing them back, he sat down and took a gulp of his wine.

'What's up?' he asked, 'You sounded a bit low earlier.'

Lucie held her wine glass and fingered the stem but she didn't drink. 'Work. I'm just up to my eyes in it.'

'Lucie, you are always up to your eyes in it. I don't know how many times I've heard that refrain.' Alex tried to keep the irritation he felt out of his voice, but Lucie picked up on it.

'You're right, of course, I am always up to my eyes in it, but recently I've started to feel, oh, I don't know, sort of isolated by it. As if I'm just on my own struggling with it.' She sighed and ran her fingers through her hair.

Alex looked at her; this was more about Marcus than about work as he'd thought it would be. He said, 'D'you want to talk about it?'

She shrugged. 'Can't,' she said, 'it's a bid situation, or it will be anyway, shortly.'

'So what do you want me to do about it?' Alex asked. He was trying to be patient but there was something so annoying about someone who was down about things when he was on the up.

'I suppose I just wanted a bit of company,' Lucie said.

'And a whinge,' Alex added.

She looked at him. 'Does that bother you?' She took a sip of wine. 'I thought that was all part of the relationship thing – sharing problems, bemoaning one's lot, someone to rely on for comfort.'

275

Alex said, 'This is an affair, Lucie, not a full-blown relationship.'

Lucie took a sharp intake of breath and looked away. Stupid, stupid, stupid, she thought, of course it's only an affair, you never wanted more, you never asked for more. But that didn't help. She felt lonely and pitifully sorry for herself.

Alex continued to drink and wrestle with his conscience. He wasn't unkind by nature but he was at that moment when irritation had got the better of him and Lucie's sorrow was more irksome and embarrassing than distressing. He felt very little sympathy

'Don't take it all so seriously,' he said at last.

'No, you're right. I should lighten up.' She stood. 'I must go to the loo and then I've got to get going, I'm afraid. I've got loads of work to do tonight. No point in whingeing as you say, I must get on with it.' She gave a self-deprecating laugh and Alex winced. He'd been too harsh on her, but there was no way of retracting his words so he promptly dismissed his fleeting regret. As Lucie moved off he took a ten-pound note out of his wallet to pay for the drinks and went to stand. As he did so he dropped the note and bent to pick it up again. He saw Lucie's open briefcase, pocketed the ten-pound note and, simply unable to resist the temptation, pulled several files out of her case to look at them. It wasn't that he was dishonest by nature, or even an opportunist, it was more that the urge to take advantage of something like this was too great to beat back. He just had to look; it was basic human curiosity. He opened the top file, saw the title and felt the blood rush to his face. Glancing up to check he was out of sight, he flicked through the rest of it. How could he not? The opportunity was too staggering to be missed; the chance of ever being caught so remote that it needn't even be considered. He flicked through the file, read the various headings, then dropped it, along with the others, back into Lucie's case. He stood up, went across to the bar and paid for the drinks. Lucie appeared while he was waiting for his change and said, 'I'll be off then.'

Alex turned. 'OK.' He reached for her hand below the bar and gave it a squeeze. As a general rule they never kissed in public, it was too risky 'I'll see you?'

She nodded. 'Ring me,' she replied. Then she smiled, a rather sad, pathetic smile, he thought later, and disappeared out of the wine bar. Alex stood where he was. The blood was pulsing round his body to his brain and he was thinking more clearly than he had done all day His thought process was so rapid and so intense that he stood motionless for over five minutes, not even registering the change that had been put on the bar in front of him. Finally Alex ordered himself another drink and went to sit down in the corner. He took out his Filofax and started to work through some figures, making small, neat calculations on the page. He sat there alone for a long time, over an hour, absorbed in his work and drinking virtually nothing. Then he stood, put some money for the wine on the table and left the bar. Outside, he took out his phone and brought Sarah's number up on to the screen. He pressed dial, got through and made his arrangement. He rang off and started for home. It never, at any time that evening or in the following week, occurred to him to question things. Why should it? Some things were simply the working of fate and fate, Alex believed, could catch you out or help you up at any given moment in your life. This, he assumed, was his.

On the way to the tube station, Lucie got a call. She took it and said, 'Oh blast, and just when I thought I might get an early night.' She laughed, rang off and dialled home. Marcus answered straight away

'Hi, it's me. I've got to work late, I'm afraid, might be very late. It looks like this deal's going through in the next week.'

Marcus leant against the fridge in the kitchen area and flipped the top off his beer on the edge of the granite work top. 'The Wye Valley Foods one?'

'Marcus!' Lucie still occasionally confided some of her work problems to Marcus, but only in the security of their own home. 'I'm on the mobile,' she warned.

'Sorry. What time will you be in then?' he asked. Not that he was interested, he would be in bed when she got home.

'I've no idea. We might be going into a bid situation so who knows?'

'I won't wait up.'

'No, of course not.' Why had she rung him, why did she bother? He couldn't have cared less if she didn't come home at all. 'See you in the morning then.'

Lucie rang off and carried on walking to the tube. How could a woman with two men in her life feel so very alone, she wondered, as she passed the barrier and headed down to the trains. It's that age-old adage, she thought, waiting in the warm, stale air on the platform for a train. Better to have one man that loves you than two that don't.

In the house in Notting Hill, Marcus drank his beer, then dialled the travel agent. He gave his booking reference and changed the date of travel. He would leave on Wednesday night. He was on top of things at work – a couple of extra days' holiday wouldn't make any difference. He hung up, having given his credit card details in order to pay extra for the flights, and went into the bedroom to pack a bag.

Chapter Fourteen

The meeting at Sarah's started on Tuesday night when Alex Stanton got there. He was late, half an hour late, but Sarah didn't want to start before he arrived. So she served wine, the women chatted and the sense of expectation escalated.

When he had arrived – offering no excuse for his lateness – they got straight down to business. Sarah talked about Wye Valley Organic Foods, outlined what it did and the facts and the figures and Alex added certain things that he'd gleaned over the past twenty-four hours. He had been working hard and he'd found every scrap of information there was to be had on them and had analysed the entire operation. He had also looked at the bigger food companies, trying to ascertain who might be on the look-out for a small organic food group and had several ideas marked out. The one thing he was certain of, after hours spent working on the Wye Valley project, was that the more he researched it, the more the whole proposal stood up.

'So why invest such a large sum of money?' Roz eventually asked, after an hour of discussion. 'I mean, I get the point that it looks like a very good opportunity, but the words "looks like" still pre-fix the "good opportunity", don't they? I mean, why not stick with a percentage of what we've already made and see what happens?'

'Don't put all your eggs in one basket,' Janie said. They all smiled at Janie's choice of proverb. 'Sorry about that, but you get my meaning. Roz is right, what makes this stock such a sure thing? We've done incredibly well so far, why take unnecessary risks?'

'Because I don't think this is an unnecessary risk. I think this is as sure as it can get.'

Roz narrowed her eyes. 'Do you know something that you're not supposed to, Alex?'

'What on earth do you mean?'

Roz shrugged. 'Well, insider trading or whatever that phrase is.'

'Good Lord, no!' Alex was aghast. 'I'm staggered that you could even suggest it. How in God's name do you suppose I would come across insider information anyway? I'm a broker, I have no connection with the company whatsoever.' He was affronted and he let his offence show.

'I'm sorry,' Roz said, 'but you never know...'

Sarah stood to open another bottle of wine. 'As far as I'm concerned,' she said, digging the corkscrew in and twisting, 'this looks like the best opportunity we've come across so far. Wye Valley's virtually out on its own in the market in terms of value and product line, not to mention management strength, and it's sitting there just saying "buy me, buy me, buy me". There's been loads of stuff recently on organic foods being the highest-earning product line in supermarkets, there's at least three articles about how Grand Met and Unilever are both vying for top position in the food market and neither have a good organic outlet on board, and so we do as we've

281

always done.' She popped the cork and poured the wine. 'We make a decision based on what we know.'

'But this isn't three thousand pounds, Sarah, this is...' Janie looked at her. 'How much did you say you want to invest?'

'Seventy-five thousand pounds.' Sarah replied. 'We each need to put in seventy-five thousand pounds and Alex wants to put in a hundred and fifty thousand. That way we'll have a small percentage of the company, at current prices roughly up to two and a half per cent, and then our vote is worth having.'

'A small percentage of the company in one shareholder's hands can definitely have an effect on the price in a bid situation. It can only work to our advantage, plus when the company is sold, the bigger the investment the bigger the return.' Alex looked round the group. 'It's the chance to make some serious money. The price could rise as much as two or three pounds a share.'

Everyone was silent, each locked in their own thoughts. After several minutes, Alex said, 'I don't think there's anything else I can tell you to convince you except that I intend to invest as much money as I've got in this stock whether you decide to go ahead or not.' He shrugged, then stood up, 'I'd better go, Sarah. I took the opportunity of coming down here to fix up a supper with an old mate in Petworth.' He picked up the jacket of his suit and slung it over his arm; he had come straight from work. 'I'll leave everything with you and if you have any questions call me on my mobile, not at the office.'

'Why not the office?' Roz asked.

'Because if I'm going to invest a reasonably big sum of money into Wye Valley, I want it to be between me and my bank manager, not me and the stock exchange surveillance team. They tape all the brokers' calls, it's standard procedure, and I'd just like to keep this as a personal investment.' He smiled. 'OK?'

Roz smiled back. 'That's fine,' she replied, just checking.'

Alex headed for the door. 'Thanks for the wine, Sarah. Call me and let me know how things develop, won't you?'

'Of course.'

'You've got my number?'

'Got it.' She opened the front door, saw him out and waved as he drove off. Then she went back to Roz and Janie.

'What d'you think?' she asked, sitting down.

'What do you think, Sarah?' Roz threw back at her. 'It's a hell of a lot of money. I've just been doing my sums and we can net thirty-one thousand pounds each from what we've made so far, but how are you going to get the extra forty-four thousand? It's not the sort of sum you can raise from selling your Grannie's old pearl necklace, is it?'

'I'm going to cash in my endowment policy,' Sarah replied. Both Janie and Roz stared at her. 'It's currently worth sixty-five thousand pounds,' she went on, 'and if I cash it in then I'll get about two-thirds of its value back, which is roughly forty-eight thousand. That's more than I need, but I'm going to invest the whole lot in Wye

Valley.' Roz and Janie continued to stare at her, but neither of them said a word.

Sarah returned their stare for a few moments then looked away 'You think I'm mad, don't you?' The silence lengthened. 'You're thinking, why can't she just invest a bit to make a bit? Well, I probably am mad, but I've seen a way forward for Rory and me; I've seen a chance to make some real money and change Rory's life. Not just new hearing aids but a new school – a small private school where he can flourish, not simply survive. I'm sorry, but that's a chance I can't turn down. This for me isn't about investment, a small business on the side, this is about changing our life. It's an opportunity to realise a dream.' She looked up at them again. 'And I'm not going to let it pass me by. I'm prepared to take the risk; I've calculated it and I'm prepared to do it. If you come in with me then we could really make it work for us, but if you don't then I'll do it on my own or with Alex.'

Janie glanced round at Sarah's small, unassuming house, at the worn-out throw over the sofa, the spotless but threadbare carpet, at the curtains re-hemmed to fit the windows of a house she never thought she'd find herself in after the divorce. She looked at the microphone aid on the coffee table, on top of a book about speech therapy. Finally she looked at Sarah, at the face that had never really shown the signs of distress or loneliness or struggle that she must have felt, and Janie thought, of course, of course you'll take the risk and so would I in your shoes. She said, 'If I can raise the money, Sarah, I'll back you.' She had her own reasons, her own dream, not as noble as Sarah's but valid to her none the less. She wanted to prove to herself, to Andrew, to Marcus even, that she could do it, that she could make money with the rest of them and really achieve something. She wanted to refill that empty space that in the past few weeks had begun to open up again in her life, despite the investment club and all its success, and she wanted to safeguard herself against loneliness and boredom. Looking across, she asked, 'What about you, Roz?'

Roz shook her head. 'I don't know,' she answered, 'I just don't know.' She ran her hands through her hair and thought about Chadwick Farm – her dream, a dream that had never been fully realised. What could she do with the sort of money Sarah was sure they would make? What couldn't she do? If she were able to raise the sum, the return on it would change their lives too. It was the difference between making money on an investment and making a dream come true. It would mean building and renovation; it would mean finally getting the farm on its feet; it would mean comfort and no worry. It could even mean buying the Gordens' land. It would actually mean that, for once in her life, anything was possible for Roz. Who wouldn't be swayed by that sort of gain? She said, 'I think it sounds amazing, I really do, but it's not as simple for me as it seems to be for you. I can't see where I'm going to get my hands on that sort of cash. I mean, we've got investments, Graham and I, but they're for our retirement...' Her voice trailed

285

away as she thought it through. 'I could ask the bank I suppose...' She bit on her lip and Sarah stood up. 'Would anyone like more wine?'

'I wouldn't mind a coffee,' Janie said, 'if it's not too much trouble.'

'Of course not,' Sarah replied. 'Roz?'

Roz looked up. 'Please,' she said, then, 'and I know this probably seems a bit odd, but would it be all right if we went over the whole Wye Valley thing again? It's just that I want to be absolutely clear on it all before I go home and talk to Graham.' Sarah smiled as she went out to the kitchen. Roz had been the one that she was most unsure of and her talking to Graham meant she was interested. Talking to Graham meant there was some chance that it might all happen.

The following morning Sarah went to her appointment at the bank. She spoke to their financial adviser, a young man in a sharp suit who looked as if he was earning too much commission, and they discussed her endowment policy, the one she had taken out just after Nick had left. He advised her not to cash it in; she told him that she needed the money and that there wasn't any other option. He suggested that if she offered the endowment policy as security to the bank then they would lend her seventy-five per cent of the policy's value. That way she would keep the policy going, just in case anything ever happened to her, and she would also have her money.

'Does it matter what the loan is for?' Sarah had asked. Apparently it didn't, unless it was something illegal. 'And how long will it take? I was hoping for the money by the end of the week.'

'That's the beauty of us securing a loan against the policy,' the young man answered. 'It should only take a couple of days.'

Sarah was impressed. This, she considered, was good advice. The young man in the sharp suit obviously earned his commission. She left the bank excited and optimistic. Could things really work out? After so many years of disappointment, could things really make a turn for the better, just like that? She walked on to Duffields and quickly changed in the staff restroom, leaving her cardigan and handbag in her locker and fastening the overall as she walked on to the shop floor.

'Mrs Greg, you are late,' the supervisor said. Sarah apologised and explained that she had asked permission yesterday to come in half an hour late this morning.

'Well, you can stay half an hour extra this afternoon,' the supervisor remarked, 'to make up the time.'

'Of course,' Sarah murmured. No, perhaps things couldn't really change just like that. Perhaps that was asking a bit too much.

Janie Leighton had also been in touch with the bank. She and Andrew held their accounts at the main branch of Lloyds in Chichester and she rang them first thing that morning and asked about making a withdrawal. Andrew and Janie shared a savings account there, along with their joint and separate current accounts, that could be accessed immediately. It was their emergency fund, made up primarily of a lump sum that Janie's aunt had left her in her will and some money that Andrew had been given from his father. It was a fund that was untouchable except in an emergency; it was there as a safety net and was particularly important to Andrew because of his two older children. He wanted to be sure that if they ever got into any trouble, as teenagers sometimes did, or needed emergency medical help then he had the funds to cover it. It was almost, Janie thought as she talked to the bank clerk, sacred money as far as Andrew was concerned – virtually untouchable and as a result a wasted asset. But although it might have been untouchable in Andrew's mind, to the bank it was simply funds that Janie had as much access to as he had. It was in an account with an instant withdrawal facility and she could take money out whenever she wanted to. Without Andrew's signature.

This she arranged to do. She asked for a banker's draft to be made up in the name of the broking house that Alex Stanton worked for and which processed all the investment trust's deals, then she told them she would pick it up the following morning. A draft was duly made out in her name for the sum of forty-five thousand pounds.

The process of securing funds for Roz was not quite as easy. She too rang her bank that morning and spoke to their financial adviser about their personal equity plans, the savings accounts she and Graham had been nurturing every year for the past five years. Every penny of profit that Graham had scraped out of his antiques business went into the PEPs. They were by way of a pension for them – good returns, tax-free savings and it was the only money, apart from a small balance at the bank and Graham's buying account, that they had saved up. Not an easy decision then to phone the bank and talk about cashing them in, but a decision she had come to in the early hours of the morning, having talked long and hard with Graham about what to do.

'I don't agree with it,' Graham had told her. 'You know my views, Roz, it's tantamount to gambling and I don't like it.'

Roz had outlined all the points that Sarah had put to her but still Graham wouldn't budge. It was, he felt, taking things too far. Roz had made some money, she'd done bloody well in fact, and now it was time to call it quits. He wasn't wooed by large sums of promised profit. This was money that he had slogged for, driving up and down the country in the van, wheeling and dealing and hard bargaining with the trade, then charming and schmoozing Americans into buying things they didn't need or really want. The PEPs were Graham's only insurance against having to rely solely on the pathetic state pension that his parents received and he wasn't about to give them up easily

'But we can't lose,' Roz had said at three a.m., when the argument had been round the block and back again. 'Even if the share price falls then the profit from the investment fund will cover the drop and we're still left with the money from the PEPs intact. I just don't see the problem, Graham, I don't see why you're so dead against having a go.'

'It's the principal,' Graham told her. 'I am not a gambling man.' But he was beginning to weaken and he knew it. Roz drove a hard bargain; she was an expert at turning the tide of opinion and he felt himself being swept away by the undercurrent.

'You took a chance on Chadwick Farm though,' Roz countered, land that was pretty high risk.' But as soon as she had said it, Roz knew she'd made a tactical error. Graham had looked at her and she had been forced to acknowledge all that was in his look. Chadwick Farm had not been a success, it had been an uphill struggle and every day was an effort. It was a risk that hadn't paid off. Roz bit her lip then and moved away from Graham in bed. She went to turn the light off, knowing that there was nothing more to be said, but he stopped her.

'Yes, I did take a chance and look where it got me.' Roz's face fell and she looked away. There was a silence and again Graham felt the force of her want and need lifting him up and towards her. She was able to manipulate him without even knowing she was doing it. It was, he supposed, part of loving her, wanting to please her. He wasn't a weak man; quite the contrary, he'd stood his ground on many, many occasions in the past. But finally, after a difficult few minutes, he sighed and said, 'Life is all about striving to achieve what we want to, Roz. Sometimes – and this is rare – we do it and it's effortless and takes us by surprise, but more often than not we don't achieve even half of what we'd hoped to and what we do achieve turns out to be nowhere as easy as we thought it would be. That's the case with Chadwick Farm; it's not lived up to expectations at all, it's been bloody hard work but it was what we wanted to achieve and we've done it.'

Roz turned to him. 'I don't get your point,' she said sharply 'I know all this, I know how hard it is, I don't need reminding of it.'

'My point,' he said wearily, 'is that if you really want to do this investment thing then go ahead, if you really think that's the way to go, but...' Roz's stomach had begun to churn. That was her physical reaction to excitement; not a fluttering in the chest or an increase in the pulse rate but a full-blown gut rot – churning nausea and a racing heart, the sweats, the shakes, the whole thing. 'But don't expect it to be a doddle. It might not – in fact probably won't – live up to your hopes for it.'

Roz stared at him. 'Are you saying that I have your blessing?'

He shook his head. 'No, I'm saying that it's up to you. Use the money from the PEPs if you really have to. I'll leave the decision to you.'

That's not fair!'

He shrugged and turned round to remove one of the pillows and plump up the one underneath ready for sleep. Roz reached over and turned off the lamp. She lay in the dark and watched the shapes in the room come into focus as the light from a crescent moon shone through the gap in the curtains. It was wrong of him to leave the ultimate responsibility to her, she thought, but then it wasn't right to even ask Graham to surrender money he had saved religiously over the past five years. Life wasn't fair, but then she'd known that for a while. And because it wasn't she made her decision. As the clock crept towards the dawn of a new day, she knew that she would phone the bank and sell the PEPs, credit the profit to her bank account and buy into Wye Valley Foods. Because life was arbitrary she knew that she would take any opportunity offered to her, that she would take the risk. Why not? Get it while you can, girl, she told herself as she drifted off to sleep. Get it while you can.

The investment club met that Wednesday evening at school. They stood in the playground together, all three women, while the children ran around, and collectively decided to make the purchase of Wye Valley Organic Foods. They had all raised the money, a feat in itself and as far as they were concerned a good omen. Sarah would ring Alex in the morning and ask him to purchase the stock on Friday. That would leave sufficient time before settlement for the funds to come through.

The deed was done. They all shook hands and went their separate ways, but they were all headed, metaphorically speaking, forward and upward. They were chasing the dream and the catcher was just a phone call away.

Marcus called Lucie at the office. He left a message for her as she was in a meeting and five minutes later she called back.

'You told my secretary it was urgent,' she said. 'Are you all right? Is anything wrong?'

'No, but I needed you to call back because I'm leaving in a few minutes for the airport.'

'Airport?' Lucie's mind went blank. 'Why?'

'I'm taking a break, Lucie. I need some time away and I'm taking a few weeks off.'

There was a silence and Lucie sat still in her chair. She looked beyond the noise and faces of the office at the window and the sky beyond, the big, grey, empty sky. She couldn't even utter a word.

'I've left everything on in the house, I suppose you'll be going home?'

'Where else would I be going?' Lucie managed to say.

Marcus looked at his ticket and passport, out on the work surface in front of him, then he glanced at his watch. 'I'd better go,' he said, 'my taxi will be here in a few minutes.'

Lucie tried to swallow down months of sadness and loneliness, months of mistakes and deception and of words that should have been said and never had been, but the lump in her throat was impossible to budge and the swallow got stuck halfway. Her eyes filled. She put her head down and her hair fell forward over her face so that no one could see she was crying.

'I'll see you when I get back,' Marcus said.

'Yes.' That was all she could answer. She put the phone down, stood up and walked out of the office and down to the ladies' toilet. Once there, she locked herself in a cubicle and began to cry.

Marcus, on the other side of the City, collected his bag from the cloakroom, said goodbye to the girls on reception and climbed into his taxi for Heathrow. The deed was done. The dream catcher had a job to do; he didn't need any more help from Marcus.

Chapter Fifteen

Jack Lowe sat reading the paper in his car which was parked on a yellow line outside the district council offices in Hersley on Friday morning. He kept an eye out for the traffic warden and frequent glances in the direction of the building made sure that no one drove out without him noticing. That was important because from the taped conversation he'd picked up at the lunch table at Goodwood the previous Saturday he knew that Gamley was off for the weekend but he didn't know where to. That he was waiting to find out.

Another thing that Jack was conscious of was a bloke with a newspaper standing across the road outside the station, supposedly reading. A bloke who hadn't taken his eyes off Jack since he'd arrived. Not that he looked particularly suspicious, more that he didn't really fit and Jack had a nose for things that didn't really fit. That was something he'd discovered over the last five or six weeks.

He may not have been the sort of private investigator his father was, doggedly hounding the job until he got a result, but he did have a skill at honing in on small peculiarities, like Gamley's relationship with Redfern – nothing obvious, but odd nevertheless. He'd picked up on that one through watching and listening, staking out the pub they all used, making the connection between the number of times Gamley was the planning officer for Glover Homes. But despite the video tape from the gents' at Goodwood – which he had now destroyed to keep inside the law – and despite feeling absolutely sure there was something going on, Jack just couldn't pin it down. There was nothing else to connect the two men together; no showy gifts, no conspicuous spending from Gamley or from anyone else in planning. There was nothing to go on except talk which, without hard evidence of corruption, was exactly that: just talk.

So here he was, hoping that Gamley's weekend away might offer up some kind of clue and wondering why the hell the bloke in the beige mac kept looking over at his car. Of course he'd heard from other people in the business about intimidation and he knew the likelihood of getting beaten up at some stage of his career was pretty high, but this case wasn't sinister, was it?

Jack shifted nervously in his seat and checked the rearview mirror again for the bloke by the station. Yup, he thought, still there, still watching me. Perhaps, he wondered, I might not have been as clever as I think I have, but he didn't have time to review his possible mistakes. Across the road, Gamley came out of the main entrance of the building and walked across to his car. He was carrying a small holdall. Jack shifted into gear and waited. As Gamley drove out of the car park, Jack indicated, saw a space in the traffic and pulled out. He was three cars behind Gamley and heading on the A264 towards Crawley.

Gatwick, Jack thought, sensing something going down. He's headed for Gatwick.

At the North Terminal, Jack, still three cars behind, followed Gamley into the short-term car park. They went up to level three where the spaces were abundant and Gamley parked. Jack, turning three rows away, did the same. He waited, watched Gamley get out, take a small case from the boot and walk towards the lifts. He was headed for departures. Jack climbed out, dropped the parking ticket into his pocket and ran for the stairs. He got to the top, after a short, sharp sprint, just as the lift doors opened. Gamley went towards the BA desk for the Channel Islands. Jack hovered, just out of sight, but close enough to see what was going on.

Gamley checked in. He greeted the ground staff, who obviously knew him, handed over his suitcase and his holdall to put in the hold and took his boarding pass. The flight was for Guernsey and, by the look of the chat going on at the desk, it was a flight that Gamley took regularly.

'Halfway there,' Jack murmured under his breath, and as he turned from his vantage point behind a notice board, he walked smack into someone, knocking himself backwards and winding himself for a couple of moments. 'Shit!' he exploded. He stared up at the bloke in the beige mac, who took one look at him and turned on his heel, half-walking, half-running across the concourse.

'Hey!' Jack called after him. 'Oi! You!' He started to jog, then realising the bloke was running, sprinted after him. The bloke headed for the escalator, Jack took the lift. He descended, came out and looked right and left. No sign of him. He stood for a moment then headed out to the car park. If he'd followed them in then he'd have to be parked. Jack ran towards the cars, sprinted up to level three and saw the bloke climbing into a 2CV. He ran across and threw himself on to the bonnet of the car, eyes closed, body tensed. The bloke inside, instead of shifting gear and accelerating off as Jack had expected him to, threw his hands up over his face and shouted, 'All right, all right ... don't hurt me, please don't hurt me.'

Jack turned, his face pressed up against the windscreen, and opened his eyes. The bloke was gibbering and shaking his head, his face covered; it was pathetic. Jack climbed off the car, brushed himself down and felt like a complete prat. He opened the car door and said, 'What the fucking hell is going on? Why are you following me?'

The bloke removed his hands from his face. Jack's voice, though stern, lacked menace.

'Get out,' Jack said, 'and tell me what's going on.'

The bloke climbed out, still in his mac, and stood with his head hung. He couldn't have been more than twenty, twenty-two at the most. 'Who are you?' Jack demanded, although at the sight of such youth and trembling fear he had lost a good deal of his aggression. 'Come on, spit it out. Who the hell are you and what are you doing following me?'

The bloke lifted his eyes, but not his head. He

had a nasty bout of acne on his forehead, Jack noticed. 'My name's Rupert Sayer, I work for the *West Sussex Gazette*, freelance. I'm a journalist.'

'A journalist?' Jack's mouth fell open. He shook his head.

'Undercover,' Rupert added, lifting his head.

'Undercover?' Jack stared at him. 'Undercover? What the hell do you mean, undercover?! What's going on?'

Rupert dug his hands in his pockets. Now he knew that he wasn't going to be shot, his natural confidence – arrogance the editor called it – expanded to its normal proportions. 'I'm on to a story; something big, and I reckoned you might be involved.'

'Your paper is doing a story that involves me? How bloody ridiculous!' Jack snapped. 'I'm going to speak to my lawyer about this. If you write anything about me then I'll have a lawsuit on the West Sussex Gazette as quick as you can say bloody Fleet Street!' he boomed.

Rupert flushed and his spots stood out angrily on his face. 'I, erm, I wasn't planning to write about you,' he stammered, 'and, erm, at the moment it's not, erm, anything to do with the, erm, paper, erm, as yet, that is...' His voice trailed off and he hung his head again.

Jack took a step back and looked at him. 'I see,' he said, with more authority than he felt, letting the words hang in the air. Rupert chewed his lip. 'What's the story then?' Jack finally asked. 'Big, you say?'

'I think so...' Rupert eyed Jack, then said, 'Why you following Gamley? Is he a mate of yours?'

'My name's Jack Lowe and I'm a private investigator,' Jack answered. 'I'm on a case.'

Rupert was impressed, as Jack had meant him to be. He didn't care much for the job, not in the way that he loved his gardening, but he was making a good go of it now and he had to admit, standing there in the North Terminal short-term car park at Gatwick airport, it gave him a thrill to say what he did. It was a hell of a lot better than saying he was a gardener.

'Bloody hell,' Rupert murmured. Suddenly assured of his safety, he leant back against the car and said again, 'Bloody hell. What sort of case?'

'I'm not at liberty to say,' Jack replied.

Rupert looked at him. 'Dodgy town planning?' he said. 'Carving up green belt land for no reason I can see other than greasing Gamley's palm – dodgy bastard.' He narrowed his eyes. 'You're on to him, aren't you? Like I am.'

Jack didn't answer. He wasn't in the habit of forming confidences and who the hell was Rupert Sayer anyway? He could be anybody. He shook his head. 'I've got no idea what you're on about,' he said. 'Sorry, mate, but you're way off the mark.'

Rupert stood straight. He might have been young and naïve but he certainly wasn't stupid; he'd got Jack's number. 'Whatever you say,' he remarked, opening the car door. He bent inside and took out a business card. 'Give us a ring sometime. I've got a wad of stuff on Gamley.' He handed the card over and Jack took it. He noticed that it didn't have any mention of the paper on it. 'Are you working independently or with the paper on this one?' he asked.

'Independently, actually. I don't want to be tied in to a local rag when this one hits the fan.' The truth was he didn't have enough of a story to take it to the paper. It was mostly a hunch and a few coincidences.

'Well, you watch your back, Rupert Sayer,' Jack said, turning towards his car. 'If you're on your own then you make sure you take care, all right?'

Rupert nodded, but his look was arrogant and Jack thought, why am I telling him this, why am I bothering? Jack walked off towards his car, opened it and climbed inside. He put the keys in the ignition and started the engine. He saw Rupert drive off and went to drop the card out of the window but for some reason thought better of it. He shoved it into the side pocket of the car door instead and then pulled the car out of the space. He didn't give Rupert another thought. Perhaps he should have done; a stray young journalist with too much curiosity and too little knowledge was a dangerous thing.

Jack pulled into the long drive of Chadwick Farm and approached the house at ten miles per hour as the sign on the gate told him to. The sign read, 'Slow children playing', which always made him laugh because the Betts children were anything but slow.

He stopped in front of the house, swung the car round and reversed it up to the back gate. He was here for two reasons: to finish a job he'd started several evenings ago and to update Roz and Graham on the Gamley case. He climbed out of the car and went through the gate into the courtyard at the side of the house, formerly the bit of paving where the bins were kept. He stamped his foot down hard on the brick terrace he'd laid two days ago to cheek it was solid and called out to Roz. The kitchen door was open so he popped his head round it and shouted again to her.

Minutes later she appeared, drying her hands on a towel. She was followed, as she always was, by Kitty and Oliver.

'Hello, Jack!' She threw the towel over the back of a chair and said, 'I'll put the kettle on, shall I?'

Jack smiled. It was a constant refrain in this house – every situation seemed to demand that someone put the kettle on.

'Thanks, Roz, but I'll get on if you don't mind. What time's Graham back?'

'He rang early this morning to say that he was leaving Newcastle at lunchtime.' She looked at her watch. 'Depending on the traffic, I'd say about six-ish, hopefully.'

'Good, that gives me plenty of time.' He began rolling his sleeves up as he headed back out to the car.

'D'you need a hand?' Roz asked. Jack looked at her and then at Kitty and Oliver. He remembered Jamie's marvellous but infuriating idea of help when he had been a toddler and said, 'I can manage, thanks. You just carry on and don't mind me.'

Roz stood in the doorway 'Hardly,' she remarked. 'A six-foot, good-looking, horny-handed son of the soil toiling away on my new

302

courtyard garden. I don't think that's something I can ignore. Couldn't I just sit and watch you?'

Jack suddenly laughed. 'No you bloody well can't. You're a married woman, Mrs Betts, and this is hubby's birthday present.'

Roz pulled a face. 'Spoilsport,' she said. 'On with the washing-up then...' She turned inside. 'Come on, kids.'

Jack opened the boot of the car and looked inside. He had more plants than he'd been paid for but then that was his present to Graham. It was his way of saying thanks, not only for the work – a case that was at last something decent to work on – but also for the numerous pints down the pub, the kitchen suppers, the first overtures of friendship that he'd had since he moved down almost a year ago. He liked Graham Betts, he liked Roz too. They were, he thought, the first people that he reckoned he could call friends.

And for friends he did favours. This – creating a courtyard garden for Graham's birthday present during the three days he was away on a buying trip to Newcastle and on a minuscule budget – was the sort of thing he did only for mates. And mates they had become; hell, he had no one else to talk to.

Jack unloaded the car. Ten terracotta pots in varying sizes, made from your basic ordinary clay, bought wholesale for peanuts and aged with a pot of natural yoghurt painted on and left to dry in the sun. One old sink, found on the tip. Two chimney pieces, the most expensive things at a tenner each, and a French fold-away bench made of rusting wrought iron, sanded down and painted over in mint green. He carried everything through to the courtyard and started arranging the pots in sets. One set in the shady corner, to be filled with hostas and ferns, a couple of grasses and a shade-loving camellia japonica, two either side of the door filled with herbs so that Roz could nip out and cut a bunch to cook with, and the rest arranged at different angles to be filled with the incredible array of plants in the boot.

Jack heaved out six bags of compost, then the plants and finally his shovel and fork. He knelt by the first set of pots and went to work.

Sarah received the call from Alex mid-morning at Duffields as she manned the customer services desk. He had bought four hundred and fifty-nine thousand shares in Wye Valley Organic Foods that morning, just as the price slipped from fifty-one pence a share to forty-nine. He had invested the total sum of three hundred and seventy-five thousand pounds, which was not a huge amount in comparison to the large institutional funds, but was big enough for a private client broker to feel slightly uneasy about. He was covered though. It was all legit, the Housewife Trust and his own involvement in it, and there was nothing – as far as he could see – that would catch him out.

Sarah's reaction wasn't what she had expected it to be. She had been excited and filled with optimism until the moment Alex had rung, then the full reality of her decision hit her and she had to sit down. Stupid, she thought, stupid, stupid, stupid. What on earth have I done? She was, for a few moments, almost paralysed with anxiety She had taken out a forty-four-thousand-pound loan from the bank and invested it in the stock market on a tip, a whim. Was she mad? Was she completely mad? Her heart hammered in her chest and she felt faint. What if the market crashed? What if the stock dropped? What if she lost the whole lot? It would ruin her; it would ruin her and Rory's life. She dropped her head in her hands and closed her eyes.

'Oh God,' she murmured, 'oh God.' A customer appeared and she immediately stood up. 'Can I help you?' she asked. Internally she thought, what are you doing? You made the decision, you've bought the stock and it's done. She smiled at the woman returning a bunch of tulips with three of the heads broken and took the attitude that she had always taken. It's bloody done, she thought, and taking the flowers she just got on with it.

Alex put the phone down to Sarah and, as mobile phones weren't allowed in the office, went along to the coffee machine to ring Lucie. He too was edgy. He was far more certain of what he was doing than Sarah, but he'd invested a hell of a lot in this, all of the profit he'd made on the market so far, and if it didn't go then the Beemer would.

Lucie answered the phone immediately She was in a meeting and thought it might be Marcus. Excusing herself from the table she said, 'I can't talk now, Alex, I'm in a meeting.'

'Are you coming over tonight?' he asked.

'I can't,' she said, though she wanted to, God knows she could have done with a bit of comfort. 'We're about to go into a bid situation. There'll be an announcement this afternoon so I'll be working most of the weekend.'

'I see,' he said, then: 'Ring me when you can.' Lucie sighed on the other end of the phone. What for, she wanted to ask, when this isn't a relationship? 'Will do,' she replied, then she hung up. Alex put his mobile down and stared at the coffee machine. He tried to think back over all the times he'd spoken to Lucie and whether or not either of them had ever used the land line at work. He couldn't honestly remember, but he doubted it. He'd been having an affair with a married woman, it was unlikely either of them would have taken the risk. Alex slotted a couple of coins into the machine and pressed the 'coffee, white with sugar' button. He put his phone in his pocket as he watched the cup drop down and fill with a murky brown liquid. All he had to do now was wait. But as easy as it sounded, that was actually the most difficult thing to do.

Sarah decided to go and see Roz on the way to school to pick up Rory. She had to pass Chadwick Farm anyway, so she stopped and called in to tell Roz that the deal was done. What she actually wanted was for someone to reassure her and Roz was the perfect person for that. She never seemed to buckle under the strains and stresses that defeated everyone else. She just seemed to coast along, although 'seemed', Sarah knew from her own experience, was a word that covered a multitude of emotions.

Pulling up outside the house, Sarah parked next to the estate car already there and went round by the bins to the back door. Only it wasn't the bins any more; it was a small brick terrace filled with flowering terracotta pots and a beautiful old bench. Sarah stood still. It was as if someone had created a small, neat square of peace and colour set off against ageing terracotta and grey-green wood and iron. She wondered for a moment if she was in the wrong house, knowing Roz's usual clutter and mess, and called out, 'Roz? Hello, Roz? Is anyone in?'

'Hello!' Roz shouted back, in her clear, deep voice. 'Hello!' She appeared in the doorway with a teapot in her hands and beamed. 'Sarah! What a nice surprise. Come on in, I've got the kettle on. We're going to have tea in our new courtyard.'

Sarah said, 'Roz, it is absolutely beautiful. Where on earth did you find the time to do all this?'

'I didn't,' Roz answered, leading the way inside, 'Jack did it.' Jack stood up as Roz came into the kitchen, not seeing Sarah following after. 'I've been wanting you two to meet,' Roz continued. 'Jack Lowe, this is Sarah Greg; Sarah, Jack.' She turned and looked at them both expectantly Sarah's smile froze on her face and Jack blinked rapidly several times. There was a short, tense silence, then Jack said, 'Sarah and I have met actually, Roz, once or twice in Duffields.'

'Have you?' Roz smiled. 'You never told me, Sarah! She's a bit of a dark horse you know, Jack, she's difficult to pin down is our Sarah...' She went on smiling for a few seconds then realised that there was something wrong.

'I know,' Jack said. The painful memory of that night came back to him – sitting alone in the pub waiting, getting slowly and surely out of it. 'Or rather, I gathered that...'

Sarah forced herself to smile. You never rang, she thought, you never rang to see if I was all right and find out why I hadn't turned up. I could have had an accident. I could have been in serious trouble and you never even checked on me in Duffields. She eyed him. I bet you weren't even there! She felt indignant seeing him now, scruffy and relaxed, comfortable with himself, moving in on her friends. You didn't turn up yourself and if it hadn't been for Rory then I'd have been sitting there like a lemon, waiting for you to arrive.

'You'll have tea, won't you, Sarah?' Roz asked. She sensed a certain tension and it puzzled her. She put it down to her imagination; that or sexual attraction and, frankly, why not? Those two were perfect for each other.

'I can't stop,' Sarah said, 'really I can't. I just called in to tell you that Alex bought the stock this morning.'

Roz spun round. 'Blimey,' she said. She held the teapot full of boiling water in her hands and didn't even notice the heat. She stared at Sarah, then suddenly said, 'Ouch! Bloody hell, that's hot!' and plonked the teapot down on the side.

'Scary,' Sarah said.

Roz nodded.

'Shall I pour the tea? Jack interrupted. He walked across and took the teapot over to the table, placing it on the tray Then he turned to Sarah and, briefly meeting her eye, said, 'Stay for tea, we have to christen the courtyard.'

'I can't, really, I've got to get to school to collect Rory.' She was being rude, she realised that, but she couldn't help herself. She didn't want to have tea with this man – it was as much as she could do to be civil to him – although why she was so angry she didn't quite know.

'Please stay,' Roz went on. 'I'll give Janie a quick buzz and ask her to collect Rory as well as Justin and Katie. She's coming back for a cuppa herself. Stay and we can have a bit of a tea party.'

Sarah was caught. She blushed, searching for a way out, and said, 'I don't think I can, Rory hates it when I'm not there, he–'

'Nonsense!' Roz cut in. 'He'll be fine.' She looked up. She didn't want Sarah to go, she didn't want to be left alone to think about the enormous risk she had just taken. The moment Sarah had told her that Alex had bought the stock her mind had flown into a panic. The reality of it was just too daunting and she wanted company, she wanted to extend the noise and keep the actuality of what they had all just done at arm's length. 'Come on, Sarah, I've made a cake. Please stay.'

'OK. I mean, thanks, I'd love to.' Not true; she wouldn't love to at all.

'I'll ring Janie then,' Roz said, 'she'll be on her way to school.' She disappeared out of the kitchen and Sarah was left alone with Jack. 'Tea?'

he asked.

'Yes, thanks.'

He poured Sarah a mug of tea and added milk. 'I didn't know you knew Roz and Graham,' Jack said, as he passed the tea over. He felt that he had to say something to fill the silence.

'Yes,' Sarah replied, 'Rory is in Justin's class.'

'School, of course.' Jack picked up his own tea and took a sip. Both he and Sarah made a conscious effort not to look at each other. She stared out at the new courtyard and he counted the number of cobwebs in one corner of the kitchen. This can't continue, they both thought separately, it's painful. Sarah turned to him, Jack looked at her and they both spoke at the same time.

'Sorry...' Sarah stared down at her tea.

'No, please, you first.'

She coughed. 'I was going to say that the courtyard is lovely.'

'Thank you.'

'It really is. You are very clever.'

He shrugged. 'Not really. Basic stuff – a bit of brickwork, some pots, nothing too spectacular, no water feature, no constructions, I didn't do much at all really...' His voice tailed off. He'd meant to sound modest but instead came across as dismissive, arrogant almost. Sarah longed for Roz to reappear.

'That night at the pub,' Jack said suddenly He had to clear the air. He couldn't leave it, he was too honest, too open for that. 'The night we were supposed to meet.'

He's going to apologise for not turning up,

310

Sarah thought with panic. He feels sorry for me, I can tell just by looking at him. He thinks I'm pathetic, he imagines that I was sitting alone in the pub waiting for him to arrive, like a fully paid-up member of the lonely hearts club. Oh God. She said, 'Forget it, it should never have happened.'

Jack blinked. He stared at her and she said again, 'Forget it. I have.'

Roz reappeared and said, 'Janie's on her way over. I caught her just as she got to school and she's bringing all three little darlings with her. Ah, I see you've got your tea. Shall we go outside?' Sarah made to move but Jack stood stunned for a few seconds. Is she for real? he thought, watching the back of her. Not a word of regret, not a hint of remorse. Hell, she couldn't give a stuff. He took another swig of tea and decided to abandon the christening of the courtyard. He would call Graham later and discuss the case; for now he just had to get out of there.

'Roz,' he said, walking outside, 'sorry, but I've got to go. I've just realised the time and I've got to get back to the office.'

'But Jack, I–' He headed towards the gate before she could finish.

'Thanks for the tea, let me know what Graham thinks. Wish him happy birthday for me, will you?'

He waved and shut the gate after him, climbing immediately into his car and starting the engine. As he drove off, Roz stood up and frowned. 'What on earth was all that about?' She turned to

Sarah who shrugged and studiously avoided her eye. 'Oh well.' She sat down again and picked up her tea. 'Just us then,' she said, then: 'But don't talk to me about Wye Valley Organic Foods. Anything other than that, OK? Now that we've done it, it's not up for discussion. Right?' Sarah nodded, feeling reassured. What's done is done. That was just what she wanted to hear.

Alex was on the phone when the announcement came up on the screen. He was talking to a client, running through their portfolio, when it flashed up. Wye Valley Organic Foods were subject to a take-over bid from the multi-national giant Unilever. He stopped listening and stared at it. On the other end of the phone his client, still rabbiting on, sensed that he wasn't being listened to and stopped talking. There was a silence as Alex watched the share price of Wye Valley rise six pence and then the client said, 'Hello? Alex? Are you still there?'

Alex shook himself. 'Oh God, yes, sorry, David, I was watching some movement in the market. You were saying?' With great difficulty he listened to the rest of what his client had to say then made his own suggestions for changes to the portfolio. His mind wasn't on it though and to his relief the client said he'd think it over and call back. Alex hung up, then rang Sarah. She was out and didn't possess an answer phone. He tried Janie; she too was out, but her answer message gave out her mobile number so he rang that.

In the courtyard at Chadwick Farm, no one took

much notice of Janie's mobile going off in her handbag. She lifted it out and answered it, walking round to the front of the house to get a better signal. She spoke to Alex, just briefly, then pressed end and returned to the tea party. The noise was relentless. Roz and Sarah were talking, Roz was shouting to the children every now and then to watch out for the pots as they threw a tennis ball around, Kitty and Oliver were washing up in a big plastic bucket and kept arguing about the mop, the older children were screeching and yelling with delight if one of them missed the ball and into all this walked Janie, her face white. Roz looked up.

'What's up?'

'That was Alex,' Janie said. She slumped back against the wall and stared at them. 'Unilever made a bid for Wye Valley Organic Foods. It's just been announced and the share price is on the up.'

Roz let out a yell and all the children immediately stopped what they were doing. 'I don't believe it!' she suddenly cried. 'It's happened, it's bloody happened, Sarah!' She jumped up and rushed towards Sarah. Sarah put her hands up to her face. The relief, coupled with excitement, overwhelmed her. Rory appeared by her side. 'Mummy?' She swallowed and wiped her face on the back of her hands. 'I'm fine, darling, really, I'm fine.' She smiled, then she caught Roz's eye and the smile widened.

'Fine!' Roz shrieked, her eyes alight with excitement. 'I should think you feel absolutely bloody marvellous!' She shook her head. 'I know I do.'

Janie stood straight. 'A drink,' she said, 'we need a drink.'

Sarah looked at her watch. 'It's four-thirty, Janie.'

'Then we're only an hour and a half off six o'clock. Roz? What have you got in your fridge?'

'Some rather tired-looking vegetables, butter, cheese, left-over baked beans and a very odd assortment of condiments, all half-used.' She smiled. 'But I've got a bottle of red in the cupboard.'

'Then fetch it,' Janie said, 'at once.' Roz laughed and went into the kitchen. Sarah looked at Janie. 'Is it going to work?' she asked quietly 'Do you really think it's going to work?'

Janie nodded. 'I do,' she said. 'Yes I do.'

At four forty-five that afternoon, in the highly secure surveillance unit at the Stock Exchange, a young woman called Janice Stimpson picked up an alert signal on her screen. She and a large team of people were trained to watch the monitors of IMAS, the sophisticated surveillance system operated by the Stock Exchange. The system built up a profile on every company traded on the Stock Exchange and any unusual share dealings came up as an alert. That afternoon, Janice had been watching the monitor for Wye Valley Organic Foods when the alert sounded. She immediately requested a back-dated profile and took a print-out. Someone had bought just under three per cent of the shares only hours before the announcement of a take-over bid. It may have been a lucky coincidence, or it may have been planned. Whatever it was, Janice Stimpson would find out. Janice was tenacious in the extreme and she always got her man.

Janice Stimpson was thirty-eight. She had been pensioned out of the Metropolitan Police three years ago with a back injury, a dislodged disc in the lower spine, sustained whilst on duty. She had been chasing a joy-rider, who had abandoned the car in an alley and tried to make a run for it on foot. Janice had caught him, grabbed him by the left arm and yanked it up his back to hold him. But this particular youth had done years of judo as part of a young persons' training scheme operated in the area and he twisted his body in a half-turn, then hooked his foot around Janice's ankle and performed *tia toshie*, throwing Janice flat on to her back. It was December, the ground was icy and as she fell on to the concrete she broke her arm in three places and dislodged her spine. Out popped the disc. She was in traction for six weeks, her arm had to be operated on twice and finally pinned with a metal plate. She was discharged from the police force on medical grounds the following June, with a very substantial pension indeed.

Janice didn't need to work. She had an ample enough income to be able to devote her time to gardening and cooking, or helping handicapped children, or looking after her elderly mother who had a small flat a few roads away from Janice in Barnet. But Janice wanted to work. She had looked hard for the right sort of job, nothing too physical but something that would be an outlet for the strong sense of justice she had, a sense that she had carried with her since childhood. She had applied originally for a job as a traffic warden but the time spent outside in all weathers would have been detrimental to her injury, the cold making it much more painful and playing havoc with the metal plate in her arm. Then a friend had mentioned that the Stock Exchange were recruiting people to train for their computer surveillance system, IMAS, and Janice went for an interview. Once inside the door, once keyed into the very great responsibility that she would be given for sniffing out financial fraud, insider trading and the rest, Janice knew she had found what she wanted to do. This was her mission. She took the job.

And she was good at it too. In the past two years she had been assigned to twenty special cases, one of which had made it to prosecution – a rare occurrence. Once she got her hands on a case she went at it like a ferret up a drainpipe – an expression her supervisor used – and couldn't rest until she had done her all. She was punctual, diligent and meticulous. She was also not very well liked. She was too good, and being too good did nothing to inspire friendship. Nobody likes a holybody. So Janice worked long and hard, with few lunch hours and no knocking off early to go to the pub. She spent hours in front of the screen and her particular speciality was insider trading.

On that Friday afternoon, once Janice had spotted the anomaly in trading for Wye Valley and looked up the purchaser, a nominee company called the Housewife Trust, she took her print-out and went immediately to see the supervisor.

Knocking lightly on his open door, she put her head round it and said, 'I think I've got something on Wye Valley Organic Foods.'

The supervisor stopped what he was doing and beckoned her into the room. He didn't like Janice any more than the rest of the team did, but since she'd joined them they had won three awards for best performance and now he gave her his attention whenever she needed it.

She placed the print-out on the desk and he looked at it. 'Two point eight per cent of the shares,' she said, 'bought this morning. Either someone likes organic yoghurts a lot and they were born lucky or there's something odd about this one.'

The supervisor smiled. 'Look into it then, Janice,' he said. She nodded. She would do more than that; she would look under it and over it, around it and through it. She would find every last scrap of information that she could on the deal and then she would begin to piece it all together, with the same laboured patience that she employed for her jigsaw puzzles. 'Thanks,' she said, flashing a rare smile back at him. 'I will.'

Chapter Sixteen

Jack walked into the office early on Saturday morning and sat down at his desk. They sometimes worked a half-day at the weekend especially if Jack had been out a lot in the week – to catch up with the paperwork. He felt lousy; he'd hardly slept, drunk too much wine, eaten nothing and the net result was a crummy hangover and a nagging feeling of failure. It was the same feeling that had dogged him for years after Sandra had left. Sarah, he thought, Sarah Greg. Nice smile, pretty but not stunning, warm and soft but not a pushover, a woman who knows her own mind and who gets on with life, a woman he had been immediately attracted to – despite the turquoise Duffields overall – and a woman he had risked his self-confidence on. Sarah. He'd failed though, blown any scrap of self-assurance he had developed over the past few years and made a complete asshole of himself. In fact, she held him in such low regard that she was painfully embarrassed about ever having made an arrangement with him and wanted to forget it, the very mention of it putting her on edge. Sarah. And he'd really thought it was worth the effort. What a mistake. Jack put his head in his hands and closed his eyes. That was how Dodi found him when she came in.

'All right, Jack?'

He lifted his head. 'Oh, yeah, sorry, Dodi, I didn't hear you come in.' He busied himself by shuffling papers. Dodi crossed the room and sat on the edge of his desk. 'D'you mind?' he said, tugging an invoice out from under her bottom.

'What's up?' she asked, ignoring his pique. 'You went off yesterday on the Betts case like a terrier after a bone–'

'Alsatian, please. Not a terrier, terriers are so...' He searched for the right word. 'So short and comical,' he finished. He looked at her. 'I'm not comical, am I, Dodi?'

'Very,' she replied and Jack looked away. She nudged him. 'Only joking, sport.'

He smiled. 'Less of the outback please, Dodi.'

'So what's up? What did you get on Gamley? Any leads?'

'Ah.' Jack sat back. 'Possible leads, I think. He was off to Guernsey for the weekend and by the look of it it's a trip he does pretty regularly. The ground staff were all over him, like he's a top customer.'

Dodi chewed the end of a pen. 'Guernsey. Tax-free, right?'

'Tax-free, so it's known as the land of dodgy earnings and missing money. Off-shore banking I think it's legitimately called.'

'So how does that fit? You think he's got accounts there and is stuffing money away?'

'Maybe.'

'How do we find out?'

'I don't know at the moment, but I'll get on to it.' He looked at her. 'There's got to be something, Dodi; there's got to be some financial connection with Redfern, money under the table, I'm convinced of it.' Dodi slid off his desk.

'But that's not the problem, right?' She narrowed her eyes and looked at him. 'There's more.'

'Dodi, you should know by now that with me there's always more.'

Dodi groaned. 'Come on, spit it out.'

'If only I could.'

Dodi folded her arms across her strapping chest and looked at him. 'Whoever she is, Jack, she isn't worth it.'

'No, perhaps you're right.' He had tried telling himself as much last night. A night in front of the footy, nice bottle of plonk, a frozen pizza waiting to be eaten. What more could a man want? Why spoil all that for a woman? But there was something about Sarah, something that he connected with, something he recognised, although the feeling wasn't in the least bit reciprocated. 'I'll forget her,' he said, 'delete her file from the great computer that is my brain and move on.'

Dodi suddenly laughed. 'Now I know you're joking. Your brain a computer? Ha!' She headed over to her own desk still chuckling. 'Your brain a computer...' She sat down and switched on her PC.

'It wasn't that funny!' Jack called across to her.

She looked at him and shook her head. 'Oh yes it was,' she said.

Janice Stimpson was also working on a Saturday morning but, unlike Jack and Dodi, she had no plans to take a half-day. She had a round of sandwiches in her bag, an apple and a can of drink. She didn't intend to move from the screen. She was on to something here and she was going to find out what.

The first thing she did was to look up all the trades in the name of the nominee company, the Housewife Trust. That took nearly five hours because once she had the name of the stock, she then had to build up a profile of it to see if there was anything unusual about the dealings. For the five dot com companies that the trust had invested in there was a good deal of shrewd purchase and luck involved. All five stocks had performed outstandingly well – Janice had even been tempted to invest a thousand pounds herself in the IT revolution – and were bringing excellent returns for investors. All five were absolutely normal in their profiles and although the dealing by the trust had been swift, in and out in just over a week, there was nothing that pointed to fraud. Then, at around three p.m. that afternoon, after a sandwich and a walk around the park, Janice uncovered her first small irregularity. So small she might even have missed it. The Housewife Trust had bought sixteen thousand shares in Sarasota plc, a small communications company, back in April, just before the announcement that it was subject to a take-over bid. The shares were purchased and sold within a couple of weeks. The share price during that time had risen rapidly and return on investment could have been up to as much as six hundred per cent. It seemed that the Housewife Trust were very lucky indeed.

Janice sat back and stared at the screen. Twice then, twice this nominee company had invested in a stock that was subject to a bid, twice they had made a substantial profit but the first time cleverly; the amount invested was not large enough to draw attention. Janice decided to look through all the bid announcements on the Stock Exchange over the past three months. She started in April and worked forward. It took half an hour and by the end of it she had matched up two other incidences of the trust dealing in shares before an announcement. Luck again? She very much doubted it.

Janice stood up and walked around a bit to stretch her legs. The pattern of dealing was clever and well-spaced and the rise in IT stocks had camouflaged things very nicely. But, as sure as she had a mole on the inside of her left arm, Janice was certain there was something going on here. Insider trading. It was as simple as that. Insider trading, the penalty for which, if convicted, was seven years inside. She went back to her desk and began to pack her things away. She would find out who and how and why. That was stage two and the stage that really fascinated her. Why, when so many of these people earned far more than she could ever hope to, did they risk it all? Greed, she supposed, greed and beating the system.

She tossed the empty Mars Bar wrapper on her desk into the bin – she always had a Mars Bar mid-afternoon – and stuffed the print-outs from what she'd discovered today into her briefcase. It was five-thirty and she was going out tonight; she had to get home. She liked to make an effort did

Janice, she enjoyed looking nice, even if it did take half a ton of slap and the best that Principles could muster. She was on the pull too. She was conscious that time was slipping by and that she didn't want to spend her life alone in a flat in Barnet. So by six she was on her way back home to prepare for a good night out and a Sunday at her mum's, reading the papers and working out a five-point plan to show to her supervisor on Monday morning.

Stan Gamley was sweating. It was too hot in his hotel room. He had the windows open and the fan going, so that every now and then cool air blew across his backside, but it wasn't really helping. He had also eaten too much at dinner. That was the trouble with hotel food, there was so much choice that you simply had to stuff yourself – it was rude not to. He had the faint burn of indigestion in his chest and could feel a trickle of sweat running down the side of his face. He was on his knees with his pelvis rammed up against the large, white, naked bottom of a lady he had met at dinner, a forty-something divorcee who was on her own for a weekend break in Guernsey, with whom he had shared a bottle of wine and who had then insisted on coming up to his room to see the view. Of course he'd had to perform, it would have been rude not to. The moment she'd sat on the edge of the bed and unfastened her blouse, showing a creased but still pert bosom trussed up in a black lace number, he'd known she was up for it. It would have been wimpish to ignore the signals. 'Oh, it's hot up here, Stan,' she'd said, reclining on the pillows and opening her blouse to let the air get to her chest. 'I think you should take some of those clothes off and get yourself more comfortable.'

Stan had done as she'd asked and stripped down to his jockeys and new navy wool M&S socks – a present from his wife Moira for the trip – and joined Brenda on the bed. A tussle had taken place as Stan struggled with the black lace and then the zip on her skirt, but he had succeeded finally and had ended up in this position, his heartburn increasing and his mind not really on the job in hand.

Brenda moaned and panted and Stan speeded up the rhythm – as much as he could physically manage – but he was having trouble keeping it up. He closed his eyes and concentrated hard, anxious not to let himself down, and after several minutes he began to pick up momentum again, to feel he was getting there. He started to grunt, Brenda set up a high-pitched sort of growling noise and it was all nicely coming together when the phone by the side of the bed rang.

'Oh shit!' Stan exploded. He stopped, his rhythm gone completely, and tried to bring his breathing under control. The phone rang on and Stan slipped limply out of Brenda. He covered his pelvis with a sheet and sat back on his heels. 'Sorry, love,' he muttered and reached for the receiver. 'Hello?'

On the other end of the line, Derek, a junior member of the planning department, took a deep breath and said, 'Hello, Stan? It's Del, from planning.'

Stan turned away from Brenda and spoke right into the phone. 'Del? What the hell are you doing phoning me here? How did you get my number?'

'I called your wife, Mrs Gamley, and told her that I needed to speak to you urgently, Mr Gamley, I mean Stan. I'm sorry but I thought I'd better ring you. It's about this bloke, this bloke I met in the pub last night.'

Gamley was having trouble keeping his temper. He had turned his back on Brenda but he could see her reflection in the dressing table mirror as she moved about collecting her clothes up and beginning to dress. 'What bloke?' he snapped.

'A young bloke, Mr Gamley. I dunno who he was, but he was asking questions about you, like did I know you and did I know exactly where you'd gone for the weekend and did you have a house in the Channel Islands. He was dead nosy and he seemed to know quite a bit about you. He was ... I dunno, suspicious, I guess.' Gamley was silent for a few moments.

'What did you tell him?'

'Nothing. I kept me mouth shut.'

'Right, Del, you did well to call me, son, well done. Where are you? If you're at home then let me have the bill for this call, I wouldn't want you to be out of pocket, son.' Brenda was dressed now and Gamley turned and looked at her, mouthing the words, 'Please stay.' She was no spring chicken but she wasn't bad looking; fantastic ass, he thought.

'That's very nice of you, Mr Gamley, I mean Stan, but I'm at the office. I didn't want to make a call abroad on my phone so I thought it would be better from...'

'You bloody twit!' Gamley growled. 'Haven't you got any bloody sense? Any calls from the office are traceable and I don't want my dealings in Guernsey traced!'

'Sorry Mr Gamley, I didn't mean to...'

'Forget it!' Gamley snapped. Brenda had slipped out of the room and his indigestion had flared up painfully in the top of his chest. 'Just get off the phone and don't talk to anyone about where I am, all right? That includes anyone from work or strange blokes in the pub. Gottit?'

'Yes, Mr Gamley, Stan. Of course. See you Monday then.'

Gamley sighed and without replying hung up. He sat back against the bedhead. He could smell Brenda's perfume on the sheets but he had to admit he was relieved that she'd gone. He was too old for this kind of malarkey: too old and too fat. He stood up, reached for his jockeys and, pulling them on, walked across to the mini-bar. He took out a miniature gin and a small can of tonic, poured them both into a tooth mug, then went out on to the balcony in his socks and pants to drink it. He had a problem and he was going to have to sort it.

Bill and Sheila Redfern were entertaining. They had invited Bill's director for dinner, along with a few friends from the golf club, and Sheila had been cooking all day. Most of the guests had just arrived and Bill had mixed a jug of Pimms and was serving it in the garden, anxious to show off the new gazebo they had had built for the summer. Sheila was in chiffon: a long skirt and matching top which tied at the waist and showed how much tennis she played. Bill was in an open-necked shirt and a pair of immaculate chinos. They were both perfectly dressed for a casual but smart summer evening dinner party, both manicured, massaged and relaxed after their weekly Saturday afternoon sex. They were a couple without children who liked to focus very much on themselves, and tonight was a testament to how much they had achieved.

Sheila was just handing round a large Portuguese plate layered with the best selection of nibbles that M&S could provide – she liked to cook but she had never been one for fiddling – when the phone rang. They didn't get calls on a Saturday night, not at eight-thirty anyway, and as the high-pitched bleep trilled out from the open French windows of the kitchen, Sheila and Bill exchanged a look. She said, 'Hand the nibbles round, darling, and I'll get it.'

'Would you, sweetie? Thanks. It's probably Ralph,' which he pronounced 'Raiff' to posh it up a bit, 'phoning to cancel the round tomorrow...'

Bill glanced towards the house where Sheila was taking the call. She had put her hand over her mouth and was beckoning him in. 'Scuse me,' he murmured, leaving the plate on the table. 'Back in a jiffy...'

Once inside the house, Sheila, with her hand over the mouthpiece, hissed at him, 'It's that odious little man, Stan Gamley. He sounds drunk!' She was irritated and Bill smiled to try and ease her mood. 'You pour the Pimms,' he said, 'and I'll be out in a moment.' Sheila nodded, but her nostrils flared. She was forty-three, she'd had a very neat and predictable life and the unexpected really put her on edge. Bill squeezed her arm. 'Go on, darling, our guests are waiting.' Her face changed as she plastered a smile on to it and took a deep breath before stepping outside. 'Who'd like more Pimms?' he heard her call, then he uncovered the receiver and said, 'Bill Redfern.'

'Bill? It's Stan. I think we've got a problem.'

Bill bristled at the intimacy of the statement. '*We* don't have anything, Stan,' he replied coolly 'If there is a problem then I'm afraid that it has nothing to do with me.'

Gamley, who had downed all three miniature gins from the mini-bar, along with a brandy and coke, was clearly drunk and not taking any nonsense. 'If it's my problem, Bill, then it's your problem. There's a bloke, he's been asking about me. Knows I'm in the Channel Islands, he's been asking questions, about me, down the pub, he...'

'Stan, you're panicking about nothing!' Redfern cut in. 'Of course people ask questions about you. You're an important man, you've got a high profile, you're head of town planning.' Redfern smoothed his voice to lull Gamley into a sense of security. He wanted Gamley off the phone; if there was a problem then now wasn't the time to talk about it. 'Everything is fine, Stan,' he continued. 'Come on, calm down. We're careful and we know what we're doing. Now, why don't you just forget all about this until Monday

328

and we'll meet for lunch then and discuss it. OK?'

Gamley, who was beginning to feel the full effect of the warmth, the food and the alcohol, slumped back against the bedhead and let out a silent belch. He'd phoned on a drunken impulse and now regretted it. 'You're right, Bill,' he said, concentrating on not slurring his words.

'Of course I am, Stan,' Redfern said gently 'I'll speak to you Monday.' Then he hung up without waiting for an answer and bent to disconnect the phone. Back out on the patio, he took his glass of Pimms and raised it. 'Cheers everyone,' he said, taking a large gulp.

'Here's to the land buyer with the magic touch,' his director proposed, smiling and raising his glass. 'Long may it continue.'

'Here, here,' Bill replied and the words seemed to echo in his head.

Chapter Seventeen

Monday morning first thing, Janice Stimpson was in the office and on the phone to the Financial Services Authority to check on a broker at White Lowen. His name was Alex Stanton and he had a so far unblemished record. She made an appointment to see the head of human resources to discuss Mr Stanton, telling her that it was a matter of the utmost confidentiality and that under no circumstances must it be discussed with anyone other than a direct supervisor. Then she went back to IMAS to find a record of his trading over the past year. Janice was on the hunt and, as always, she knew exactly what she wanted to find.

At nine-fifteen on the same Monday morning, Sarah was shown into the headmaster's office at Ledworth House and asked if she would like a coffee while she waited. She said yes, coffee with milk and sugar, and would the headmaster be long because she had to be at work by ten-thirty?

The secretary said, 'I'll go and get him right away and I'll let him know that you've got a deadline.' She smiled and disappeared, leaving Sarah to look at the book-lined study and wonder what she was doing here. She had made the appointment Saturday morning on an impulse after a row with Rory about pronouncing a word.

Stupid really; a stupid, pointless row because he wouldn't – and of course couldn't – say the word 'think'. A basic word, she'd told him, a basic word that he should be able to say. What was she spending all her hard-earned money on if he wasn't paying any attention to what he was being taught? It was an explosion, not really a row, and it had come from out of nowhere as these things sometimes do.

'Think,' Sarah had said loudly to him as they chatted over breakfast on Saturday morning. She had interrupted what he was saying because he said 'fing'.

She looked at him and tilted his face towards her, her hand on his chin. 'T, T, Th ... Think. Say the "th", Rory It's the "th" sound, not the "f" sound and it ends in a kicking k...'

Rory had turned away and ignored her. 'I don't fing that I want to...'

She cut in again. 'Rory, it's the "th" sound. Come on, please, say it after me...'

But Rory had abruptly stood up, knocking his chair over, and slammed out of the kitchen. That had done it for Sarah, she'd well and truly lost her temper. Although later, when she'd analysed it, she didn't really know why. He'd done it before, gone off in a strop, only this time she couldn't take it. She had stormed out after him and shouted up the stairs. He had shouted back and the whole thing had escalated into the sort of angry slanging match that she had always dreaded. She had fled the house in the end, fled out into the garden, tearful and angry, Rory yelling after her that he wasn't ever going to be

331

normal no matter how much she tried or how much she spent and that he was sick of her pretending that he would be.

Sarah had dug the flower beds. She had taken a garden fork and dug the earth over and over until she had a blister on her right hand and her face was wet with tears. Then she had walked inside, dried her eyes and phoned Ledworth House. It was a premature, rash gesture and nowhere near available to her yet, but she felt she had to do something.

'Ah, Mrs Greg.'

Sarah turned from the books and looked at the man who had just entered the room. He was tall and slim, dressed soberly in a grey suit, and he was smiling. He was relaxed and smiling and so used was she to harassed headteachers who could spare – and this seemed to be a universal refrain – just a few minutes, Sarah was taken aback. She blinked in surprise, then smiled back and shook the hand offered to her.

'Thank you for seeing me at such short notice,' she said.

'It's my pleasure,' he replied. 'You wanted to talk about your son, Rory, who is seven, nearly eight, and partially deaf; is that right?'

'Yes...' No stammering over the name then, no prompting, no reminding the headteacher of who she was and what her problem was. 'Yes, that's right. I wanted to talk to you about a place for him. He's doing well at school, but I think he could do much, much better. He needs a smaller class and more individual attention and that's really what I'm here for.'

The headmaster, Mr Tully, smiled again. 'Then let's discuss it,' he said. 'Please, Mrs Greg, take a seat.'

And Sarah sat. It was the first time she had ever been asked to sit and discuss the needs and wants of her son and it felt good. She began to talk about Rory. It felt very good indeed.

Janice Stimpson had a sizeable print-out of the share dealings of Alex Stanton at White Lowen and nothing looked in the least bit unusual until April of that year. In April he had started trading for the Housewife Trust and from that moment on things began to look odd. Whoever the Housewife Trust were, they were involved. It was almost certainly a case of secondary insider trading and very much a convictable offence. Janice was pleased. She had her hypothesis, now she had to prove it.

Leaving the office mid-morning, she went along to White Lowen and met the human resources director. She asked the standard questions and checked Alex Stanton's C.V. It was all exactly as she had expected it to be; there had been no earlier offences, there seemed to be no tangible connection with any source of inside information, in fact no indication at all that this was anything other than a normal financial career. Janice made a note of a couple of colleagues that Stanton spent his lunch hours with, took their numbers from the switchboard list but that was it; there was nothing more to go on. Often the case, she thought, thanking the woman and saying goodbye. If he was insider trading then he had to be obtaining insider information from somewhere. The question was where?

Janice made her way back to her office and requested copies of all the tapes of Stanton's calls from the last eighteen months. People who dealt on price-sensitive information rarely used the office phone, but it was procedure to check. Once she had that out of the way, and she was certain it wouldn't yield anything at all, then she could get on with the investigation proper. It was like jumping through hoops, Janice thought, entering the Stock Exchange; once through them all it was a clear run to the finishing post. And it was a clear run that she relished.

Roz put the phone down having just spoken to Jack and sat staring at it for a few moments. Still no further on, she thought; then, bugger it, it's worth a try. She picked up the receiver again and dialled Cecil Gorden's number, speaking briefly to him before hanging up and shouting to the children in the playroom.

'Kitty? Oliver? Come on, let's get going.'

Both of them looked blankly at her as she walked into the playroom. They were building some kind of monster construction out of Duplo and didn't want to be disturbed. 'Come on!' she repeated. 'We're going to see the Gordens.'

'Whodey, Mummy?' Kitty said.

'Nice Major Gorden up the road,' Roz replied, kneeling in front of her daughter to fasten her sandal. 'Come on, other foot and let's get going.'

Oliver looked distressed at leaving his tower.

'It'll still be here when we get back,' Roz said. 'Come on, let's go!' She hurried the children outside and along the drive towards the lane. They were slow and she was impatient, but finally they managed to walk the half-mile to the Gordens' house and Roz called out to Cecil who was weeding in the front garden.

'Hello, Roz dear,' he said, getting slowly to his feet. 'The old knees aren't what they used to be.' He walked stiffly over to the front gate and unfastened the latch. 'Come on in, I'm sure we can find something for the children in our biscuit tin.' Oliver, who had sulked all the way there, perked up at the word 'biscuit'. It had magic powers that word, Roz thought, following Cecil into the house – along with the word 'sweetie' it was able to stop a tantrum and change a mood in five seconds flat. Or maybe it's just my kids who are so addicted to sugar, she wondered, as Kitty and Oliver stared awestruck into the wide circular tin filled to the brim with all sorts of biscuits.

'Nice to see you, Roz dear,' Cecil said. 'Daphne will be disappointed to have missed you.'

Ha, thought Roz, but she just smiled.

'She's having her hair done, always does on a Monday. Sets her up for the week. Monday and Friday.'

'Nice,' Roz murmured.

'Coffee?' the Major asked. 'I was about to have one myself.'

Roz spotted the empty coffee cup by the sink and realised that she'd missed Cecil's coffee hour. She didn't want to put him out, so she said, 'No thank you, Cecil, I had one before I left the

335

house. I just popped in actually to ask you something.'

Cecil turned from the sink and replaced the kettle on the side.

'Ask away, my dear.'

'Well, it's a bit delicate actually, it's a financial question. I, erm, I just wondered, if you don't mind me asking, exactly how much you had been offered by the developers for the land at the back. It's just that I might have come into a bit of money and, well, I might just possibly, perhaps, be interested in buying it myself.' There, it was out. The thing that she had been mulling over in the back of her mind all weekend was out. She hadn't told Graham, hadn't even had the courage to think it out loud and now she'd said it. She'd said it and was waiting for a response. Apart from the fact that her hands shook, she felt pretty good about it.

The Major looked at Roz, then at Kitty and Oliver, now both tucking in nicely to the tin of biscuits, and said, without any consideration, 'Two hundred and fifty thousand pounds.' Daphne wouldn't approve, of course. In fact she'd be furious. The last thing she wanted was for the Bettses to own all the land around or for the pig farm to expand, but the Major, well, he felt differently on these things. He liked Roz and Graham, they deserved a break, and if asked an honest question he gave an honest answer. He'd never been the sort of social politician that Daphne was.

Roz took a deep breath. It was more than she'd been expecting but, if things worked out, it might

336

not be unreachable. 'Thanks, Cecil,' she said, 'I appreciate your honesty.'

'Not at all. Was there anything else?' He glanced nervously in the direction of the children, who were now both covered in chocolate in the midst of Daphne's immaculate kitchen.

'No, I'll let you get on with your garden,' Roz replied. She crossed to the biscuit tin and removed it from the children's grasp, placing the lid firmly on and tucking it away on the top shelf. There was a loud vocal protest but, taking two sticky hands, she tugged the children out of the kitchen, very mindful of the paint-work and hissing, 'Don't touch anything!' under her breath. She pulled them through the hall and out of the house. Cecil saw her to the gate.

'Goodbye, Roz,' Cecil said, 'bye, Kitty, bye, Oliver.'

She smiled at him and nudged the children. 'Bye, Cecil,' she replied, feeling far more cheerful than she had when she'd put the phone down to Jack. The children both mumbled, 'Bye-bye' and Roz added, 'Thanks again.'

With that, she made her way back to Chadwick Farm.

Aiden Thornton sat anxiously flipping a coin over and over in his hand outside the meeting room on the third floor of the Stock Exchange building. To be called in by the surveillance team for an interview was serious and the phone call he'd had at midday had thrown him completely off-balance. He'd never done anything even remotely wrong but he was still as nervous as hell.

'Mr Thornton?'

Janice Stimpson appeared in the corridor clutching a file.

'Yes?' Aiden stood up.

'Hello, my name is Janice Stimpson. I'm investigating one of the brokers that you work with and I'd like to ask you some questions. Is that all right?'

Aiden blinked; it wasn't him. The relief flooded his face and he smiled. 'Yes, yes, that's fine.'

'Good, follow me please.'

Janice led the way into the meeting room and switched on the lights. 'Please, take a seat,' she said over her shoulder while she fiddled with the air conditioning. Finally blasting some cool air into the stuffy atmosphere, she turned and pulled out a chair.

'This is an informal interview, Mr Thornton, more of a chat really, to try to find out a bit more about the background of the broker involved. His name is Alex Stanton and we are concerned about some of his dealings on the Stock Exchange of late.'

Aiden wasn't surprised and that too showed on his face.

'Your personnel director told me that you're friends with Mr Stanton, is that right?'

'Not friends exactly. We don't socialise outside of work but we do have the odd beer at lunchtime and after work. He's a good bloke, Alex; charming in fact.'

'Has he got a girlfriend?'

Aiden hesitated. Alex obviously had a girlfriend, the woman he'd seen him with several weeks ago, but he'd flatly denied it and Aiden didn't spread gossip. 'Not that he's ever told me about,' he replied. He glanced away. It wasn't a lie – Alex had never admitted to a girlfriend – but then it wasn't the whole truth either.

'He hasn't mentioned any deals to you recently, offered you any tips for the market?'

'No, not at all.'

'Has he talked about anything he's recently bought? Like a new car, a property? Has he mentioned any holidays?'

'No, he...' Aiden broke off. He hated the idea of snitching on his mates but then he did know about the car, he had seen the car.

'I should remind you, Mr Thornton, that withholding information won't do you or Mr Stanton any good at all.'

Aiden swallowed. This was an informal chat, she'd told him – he wasn't under any oath. Besides, Alex had told him he'd had the car for some time. It wasn't new; he'd expressly said it wasn't new.

'No, he's not said anything to me about any of that.' That wasn't a lie. Aiden was satisfied that he wasn't lying.

'So there's nothing out of the ordinary about Mr Stanton's behaviour as far as you can tell?'

'No. He seems completely normal to me, there's nothing out of the ordinary at all.' That wasn't the truth either. The last time they'd seen Alex at the health club he'd been distinctly odd, dead cagey about the girl he had been with, but also kind of smug. What had Sophie called him? The smug bastard in the flash tennis kit. But

Aiden didn't mention that, he said nothing about it at all.

'I see.' Janice made a note on her pad. It read: Not admitting all he knows. Find out more. 'Well,' she said, 'to sum up then, you are absolutely sure that Mr Stanton has not mentioned anything to you that might be construed as out of the ordinary. Is that right?'

'I'm not "absolutely sure", no. I think, "to the best of my knowledge" is a better phrase. I'm not absolutely sure about anything to be honest with you, Ms...'

'Stimpson.'

'Ms Stimpson.'

Janice made another note. It read: Will buckle under pressure.

'OK, then there's nothing more to add.' Janice stood up. 'Thank you for your time, Mr Thornton. Perhaps we might be able to talk to you again in the course of this investigation.'

'Yes, certainly.'

'And if there's anything at all that you think might be relevant to our enquiry, then please...' Janice held out her business card and Aiden took it. 'Do give me a call, won't you?'

'Yes, thanks, I will,' Aiden headed for the door, but before opening it he turned and said, 'What exactly are you investigating Alex for?' Janice looked directly at him. 'Insider trading,' she said. Aiden took a breath. 'Right, I see.' He left the room and made his way outside. He did see too. He took out his phone and immediately called Sophie. He had the awful feeling that he saw only too well.

Bill Redfern swung his Mercedes – silver, series 500 – into a space at the opposite end of the car park to Stan Gamley's Rover and climbed out. Stan was waiting for him on the wall by the cafe, drinking tea from a polystyrene cup.

'Stan.'

Gamley stood up and chucked the last of his tea on to the ground.

'I'll just get myself a drink and then we can go for a little wander,' Redfern said. He went to the cafe and bought a carton of orange juice. It was warm today and he had no idea how Gamley could drink hot tea in weather like this. He dug the straw into the carton and took a sip as he approached Gamley. 'Come on,' he said, 'let's walk.' The two men headed up the path towards the woodland.

'I took a trip to the pub this morning,' Redfern said, 'spoke to the young girl behind the bar. She told me quite a bit about your young man.'

They were walking uphill now and Gamley was short of breath. He didn't answer.

'His name's Sayer, Rupert Sayer, and apparently he's a freelance journalist, or so he says.'

'Yeah? What's that got to do with me then?'

'He's working on a story, Stan, undercover, about local council planning.'

Gamley stopped and looked at Redfern. 'What the fuck's going on? How the fuck has he got anything on fucking town planning? Jesus! If any of those little bastards in my office have been shooting their mouths off, then I'll...'

'Calm down!' Redfern snapped. Gamley

341

stopped, the physical exertion of his anger and the walk leaving him breathless. 'He's got nothing on you, it's all speculation at the moment, hence the snooping around. No one's said a word, he's just some interfering snotty little prat who's got big ideas. OK? He's got nothing on you, Stan, nothing on you and nothing on me. He's been cataloguing development over the past year and he thinks he knows something, thinks he's made some kind of connection. He knows fuck all!'

Redfern started walking again. Gamley hurried to catch up.

'What if he does find something? What if he gets lucky?'

'What is there to find out, Stan? Who the hell knows about this whole thing? You, me, and that young bloke; what's his name? Dave or Darren?'

'Derek.'

'Yeah, Derek. There's a couple of people on the council who I deal with but they're not likely to blow their own cover; too well-paid for what they do to want to mess things up. So how can there be a problem, Stan? Everything is under control.'

Gamley went quiet for a moment and Redfern turned to him. 'If there is a problem, you'd be advised to tell me now, Stan.'

'There's no problem,' Gamley answered.

'Good.' Redfern took the path to the right and cut down through the trees. He walked at quite a pace and Gamley struggled to keep up with him. 'So what do we do?' Gamley asked, as they reached the path on the other side of the patch of woods and started back for the car park. 'We don't do anything,' Redfern replied. 'You just wait. If things start to get out of control then I'll handle it.'

Gamley didn't really know Redfern that well. They did business, that was all there was to it, but he had always sensed that Redfern had a ruthless streak. He let very little get in his way. So Gamley said, 'What's that supposed to mean, Bill?'

Redfern shrugged. They were back in sight of the car park now and he cut off the path across the grass towards his car.

Gamley stopped, watched him for a moment and wondered about running after him, demanding an answer. He dismissed the idea as ridiculous and turned away. Whatever it meant, perhaps it was better not to know. He followed the path and made his way to his car. By the time he looked across the car park Redfern had gone.

Janie was in the kitchen when Andrew came home. It was early, six-thirty, but Katie was in bed reading and the house was quiet. She was cooking. She had been cooking all day

'Hello.' He came in and across to her, without kissing her cheek. 'What's all this?'

'I'm filling the freezer,' she said. And filling my life, she thought.

'Why?'

She shrugged. 'Something to do really.'

'Ah.' Andrew took his jacket off and hung it over the back of a chair. He seemed tense, upset even, but Janie didn't ask why; she wasn't sure she wanted to know. He went to the fridge and

343

took out an open bottle of wine. 'Drink?'

'Yes, thanks.'

Andrew poured some wine and left the glass on the side for her. Janie washed the pastry off her hands and took the glass. She sipped, waiting for Andrew to speak.

'I had a call from the bank this afternoon,' he said. Janie started. He'd said it so casually that it almost misled her, it almost sounded like a normal comment. She looked down at her hands. 'Why, Janie?' he asked. 'What on earth do you need forty-five thousand pounds for?' His voice was calm, restrained, and it unnerved Janie. Andrew wasn't angry, he had gone past that. He had a contained, deep-seated fury that had hardened into something much worse than anger and Janie knew it. She couldn't even look up at him.

'If you had perhaps explained what the problem was we might have talked about it. If you had told me why, then perhaps we could have discussed it. That is, or was, our emergency money – it is there in case the children ever need it, in case we ever had to bail any of them or ourselves out of serious trouble. It is there, Janie, as our security. You took it away, you took our security away. I presume it was for investment into the stock market?'

She nodded.

'I thought so.' Andrew finished his glass of wine and walked over to the sink where he rinsed the glass and placed it on the draining board. Just like him, Janie thought, to finish everything so neatly. He walked out of the kitchen. Janie went after him. In the bedroom he had put a sailing bag on to the bed and was filling it carefully with his clothes.

'Andrew? Andrew, what are you doing?' Janie came across to him and tugged at his arm. 'Andrew?' He shrugged her away and carried on. 'Andrew, stop it!' she suddenly cried. 'Please stop all this nonsense. Please, can't we talk about it?'

He stood and faced her. 'Janie, that is exactly what I have wanted to say to you for a long time, and not just since you started all this stupid stuff about the investment club and making money and having a life of your own. For over a year, all I've wanted to do was talk to you. But you wouldn't; you didn't want to talk and you wanted to do your own thing. Fine, OK, that's fine. Well you've done your own thing, you've gone ahead and pleased yourself without any regard for anyone else. It's been all about you. And this...' He walked into the bathroom and took his toiletries bag off the shelf. 'This is about me.' He put it into the holdall and zipped it up. 'I need some space. I need to think.' He picked the bag up and headed for the door, but Katie stood out on the landing in her nightie, blocking his way. She said, 'What's the matter, Daddy? Where are you going?'

Andrew knelt and dropped his bag down on the floor. He took both her hands in his. 'I've got to go away for a little while, for work. I'll ring you though, tomorrow night after school, and I'll see you maybe at the weekend...' He broke off as his voice cracked and Janie had to turn away. She wiped her face on the sleeve of her shirt and said,

'Jump into bed, poppet, and I'll come and tuck you up in a few minutes, OK?' Katie stood where she was. She didn't know what to do. She could sense that there was something horribly wrong, she could feel the stress and emotion that hung in the air, but she didn't understand it. She was confused. Both her parents were denying there was anything wrong; acting so strangely but saying normal things. She stood her ground for a few moments longer, then she turned and went back to her room. Janie's heart ached.

'Andrew, please...' Andrew headed down the stairs and opened the front door. In the hallway Janie held on to his arm. 'Andrew, please don't be rash, please don't...' But he pulled himself away and walked out of the house. Janie started to cry. He climbed into the car, started the engine and reversed round. Minutes later he had driven off and Janie stood, still in the open doorway, staring at the empty drive.

'Mummy?' Katie called from upstairs. Janie closed the door and went into the kitchen for a tissue. Blowing her nose and hurriedly wiping her face, she checked her reflection in the mirror before she climbed the stairs. 'I'm coming, darling,' she called back, 'don't worry, Mummy's coming.'

Aiden met Sophie for a drink straight after work. He told her all about his meeting with Janice Stimpson, from the Stock Exchange surveillance team, and all the time he was talking he turned her business card over and over between his thumb and forefinger.

'Will you ring her?' Sophie asked.

'And tell her what? That I think Alex might be up to something or that he might be having an affair with someone he shouldn't?' He stared morosely into his beer. 'It's all might bes and hearsay, Soph. It's not enough to snitch on your friends for.'

'Sorry, I didn't realise he was a friend,' Sophie said. 'I didn't realise that he'll be helping you out if you get done for withholding information in the course of an investigation.'

'They can't do that, can they?'

She nodded. Actually she didn't know, but she wasn't going to have Aiden take a chance for that arrogant, smug bastard they'd met at the Riverside. 'Look, Aiden,' she said, 'as far as I can make out you know two things. Firstly that Alex Stanton is seeing someone but he flatly denied it, which is suspicious in itself, and secondly that he's making an awful lot more money than you, either legitimately or not. That's all you have to tell this woman. Both of those things are not hearsay, they're things you know. Let her decide what they mean.'

Aiden shook his head. He really didn't know what to do.

'Aiden! I really don't see your problem. It's him or you. Do you really want to get done for perverting the course of justice? Insider trading is a criminal offence, you know!'

Aiden stood up. Sophie was right, of course she was right, but he was sick of hearing she was right. 'I'm off home,' he said.

'But you haven't finished your beer.'

He shrugged. 'You have it,' he said and he walked out of the pub.

Half an hour later, when he got home, Aiden Thornton rang Janice Stimpson's mobile number and spoke to her direct. He told her what he knew, nothing more, but he hated himself for doing so. When he'd rung off he poured himself a large glass of whisky and downed it in one. Then he went down to his local and got completely off his face.

Chapter Eighteen

Janice Stimpson was in work early; after the phone call from Aiden Thornton last night she was eager to get started. The first thing she did was to re-work her way through the list of phone calls that Alex Stanton had received in the period from February through to the present day. Even though she had done it already she was now looking for clues as to who Stanton might be involved with. It took her all morning, but by lunchtime she had something to go on; by lunchtime she knew that if Thornton was right and Stanton did have a girlfriend, it certainly wasn't a relationship he was admitting to. He'd had a fair number of personal calls, but none intimate as far as she could tell. Janice sat back and chewed the end of her pencil. Why not if he was seeing someone? Chatting on the phone – in Janice's limited experience – was a relatively large part of romance. He was obviously as careful with his personal life as he was with his professional life and that begged questioning.

Janice went to see her supervisor.

'I'd like to request some time off for surveillance,' she said, as he glanced at her notes.

'It's not customary, Janice,' he replied.

'I realise that, but I think I could get a handle on this if I had some time on surveillance. There are some answers that I'm not going to find unless I get out there and start searching.'

Her supervisor put down her notes and looked at her.

'Janice, this is not within my jurisdiction, you understand that, don't you? I cannot give you permission to do surveillance work, it is not something that we recognise.'

Janice sighed. 'But in the past I've...'

The supervisor held up his hands to stop her. 'In the past you have requested time off to work at home on the case, Janice, and I have always granted it.'

She looked at him. 'I see. So I need to request some time off to work on this case at home, right?'

'In writing please, Janice. If you can put a note on my desk within the next hour or so, I can grant you time off with immediate effect. I'm out for the afternoon after one o'clock, so you need to do it before then.'

Janice smiled. 'Thank you,' she said. 'I'll do it right away.'

It was just before lunch and so far that morning Alex had done bugger all. He had sat for nearly three hours now and watched the screen. The price of Wye Valley Organic Foods had gone bananas, just as he'd expected it to after the frenzy of coverage in the weekend press about the take-over. It had shot up from fifty-five pence at the close of play on Friday night to one pound at the end of play on Monday. And Alex had watched it climb steadily since then to its current price of one pound eighty pence. He was mesmerised by the screen; every call he'd taken he had cut short so as to be able to get back to the small yellow numbers on the right side of it, the ever-changing, ever-increasing numbers.

But Alex was nervous. He didn't feel excited or triumphant or even comfortable about his investment, he just felt nervous. To take a big position in a stock almost immediately prior to the announcement of a bid situation was always cause for speculation and sometimes even investigation by the Stock Exchange. That was the last thing he needed. Investigations, no matter how innocent the party involved, left a sour atmosphere and the atmosphere in the office this morning was certainly odd. It was nothing tangible, just an undercurrent of tension, and ridiculous as he knew it was he couldn't help feeling that everyone knew what he was doing, that everyone knew he'd taken a massive position on Wye Valley Organic Foods just before their announcement. It made him uneasy, self-conscious and uneasy. Perhaps he should just get rid of the stock, call it a day and sell at one eighty. Hell, it was a phenomenal profit with that amount of stock, even after the capital gains tax. He fiddled with his pencil and jotted a few figures down on a piece of paper. They looked good. He tore the piece of paper up, then scrunched the pieces into a ball and chucked it at the bin. He'd ring Sarah, that's what he'd do. He'd call her and see what she wanted to do. He took his mobile out of his case, left the office and in the corridor rang Sarah's home number. She answered straight away.

Sarah had come in from Duffields with four bags of shopping, all sopping wet from the sudden torrential downpour of rain that had hit just as she'd climbed out of the car. She heard the phone, dropped the shopping just inside the front door and ran to pick up the receiver, leaving a trail of wet footprints on her newly hoovered carpet. 'Shit,' she muttered; then, 'Hello?'

'Sarah, it's Alex Stanton. I'm just ringing with the latest on Wye Valley.'

'Oh, great! I had a look on Ceefax this morning before I left for work. I just can't believe it, it's doing incredibly well, isn't it?'

'That's why I'm calling. It's up to one eighty and I was thinking that perhaps, if you agree, we should get out sooner rather than later.'

Sarah sat down. 'How soon?' she asked.

'Possibly by the close of play.'

'Why?'

Alex thought, because I'm nervous; because I'm stretched to breaking point on this one and I don't know if I can take the stress. I just want out and done with it before anyone from Stock Exchange surveillance starts sniffing round me and ruining my job prospects. But he said, 'Because we've done bloody well and I don't want to take the risk any further.' Because, he suddenly wanted to confide, I have the oddest feeling this morning that things aren't too good. No one is chatting, no one is stopping by my desk, something is going down. I can just sense it and I hope to God it's nothing to do with me.

Sarah held the phone and tapped the wire

against her leg. Alex was edgy. They had a hell of a lot at stake and he was edgy, but then they'd bought all that stock in order to be able to use it to their advantage and they hadn't even got close. What was the point in taking such a big position if they weren't even going to use it? She said, 'I'd better ring round, Alex. I'm not sure it's the right time to sell. Let me make a few calls and ring you back. OK?'

Alex wanted to say, no, it's not OK. I'm the broker, take my advice. But he had always been deferential to clients and old habits die hard. 'OK,' he said. 'We'll speak after lunch.' He hung up and Sarah got on with bringing her shopping in.

Janie was in bed when the phone rang. Organised, diligent Janie had left the house in a mess, last night's supper – if you could call it that – still on the plates in the kitchen, the chaos of breakfast things untouched, no curtains drawn, no cushions plumped, washing left dirty on the landing, beds unmade, nothing done. She rolled over and tried to ignore the bleeping, then sat up and swore when it carried on. The room was half-dark and smelt of smoke, alcohol and bad breath. She stood up, the phone rang on and in the end she answered it.

'Hello?' Her stomach turned. The full ashtray on the bedside table made her feel nauseous and her head was thumping.

'Janie? It's Sarah. Are you all right? You sound terrible.'

Janie sat down on the bed, knocking a half-full

wine glass over as she did so, and tears welled up in her eyes. She wiped them on the hem of her night-dress and blew her nose. 'I'm fine,' she said, but Sarah on the other end knew she wasn't. 'I just feel a bit...' but a sob caught in her throat and she couldn't finish. 'A bit weepy...' she said finally. Sarah bit her lip. She looked at her watch and thought that she could probably get over there for an hour before she had to pick Rory up from school.

'I'll come over,' she said.

'No,' Janie answered, 'no don't, please, I'm fine.' Pride. Janie, perfect Janie who had everything, couldn't bear to think of anyone seeing her with less than that. 'I'll be at school,' she said, 'I'll see you then.' She reached for the lamp switch and turned it on, the light hurting her head. 'What did you want, Sarah? Was it anything important?'

'Wye Valley,' Sarah answered. 'Alex Stanton wants to sell today. The price is one eighty and for some reason he wants to get out. What d'you think?'

Janie sighed. What did she think? She thought that she had been stupid, that she had risked everything for nothing. She thought that Andrew had done what he'd always done, walked away from a situation, only this time physically not just mentally She thought that she had been trying to fill a void in her life that she would never be able to fill. It was there, whatever she did, whatever she thought. It was always there – a big gaping hole waiting for her to fall into it, waiting to swallow her up, to cover her with darkness. She said, 'I think we should do what Alex says.' And she said it because it meant that she didn't have to think.

On the other end Sarah worried. This wasn't Janie, this wasn't what she had expected. 'Are you absolutely sure, Janie?' she asked.

'Yes,' Janie replied. There was a silence; Sarah didn't know what to do. Then Janie said, 'I've got to go, Sarah. I'll see you later.'

'OK, fine.' They said goodbye and Sarah rang off. Janie lay back on the bed and stared up at the ceiling. Was she sure? Was she absolutely sure? Janie wasn't even sure that she knew who she was anymore. She closed her eyes. How could she be sure of anything? Nothing was ever what it seemed.

Sarah rang Roz, but caught her at a bad moment. Kids screaming, Graham moaning and the cow with some sort of infection that threatened the birth of the calf. She listened to what Sarah had to say, then made her decision. She didn't want to hang around, to take any more risk than they had done already. She had enough on her plate; if the deal was ready to be closed, then close it, don't piss about. She said exactly that to Sarah and Sarah rang off, not offended, but uncertain that anyone was thinking straight. She sat on the bottom stair in the hallway of her small, neat house and wondered what to do. Then she had an idea. She went to her bag and took out her diary. In it she had Marcus's mobile phone number. It was a bit of an imposition, she realised that, to interrupt his holiday, but this was important. It would be crazy to make the wrong decision just because Alex said so. She dialled the number, waited for the connection and was mildly surprised to hear the line ring; she hadn't really expected to get through.

'Hello, Marcus Todd.'

'Marcus, hello. It's Sarah.'

'Sarah?'

The line was clear so he couldn't have mistaken her name. Sarah blushed. 'Sarah Greg,' she said, 'from the investment club.'

'Oh, of course.'

Sarah waited for something else, some sort of warm and friendly greeting, but nothing was forthcoming so she said, 'Sorry to bother you, Marcus, on your holiday, but I've got a bit of a problem with this Wye Valley Organic Foods investment.'

There was a silence and Sarah waited. 'The one you recommended?'

There was another silence, then Marcus said slowly, 'I don't remember recommending anything to you, Sarah. I might have mentioned something in passing, but I certainly never make recommendations outside of my job.'

Sarah's first reaction was surprise, her second was embarrassment. She had made an error, called at a bad time.

'No, no, of course not, it's just that...' She broke off, losing her nerve.

'Just that what?'

'Oh, I, erm, I just thought, wondered, if you might know whether it would be right to sell them now or...' Her voice trailed away. There was an icy silence on the other end, then he said, 'I am afraid that I really have no idea.'

'No, no, of course not,' she murmured.

'Was there anything else?'

'No, nothing else.'

'Goodbye, Sarah.' Sarah stared at her hands as the faint click on the line told her that Marcus had disconnected, then she replaced the receiver and stood up. That, she thought, had to be one of the most painful phone calls she'd made in a long time. She took a long deep breath to calm herself, then picked up the phone again to call Alex.

Alex sold the shares in Wye Valley for a total of one pound ninety-five pence a share at two o'clock that afternoon. He did the deal and immediately afterwards called Lucie and arranged to meet her after work. He needed some company and was hoping for sex: he could do with a little physical comfort. They usually went up to the West End to drink, but tonight Lucie didn't have time. She could only spare an hour and, disappointed but still desperate to see her, Alex arranged to meet her at a wine bar in St Paul's. He wouldn't normally have taken that kind of risk, but he was tired, stressed and not thinking straight. So they made a date and after that he called Sarah to let her know that he had sold the shares and to tell her how much profit they had collectively made.

In the Stock Exchange surveillance room, IMAS picked the transaction up and Janice Stimpson, just going off for the day, knew that she was on to something substantial. She took a print-out of the sale and added it to her file, then she packed up her desk and went on her way. She had work to do and she was really looking forward to it.

Sarah called Janie. She called Janie and said, 'Alex sold the shares at one pound ninety-five pence a share. That means we've each made roughly two hundred and twenty-three thousand pounds.' She was breathless as she said it, hardly able to contain her excitement. 'Janie, it's amazing and it's all down to you! You were the one who started all this, you were the one who made it happen. I can't believe it, I...' Sarah stopped. 'Janie? Janie, are you still there?' But Janie wasn't. The line was dead and when Sarah tried to ring straight back all she got was the engaged tone. She tried several times more, then she called Roz.

Roz put the phone down in the kitchen and stood for quite some time looking out of the French windows at the small courtyard garden where Graham was sweeping away the rain debris. But she didn't see Graham, the brickwork or the pots or the rain still drizzling down as he swept. Roz saw the fields at the back of her land, she saw the green horizon stretching out far beyond her line of vision and she knew that it could be hers. The relief made her want to cry. She went outside and stood in the shelter of the doorway for a moment, until Graham had swept the pile neatly against the wall.

'Don't just stand there, woman,' he muttered,

bending with a piece of card to scoop the debris into the wheelbarrow.

'Why not? You do it so beautifully it seems a shame to interrupt you.'

Graham flicked a dead leaf at her and smiled. 'White, one sugar please, love,' he said.

'You'll be lucky.'

He finished the job in hand, then looked up at her. 'Can I help you?'

'The shares,' Roz said, 'in Wye Valley Organic Foods?'

Graham folded his arms and stared at her. She noticed that his face had set, waiting for disappointment, and she wondered if that's what he had come to expect from her; disappointment.

'Alex sold them this afternoon. We made a profit of one pound fifty-five pence per share.' Graham dropped his brush and came across to her, taking her into his embrace. He said nothing and neither did she. They stood like that, hugging tightly, then she pulled back and said, 'Shall we buy the Gordens' land? We've got enough money, you know.'

Graham stroked her cheek. 'Not at developer's prices, no. We'll wait until Jack's done his bit and then we'll offer them what it's really worth. OK?'

Roz nodded. 'OK.' She turned away back towards the house and as she did so Graham let out a roar of triumph.

Janice sat in the foyer of the Chartered Municipal Bank which was opposite White Lowen and waited for Alex Stanton to leave the building. She had been there since five, it was now six-fifteen

359

and, as she glanced down at her watch for a time check, then up at the building again, she saw someone she thought might be him come down the steps and fasten his raincoat before heading off. She checked the photo the bank's human resources director had given her and saw it was definitely Stanton. 'Bingo!' she muttered and, glancing at the security man, she was on her way. Janice had done this before, several times, and of course she was a great fan of crime novels and thrillers on the telly. She knew what she was doing. She kept her distance and followed Stanton down through the City, up Cornhill and towards St Paul's. She saw him enter the Corney and Barrow wine bar on the corner of Paternoster Row and bought herself an *Evening Standard* before following him inside. She took a seat at the other end of the bar, ordered herself a glass of wine and took out the paper to wait.

Lucie was feeling frail. She had been working long hours, she was tired and lonely and she needed this time with Alex. It had been over a week since she'd seen him and she needed it more than she was able to say. Coming into the bar, she saw him just inside the door and smiled. He smiled back, hands in pockets; a warm, charming grin that made her heart melt. Lucie had always been tough and given as good as she got, but she had also always had a fatally romantic side. Perhaps it balanced the toughness, perhaps it was just escapism from the harsh reality of her job, but whatever it was, without thinking at that moment it got the better of her.

When she saw Alex she went across and kissed him, forgetting completely where she was.

He kissed her back. He was relieved, he was feeling euphoric with success and for a moment he didn't give a shit about being careful. For a moment he just wanted to feel the warmth of her lips and breathe in that wonderful, sharp scent that she wore.

'Hello.'

'Hi.'

'Drink?'

'Wine, please. No, stay there, I'll get it. Shall I get a bottle? I could do with a couple of glasses myself. I've got to work tonight, but it'll help get through the boredom, waiting for documents to be checked.' Lucie went to the bar. She ordered a bottle of Meursault and took out her credit card to pay for it. Normally they had the house white, it was perfectly acceptable, but tonight she wanted to treat them both so she picked the expensive white burgundy and paid for it on Visa.

She took it back to the table with two glasses and Alex poured. Lucie slipped her raincoat off and sat down.

'You look tired,' she said to Alex.

'Not really, just a bit stressed.' He wanted to tell her about Wye Valley, but he couldn't. She hadn't wanted to know about the investment club from the first; it was a subject they simply didn't discuss. 'And you,' he went on, 'look wonderful. It's good to see you, Lucie.'

She smiled again, enjoying the moment. She didn't know what was going on in her life, what Alex wanted from her or indeed what she wanted from him, and perhaps that made her more reckless. But she did want this moment; it had been an unhappy week and she wanted to enjoy every second of the time with Alex. They tapped glasses and drank to each other, then Alex said, 'Move a bit closer, or as close as we dare.'

Lucie shuffled her chair in towards him and under the table he put his hand on her leg and gently stroked it. Why not, he thought, no one can see us. That was his biggest mistake.

Across the bar, Janice didn't miss a trick. She had perfect eyesight and was incredibly observant. She could describe a place almost to the last detail once she had seen it and now, watching Alex and Lucie, she took in every movement made, every intimacy shared, and she knew that once again surveillance had paid off. She observed them for the whole hour they spent in each other's company. She watched them leave the bar, part company, saw the goodbye kiss and waited where she was for five minutes to make sure that they didn't come back. Then she went up to the bar.

'Hello, can I help you?' The young woman behind the bar was Australian. They get everywhere, Janice thought briefly. I wonder why when they have such a nice place at home.

'Can I have a word with the manager?'

The girl's face clouded and Janice added, 'No complaint, I'd just like to ask him something.'

'Oh, sure.' The young woman disappeared and a man returned in her place; mid-thirties, Janice thought, public school.

'Can I help you?'

362

'Yes, I hope so. My name is Stimpson, Janice Stimpson.' Janice took out her card for the Stock Exchange and held it up. 'I work for the Stock Exchange surveillance team and I'm currently investigating a case of insider trading. There was a young woman in here a few minutes ago who paid for a bottle of wine on her Visa card. It was a bottle of...' Janice glanced down at the note she had made on the back of the *Evening Standard*. 'A bottle of Meursault.' She pronounced it Meee-r-salt and the manager felt duty-bound to correct her.

'Meursault,' he said in his best French. 'What about it?'

'Could I possibly have a look at the credit card slip?'

The manager raised an eyebrow 'I'm not sure,' he replied. 'This is a very peculiar request.'

'Not at all, it is simply part of an enquiry.'

'Can I see your card again, please?'

Janice took her ID out of her pocket once more and held it out. The manager took it, stared hard at it, then, after hesitating for a few moments, finally agreed to her request. He opened the till, rifled through some of the slips of paper, then found the one for the Meursault. He handed it over, glancing round the bar as he did so to make sure no one was looking.

Janice looked at the slip. Lucie Croft. She took her notebook out and began to write down the number, but the manager stopped her. 'I'm terribly sorry,' he said, 'but I really can't let you take down the number. It would be foolish, you could be anyone. You've seen the name on the

363

receipt, that's as much information as I'm prepared to give you. If you'd like to come back with the police, then...'

Janice smiled. Uptight bastard, she thought, definitely public school. She put her notebook away and said, 'Of course.' She hated to be thwarted in the course of her investigation, no matter how sensible the reason. 'Well, thanks anyway, that's been a great help.'

He nodded, turning to make a note of her name on a slip of paper. 'You won't mind if I contact the Stock Exchange tomorrow morning and just check on who you are, will you?' he asked, turning round. But it was a rhetorical question. Janice had gone.

The office was empty when Janice got back there at eight p.m. She could have just gone home, thought about this and dealt with it in the morning. That's what any normal person would have done, but then Janice wasn't normal, not when it came to work anyway. She had a kind of evangelistic zeal – she was on the crusade for justice and she thought of it as her goal, her mission.

So, at eight that evening, Janice sat at her desk and set about finding out who Lucie Croft was. She was prepared for a long haul; she had sandwiches and a can of drink and had stacked up on change for the drinks machine. Everyone who worked in the City could be traced, one way or another, through the Stock Exchange or the Financial Services Authority. There were lists from the banks and finance houses, there were lists of analysts and accountants. Everyone could be traced. It was a mammoth task but it was not insurmountable. If Lucie Croft worked in the City – and Janice was convinced by her weird sixth sense that she did – then Janice would find out who she was.

Then she would nail her. Just like she'd nailed every other thieving bastard she'd uncovered in her work at the Stock Exchange.

Chapter Nineteen

Bill Redfern stood at the front door of his executive home – three years old and built by Glover Homes, with four bedrooms, a luxury kitchen and top of the range specification – and waved to Sheila as she reversed out of the drive in her soft-top black VW Golf GTi. He glanced down at his trousers – Hugo Boss, khaki, front pleat with turn-up – and shifted his belt – black leather, silver buckle, Giorgio Armani – so that it sat perfectly in the centre of his waistband. Things mattered to Bill. People he could live without, but things, where they came from, what image they created and what label they carried, were paramount. He liked to have the best and he was under the misguided – but popular – impression that a designer label meant he had made it. And all Bill Redfern cared about was the fact that after years and years of struggle he had arrived. That was something he was certain of. That was something that he would never, not for anything, give up.

Bill Redfern was forty-one. He was a well-groomed forty-one, with all his hair intact and a still reasonably firm six-pack in his abdominal region. Appearances were important; he kept himself in good shape. He was happily married – or at least contented – to Sheila, a woman who shared his energy and drive for materialism and who he felt had taken him into the higher rungs of management and would continue to do so as the years went on. Bill was ambitious; he was doing well now, but he wanted to do better. He had worked for Glover Homes for twenty-one years. Twenty-one years of hard graft, of careful and clever manoeuvring, of always being in the right place at whatever time. He was the land buyer now, he earned a high five-figure salary, had an excellent pension plan and looked forward to a good eight to ten per cent bonus every year. But it hadn't been easy. He'd joined Glover Homes straight from technical college with a City and Guilds in building and he'd worked his way up from the bottom. He had done well in the boom time and ridden the late eighties property depression with all the skill and cunning he could muster. He was a clever operator was Bill Redfern, and he became more clever the more he achieved. He wasn't an honest man, but then who was in business? He got the job done, achieved the best results and that's all that mattered – certainly all that mattered to Bill. With his careful land buying, Glover Homes had made some insightful decisions over the past ten years, decisions that had taken them up into the top league of builders.

Yes, Bill Redfern had made it. Three holidays a year, weekends away, designer clothes and restaurants, silver Merc; in short almost anything that he wanted. Almost. Only recently, in the midst of all this success, there had developed the tiniest irritation in Bill Redfern's life, like a small mosquito bite on his arm. It was an irritation that he would not tolerate.

So, standing at the doorway of his home, he waved to Sheila, then went inside and into the study that she had just finished decorating for him. He sat at his Victorian partner's desk – reproduction, but who'd ever notice – and admired its mahogany veneer with dark green embossed leatherette. He switched on his PC and sat down to answer his e-mails. He was working from home today; he had something to sort out that he didn't want to do at the office. So he replied to the mail on his system, filed some personal finance papers away, then began making his calls. He started with the Glover office in Lewes, East Sussex. Glover Homes had seven regional offices and Bill needed to call every one of them. Something was going on; the bite was beginning to itch.

'Hello, planning and development please,' he said when the line connected. The switchboard put him on hold, he heard the first few bars of a popular classic and was then put through to the office he needed.

'Hello, Pat Belling please...'

'I'm sorry but he's in a meeting. I'm the office secretary, can I help at all?'

Bill already knew this; he had all the planning meetings in his diary and Sharon was the one he really needed to speak to. He wanted to keep this thing very low-key 'Oh, yes, hello Sharon, I wonder if you can. It's Bill Redfern here, from head office.'

'Hello, Mr Redfern, what can I do for you?'

'Sharon, I've had a couple of calls from some of

my people saying that there's been some journalist bloke ringing round the planning and development offices asking questions and I just wondered if he'd got through to you at all?'

'Yes, Mr Redfern, he called on Monday He wanted to know who dealt with our land buying for this area so I gave him Mr Belling's name and number. I told him as well that most of the decisions were made by yourself and Mr Ashby, the director.'

Shit, Bill thought. 'You told him, did you, Sharon, that we have a strict land-buying policy and that it is always adhered to?'

'Yes, Mr Redfern.' Actually she hadn't said that at all, she'd had quite a nice chat with Rupert Sayer. He'd been so easy to talk to and they'd arranged to meet for a drink a week on Wednesday. He was really nice – if you could tell that from a voice and Sharon believed you could. He certainly sounded a lot nicer than the blokes she met down the Hand and Spear. And he was a journalist too, he was going places; further than the seventies night at Rafters, the local night club, anyway.

'Well done, Sharon. Did he want to know anything in particular, ask about anyone in particular?'

'No, not really, Mr Redfern, just general stuff.' That wasn't true either. He'd asked quite a bit about the decision-making process for land buying and how involved Mr Redfern was and whether she knew of any connections he had with the district council. He'd had a list of names which he'd read out and she'd recognised one or two of them. He'd said he was doing a feature on local development and the benefits for the community, so she'd told him about the funding for the leisure centre and the proposal for a small, covered shopping area, which she wasn't supposed to know about, but then when you typed things you couldn't help reading them, could you?

'Good, glad to hear it. Now, if he rings again could you possibly give me a call, Sharon? I'd just like to keep abreast of the situation, just in case he writes something he shouldn't.'

Sharon looked at her nails, false and bright red. She was pleased with them, they made her look sophisticated. 'Of course, Mr Redfern.' It wasn't that she didn't like Bill Redfern, or that she didn't have some kind of feeling for the job, but she had no intention of telling him if Rupert rang again. Why should she? She was only a secretary, she owed the company nothing.

'Thanks, Sharon. Take care now.'

'Yes, Mr Redfern. Bye.'

Bill hung up and looked at the phone. He had been an expert liar all his life and, being such a good one, he found it easy to spot anyone who wasn't up to his standard. And Sharon was very naïve; she couldn't tell a lie to save her life. Rupert Sayer had been on the phone and chatting her up, that much was obvious, and she had fallen for it, for whatever line he'd spun her: dinner, perhaps, at somewhere other than Pizza Hut. He had probably, if not certainly, asked questions about Redfern and possibly, if not probably, had a good idea by now that there were many things that influenced a decision to buy land, not just price, location and availability. Redfern drew a couple of rectangular boxes on the sheet of paper in front of him – his usual doodle – and began filling them in with black ink. He broke off for a few moments to make a note under Sharon's name and the office, then reached for the phone to make his next call. As he did so it rang and startled him. Bill was oddly superstitious about this sort of thing; fate and all that. He picked the receiver up.

'Hello, Bill Redfern.'

'Bill, it's Peter Ashby.'

'Hello, Peter, how are you?' Bill's voice took on a slightly deferential tone. Peter was his director.

'Fine.' Ashby was short and abrupt; it was his manner. 'Bill, there have been a couple of calls, to various offices, from some journalist chappie.'

'I know, I'm on to it.'

'Good.' There was a brief silence, then Peter said, 'Make sure you are, Bill, because Glover Homes has a reputation and we can't afford for any members of our team to be caught doing something that they shouldn't.'

There was another brief silence, then Bill said, 'Of course.' He'd got the message. Everyone knew how land buying went, all the senior management knew the way it worked and if they didn't then they were bloody stupid. How else had Glover Homes got to where it was today? Quality land didn't just appear, it had to be worked for, bargained for and it involved risk. Bill looked at his screen. There was an e-mail from the MD waiting for him; another warning.

So the risk's all mine, he thought; whatever's been done in the full knowledge of the senior management is now something I have to take sole responsibility for. Bill well and truly got the message. He said, 'I've got it completely under control, Peter. Please make sure everyone knows that.'

'Thank you,' Ashby said, 'I will.' And he hung up.

Bill stared at the screen and thought about reading his e-mail. He thought about what he'd done for Glover Homes, about how the MD had once called his land buying inspired but would just as easily call it corrupt in the next breath. He thought about what he'd achieved, where he was and where he wanted to be and then he stood up and walked into the kitchen. He wouldn't finish the calls, there was no point. He had other things to do now, more important things. He went back into the study to switch off his PC before he left the house and as he did so he glanced down at the sheet of paper he'd had in front of him whilst talking to Ashby. He blinked. Perhaps that too was fate, because all the little rectangular boxes he had drawn, all neatly filled in with black ink, looked just like coffins.

Rupert Sayer stood in the lounge of his small terraced cottage and surveyed the landscape of papers strewn across the floor. There were small neat piles everywhere, maps, flow charts and brochures for housing developments. He had everything worked out. It all fitted together and, with the arrogance of youth, he was extremely pleased with himself. Now he had to find the hard evidence and that, he had to admit to himself, he needed help with. It was all very well putting together a theory but he needed to back it up with proof. So far it was all circumstantial and he needed Jack's resources to change that.

Stepping over and through his filing system to the phone on the desk in the corner, he picked up the receiver and dialled the number he'd found in the phone book. He waited. The line answered and he said, 'Hello, Jack Lowe? This is Rupert Sayer. You probably don't remember me, but we met at the airport. I'm doing a story on Glover Homes.'

In his office, Jack, pleased to have an excuse to stop working on the mound of invoices Dodi was making him do, leant back in his chair, put his feet up on the desk and said, 'Of course I remember you. You run like a bloody whippet, nearly didn't catch you actually.'

Rupert smiled.

'How are you doing, Rupert? Keeping out of harm's way I hope.'

'I'm doing pretty well actually, Jack, I've made good progress with this story I think I'm on to something.'

Jack was wary 'Really?' If Rupert was on to something he hoped to God he was keeping quiet about it.

'Yes! You wouldn't believe what I've managed to wangle out of the secretaries on the phone. I've called every single Glover regional office and I've got some ace stuff out of it. I've...'

'Hang on a minute, Rupert,' Jack interrupted.

'Are you saying that you've been ringing the Glover offices personally?'

'Yes! I spoke to the secretary of each planning department and in three cases out of seven I've managed to...'

'Shit!' Jack sat up. He took a deep breath and held it for several moments, then, as slowly and as calmly as he could, he let it out.

'What's the matter?'

'Nothing! Only the fact that you've probably blown my whole bloody case!' Jack was angry but was trying hard to keep a lid on it. 'Do you really think that all these calls won't get back to Redfern and then Gamley? They'll be on to you by now and running shit-scared. They'll tighten up every tiny little crack in the operation and that'll be it, there won't be even a sniff of any wrongdoing! God, Rupert, this isn't some *Boy's Own* adventure. This is bloody serious. We're talking major bribery and corruption charges, not some tabloid scoop! The chances are that you've gone and ruined everything I've done so far!'

'Yeah? So you already know about Redfern's involvement in four other counties, do you? You already know that all land buying decisions have to go through Redfern, despite the fact that there are separate offices for Kent, East Sussex, West Sussex and Surrey and he's not even area director. You knew all this, did you? I suppose too that I didn't need to find out that in East Sussex Glover Homes funded the building of a new leisure centre and there are plans underway to fund a new shopping area, although nothing has ever been released for public knowledge on the subject.'

Jack was silent. He was thinking, shit, this boy really has done his stuff. He said, 'Rupert, I didn't know any of this.' That wasn't what Rupert was expecting and it took the sting out of his anger. 'Yeah, well...' he murmured.

'You've done an amazing job,' Jack said, 'incredible, I'm impressed.' Jack hesitated, then added, 'But you've put yourself in a difficult position, Rupert. This was hardly covert, was it?'

'I told them I was from the *Telegraph*.'

Jack rubbed his hands wearily over his face. Naïve was a word that sprang to mind, it was kinder than stupid.

'Look, Rupert, I don't know how to say this, but...' Jack took a breath. 'I don't think that will have fooled anyone. If Redfern wants to find out who you work for all he has to do is trace your calls, which I'm absolutely certain he will have done already. You, no, we are dealing with a big corporation that has a good reputation it will want to protect. Whatever is going on, it will go to extraordinary lengths to cover it up. Believe me. You should drop it, Rupert, at least for now. Leave it alone. Take a break and let things settle down.'

Rupert looked down at his work on the floor. Jack's words didn't frighten him, they just added fuel to his already burning ambition. It was a case of David and Goliath, he thought, of the weak overpowering the strong in order to seek justice. It was a romantic view, misguided and immature, but Rupert wasn't to know that. He was too

375

young to know that. Besides, this was his fortune, this was his passport into the world of investigative journalism and he wasn't about to relinquish it.

'I rang you for some help,' Rupert said. 'I thought you'd be only too happy to take advantage of my knowledge in return for nailing Redfern and Gamley.'

'I'm sorry,' Jack said, 'I can't give you any help, not at the moment, not with the situation as it is.'

'That's a shame,' Rupert said. 'I'll have to do it on my own then.'

Jack went to say something; he wanted to warn Rupert, to offer advice, to try to talk him down, but he reckoned it was pointless so kept his mouth shut. Whatever he said would go right over the boy's head; he was too young to listen, too impetuous, too arrogant. He did say, 'Rupert, be careful. Whatever you do, please, be careful.' But it wasn't enough. Later, when he went over and over that sentence in his head, he knew it wasn't enough. He could have said so much more and he didn't.

'Yeah,' Rupert said, 'thanks.' And he hung up. He dropped the receiver back in its cradle and stared at the phone for several minutes, angry and frustrated, before heading for the hall. There he took up his car keys, opened the front door and went out to his car. If Jack wasn't interested in helping then he'd have to go it alone and he might as well start immediately. He was halfway there and, despite what Jack said, he wasn't going to give up now because someone might be on to him. He wasn't going to give up full stop. Why should he? He had everything to gain from this, he thought as he climbed into his car, and nothing to lose. The arrogance of youth.

It was eleven a.m. and time for a coffee. As Janice Stimpson stood up from her desk and made her way past the fax machine, she saw the fax coming through with her name on it and smiled. But she didn't wait for it. She wanted to have her coffee at her desk and to read the fax slowly and at her leisure. She wanted to savour the moment.

Janice knew who Lucie Croft was. She had found out last night from one of her lists, had rung the human resources manager of World Bank where Lucie worked in corporate finance, raising finance for take-overs and mergers, and had requested, under Stock Exchange jurisdiction, a list of all the deals that Lucie had been involved in over the past year. The fax had the details and Janice knew she was home and dry. She would have bet her last pound on what was on that list. She was certain that one of the names was going to be Wye Valley Organic Foods.

So Janice pressed her coins into the machine, requested a cappuccino – nothing like the real thing of course – took it without spilling any from the little slot where it came out and went along for her fax. She collected it from the pile that had come through but she didn't look at it, not even a glance. She sat down at her desk, sorted the sheets into order and took a sip of coffee. Then, and only then, did she look at the list. She read down it and smiled again. There it was, just near the bottom: Wye Valley Organic Foods.

'Done it,' she said aloud. And alongside her a colleague raised his eyes heavenward and wished that Janice would get a life.

Janice's supervisor was in a meeting when Janice knocked on the door. He looked up, saw her standing outside and said to his associate, 'Ms Stimpson is outside. I'm afraid I'm going to have to postpone our meeting until later.' He could see the brown file under her arm and he knew what was coming. In one way it filled him with awe that someone could be so diligent, so meticulous and so successful, and in another it annoyed the hell out of him. He too wished that Janice would get a life.

The associate left and Janice came in. She was smiling and that also irritated him. It was one thing to take pride in one's work but this was almost a perverse joy. Somehow he couldn't quite see the glee in catching people out.

'I've got a case,' she said, 'for primary insider dealing and very probably for secondary insider dealing as well.'

The supervisor nodded. 'Well done,' he said, without returning her smile. 'Sit down, Janice, and let's see what you've got.'

Janice sat down and opened the bulging brown file. She put it on the desk in front of them both.

'I have here a list of trades for Alex Stanton, a broker with White Lowen, done for a nominee company called the Housewife Trust as well as in his own name. These trades, I believe, were made when he was party to price-sensitive information on each company. This information, I believe, was given to him by Lucie Croft, a corporate finance manager for World Bank, who was part of a team working on the take-over bid for each company. Stanton has been having an affair with Ms Croft for six months.'

The supervisor raised an eyebrow. How, he wondered, did Janice get access to that sort of information?

'And the secondary insider dealing?' he asked.

'The Housewife Trust.' Janice sat forward a little in her seat. She was excited; she had worked hard on this bit and she was pleased with herself. 'The Housewife Trust is made up of three names: Sarah Greg, Roz Betts and Janie Leighton. They are, I presume, friends or colleagues, but Janie Leighton is the clue. Leighton is her married name, Todd is her maiden name. I found that out when I was checking her bank details. Anyway, Todd is also the name of Lucie Croft's husband – he's called Marcus Todd – and it's my betting, although I haven't been able to find this out yet, that we'll discover that Marcus Todd is the brother of Janie Leighton and that Lucie Croft and Janie Leighton are sisters-in-law. That's the connection, and it's all we need.' She sat back triumphant, waiting for praise. There was a pause; actually her supervisor didn't know quite what to say.

'Well,' he began, 'Janice, you have surpassed yourself.' He didn't mean it as a compliment exactly, more as a plain statement of fact. How in God's name did she get all this? It pained him to even think about the methods she must have employed; pained him so much in fact that he didn't even try. 'That really is a remarkable piece of work.' He wasn't exaggerating either, he was amazed; only Janice could have done it. 'I think that the next stage is a foregone conclusion, Janice, don't you?'

She tried not to look eager, to keep her tongue in her mouth, to keep her breathing regular. 'Sir?'

'Let's hand it over to the DTI for a prosecution.'

Janice nodded. 'Quite right,' she replied.

He finally smiled, albeit wearily He had to, it would have been rude not to. 'Congratulations, Janice,' he said; then, 'Let's prosecute.'

Rupert Sayer was a good driver but not particularly cautious; he was too young to be cautious. He drove at speed and he drove with his music blaring. Whether this made a difference to his concentration no one would ever know.

At eleven-thirty that morning, on his way back from Chichester, he took the road to Storrington with the intention of calling in at the Boatman just outside Amberly for a drink. It had rained overnight, a heavy summer shower, and the roads were wet and slippery, the water coating the surface like oil. Rupert drove fast as he sang along to Travis on his stereo, with the window open on the driver's side and a cigarette in his right hand.

Behind him a silver Mercedes came up close. He saw it in his rear-view mirror – it had its lights on and he couldn't clearly see the driver. The Mercedes came up so close that it touched his rear bumper and Rupert momentarily lost control of his car. He swerved. He was coming into a sharp bend and he straightened rapidly, oversteering and hitting the grass verge. His car was small, a Citroën 2CV, and it over-balanced easily. The wheels went out of control and on the hard part of the bend the slick road was like an ice rink. The car swerved right across to the other side of the road as Rupert tried desperately to steer, but he had no real experience as a driver and couldn't do it. In a reflex action his foot jammed down on the accelerator and, just before a spot in the road where people stopped to take photographs of the stunning views over the River Arun, his car left the road and plummeted over the edge. It was a sheer drop. The car bounced twice, turning right over and crumpling on impact. It fell a total of one hundred and fifty feet, then stopped. There was a moment of silence, then Rupert's head fell forward on to the horn and its shrill sound split the air.

The silver Mercedes didn't even stop.

AUGUST

Chapter Twenty

It was the first day of August and it was miserable. Arctic winds blew in from the North Atlantic, dropping the air temperature down to the low sixties, and there was thick cloud overhead which blocked the light and made everything dark and grey. As Lucie made her way along to the bank from the tube it began to rain. She didn't have an umbrella and her pale fawn linen suit took on a pattern of small, dark stains.

She reached the bank and went inside, shaking the water out of her hair and greeting the reception staff. The two girls smiled back, but Lucie knew what they were thinking. By now it was all round the bank and she knew that they thought exactly as she had done when it had happened two years ago to someone else.

Stupid prat, they thought; as if earning a quarter of a million pounds and a one hundred per cent bonus wasn't enough.

She made her way to the lifts, went up to the third floor and across to the meeting room. She was bang on time – as she always was – and knocked on the door. She was told to come in and did so. Her director was there, James Colley, along with the MD of the corporate finance division and a board director of the bank itself; a face she had seen only a few times at corporate events.

'Lucie, come in and sit down please,' her director said. He was a man only a few years older than herself, but he looked habitually tired and worn down by the pressures of the job. Lucie sat down. She looked across the table at the three men and waited. She was outwardly composed, that was her training, but her mind was blank and her hands shook.

'Lucie, you know Michael Steadman, of course, and I think you've met Henry Trotten a few times, haven't you?'

'Yes, yes, of course.'

'Good.'

She tried to smile but it didn't really work, so she let her face fall again into its sad and anxious expression.

'Lucie, as you are obviously aware, the Department of Trade and Industry has decided to go ahead with its investigation into this alleged illegal trade in Wye Valley Organic Foods and Sarasota plc.'

She was aware, but the sound of it still chilled her to the core. She nodded.

'Of course, I've listened to what you have to say about your own involvement in the case and have discussed it at length with both Michael and Henry, but I'm afraid, Lucie, that although we are all very much on your side, we have to think of the bank's reputation and our clients. You work in a very price-sensitive environment and any doubt on your integrity, no matter how misguided, will reflect on the bank. I'm sure you understand that.'

Again Lucie nodded, but she couldn't speak.

Ten years, she thought, ten years I've worked for you and you don't believe me.

'We have decided, Lucie, that it would be best for you and for the bank if you took an extended period of leave.'

Lucie swallowed and blinked several times as her eyes filled with tears. James Colley looked away

'You will, of course, be on a full salary, with all your benefits intact, until the matter is resolved.'

Lucie stared down at her lap and willed herself not to cry. She didn't cry. She had never, not once in the last ten years, shown her emotions at work. She was a professional; she knew what she was doing, what she was worth. But even as she told herself all this, a small tear fell and splashed on to her skirt, staining it as the raindrops had done. She bent, took a handkerchief out of her handbag and blew her nose.

'Is there anything that you would like to ask me, Henry or Michael?'

'No...' Lucie coughed to clear her throat. 'No thanks, James.' She made a move to stand and James said, 'Thank you for coming in, Lucie. If you'd like to clear your desk now it'll save you having to make another journey.'

She glanced up, shocked. 'Oh, erm, I'm ... I'm not prepared, I've not brought in any boxes or...'

'Molly, the group secretary, has some boxes for you, Lucie, and she'll give you a hand with your things. I've asked her to book you a cab home when you're ready to leave.'

'I see.' Lucie picked up her bag. She saw that this was as good as a dismissal, that the bank couldn't fire her because it would be an admission of her guilt, so they were letting her go on extended leave and when everyone had forgotten about her, when this whole thing had been cleared up and she was found not to have been involved at all, then they would terminate her contract and pay her off. They would dismiss her, simply and quietly, with the minimum of fuss. She turned and held out her hand. 'Goodbye,' she said, shaking each man's hand. 'And thank you.' Though what she was thanking them for she had no idea. She had been shown no loyalty, no trust. She had made them a great deal of money in the last decade, done deals that had cost her more than just her time. She walked towards the door and saw Molly waiting in the corridor for her. Escorted off the premises, she thought, but with more sadness than anger. What did D.H. Lawrence call it? 'The bitch-goddess Success.' She shook her head. How right he was.

Sarah stood by the French window in Roz's kitchen and stared out at the rain which was coming down in sheets. It hammered on to the brick courtyard outside, knocking the heads off the red geraniums and drenching the calico umbrella, making it limp and sodden. It was dismal but it was somehow fitting. It was appropriate weather for the mood of anxious depression that had engulfed Sarah and Roz.

Roz came in and went straight across to switch on the kettle. She carried a packet of cigarettes and took one out and lit it with the kitchen matches, taking a long, deep drag.

Sarah turned. She wanted to say, Oh Roz, that is such a shame, but she didn't. 'Seven years,' Roz said angrily, 'seven years I've not smoked and because of all this fucking mess I've started again. I tell you, if I ever get my hands on that Alex Stanton, I'll bloody kill him.'

'Ditto.' Sarah came over to the dresser and took two mugs down for coffee.

'I'll be better when Graham gets here,' Roz said. Graham was on his way back from a buying trip in Ireland and the first ferry he'd been able to book on to was that morning.

'What time did Andrew say he'd come over?' Sarah asked.

Roz glanced at her watch. 'Ten-ish. Apparently he's taken the morning off.'

'Bully for him,' Sarah retorted and Roz looked at her. 'I'm sorry, Roz,' she went on, 'but he's hardly being supportive, is he? He walks out on Janie, for God knows what reason, though I very much doubt an affair, and then when all this blows up two days ago he doesn't even ring her. The caring, sharing husband, local GP, pillar of the community.' She clenched her jaw. 'What a farce!'

Roz took the hissing kettle off the Aga and said, 'I think your anger might be a bit misguided, Sarah.' But Sarah ignored her. That might be the case, but she really couldn't care if it was.

Roz spooned coffee into the mugs and poured on the scalding water. 'Milk?'

'Thanks.' Sarah helped herself to milk from the bottle on the table and Roz went to the front window as a car drove up.

'He's here,' she said. 'I'll go and let him in.'

Sarah took down another cup, heard voices in the hall and made a third coffee. Andrew walked in.

'Hello, Sarah.'

'Hi. I've made you a coffee if you want it.' She placed it on the table and Andrew shrugged his waxed jacket off and hung it over the back of the chair. He took his coffee, added milk and sat down. 'So,' he said, 'what's this all about?'

Sarah and Roz exchanged glances.

'You said last night, Roz, that we needed to talk urgently so I've taken the morning off. What is it? I hope it doesn't involve Katie.'

Sarah chewed her fingernail and looked at Roz. He didn't know; Janie hadn't told him.

'Have you spoken to Janie in the last forty-eight hours, Andrew?'

'No. I collected Katie on Saturday night and returned her yesterday, but we barely spoke. Why? What's up?'

Roz stubbed out her cigarette and came to sit opposite Andrew. 'The broker who has been dealing for us, for the investment club, has been suspended pending an enquiry by the DTI into an allegation that the Stock Exchange surveillance team have made of primary insider trading.'

Andrew narrowed his eyes. 'I don't understand.'

Roz reached back for her cigarettes and matches. 'You will,' she said and lit another one. She took a drag and went on. 'It appears that Alex Stanton was having an affair with Janie's sister-in-law, Lucie Croft, who is also being investigated by the DTI on the same charges. As you know, Lucie works for a bank and apparently had access to price-sensitive information on two of the stocks that we invested in. It is alleged that Alex Stanton dealt in the shares knowing that they were about to be the target of a take-over bid. A primary insider offence. It is also alleged that – because of our connection with Lucie Croft – we allowed Alex Stanton to invest money in shares that he had price-sensitive information on, a secondary insider offence. We too will be investigated by the DTI.' Roz stopped and drank some coffee. 'All of us.'

Andrew's face had clouded. He looked momentarily confused. 'Let me get this right, Roz. Are you saying that the broker you put your trust in has been insider trading?'

'Correct.'

'And that this in turn means you could be liable for charges of the same offence?'

'Correct.'

Andrew threw his hands up. 'It'll never wash. No way!'

'Oh, but it will. We are all connected to Lucie Croft and apparently Lucie knew that both Sarasota plc and Wye Valley Organic Foods were about to be taken over before it was announced. She was part of the team that was working on the bids. She passed this information to Alex, he dealt on it and voila! We're all in the shit!'

'Oh Christ!'

Roz shook her head. 'Exactly!' She finished her cigarette and thought about another. Reaching for the packet, she caught Andrew's eye and remembered that he was a GP

'I can't believe you don't know!' Sarah remarked. 'I can't believe that Janie didn't tell you.'

Andrew put his head in his hands for a few moments, then he looked up. 'Janie doesn't tell me anything, Sarah, at least not anything important.' He drank some coffee and stood up. 'I'd better get over there and talk to her. She must be in one hell of a state.' He reached for his jacket, looked at Sarah and Roz, then thought better of leaving and sat down again.

'Right,' he said, 'the first thing you need to do is contact a lawyer. I'll get home and on the phone. Katie's godfather is a lawyer, he'll be able to root around for the right person to help you. The next thing you need to do is sit and talk through every meeting, phone call and conversation you had with Alex Stanton and Lucie Croft. You need to write it all down, every tiny detail that you remember. Get records of your phone conversations: phone BT and get them to print out an itemised bill or something and do the same for the mobile phone company, and then we'll talk later. I'll come over again this afternoon when I've found you a lawyer and we can talk it all through.' He stood a second time. 'OK?'

Sarah nodded. 'OK.'

'Roz?'

Roz looked up at the ceiling where the most almighty crash had just thundered from Justin's bedroom upstairs. 'God and children willing, OK.'

Andrew took his coat off the chair and pulled it

on. 'I'll see you later,' he said. 'I'll ring and let you know what time I'll be back.'

'Thanks, Andrew.' Roz stood to see him out but he said, 'Stay where you are and get going on that list.' She smiled and he left the room. Sarah said, 'God, I feel awful about what I said earlier.'

'Don't,' Roz told her. 'We all make a misjudgement some time.' She stood and went across to the drawer for a piece of paper and a pen. 'Hell, I thought you were quite nice until I got to know you.'

Sarah smiled. Good old Roz, she thought, she wasn't going to be easily defeated.

Lucie opened the front door of her house, walked in, closed the door behind her with the heel of her foot and stood for a while in the rain-drenched half-light, wet and cold and numb. She took her jacket and skirt off, both soaked, and left them on the floor by the front door. In the kitchen she opened the fridge and took out the half-empty bottle of wine she hadn't finished last night, reaching up into the cupboard for a glass. She poured, took a sip and turned.

'It's a bit early for the booze, isn't it?'

Lucie jumped and spilt the wine. 'My God, Marcus! You gave me a bloody fright!' She put her glass down and tried to catch her breath. 'What are you doing here? You're supposed to be on holiday somewhere, aren't you?'

He smiled but his eyes were cold. 'That's a nice welcome.'

She took up her wine again and drank, avoiding his eye.

'Janie rang me,' he said. 'Last night. I got on the next plane home.'

'I see.'

Marcus walked into the kitchen and took down a wine glass for himself. He poured, then took a swallow. 'Are you all right?'

Lucie shrugged. She drained her glass, then finally looked at him. 'What do *you* think, Marcus? My life is a mess, I'm being investigated by the DTI for primary insider trading, something I am certainly not guilty of, I've lost my job and I feel like shit. Apart from that, yes, I'm fine.'

Marcus held her gaze. 'And Alex? How is he?'

Suddenly Lucie's face flooded with colour. She dropped her eyes away and stared hard at the ground.

'I told you, Janie called me last night. She told me everything. I presume it's true?'

Lucie couldn't answer. There was nothing sharp or clever she could say, so in the end she simply said, 'I'm sorry, Marcus,' and Marcus said nothing. They stood like that for some time until finally Lucie began to shiver and Marcus told her to go and have a warm bath.

Some time later, when she was dressed and lying on the bed, Marcus brought her a cup of tea. He put it on the bedside table and sat down beside her. 'Thanks,' she murmured.

'Drink it,' he said, 'it's better for you than wine, at least at eleven a.m. it is.'

She shuffled up the bed, stuffed some pillows behind her back, then reached for the tea.

'So,' Marcus began, 'it looks like you've all been used by Alex Stanton.'

Lucie closed her eyes. That's what she'd been telling herself for the last forty-eight hours, that was the reality of it; she had been well and truly used by Alex. But somehow it hadn't sunk in yet, somehow she just couldn't see it. Not Alex, he didn't have the drive.

'How did he do it, d'you think? He must have had access to your briefcase and looked at files, that's the only way I can think...'

'I am extremely careful with price-sensitive information, Marcus. I don't go leaving my brief-case open for all and sundry to look into.'

'I know, but there must have been times, I mean, during your affair, when he had the opportunity to...'

Lucie turned and stared at him. Was he doing this on purpose to humiliate her? 'I don't want to talk about it,' she said. 'I'm surprised that you do.'

Marcus shrugged. 'You have a charge hanging over your head, Lucie, and if you get convicted you could get seven years. I think we should talk about it, don't you?'

Lucie shook her head. Talk? What the hell was wrong with him? Where was his passion, his anger? 'OK,' she snapped, 'yes, he must have had access to my briefcase at some point. Yes, I did carry documents to and from the office to work on at home and very probably had them in my case when I met him on more than one occasion. That's how he did it, I can't think of any other way. I never talked about my work, the only person who ever knew anything about my job was you. So yes, you're right, Marcus, he must

395

have been snooping in my briefcase. You're right, OK? Does that make you feel better?'

'It's not a question of feeling better about it, Lucie, it's a question of getting you off this charge, of getting you through this investigation.' He spoke calmly and rationally and again Lucie couldn't help wondering how he could be so relaxed. 'I can help you, Lucie, if you'll let me. We can work through this together.'

She hung her head and stayed like that. Again she couldn't answer him; she was too humbled in the light of such forgiveness. Marcus stood up and left the room and Lucie began to cry.

Janie saw Andrew's car from the bedroom window. She had been having a lie-down while Katie watched a video and as she opened the curtains he pulled into the drive. He looked up at her but he didn't smile or wave. She went into the bathroom to splash some cold water on to her face and was bent over the sink when he came upstairs and to the door of the bathroom.

'Are you all right?' What was she doing lying down in the middle of the morning?

She straightened, reached for the towel and covered her face. 'I'm fine,' she said, replacing it on the radiator. She walked past him into the bedroom and began to find some clothes to put on. Andrew watched her. She had lost weight and her skin had a pallor to it from not enough fresh air. Her hair was dirty too, something that was unthinkable in Janie.

'Why didn't you tell me?' he asked.

'Tell you what?'

'About the DTI investigation.'

Janie finished laying her clothes out on the bed – yesterday's underwear, tracksuit bottoms, a grubby tee-shirt – and slipped her dressing gown off. She began to dress.

'Janie?' Andrew caught her arm as she reached for her trousers. She looked blankly at his hand and then shrugged him off. She's not connecting, he thought. 'Janie, please,' he said, placing both his hands gently on her shoulders, 'please talk to me.'

Janie looked at him. 'What's the point?' she asked. 'I've tried talking to you, Andrew, over the years I've tried, but you don't listen. You think you've heard but you haven't, you walk away, both emotionally and physically So, what's the point?'

Andrew let her go and she continued to dress. In many ways she was right and he knew it. He spent his life listening to things that he didn't want to hear, to other people's problems, problems that sometimes he couldn't solve or cure, and when Janie spoke he only listened to what he wanted to; he blanked out the rest. He made decisions for her too, did what he thought was best. Occupational hazard he had always called it, but was it more? To Janie had it meant something else altogether? Arrogance, control?

Janie finished dressing and made for the bedroom door. Andrew called out to her. 'Janie, we have to sort this thing, we have to sort this investigation, there isn't any time to waste.'

'Of course,' she said, 'whatever you say.'

He crossed to her then and stopped her from

leaving the bedroom. 'What the hell is it, Janie?' he suddenly snapped. 'What has been eating you for all this time? What has come so far between us that we can't even speak to each other any more?' He grabbed her arms and forced her to look at him. 'Tell me, for God's sake, tell me!'

Her face set and her eyes hardened. 'You really can't see it, can you?'

'No! No, I bloody well can't!'

'There's a gap in my life, Andrew,' Janie said, 'no, not a gap, more a gaping chasm that is threatening to swallow me up. I look at the next twenty years of this, of losing Katie as she grows up, of fiddling around the periphery of your life as a country GP, of mindless gardening and cooking and cleaning, and I can't bear it. When I think of what's in store for me I just want to kill myself.'

Andrew took a sharp breath. He felt like he'd been slapped with her words. He looked at her for a few moments, then he said, 'Do you care so little for me and Katie?'

She shook her head. 'It's myself I don't care for, Andrew. I'm valueless, unfulfilied. I will grow old and wizened and dried-up like a barren wasteland.'

Andrew moved his hand to her face and touched her cheek. 'What do you want, Janie? Tell me what it is that you want and I'll try to give it to you.'

'I want what I can't have,' she said slowly 'I want a baby.'

Andrew looked away He was silent for a while, then he said, 'Is that what all this has been about?

398

All this investment thing, taking our money? Has it all been about having a baby?'

'Yes! No, I...' Confused, Janie shook her head. 'I don't know. Not on the surface, no, but underneath, maybe I think it has. You know, when I took the money out of our emergency account, all I could think of was filling the gap. It obsessed me. I thought that making money would do it, or taking a risk, doing something radical, but I was wrong. After I'd invested the money, even after we knew that a take-over bid had been announced, I felt nothing. It was the same as before. I was empty.'

'Oh Janie...' Andrew released her and moved away to look out of the window at the endless rain.

'And even now you don't listen,' she said. 'You are turning away from me because you don't want to hear what I have to say I am just another problem that you can't solve.'

'No, no, that's not true, Janie. I am turning away because your pain overwhelms me and I don't know how to deal with it. I never knew, I thought you had got past it. I thought after the last miscarriage that you had...' he shrugged, 'I don't know, come to terms with it, I suppose.'

Janie let out a long deep breath. 'So did I.' She looked at him and wondered, was it that he hadn't listened or was it that she had stopped talking? He took her hand and held it in his own.

'Janie, we've got to put this on hold, you know.' She nodded. 'We've got to sort this investigation thing out first, you understand that, don't you? But I am listening to you, I have heard what you've been saying and we will deal with it, I promise. We'll deal with all the emotions you've got stored up inside you, I promise we will.'

She nodded a second time, but she thought, no baby. Then she thought, so how? How, Andrew, will you do that?

'Why don't you take a shower now, wash your hair, put some clean clothes on and I'll get on the phone to Ed and see if he knows a lawyer who could help us. Then I think we should get over to Roz's house and start to try and make some sense of this whole thing.' He kissed her hand. 'Does that sound OK?'

'Yes, Andrew,' she replied, knowing that she cared neither one way or another what happened. 'That sounds fine.'

'Right,' Andrew said, finishing his note. 'So we're agreed on priorities then?'

Roz, Graham, Janie and Sarah all nodded. They were sitting around Roz's kitchen table, with a couple of empty wine bottles in front of them and the remains of a take-away curry. Five children were asleep in various bedrooms over the house, it was late and they were all worn out.

'First, you need to get copies of the phone calls that Alex Stanton made to you, Sarah, and to you, Janie, both on the BT line and on your mobiles. Second, you need to think hard about what went on between you three and Alex. That meeting you had at Sarah's when you decided on Wye Valley; did you make any notes? Can you remember exactly what was said? What reasons did he give you for investing in Wye Valley? The same for Sarasota plc, go through the same procedure for Sarasota plc. The key to all this, I think, is going to be cataloguing in detail exactly what was said and when. If you can categorically state that no mention of inside information was ever made to you, then I think it has to be a strong point in your favour.'

'And there's the whole Lucie thing as well,' Roz said. 'I mean, Janie might be related to her but we never saw her, we had nothing to do with her. Hell, none of us had any idea that she was having an affair with Alex. You didn't, did you, Janie?'

Janie shook her head. 'Nor did Marcus. I rang him last night and he was shocked.' She looked round the table, then added in her defence, 'I had to tell him, someone did.'

There was a murmur of assent.

'Do you think that Lucie is involved, Janie?' Graham asked. 'You know her better than any of us do.'

Janie shrugged. 'I have no idea,' she replied. 'I keep asking myself why, why would someone with such a dazzling career, such a huge income, risk all that for peanuts? Even with our money combined we didn't make half of what Marcus and Lucie earn in a year. Why would she do it and why would she involve me?' Janie's face creased into a frown. 'In my heart I don't believe it, but everything points to her. She was the one with the information; Alex couldn't have done it without Lucie.'

There was another murmur of assent, then Graham said, 'It doesn't really add up, does it?'

'No,' Janie said, 'no, it doesn't.'

401

'Well, I think we need someone professional on this, you know,' he said. 'I think we should get Jack Lowe involved...'

Roz groaned. 'You and that bloody Jack Lowe! Leave it out, Graham, What good would a private investigator be on this?'

'He'd get to the bottom of it, that's what good he'd be.' Graham liked Jack; they were similar characters and had made the sort of connection that men rarely do. 'He's bloody good at what he does and he's fond of us. I bet he'd do it if we asked him.'

Roz stood up to put the kettle on. 'I think he's made enough money out of the Betts family for one year, Graham. Besides, we don't really need to get to the bottom of it, we need to get ourselves off it.'

Sarah looked at Roz. 'Graham's got a point, Roz. How can we get off this thing unless we find out what really happened? If, by some chance, Lucie isn't involved, then presumably we can't be involved either, can we?'

'Good thinking, Sarah!' Andrew stood to help Roz with the coffee. 'Who is this Jack chap then? Have I heard of him?' He began to wash the mugs that Roz took off the table.

'He's someone who's been helping with the Glover Homes land thing,' Roz replied. 'He's been investigating the whole business for us.'

'Is he good?'

Roz glanced over her shoulder at Graham. 'I'll answer this, love. Jack is Graham's new B.F. so he's a bit biased.' She picked up a teatowel. 'Yes, he's good. He's certainly done a great job for us, uncovered some incredible stuff about corruption in town planning, but he hasn't got a result yet and it's taken quite a long time. I don't know that we've got the time to be messing about with Jack Lowe.' She dried five mugs and brought them back to the table.

'Graham? D'you agree?'

Graham shrugged and Andrew sat down. 'I think you should talk to him,' Andrew said, 'and get his angle on things at least. It won't cost anything to just talk to him, will it?'

'No.'

'Good, I'll put that down as your priority then, Graham. As for me,' Andrew went on, 'I'll get back to Ed tomorrow morning and try to get a lawyer on our side. I'll also call the DTI and find out exactly what an investigation involves. Then at least we'll have some idea of what to expect.' He took a sip of his coffee and looked round the table. 'For the moment,' he said, 'I think that's it. I can't think of anything more that we need to talk about. Can anyone else?'

No one could. So Andrew made a few final notes on his list and everyone drank their coffee in silence.

It was well after midnight and Jack Lowe was working in the dark. There was a full moon, so it wasn't really black, not like it usually was, but even if it had been he would still have been digging. He had been digging for hours, three hours to be precise, and he had dug a bed twenty foot by twenty. He was sweating, the air was thick with moisture and his tee-shirt was wet. It clung to his body and every now and then he would wipe the sweat out of his eyes with a towel he had on the ground beside him. He was oblivious to it though; he was oblivious to the time or the energy it was costing him to do such a task and to the fact that it was the middle of the night. He saw nothing but the soil and he thought of little else; his mind was blank save for just a few words that went round and round in his head.

And in the kitchen was the weekly local paper, half-read on the table, abandoned. On the third page, the page it was still open at, it carried the tragic story of the fatal accident of one of its freelance journalists, Rupert Sayer. Just twenty, he had been killed when he lost control of his car on the bend up at the Hersley beauty spot.

It wasn't enough, Jack told himself as he dug; what I said to him the other day simply wasn't enough.

Chapter Twenty-one

Lucie watched Marcus as he made her some toast, but she watched him with the wary unease of someone who felt threatened. For the past twenty-four hours he had been almost unrecognisable from the Marcus she had got used to, the Marcus who had begun to lead a separate life to her, and it unnerved her. She didn't understand it. He should have been upset, distressed, angry and humiliated; anything but this cloying concern, this suffocating kindness, this forgiveness. Did he care so little for her that her affair didn't even matter? Or was he really capable of such largesse? Lucie didn't know. But she did know that Marcus operated a strict code of justice in his head. He scored people on their misdemeanours and punished them accordingly. Some friends she knew had been banished entirely for doing the wrong thing, failing to return a kindness or not living up to expectations. So this, this didn't make sense at all. Marcus caught her staring and asked, 'Jam or marmalade?'

Lucie blushed. How could she harbour such unkind thoughts?

'Marmalade please.'

He passed her the plate and put the kettle on for tea. Tea, she thought, from the man who could previously hardly be bothered to turn on the tap. Lucie stopped herself. Why was she directing all her anger at Marcus?

'I thought I might pop out and get some magazines,' she said, 'maybe go to the gym for an hour or so.'

'Fine. Are you feeling up to it?'

She looked at him. Perhaps that was it, perhaps he thought that under all this pressure she might crack up. 'I think so,' she replied, 'it's just up the road.'

He smiled. 'I was thinking of Cannons.'

'I don't think I'll be going back to the City for some time,' Lucie said.

'No, perhaps not.'

She took a bite of toast. She wasn't in the least bit hungry, but made an effort for his sake. 'What time are you off to work?' she asked.

'I don't think I'll go in actually, I think I'll stay here and keep you company. I've got a couple more days of my holiday left anyway.'

'I see.' A month ago she would have been pleased, would have taken it as a sign that things were improving between them, but now, now she wondered if things hadn't gone too far to ever recover properly. She stood up and left her toast uneaten. She had been waiting for him to leave for work but if he wasn't going then she might as well just get on. 'I think I'll get going,' she said.

'But you haven't eaten your toast.'

She glanced down at it, then looked up at Marcus and shrugged apologetically 'Sorry,' she said, 'I'm not terribly hungry.'

'Maybe I'll come,' Marcus said, 'have a swim.'

Again Lucie shrugged. She didn't really care,

one way or the other. 'No, perhaps not,' he finished, 'I'll get on and deal with some of my mail.'

She went into the bedroom – which they now shared again – and sat to pull on some trainers. What the hell is going on, she thought, just where is he coming from? But she didn't have any answers. At the moment, Lucie didn't have any answers to anything.

Alex was waiting across the road from Lucie's house, wearing a jacket and a hat pulled down over his eyes. He had been there since eight a.m. waiting for her to come out. Finally at nine-thirty he got his chance. Lucie came out of the house carrying her sports bag, turned right when she got to the pavement and started out for the health club. Alex set off after her. He wanted to get in front of her, to head her off, so that at least he'd have some chance of stopping her and making her listen to him. He'd been calling for the past three days but she just wasn't answering her phone. He had to speak to her, to make her understand. He had to also somehow convince her to help him, because if she didn't then he was going down for several years and that was unthinkable.

He crossed the road several yards in front of her and at the first turning off the main road he stopped and stood by a low wall. As Lucie came into view he stepped out directly into her path. She jumped back, suddenly startled, and he took hold of her arms.

'My God, Alex! What the hell are you doing

here?' She looked at his face, unshaven, tired, wretched. 'You gave me a fright, you stupid bastard!' She yanked her arms away from his grip and went to move off. She was incensed at the very sight of him.

'Lucie, sorry, oh God, sorry, I didn't mean to scare you, Lucie...' She set off and he turned after her. 'Look, Lucie, we've got to talk, please, you've got to talk to me, please?' He shouted the last plea and something in his voice made her stop and turn round. 'I can't help you, Alex,' she said. 'You used me. I don't know how you did it and I'm still trying to come to terms with it, but you used me, abused my trust and I can't help you out of this mess. I've got enough to do trying to help myself.'

'I didn't use you, Lucie, I swear I never did anything wrong, never.' He stood where he was and looked at her. 'I don't know what the hell has happened, I keep trying to work it out but I can't. I never used you, Lucie, I had no idea that you were working on Sarasota or Wye Valley, how could I have done? You never said a word, you never once told me anything about your work.'

She turned and walked back to him. 'No, I didn't, but there was always my briefcase. You had countless opportunities to look in my briefcase, Alex, and you took them.' She shook her head. 'Why? Why did you ever think you could get away with it?'

'But I haven't done anything,' he cried. 'I never looked in your briefcase, I knew nothing about your involvement with Wye Valley.'

'You swear that you never looked in my briefcase, Alex? You swear it, on your life?'

Alex stared at her. He stared and stared and then dropped his eyes. 'I thought so,' she said and turned to walk away But he grabbed her and swung her round. 'All right, I did look in your briefcase! I did it once, the night we met for a drink in Red's wine bar. I dropped a tenner on the floor and when I bent to pick it up I couldn't resist looking in your briefcase. It was open and it was too much of a temptation. I looked and I can tell you what I saw, I saw a document on a merger between Rightson Electronic plc and the KEC group. I saw it, I glanced at it and I thought shit, I could do something with that. Christ, I even worked out some figures! But I didn't do it, Lucie, I didn't do it because you trusted me and because I'm not fucking stupid. Anyone could put two and two together about us. Besides, I was making money legitimately, or so I thought, with this investment club!' He held her arm so tightly that it hurt. 'I have never dealt shares using inside information, Lucie, never.'

Lucie pulled her arm away 'Get off me,' she cried. 'Who the hell do you think you are, man-handling me like that!' She rubbed her arm and started to walk away.

'I'm an honest man, that's who I am!' he shouted after her. 'I'm someone who's been fuck-ing set up, that's who I am!' She increased her pace, hurrying away from him. 'I didn't do it, Lucie,' he shouted. 'Check your files, see what you had in your bag that night. I didn't do it...'

She ran across the road and jumped on to a bus. She had no idea where it was going but she didn't care; she had to get away from his shouting. She pushed her way to a seat and slumped down into it, covering her face with her hands. As the bus drove off she could still hear him shouting and the words 'I didn't do it' reverberated in her ears.

Graham saw that the ground-floor door of Jack Lowe's office was open and he walked in, calling out from the bottom of the stairs. There was no reply but he could hear voices, so he carried on up.

'Hello? Jack? Hello?'

Dodi and Jack stood by Jack's desk, a huge plastic crate between them which Jack was maniacally filling.

'Jack?'

Jack looked up. 'Oh, hi, Graham.' He stopped for a moment to smile, then bent and began emptying the drawers of his desk.

'What's going on, Jack? Moving offices?'

'No, he's shutting offices,' Dodi said, her face like thunder. 'He's giving up, bottling out...' She looked at him. 'The coward.'

''Tis a far braver thing I do now ... etc, etc, etc.' Jack stopped packing and returned Dodi's stare. 'I am not a coward, Dodi, quite the contrary I am showing a bit of responsibility for once, I'm looking after your interests and not just my own.'

'Oh really?' Dodi fired back. 'Well, you could've fooled me!'

'What's going on?' Graham asked again. 'Please, tell me what's going on.'

'I'm closing down for a while,' Jack said. 'I was

410

going to come and see you later to tell you that I'll have to end your investigation and will refund half my fee.'

'You'll do nothing of the sort,' Graham said strongly. 'You earned that fee, it's yours. I won't have it back.'

'Don't try arguing with him,' Dodi snapped, 'he's too pig-headed to see anybody else's point of view.'

'I do see your point of view, Dodi,' Jack snapped back, 'I just don't agree with it. Besides, this is my office and I'll do what I want with it.'

'But we've got loads of work! We've got enough house surveillance work to keep us going until Christmas, not to mention all the other stuff! Jack, we're making good money for the first time since we opened and you want to throw it all away!'

'Correction, I want to sell it, eventually.'

'But Jack...'

He held both hands in the air. 'No buts. We are packing up today and closing. That's the end of it.'

'Why are you closing, Jack?' Graham asked.

Jack turned to him. 'A young man, Rupert Sayer, a freelance journalist, was doing a bit of investigative journalism. He had a story on corruption in local town planning and he came to me with it. I ignored him. I didn't want his interference in my own investigation to make things difficult for me. Result? He's dead. A fatal car accident. Seems a bit odd, don't you think? He rings Glover Homes for information, manages to wangle God knows what out of the

411

secretarial staff and then ends up crushed in a 2CV. Sorry, but it's too much of a coincidence for me, I'm out of here.'

'Hang on, are you saying that someone connected with Glover Homes murdered this young man?'

Jack thought for a moment. 'Yes, I suppose that is what I'm saying, but how I'd ever prove it I don't know'

'Jack, that is a bloody serious accusation,' Graham said.

'Why d'you think I'm closing down, Graham? If I'm right and Glover find out that I'm on to something, how do I know that I'm not next, or Dodi, or you or Roz or one of the kids, my son or yours?'

'Jack, this is bizarre! You are totally over-reacting. Have the police talked about any wrong-doing? How do you know it wasn't a simple case of an RTA? Why are you jumping to these outrageous conclusions? Calm down, Jack, please.'

Dodi patted Graham on the back. 'Good on ya, mate,' she said. 'I've been trying to tell him the same thing myself.'

'Look, you're upset. It's always upsetting when someone young dies, such a waste of life, but Jack, is there really any need to go to these sorts of lengths?'

'I think so,' Jack replied sharply. 'I am not going to try and beat these buggers, there just isn't any point. I'm giving up, and before you say anything else, you won't change my mind, because it's as much for you as for anyone else. You too, Dodi.

412

I've already got one death on my conscience, I'm not having another.'

'There's no telling him,' Dodi said, as Jack continued to pack up his box. 'He's only thinking of himself. I mean, what's going to happen to me? Where am I going to get another job in a place like this?' She took a handkerchief with a picture of a koala bear on it from her pocket and blew her nose.

'You'll get something, Dodi,' Jack said, 'you're a bright lass. And you've got a couple of months' money so there's a bit of time.' He bent to unplug the phone. 'Anyway, what did you want, Graham?'

'I wanted to try and get you on another job, but I see there's no point now.'

'Nope, none at all. Sorry, mate.' Jack's flippancy covered a quagmire of emotions that he was finding it hard to cope with. Loading the phone into the crate, he fought the temptation to ask what the job was about and Graham said, 'I won't keep you then, Jack. Give me a ring when you've got organised and perhaps we can have a beer.'

He looked up. 'Yeah, I'll do that, thanks, Graham.' Graham smiled and left the office. Dodi stood where she was and glowered at Jack. 'It's no good looking at me like that, Dodi,' he said, 'you can't scare me. My mind's made up, it's as simple as that.' And for once, she reckoned that it was.

Sarah was loading shopping into the boot of her car when Graham caught sight of her in the car

413

park behind Duffields. She had taken leave from her job for a couple of weeks with the original intention of taking Rory away on holiday, but that wasn't going to happen now.

'Hi, how are you?'

'All right. Shopping as per usual.'

'Where's Rory?'

'He's on a football course at the leisure centre. I got him in at the last minute when I knew we couldn't go away. He loves it.'

'Good.' Graham dug his hands in his pockets. 'I saw Jack Lowe,' he said.

'Great, what did he say?'

'He said he can't help us, I'm afraid. Apparently he blames himself for the death of some young journalist and he's decided to close up shop for a while.'

Sarah frowned. 'Really? I saw that in the paper. What on earth could Jack have to do with that?'

'He thinks it's connected with the investigation he's been doing into Glover Homes. He thinks...' Graham stopped. 'Oh, it doesn't really matter what he thinks, the point is that he's giving up, so he can't help us.'

Sarah slammed the boot shut and looked at Graham. She was disappointed but she didn't want to show it. She said, 'Oh well,' and shrugged. She climbed into the car and wound the window down. 'What next?' she asked.

Graham shook his head. 'To be honest, Sarah,' he said, 'I really don't know.'

Sarah drove home and unpacked her shopping before looking through the post. She made herself a coffee, went upstairs for a sweater as it had suddenly turned cold again and sat down at the kitchen table to open the two letters she had received. One was from Nick with some money in it, but she didn't even read it, it was too painful. She left it for Rory to read when he got in. The other was from BT; an itemised list of the phone calls that she had made and received over the past three months, as requested. She unfolded it and looked down. Three to Alex Stanton on his mobile and at least eleven to or from Marcus Todd. Sarah went and got her diary to check the dates of the calls to Alex and as she did so something suddenly occurred to her that hadn't before. Almost every call from Marcus, except for one – the one to arrange the day out at Goodwood – had been about stocks to invest in. She stood in the hall with her diary in her hand and thought, it was Marcus who suggested Sarasota – or rather he didn't actually suggest it, he mentioned that something like Sarasota might be a possibility and it was Marcus who suggested Wye Valley. Could Marcus have had anything to do with all this? She went back into the kitchen, sat down and then thought, that's ridiculous, I'll be accusing Janie next. Marcus was working on a tip from Alex, he'd said so. Alex had given him the ideas – each time they'd talked he'd mentioned Alex's name. Still, it wouldn't do any harm to just ring Janie to run it past her. It might at least put her mind at rest. She dialled Janie's number and waited for the line to be answered.

'Hello?'

Janie sounded worn out and Sarah's nerve

faltered. She took a breath, then said, 'Janie, hi, it's Sarah. How are you?'

'OK,' Janie answered. She added nothing more and Sarah wondered whether to go on. She bit her lip then, without any more consideration, rushed in. She'd made the call, she might as well go through with airing her thoughts. 'Look, Janie,' she began, 'I've been thinking about this investment thing, like Andrew asked us to, and I've checked all my records and made a list of my calls to and from Alex. It's just that I know I should have mentioned this before, but the thing is that I, erm, I've had quite a bit to do with Marcus over the past few months. We've struck up a sort of friendship, nothing more, completely platonic of course, but I've been using him as a sort of sounding board for all our investment ideas and...' Sarah stopped. There was an icy silence at the other end of the phone, then Janie asked, 'What are you saying, Sarah?'

'I just wondered, I mean, you see, Marcus always gave me Alex's tips, he sort of passed on the original ideas and I just wondered if...' Sarah broke off and regretted immediately what she was about to say. 'I wondered if he might be involved in any way.'

Janie caught her breath. Sarah heard the sharp intake on the other end of the line, then Janie said, 'That is ridiculous, Sarah, utterly ridiculous! My brother has been well and truly used in this situation when all he ever tried to do was help us, give us all something to aim for. So what if he's been helping you on the quiet? I'd say that was bloody kind of him, giving up his time and

416

energy to put something in. I'm afraid, Sarah, that you're completely wrong! He's the victim here and I just don't know how you could even think, let alone suggest, that he might be involved in something dishonest. He's one of the most honest people I know, he...' Janie stopped as the blood rushed to her face and the vein in her neck throbbed with indignation. 'I think it's very poor of you, Sarah, to accuse...'

'I haven't accused anyone, Janie,' Sarah protested. 'I just wondered, that's all, because I seem to have had so much feedback from Marcus, whether...' She stopped, near to tears. There was a silence, then finally Sarah said, 'It is ridiculous, I realise that, of course it is. I'm sorry, Janie, I didn't mean to offend you, but all sorts of things are going round and round my head and I don't know what to think...' Janie remained silent. 'I'll let you go,' Sarah said. 'Sorry, Janie, I really am.' She rang off and sat for ages just staring at the phone. Finally she stood, collected up the bill from the phone company and went into the kitchen.

There she started to make notes in her diary She wrote the time and length of each call to and from Alex Stanton and tried to remember what they were about, but for some peculiar reason, she couldn't. Nothing he had ever said sprang to mind, nothing was of any note. It was a blank; she had drawn a blank. She put her head in her hands and closed her eyes. For the past three days she had been stunned by all this, dazed by the sheer extraordinariness of the whole thing, but now, alone in her kitchen with the rain beginning to pit against the windows, the full terror of it hit her and she had to clench her fists to stop from screaming. She could go to prison. The nausea rose in her chest and she took several deep breaths to try and control it. Prison.

Suddenly she jumped up, knocking the chair back, and grabbed her car keys off the table. What did he mean he was giving up? Bloody Jack Lowe, giving up when he could do something positive to help. Copping out, weak bastard. She slammed out of the house and got into her car. She drove off, her foot down hard on the accelerator, in the direction of the village. Once again her anger was misguided, only this time she didn't have Roz to tell her so.

Jack was about to lock up when Sarah banged on the downstairs door. 'Who the hell's that?' he demanded and Dodi said, 'Go see for yourself. I don't work here any more.' He went down the stairs and unbolted the door.

'About bloody time!' Sarah snapped, barging past him and going up the stairs. 'I've got something to say to you, Jack Lowe!' She was up and into the office before he could stop her and she waited for him, not even seeing Dodi hovering in the small kitchen area. 'OK,' Jack said, when he reached her. 'Say it.' He stood opposite her with his hands on his hips and she glared at him, at his arrogance and indifference.

'You are a weakling,' she spat, 'a pathetic weakling. You give up at the first sign of adversity and slink off home to your flowers and it makes me sick! You've no guts. You throw in Graham and

418

Roz's investigation because you can't handle it; with absolutely no regard for how much they could lose, you ask me out for a drink and you never even turn up without any explanation at all, and now you won't even consider helping us, at a time when we need all the help we can get. You're a...' She could feel the tears welling up as she searched for the right word. 'You're a wet!' she finally cried. 'You don't give a damn about anyone but yourself!' She turned suddenly and headed for the door.

'Now just wait a minute!' Jack shouted, jumping in front of her to block her way 'I did turn up for that drink. I turned up at eight-thirty and I sat and waited. I waited until closing time and you never came. You didn't ring to let me know and you never even apologised. In fact, you were embarrassed about having even arranged it. I could sense it – when I met you at Roz's you could hardly look me in the face!' He glared at her. 'And I'm the coward?'

'I did ring you. I rang the pub and you weren't there. They looked for you and you weren't there. Of course I didn't ring to apologise because there was nothing to apologise about. You didn't turn up, Jack, I checked, so don't try and bluff me!'

Dodi, standing in the kitchen, pressed herself back against the wall. This was going to end one of two ways. Either Sarah would hit him or kiss him. Dodi held her breath.

'I did turn up.'

'You didn't.'

'I did. I was there and I never got a call. You never rang.'

'I did.'

'You didn't.'

'Oh for God's sake!' Dodi suddenly burst out, unable to stop herself. She stamped into the room and faced them both. 'Why don't you just agree that you called and even though he was there he didn't get the message? He might have been in the karsey, or just didn't hear his name. He *was* there, all right? And you called to let him know you couldn't come, right? End of row.'

Sarah's face had dropped into an expression of shock and Dodi thought, I've overstepped the mark here, but now I've done it I might as well finish. She had nothing to lose; she didn't work here any more after all. 'The thing that you really need to be talking about, if you don't mind me saying, is this job you want Jack to do. You're in trouble, right? And you need some help, that's why you're so angry.' Dodi turned to Jack. 'She's right, you know, you shouldn't be giving up just because you think someone's got the better of you. If this Rupert bloke was murdered, then it's up to you to set the record straight, Jack, to make sure some justice is done...'

'Justice!' Jack burst out. 'What the fucking hell has justice got to do with it? When was anything ever just?'

'Oh take the chip off, for God's sake!' Sarah snapped.

Jack turned to her. 'And what's that supposed to mean?'

Sarah, who had listened to Dodi firstly with shock, then with growing admiration, thought, if she can do it, so can I. She had something to say and she was going to damn well say it.

'It means, stop moaning and get on with it, that's what the rest of us have to do.' She took a breath. 'I was given a damaged baby, Jack, not his fault, not mine, and I did the only thing I could, I got on with it. He's still damaged, but he's also a confident, strong, intelligent, healthy child. I could have given up, but I didn't.' She looked at him and, in a moment of stark realisation, knew that it wasn't him she was angry at, it was everything. She'd been angry for years and had never been able to say it. She dropped her gaze and stared down at her hands, suddenly acutely embarrassed by this painful outburst. Embarrassed and relieved too. Then Dodi patted her on the arm. 'Well said,' she remarked quietly.

Sarah nodded. 'I'd better go,' she said, 'I think I've said far too much.' She looked at Jack again. He was watching her with an expression she couldn't fathom. 'Sorry,' she murmured, moving past him to the door. She walked out and down the stairs, wondering what the hell she had been thinking, why on earth she had come, but feeling – and this was the odd part – mildly euphoric.

'Wow,' said Dodi, when the door downstairs had slammed shut and Sarah had gone, 'that is some girl.'

She turned and went to pick up her jacket and handbag.

'Where are you going?' Jack asked.

'Home,' she said, 'to start looking through the situations vacant pages.'

'No you're not,' Jack said.

'I'm not?' Dodi wanted to smile, but couldn't

quite let herself.

'No, you're going to give me a hand with un-packing this bloody crate, then you're going to get us some lunch, and after lunch we'll phone Graham and Sarah Greg to see what the hell is going on.'

'Bonzer!' Dodi said, then she grinned. 'Good on ya. At last, more man than mouse.' And she ducked as a pencil came flying across the room at her.

Marcus was out when Lucie got in from the gym and she was relieved. She made herself a coffee and sat for some time in the silence, drinking it and thinking. Then she went to the box she had brought home from the office yesterday and took out her desk diary. She sat on the floor with her personal diary and her desk diary and went back to the beginning of the year, to the time she had met Alex.

For every meeting that they had had she had marked the date with red ink. She hadn't put any names or times or places, that would have been foolish, but she had marked the date so that she didn't forget. Then she tried to match up the dates she had met Alex with the meetings that she'd had on that day or the following day, with a view to seeing what she might have had in her briefcase. It was a laborious job, but she executed it with meticulous care and by the middle of the afternoon she had a list of work that she might have had on her person when she met Alex, along with a list of their dates. There was a bit of confusion around the Wye Valley deal; she had met

Alex, but she didn't have a Wye Valley meeting specifically penned in on that day or for the day after. But she remembered working on the bid, she remembered it because she had told Alex that she was working on something that would soon be announced, they were almost her very words, she remembered them well.

She sighed. Certainly no meeting with Alex had ever coincided with a meeting at work for Sarasota plc and also, interestingly, he had been telling the truth about Rightson Electronics. She had been working on that merger the night they'd met at Red's, and she'd gone back to the office to check the documents so she'd definitely had them with her. Again she sighed. What if Alex was telling the truth? What if it really wasn't him? Lucie stood and immediately dismissed the idea; it couldn't have been anyone else. She walked across to the kitchen to find something to eat in the fridge and stopped by the phone. Still, there was no harm in making sure. She picked up the receiver and dialled.

'Hello, Molly, it's Lucie Croft here. Molly, could you do me a favour? Could you check on the PC for my chargeable hours for the following dates and let me know what they were and for whom?' Lucie read out the dates. 'Great, thanks.' She hung up and waited by the phone. Molly was thorough and quick. She waited five minutes, biting her fingernail, then Molly rang back.

'Oh,' Lucie said, when the reply came. 'Right, I see.' She had been working on the Wye Valley deal on the day she met Alex. 'Thanks,' she added, 'yes, and you.' She hung up again and slumped back against the counter. 'Bugger,' she said aloud. That put the ball firmly back in Alex's court. The trouble was that now she just wasn't convinced.

'Right,' Jack said, 'let me get this absolutely straight.' He was sitting on his desk facing Sarah and Graham, while Dodi sat at the desk and made notes. 'The big question mark is over Lucie Croft's involvement, right? She is the obvious source of the inside information but it seems unlikely to all of you that she would have taken such a risk.'

'Sometimes people do the weirdest things,' Dodi said. 'It might be that the boyfriend per-suaded her or blackmailed her into it?'

'Good point, Dodi,' Jack said. 'There are all sorts of things that might have gone on, but certainly that's our first line of investigation I'd have thought. There will ultimately be some clues along the way and I'll set out to find them. Is that OK?'

'Fine,' Graham said. 'Sarah, d'you agree?'

'Yes.'

'Good. The other thing that I'm going to ask Dodi to do is to follow up a line of enquiry about Alex Stanton. I think we need to find out exactly what he has to say for himself.'

'Bonzer.' Dodi looked up at Graham and Sarah. 'It means right on,' she said.

'And for now I think that's all we can do. I'd like to speak to your lawyer once you get hold of one. How's it going, d'you know?'

'Andrew is apparently having a bit of trouble

424

finding someone. This is a very specific case and no one seems to know that much about it.'

'Oh.' Jack jumped down off the desk. 'OK, well, if Dodi's got all the details, then I won't keep you.' Graham and Sarah stood.

'Thanks, Jack,' Graham said. 'I feel happier knowing that we've got some muscle on the case.'

Jack smiled. 'Hardly muscle, Graham, more like gristle.'

'Difficult to chew and impossible to swallow,' Sarah said.

'Yes, sort of.' Jack saw them downstairs to the main door and Graham offered to walk Sarah to her car.

'Thanks, Graham, but I'm going to the leisure centre to pick up Rory.'

'Right, well, I must dash,' he said. 'Thanks, Jack, and good luck.' He kissed Sarah. 'We'll speak soon, love.'

Sarah stood for a few moments and watched him disappear up the street, then she turned to Jack. She had something to say but she had nowhere near the courage she'd had that morning.

'Jack, I...' She broke off, very uncertain of herself, looked away, then something suddenly struck her. 'Jack...'

'Yes?'

'You know, it's just occurred to me that if you really are worried about this Rupert Sayer thing then you can always check it out.'

'Really? How?'

'I don't know, check the cars of the people you think might be involved, see if any of them have paint on them from Rupert's car?'

'I've no idea who might be involved, it'd be like looking for a needle in a haystack.' He shrugged. 'Nice try though. If you need a job any time...'

Sarah smiled back. 'Actually, that wasn't what I was about to say I was about to apologise.'

'What for?' Jack tried to act cool, tried to keep his face from looking eager and excited, but the truth was that he thought Sarah was amazing and just standing next to her threw him off-balance.

'For being rude this morning. I was out of order. And also for not turning up that night we'd arranged a drink. I did ring the pub and I did have a good excuse. I had to cope with Rory who'd had a bloody awful day and...'

Jack took her hand and she stopped. He looked at it, turned it over so that he could see the palm and then held it gently between his own long, thin fingers. Sarah watched him and held her breath. 'It's forgotten,' he said, looking up at her. 'But thanks.'

She nodded and he released her hand. 'I'll ring you and let you know how I'm getting on,' he said. 'Try not to worry too much, I'm sure we can work this thing out.'

'Yes, OK.' Sarah put her bag on her shoulder and looked up the road. 'Bye, Jack,' she said, moving off.

'Goodbye, Sarah,' he replied.

She walked away, tucking the hand that he had held into her pocket, and thinking that the last moment had been over too quickly, that she would have liked Jack to go on holding her fingers in his for a lot, lot longer.

Chapter Twenty-two

Lucie woke early, but Marcus was still asleep beside her as she slipped from the bed and into the bathroom. She cleansed her face, brushed her teeth and had a quick wash in the dark. She didn't want to turn the light on or shower because she didn't want to wake him. That done, she crept into the bedroom, gathered the clothes up that she had left on the chair and went out, closing the door softly behind her. In the living area she dressed, collected up the sports bag she had packed the previous night and left the house. It was six-fifteen and she wanted to be in the City by seven.

She was early. At six-forty-five her taxi pulled up outside the bank and she climbed out. Going in, she asked the security men if Molly Kirk had come in yet and they checked on the list.

Lucie was told that she hadn't. She left, walked the fifty yards or so down the road to the cafe that Molly and many of the administration staff used and ordered herself a coffee, taking a seat in the corner. Molly was overworked but well paid and Lucie knew that some mornings she was in at six-thirty in order to keep on top of her workload. She opened her paper and began her wait.

At seven-thirty Molly came into the cafe for her daily take-out cappuccino and round of toast. She queued and Lucie took her opportunity.

'Hello, Molly,' She stood behind her and Molly turned.

'Oh, Lucie...' She stopped, momentarily embarrassed, then said, 'Hi, how are you?'

'I'm fine, Molly. Can we talk?'

Molly looked uncomfortable. She glanced at her watch and said, 'I'm late already, Lucie, I don't think I have the time to...'

But Lucie touched her arm and said, 'Please, Molly, it's important.'

Molly shrugged. 'OK.'

'I'm sitting over there.'

Molly, at the front of the queue now, ordered her breakfast and nodded. Lucie went and sat down to wait for her.

'So,' Molly said, taking a seat. 'What's up?' She had mentally prepared herself for a sob story and was braced, ready for the outpouring.

'I need a bit of help,' Lucie said. 'I need to find out if I've been set up in this thing because I know for certain that I haven't done anything wrong.'

'Help?' Molly had gone from looking uncomfortable to looking decidedly uneasy. 'What d'you mean by help?'

'I need to find out, Molly, if I had the documents for the Wye Valley Organic Foods deal in my briefcase on a certain night in July. The only way that I can think of doing that is to check the files in the computer. It's only that one day and if, for example, they were still being transcribed, then I couldn't have had them in my bag, could I?'

Molly took a sip of her coffee. 'Which means?'

428

'Which means that Alex Stanton, the broker, couldn't have looked into my case and got the information, which is what is being alleged.'

'So how did he do it?'

Lucie shook her head. This was something that she didn't want to think about, that she had been putting to the back of her mind for the past twenty-four hours. She swallowed hard and looked at Molly. 'He didn't,' she said, 'someone else did.'

Molly looked away and continued to sip her coffee. She had always liked Lucie Croft, had been shocked when all this had come out a few days ago; yes, actually shocked. Lucie didn't seem the type, had never put a foot wrong as far as she knew. But then she was having an affair, she'd admitted it, and Molly had been shocked by that too, especially with that successful, good-looking husband of hers. Some people, Molly thought, just didn't know what they'd got.

'I don't think I can help,' she said at last, 'it would put me in a very difficult situation.'

Lucie said, 'All I'm asking is that you check the computer, Molly, and give me a ring. I'm not asking you to do anything illegal, I promise. It would...' She broke off and looked at her hands. It would what? It would raise questions that Lucie didn't know that she wanted to answer. It would, perhaps, be the end of her marriage. 'It would make things much clearer for me, Molly, it would give me a chance.'

Molly took a deep breath, then stood. 'I'll do it now,' she said, 'before anyone comes in. Give me your mobile number.'

Lucie wrote her number down on a slip of paper and handed it over. 'I'll wait here,' she said.

Molly nodded. She turned to go and Lucie called after her, 'Thanks, Molly.' Molly nodded again and left the cafe.

In the office, Molly didn't even take off her coat. She went to her PC, switched it on and went straight into the system. She looked up the file for Wye Valley Organic Foods and went into file management. She wrote down the dates and times that the document had been worked on and noticed that the file hadn't been created until the twelfth of July. It had been a rush job, she remembered that now, a deal done at the last minute. And they'd had to borrow a secretary from the pool to type it up because Molly had been snowed under with other stuff; the initials of the secretary who'd done it were there on the file. She made a note of all the dates and times for the file and sat for a few moments thinking, then she took the piece of paper from her bag and immediately dialled Lucie Croft's mobile.

Lucie took the call, made a note of the dates and times that Molly read out and listened carefully to what she had to say. She hung up, finished her coffee and left the cafe. She should have felt excited, this was a step forward, the answer that she needed, but she didn't. She set off for the tube and felt more angry and distressed than she had ever felt before in her life.

Alex wasn't sleeping well. He went to sleep all right – three pints of lager and half a bottle of wine usually took care of that – but then he would wake, any time between two and four in the morning, and he'd be wide awake, lying in the dark listening to the rhythms of the night through his open window and worrying. It was classic anxiety, the perfect pattern of stress-related sleep problems, but the solution was valium or something equally soporific and Alex would rather have clear panic than spaced-out calm. So he slept early, between eleven and two, and then got up and made himself a drink, watched some telly or sometimes wandered aimlessly round his flat. He usually went to bed again about five or six a.m. and slept for maybe an hour, if he was lucky. If not he went to bed and lay with the blind down, constantly wondering how his life could have taken such a turn.

Alex had just got up when the buzzer went for the front door. It was nine a.m. and this morning he had drifted off to sleep at about seven and slept for a couple of hours. He felt reasonably refreshed, better than he had done all week. Perhaps he was coming to terms with his fate; perhaps depression was just beginning to kick in. Whatever it was, he got up, washed his face and brushed his teeth before pulling on some track-suit bottoms and a tee-shirt, something he had got into the habit of not doing until at least midday. Then the buzzer went, he pressed it, heard Lucie's voice and opened the door for her. He stood outside his front door, two flights up, and waited.

'Hi,' she said. She didn't smile, in fact her face looked worse than he had ever seen it, ashen and tear-stained. He let her go past him into the flat and followed her in. 'What's up?' he asked. She turned. 'I've checked all my meetings and I've checked the documents at work. You couldn't have looked in my briefcase at price-sensitive documents, except for the one for Rightson Electronics, because I wasn't carrying any. On all the occasions we met I didn't have the documents on me, except for the Rightson document, which you openly admit you looked at but did nothing about.'

Alex felt the immediate pulse of excitement, then Lucie began to cry. He crossed to her, put his arms round her and attempted to comfort her. But it was half-hearted; he was too distressed himself to offer any real consolation to anyone else. Lucie cried for a few minutes, then pulled away and searched for a handkerchief in her bag. She found tissues, blew her nose and wiped her face. Alex wished he had something he could offer her – a word, a caress – but he didn't. He was as dry and emotionless as a stone.

'My group secretary checked the Wye Valley documents this morning...' Lucie said. She cleared her throat and took control of herself again. 'They weren't typed up until a few days after we met. We had a drink on the ninth of July, I've got it marked in my diary, and the documents were typed up on the twelfth. You dealt on Friday the thirteenth and we had no other meeting between the ninth and you dealing. So there's no way you could have known about that deal. I never spoke to you about it, I never even took the documents out of the office. You had no access to the files so there's no way you dealt on price-sensitive information. No way at all...' Her voice wavered again and she stopped to get a grip of her emotions. 'Unless you broke into the bank's system, which is impossible...' She blew her nose again and looked at him. 'So, I know you didn't do it and you know you didn't do it, but what do we do now?'

All the time she was speaking Alex felt the life flow back into him again, he felt his pulse begin to beat and his brain begin to clear. 'You've got proof that you didn't have the documents on you?'

'They're dated, on the system, I couldn't have taken them home.'

'Right...' He walked away from her to the window, then back to her, then to the window again. He looked out and his excitement suddenly dropped. 'But as far as the DTI is concerned, you could still have passed on price-sensitive information to me, couldn't you?' he asked, without looking at her. 'This only proves my innocence to you, doesn't it?'

Lucie didn't answer.

He turned. 'Doesn't it, Lucie?'

She swallowed, there was a silence, then finally she said, 'Yes. As far as the DTI is concerned I could have told you about the deals, but I didn't and now I know that you couldn't have seen any documentation because I didn't ever have it on me. At least that's one step forward, isn't it?'

Alex went back to the window and stared out. His shoulders were hunched as if he were in pain.

'Alex?'

'Yes?' He straightened and turned.

'Can I have a drink?'

'Shit, oh God, of course, sorry...' He went over to her and led her to a seat. She was so pale that she looked suddenly fragile.

'I'll get you a brandy,' he said, 'and some tea. Won't be a moment.' He disappeared and she could hear him putting the kettle on and opening cupboards in the small kitchen. She laid her head against the back of the chair and closed her eyes. How long would it take him, she wondered, to come to the same awful conclusion that she had? It had taken her about ten minutes, once she'd worked through the sequence of events, and then she'd been sick. She had got off the tube at Leicester Square and been sick in a rubbish bin, as sick as a dog, right in the middle of the early morning commuters.

Alex appeared with her tea and a tumbler full of brandy. She took the brandy, swallowed a large gulp and felt it burn all the way down to her stomach.

'Better?'

She nodded and he passed her the tea.

'Lucie,' he began, 'I don't know how to say this, but...' He stopped and stared at his hands for a moment. 'The thing is...'

She put her hand on his arm. 'If it wasn't you, then there is only one other person who knows anything about my work,' she said. 'There is only one person I have ever talked to about what goes on in my office and...' Again her voice wavered as her emotion got the better of her.

'Marcus?' Alex asked.

She nodded again and her eyes filled with tears. 'I'm sorry, I should be more controlled, I...' She fumbled by her feet for her bag and Alex bent for it, passing it to her. She took out her last tissue and wiped her face. Alex stood and walked away. Shit, he was thinking, what the fuck is going on? He stood by the window again and tried to work it out, then he turned and said to Lucie, 'But why?'

Lucie shrugged. 'I keep asking myself the same question. It is too awful, too terrible to think that Marcus could want to do this to me, or to you, and I keep thinking, no, it can't be him, it just can't. But then I think, who else could it be? He's the only one who knows anything about my job. He talked to you, to the investment club, to me; he's the link. He's the one that set it all up, he's the only one it could possibly be and...' She put her hands up to her face. 'And I don't know why.' She was silent for a while, then she rubbed her eyes and massaged her temples with her fingers. 'How could he?' she murmured. 'I just don't know how he could do it.'

Alex took a deep breath. 'Unless he knew about us.'

Lucie jerked round to look at him. She shook her head. 'No, that's ridiculous.'

'Is it?'

She stared at him. 'But how? How would he have found out?'

'I don't know. Did someone tell him, did he guess? Did you unknowingly give something away? I don't know, Lucie, but it seems more likely than anything else.'

'Does it? What, revenge? Does *that* make sense to you?'

'Nothing makes sense to me any more, Lucie, nothing at all.' Alex came back to her and perched on the arm of the sofa. 'Look, let's try and work this thing out carefully, shall we? Let's stop jumping to conclusions. Now, I first met Marcus in March. He was at a cocktail party at Heaton Alliance, the big insurance company, and he came over and introduced himself.'

'Did he? That's very unlike Marcus, he never usually chats to anyone unless he's forced to. Whose party did you say it was?'

'It was Heaton Alliance, a party to launch their new European fund...' Alex broke off and looked at her. 'What's the matter? Why are you looking like that?'

Lucie shook her head. 'Marcus never goes to things like that, never. He doesn't need to, he doesn't waste his time. Why did he introduce himself to you?'

Alex shrugged. 'I don't know, I think he said we had someone in common, or maybe we just got chatting, I can't honestly remember.'

Lucie stood up and went to her sports bag. She took out her diary and began flicking through it to see if there was anything in it that might possibly have given her away.

'Maybe I said something then,' Alex said, 'maybe I let something slip...'

She glanced up. 'Perhaps you called me and he took the call? Do you ever remember calling the house?'

'No, never. What about bills? Could he have

seen my number on an itemised bill?'

'I don't think so. I honestly can't remember if my bills are itemised, I usually get them at the office because it's a work phone. He might have listened to one of your messages on the mobile, though when is the question. I nearly always have it on me.' She stopped. 'You know, I've been wondering the last two days, wondering and thinking and worrying that his reaction to finding out about my affair with you wasn't normal. That his reaction to this whole insider thing wasn't right, that he was... I don't know, laid-back almost, as if he already knew, as if nothing had shocked him. He was so unemotional about it, so calm. He said he wanted to focus on me, on getting me off the charges, but Christ, what if he'd planned it all along? What if...' She wasn't able to finish. This was her husband she was talking about, a man she had loved; no, did love, didn't she? 'Oh God, Alex, I just can't believe it, I just can't.'

Alex stood up. 'Right, let's find out if he knew and then we can move on from there. You need to check that you don't get an itemised bill that he could have found and I'll call the hotel we've used quite a bit and check that no one has asked any questions about us.' He went across to the phone, while Lucie took her mobile out of her bag. She called the phone company and stood, going across to the window to make her call. A few minutes later she turned, looked at Alex and pressed end.

'Nothing from the hotel,' he said. 'Reception gave absolutely nothing away. You?'

Lucie's face had drained of all colour again. 'My husband requested an itemised phone bill earlier this year, in February. He was sent it.' Alex came across to her and held her. She laid her face against his chest, but wasn't comforted; she had gone beyond comfort. 'I have to ring Janie,' she said, pulling back.

'No, don't ring her, go down and see her.'

She looked up at him and he could see the pain in her face. He thought, how did it all come to this?

'D'you think so?'

'Yes, I do. Borrow my car and drive down today.' She moved away from him and he said, 'It's always better to see people in person. Just get in the car and go.' She nodded but he could see that she wasn't listening. She went back to the chair and picked up her tea. 'Why?' she asked, looking at him. Alex shook his head once again. 'I really don't know, Lucie,' he said gently, but he did know. It was the oldest, most raw, basic and powerful of human emotions. It was jealousy. It was love, twisted and thwarted and gone bad. It was revenge.

Jack had addresses for all of the people he considered part of his investigation; he had their addresses, their photographs and the registration numbers of their cars. After a night thinking about it, he decided that Sarah's idea was worth a shot, even if it was a long one.

He started with Stan Gamley. He went to the council offices, parked and, checking up at the windows of the building, looked first at Gamley's

438

car, then at the cars of the three people who worked for him. He looked all round the cars, under the front of each one, along the wings and particularly around the bumpers. There was nothing on any of them; just as he'd expected.

He then drove the thirty miles or so to the main West Sussex office of Glover Homes. He went in through the gates, drove round the car park looking for Redfern's car and, seeing it wasn't there, stopped for a few minutes to look at the map. Redfern lived fifteen miles from Burgess Hill and Jack thought, why not, while I'm in the area? He headed off to find Redfern's house.

It proved easy to locate, easier than Jack had imagined. It was at the end of a cul-de-sac of executive homes, a nice development if you liked that kind of thing – which Jack didn't – but poorly landscaped with cheap shrubs and not much imagination. It was probably done by Glover Homes, Jack thought. He parked halfway down the cul-de-sac and looked across at Redfern's house. The car was in the drive which meant Redfern was very probably in. Was it worth the risk? Jack sat and weighed it up. Yes, he decided, it was. Three minutes maximum; he could check the car, note anything of interest and be gone easily in that time. He climbed out of his car, walked the twenty yards to Redfern's house, glanced behind him for any prying neighbours and bent to look under the front of the bumper. He hardly had to bother. Along the righthand side there had obviously been some kind of collision. There was a small graze along the plastic and the tiniest scrape of white paint. Jack stood, looked again at the house behind him, then at Redfern's house and hurried to his car. He took his digital camera out of the glove compartment, went back to the silver Mercedes and bent to take some photographs. He took ten, from all angles, very quickly, and then walked away. Back in his own car, as he dropped the camera on the seat and started the engine, he realised that his hands were shaking. 'Shit,' he said aloud as he drove off; then, 'Got you, you bastard.'

It was lunchtime and Marcus had had no word from Lucie. He sat in the living area of their smart house on the grey linen sofa and kicked at the leg of it. He could see that she'd been through her box from work and taken her diary. Files had been looked at too, things rifled through; it unnerved him. He didn't like to be left alone, not at this crucial stage. He wanted to be with Lucie, to make sure that she found out the right things in the right order; he wanted to guide her through this. He also needed to protect himself. Without thinking any further, he reached for the phone and dialled a number he had come to know well. The line connected, it was answered after five or six rings and he said, 'Hello, Sarah. It's Marcus. I just rang to see if you're all right.'

Sarah had run in from the garden where she was mowing the grass. She was tired and out of breath. She hated mowing the lawn, but at the moment she would do anything other than sit and think. It was the second time it had been cut this week.

'Hello, Marcus.' She was cool; she remembered their previous phone conversation and almost couldn't equate this charming, smooth voice with the one she had last spoken to.

'I am so sorry, Sarah, about all this trouble,' he said, 'I just wanted to ring and let you know that.'

'Yes...' Why did it sound insincere? Sarah shook herself. 'Well, erm, thanks,' she replied, 'it must be awful for you too.'

'Yes, yes it is. Look, Sarah, I want you to know that I'm on your side, OK? That I'm here if you need anything, any advice or want to talk things through with me...'

'Right, erm, thank you.' She softened. She'd caught him at a bad time on holiday, she knew she had. 'I appreciate it, Marcus,' she said, 'I really do.'

'Good. You will let me know if there's anything I can do, won't you?'

'Yes, I will.'

'And how's it going? Have you got a lawyer yet? Do you know exactly what happened?'

'Well, we're not sure that Lucie–' The doorbell rang and Sarah could see a tall figure through the glass panel. 'Sorry, could you hang on a minute, Marcus?'

She went to the door, opened it and Jack stood there. She smiled. 'Come in, Jack, I'm just on the phone.' Going back to the receiver, she took it up and said, 'Sorry, Marcus, someone has just arrived. Can I call you back?'

'Yes, yes, of course. You didn't finish, Sarah; you didn't think Lucie what?'

'Oh nothing. I'll talk to you about it later.'

'Sure.'

'Bye, Marcus.'

'Bye, Sarah.'

Sarah hung up and turned towards Jack. Marcus hung up and said, 'Bugger.'

'Hi.' Jack stood uneasily He was tall and looked out of place in Sarah's small, pink hallway

'Come in and I'll make some tea,' she said.

'Oh, erm, thanks.'

He followed her into the kitchen and looked beyond it at the garden. 'Been busy then?'

'Oh yes, the grass. I hate it, but it takes my mind off things.'

'I'll do it for you if you like. Once a week after work.'

She turned from filling the kettle and said, 'Oh no, I couldn't possibly let you...'

'I'd like to. It would only take ten minutes. I bet it takes you over an hour.'

Sarah smiled. 'Yes, it does!' She switched the kettle on and waited. He was obviously here for a reason; she didn't know him well enough for a social call – yet.

'I came to thank you. I went to see a car this afternoon. A car belonging to someone I thought might be involved in Rupert Sayer's accident.'

'And?'

'It was.'

Sarah swung round. 'Bloody hell.' She looked at him. 'That's serious, Jack. Have you been to the police?'

'Not yet. I wanted to ask you something first.' He dug his hands in his pockets. 'I wanted to ask you if you'd help me with something tomorrow morning.'

Sarah frowned. 'What?'

'There's a bloke called Gamley. He works in town planning, runs it actually, and he's on the make. Bill Redfern, the land buyer for Glover Homes, pays him off on a regular basis. I know it and Rupert knew it, but I need proof and there isn't any. Not a sniff. I reckon he's stuffing money away to Guernsey in a suitcase.'

'So?' The kettle boiled but she left it.

'I've had an idea and I need you to help me with it.'

Sarah said, 'I hope it doesn't involve anything illegal, Jack, or even close to the mark because I really don't want to get...'

'No, it doesn't, not at all. It would involve you acting the part of a researcher at Gatwick short-term car park tomorrow and intercepting Gamley as he gets out of his car so that I can have a look in the boot at his case.'

'Oh God,' Sarah said, 'I don't know if I...'

'I've got it all scripted,' Jack cut in. 'I did it an hour ago and it'll work, Sarah, I'm certain it will. If I can find out if he's got cash in his case then I'll shop him to Customs.'

'Why not just shop him anyway and let them look?'

'Because if he's not taking anything with him this time then he'll get scared and change his routine and then I'll never get him.'

Sarah made a pot of tea. She took her time over it, stirring the teapot and laying out cups and saucers – things she rarely used. She poured milk into a jug and set out the sugar bowl. She wasn't trying to impress him, she just needed time to think. 'Is that why you've offered to cut my grass?'

Jack shrugged. He could lie now but he decided not to. 'Yes,' he replied, 'to soften you up.'

Sarah poured the tea. 'Oh why did I open my big mouth yesterday about not letting Graham and Roz down?' She glanced up at Jack and smiled.

'Does that mean yes?'

'It means I'll give it a go.'

'Great, I...' He stopped, interrupted by the phone. Sarah headed into the hall to answer it. 'Help yourself to tea,' she called on her way. Jack heard her answer the phone, say a few words, then hang up again. She came to the kitchen door. 'Actually, don't help yourself to tea,' she said. 'That was Janie on the phone. Lucie Croft has just turned up and she says she thinks that Marcus set her up.'

Chapter Twenty-three

Lucie was sitting in Janie's kitchen when Sarah and Jack arrived. They were the last ones. Everyone else was there – Roz, Graham and the three children and even Andrew, who had somehow wangled cover for his afternoon surgery. The house was noisy; Justin and Katie ran in and out of the garden chased by Kitty and Oliver, everyone was talking, Roz was smoking and there was a smell of fresh coffee above the smoke. Janie, Sarah thought, looked oddly at home amongst the chaos and it surprised her.

'I don't think you've met Lucie, have you, Sarah?'

'We met once,' Lucie said, 'at a barbecue here, a couple of years ago.'

'Yes, we did,' Sarah replied, but the person in front of her was nothing like she remembered and she had to make an effort not to stare. This frail, worn-out figure in jeans and a sweater bore no resemblance at all to the sleek, linen-draped power woman she'd met, a woman who had exuded confidence and spoken with the sharp, concise manner of someone always in control.

'I'm sorry,' Lucie said, 'for all this awful mess.' She couldn't meet Sarah's eye and Sarah shrugged; she had no reply

'Coffee?' Janie asked Sarah.

'Please.' She pulled out a chair and sat at the

table with Lucie. She didn't really want to but felt she couldn't do anything else. As she sat Roz came over and sat down as well. Andrew said, 'Shall we all sit down? I think that Lucie wants to talk to us.'

Jack, who had been talking to Graham, waited for Janie to pour the coffee and brought the mugs over to the table. Sarah thought, you can tell a man who lives on his own, he doesn't wait for anything to be done for him. He sat next to Sarah and she glanced at him, catching his eye. There was something about him that she liked, something easy and unassuming. He smiled at her and she smiled back.

'Thank you all for coming over,' Andrew said, as Janie finally sat down. 'Lucie wanted us all to be here so that we can hear from her what's happened. She wanted to explain things in her own words.' He glanced at Lucie who sat, head down, with her hands clasped together on her lap. 'Lucie?' She looked up.

'Thanks, Andrew.' She took a deep breath. 'I, erm, I don't really know how or where to start, I suppose that I need to say sorry, I...' She was still tearful and her voice broke. She took another deep breath and stared down at the table for a few moments, then went on. 'I don't know how all this happened, I really don't. One minute my life was ordinary, unhappy, yes, but very ordinary, and the next it is extraordinary I didn't do anything to change that, except...' Once again she had to stop and Sarah winced. It was terrible listening to someone else's pain. 'Except that I had an affair and that's where I think, where I can only assume, that things went very wrong.' She coughed. 'Janie, I know that this is as hard for you as it is for me, but I came here today to tell you that I am beginning to think that this whole thing has been engineered by Marcus. I am beginning to think, and Alex agrees with me, that we might have been set up.'

There was a sharp intake of breath around the table and Janie's face creased into a frown. 'I know what you think, Lucie, but I just don't understand it. How could it have had anything to do with Marcus? He told me that you had been supplying information to...' Andrew touched Janie's arm to stop her. 'Let Lucie speak, Janie. Let her say what she has to.'

'But we've heard it and...'

'Let everyone else hear it and then we'll talk.' He squeezed the arm that he held. 'Please?' Janie shut up. She reached for her coffee and took a sip, bending her head over the mug.

'I know that I didn't give any information to Alex. I took no interest in this investment club thing because I didn't agree with Alex being involved. I have never given him any details of projects I've worked on or let him have access to information that was price-sensitive. I even checked it with my secretary. I've never carried files on my person that contained price-sensitive information...' She paused. 'No, that's a lie. I did carry some documents home one night that outlined a deal for Rightson Electronics with another company and Alex looked at them. He admitted to me that he had glanced in my case, seen the files and had a look at them. But...' she looked round the table, 'he didn't do anything about them because he didn't have the nerve. It was too risky and he isn't that stupid.' She sighed. 'I believe him, I've checked and his story is true. So we started to think about who might possibly have had access to the inside information that Alex so naïvely dealt on...' She shook her head. 'And the only name we could come up with was Marcus. He is the only person I have ever talked to about my work, he knew about every deal. He also, we think – although we're not certain about this – knew about our affair.'

'No,' Janie said. 'No he didn't, Lucie. I told him about your affair when I rang to tell him what had happened and he was shocked, stunned even. He was hardly able to speak to me about it.'

'He had requested an itemised phone bill for my mobile, Janie; it had Alex's number listed several times.'

Sarah said, 'I just don't see it, Lucie, I'm sorry but I don't. I've had quite a lot to do with Marcus over the past few months – he's given me a lot of help with this investment club – and every tip that he's passed on to me, to us, has been from Alex.'

'Have you been seeing Marcus on a regular basis?' Roz asked.

Sarah blushed. 'Yes, I mean no, not seeing him like that, it's been just friendship, we've shared a common interest. He wanted to help us and he didn't want any of you to know it was him in case Janie thought...' Sarah broke off. She looked at everyone round the table and said again, 'He's been trying to help us, he's been passing on tips from Alex, he...'

'Who told you they were tips from Alex?' Lucie asked.

'Marcus, of course' Sarah shook her head. 'He's been really kind, he...'

'Why didn't he want any of us to know he was involved?' Roz asked.

'He was worried it would be misconstrued.' Sarah stared at Roz. 'And from the looks on your faces he was right!' She stood up.

'Perhaps he wanted to make sure that no one questioned his motives, Sarah,' Jack said. Sarah looked at him and her heart sank. She had never questioned the information Marcus had given her, never thought to confirm that the tips had actually come from Alex. It had never seriously occurred to her that he was anything other than completely honest. Why should it have? Her best friend's brother, why should she ever think he would lie to her? Janie had almost bitten her head off when she'd raised even the smallest doubt about him. Sarah hung her head and slipped back into her chair.

'Did Marcus tell you about Wye Valley Foods, Sarah?' Lucie asked.

Sarah nodded. 'He said that he had had a tip from Alex.'

'Alex couldn't have had any tips about Wye Valley, I never told him about it and he had no access to documents in my case or anywhere else,' Lucie said. 'I often talked to Marcus about work and I told him about Wye Valley. I discussed all my projects with him.' She looked again at Sarah. 'Did he tell you about Sarasota plc?'

'Yes.'

16PP

MAG · 32196 · THE DREAM CATCHER.1·9

'Passing on a tip from Alex?'

'That's what he said.'

'He was lying.' Lucie looked away 'I'm sorry, but I'm convinced he was lying.'

Janie put her head in her hands and Andrew touched her gently on the back. 'I can't believe it,' she murmured, her face buried, 'I can't believe he'd do it to us, to me...' There was a shocked silence around the table.

'He was the one who mentioned the idea of an investment club in the first place,' Lucie said quietly. 'He said he thought it would be good for you, Janie, to start an investment club, it would give you an interest. He knew then that I was having an affair and he needed to be able to set the whole thing up...'

'No!' Janie said. 'I just can't believe it, Lucie, I can't believe that my brother would do that. I'm sorry, but this sounds to me like an elaborate lie.'

'Are you saying,' Jack ventured, 'that you think Marcus set you up because you had an affair, because of jealousy?'

Lucie swallowed hard. 'I ... I think so, yes.'

Janie looked up and shook her head. 'He couldn't do it, Lucie, I know him and I know that he couldn't do something like this. I mean, we're talking about criminal charges! Marcus wouldn't do that...'

Jack had been thinking hard. He said, 'What if, and this is only a guess, what if Marcus knew that you weren't going to get prosecuted?'

'What?' Andrew looked at Jack. 'The woman from the Stock Exchange, what was her name, Janie?'

'Stimpson, Jan or Janet or something...'

'Janice Stimpson,' Roz said, 'old bag.'

'She told Janie that they were handing the file over to the DTI for investigation with a view to prosecution. Prosecution means criminal charges and the maximum penalty for secondary insider trading is five years.'

Jack frowned. 'Yeah, but what if Marcus knew that they wouldn't have a case.'

Andrew leaned forward. 'How could he know that?'

'I rang the DTI this morning, just a routine enquiry, and I found out from some chap there that they get thirty cases of insider trading a year to investigate and they bring probably one to trial, if they're lucky.'

'Bloody hell.' Andrew looked at Janie.

'That's the best news I've had all year,' Roz said. 'Are you sure, Jack?'

'That's what he said. That's maybe why you're having a bit of trouble finding a lawyer to take the case on. I don't know, but it seems to me that to prosecute there would have to be some kind of concrete proof, like phone tapes or video footage or witnesses. In this case there's nothing except connections and someone in corporate finance who denies having passed on insider information, along with proof that she never took the files out of the office on the occasions she met her lover. Right, Lucie?'

'Yes. It's all on the computer. The Sarasota document was being worked on at the time I met Alex for lunch and the Wye Valley Organic Foods document hadn't even been created the night we

451

met for a drink.'

'It's all hearsay and speculation. It's a good case, well fitted together, and the chances are that the DTI is hoping that someone involved will talk when they get around to interviewing you all, but if they don't, then I don't see how it can wash. Unless they can categorically prove that Lucie passed on price-sensitive information to Alex, by way of taped phone conversations, then I don't see how they can prosecute.'

'D'you mean that we might get off?' Sarah stared at Jack.

He shrugged. 'Look, I'm not a lawyer, I don't really know, but if I had to make an educated guess I'd say that if Marcus did set this all up then he knew something about insider trading before he did it. He very probably knew that they'd have a hard time pinning this one down...'

'Are you saying that you think it might all have been a ruse? What? To scare me?' Lucie couldn't keep the shock out of her voice. 'All this grief and pain and terror...' Her voice cracked and she stared hard at her hands to stop herself from crying. She wasn't sure if it was relief or hurt or anger that had brought the tears.

'I can't believe it,' Sarah said, 'I just can't...'

Jack stood and went across to the kettle. 'Mind if I make more coffee, Janie?'

'No.' Janie's voice came out as a whisper and Andrew thought, this is harder for her than for anyone. Marcus betraying Lucie I can just about understand, but betraying his sister I can't. He reached for her hand under the table and was surprised to find that she gave it and clutched his for support. They sat in silence, waiting for Jack to come back with the coffee. It was as if Jack linked them all together, offered them some outside objectivity in a highly emotive situation. He filled the cafetiere, brought it back to the table and silently poured coffee into mugs. Then he sat and said, 'If we find out whether or not Marcus did know about the affair, will that make things clearer for everyone?'

'It would at least give him a reason,' Andrew said, 'although what difference that would make I don't know'

'I don't think he did know,' Janie said stubbornly, 'and I don't think it was him.'

'That means you think it was me,' Lucie said. 'It's my word against his. There is no irrefutable proof that I didn't pass on insider information to Alex, but then there is no irrefutable proof that I did either. You have to decide who you believe.'

'I don't think it was you,' Janie protested, 'I think it was...' She stopped and looked away 'I don't know who I think it was,' she murmured.

'Lucie, was there a cafe or restaurant or somewhere that you went on a regular basis with Alex, somewhere Marcus might have seen you?'

'No, only...' Lucie flushed. 'We used a small hotel in the West End, but Alex rang them and they said they'd never had any enquiries about us.'

'I'll check it out,' Jack said.

'Would you?' Lucie was eager; she wanted an end to the speculation. She wanted to know and once she did she felt she could deal with it.

Jack looked at his watch. 'It's three-thirty now,

I could be up there by five-thirty, depending on traffic.' He'd made up his mind to go, it seemed to be the most obvious solution. He could ask questions and read things in the answers that most people couldn't.

'You sure, Jack?' Jack had stood up and Graham stood as well. 'D'you want me to come with you?' he asked.

'No, you call Dodi and see what she's found out about Alex. I asked her to get some background information and she should have done it by now.' Jack dug in his pocket for his car keys. 'I'll get off,' he said. 'I think it's the only thing to do for now, except to try not to worry.' He glanced at Sarah. 'Sarah, I couldn't have a word, could I?'

She stood, puzzled, and followed him out into the hall. He was fiddling with his keys. He glanced up and smiled at her and she knew then for certain that she liked him. 'Sarah, I've made a mistake. I realised it as soon as I said it but I can't go back on it, so I need help.'

'OK.'

'My ex-wife, Sandra, is dropping Jamie off tonight at six. They've been in Spain and he's coming to stay with me for a few days so that Sandra can go off with Billy Bright Boots to some football do and, well...' He shrugged. 'I'm not going to be there, I'm going to be in London.'

'You want me to go round and wait for Jamie?'

'Would you mind?'

She shrugged. Actually she'd quite like a glimpse of Sandra, but she wasn't going to admit that. 'I don't mind at all. I'll take Rory and then

454

we might go out for pizza or something. I hate other people's kitchens; I'm bad enough at the best of times in my own. Will he mind? He doesn't know me.'

Jack coughed. 'He knows of you, I've, erm ... I've mentioned your name a few times and of course he'll recognise Rory from school.' Jack handed her his house keys and dug in his pocket for his business card. 'Home address is right under the office address. it's dead easy to find, it's at the end of Rough Lane, you can't miss it.'

She smiled. 'OK.'

'Thanks, Sarah.'

She was still smiling when he leant forward and kissed her on the mouth. She pulled back, caught her breath and blinked. 'See you later,' he said, but before she had a chance to reply he had gone.

The meeting broke up just after Jack left. Lucie sat pale and distraught but Janie couldn't bring herself to ask her to stay; she was too upset. So Roz went across and said, 'We've got a spare room at Chadwick if you'd like to stay the night with us? It's not terribly smart but it's comfy and you look tired. I don't think you should be driving, if you don't mind me saying.'

'No, I don't mind you saying, and thanks, I'd like to stay,' Lucie replied and the relief on her face was apparent. Sarah left soon after that. She had to collect Rory at four-thirty and she wanted to pop home first. If she was going to meet Sandra then she wanted to be a bit prepared for it.

She collected Rory from the leisure centre with

an overnight bag in the car – just in case – and they made their way over to Jack's house. She had to inform Rory in detail about where they were going and why – he liked to have a good understanding of everything – but she left out the crucial information; he still knew nothing of the DTI investigation.

She pulled into the drive of Jack's home and stopped. Both she and Rory looked up at the house, a brick and flint cottage that had been extended over the years. It was covered in wisteria, all in bloom, and lilac blossoms drooped from its branches heavy with pollen and scent. There were terracotta pots out the front – not the standard neat size filled with verbena and geraniums but huge great urns that spilt a profusion of wonderful things Sarah had never seen before. Sarah saw the gate at the side of the house, made of rusting wrought iron, and said, 'Come on, Rory, let's have a look at the garden. Jamie's dad is a bit of an expert at growing things.'

And he was too. Around the back of the house the garden had been divided into several areas, each one leading off from the other, each one unique and individual. The first was a traditional cottage garden, the perfect fit for the house, but through a gap in a yew hedge there was another pocket of garden that was neatly laid out into squares and planted with lines of box hedges and lavender. In the centre of each square was a shaped box hedge: one spiral, one consisting of three balls of green, all perfectly circular, one cone-shaped and one in the shape of a bird. A

mall path ran on into the next pocket of garden
vhich was accessed by a gate. Once through this
here was a long rectangle of still water filled with
vater lilies and reeds, backed by a glass wall that
ad water cascading down it. The water and the
;lass combined to create an image of dazzling
ight as they caught the rays of the late afternoon
un.

'Wow,' said Rory He went across to the water.
There are lights at the bottom, Mum, it must be
it up at night.'

Sarah was stunned. 'It's beautiful,' she said
[uietly, 'really beautiful.' They walked on to the
ext piece of garden which was obviously in the
>rocess of being created and then turned and
vandered slowly back through it all to the
ottage.

'Can I open the door, Mum?'

Sarah gave Rory the keys. 'Go ahead.' But she
lidn't want to go in yet, she wanted to stay and
ake in the garden. So she watched Rory unlock
he back door, then turned to see the glitter of
ight bouncing off the glass wall which was just
isible through the curtain of green that separ-
ted it from the rest of the garden. When he said
;ardening, Sarah thought, I didn't realise he
neant this.

'Mum,' Rory called, 'Jamie's got the Pokemon
ifficial handbook!'

Sarah turned and smiled. 'Oh good!'

'Come and see it.'

She took one more look at the garden, sighed
nd went inside.

Jack was surprised at how quickly he'd made i
up to London. He'd driven to Gatwick, got or
the express to Victoria and jumped in a cab onc
in London. He climbed out now in front of the
hotel and looked up at the sign. Not very glam
orous but then, in his experience, people who
had affairs rarely had them with any style. He
paid the driver and had a look at the building. I
was an end of-terrace house with iron railings
bay trees and a discreet sign over the door. It wa
obviously aimed at middle-bracket American
tourists: nice and clean and comfortable with the
smart mock-Victorian look that most of them
liked. He reckoned it ran over two houses and
began to walk to the end of the street to look for
the back entrance. Things in hotels, Jack knew
always happened where the staff were. He found
the door to the kitchens, opened it and called
out. One of the kitchen staff came up and Jack
said, 'I'm looking for one of the chambermaids.
I've got a package for her. Where would I find
laundry?'

'Carry on round the back and it's through the
main door, along the corridor and second on the
right. D'you want me to give it to her?'

'No thanks, mate, I promised I'd see that she
got it personally.' Jack closed the door and
carried on. He found the main door, opened it
and went into the hotel where the smell of
laundry was overpowering. 'Hello?' He opened a
door, not the second on the right, and looked in.
Two girls were in there smoking, despite a no
smoking sign on the wall.

'Can I help you?' one of them asked.

'I don't know, maybe.' Jack came in and closed the door behind him. The air was thick with smoke. 'I need to know if either of you can remember or know of a bloke who came round earlier in the year asking questions about a couple who used the hotel regularly. He might have paid for the information, might have asked someone to keep their eye on the couple and phone him, or maybe just confirm that they used the hotel. He might even have just hung around looking suspicious...' Jack broke off. Both girls were staring blankly at him. 'No? Don't remember anything at all?'

'Nah, sorry. Nothing.'

Jack nodded and left the room. He went on, looked in the laundry, which was empty, then decided to try reception.

Back at the front of the hotel, he went in and across to reception. There was a young woman on the desk, which was a better bet than a male manager. Jack went over to her.

'Hello, can I help you?'

Jack read her name badge and said, 'Hi, Lorna, I wonder if you can. I'm trying to find out if anyone has been seen in your hotel earlier in the year making enquiries about a couple who stayed here regularly.'

'For what purpose?' She was immediately wary

'I'm a lawyer,' Jack said, 'and my clients are well known and fear that they may be the subject of a tabloid story. Untrue, of course, which is why I'm here, working on their behalf. The chap was a journalist.'

Lorna shook her head. 'I'm afraid I don't

remember anything personally, but I can tell you that it is hotel policy not to give out any information on our guests whatsoever.' She shrugged. The matter, as far as she was concerned, was closed.

'OK, thanks.' Jack turned and headed out of the hotel. He'd have to try the kitchens; maybe one of the chefs might know something. He was on his way down the steps when someone touched his arm. He turned.

'There was a bloke, he was here in February.'

Jack faced a young man, about eighteen, in full bellboy livery. He looked hot and uncomfortable.

'Really?' Unlikely, Jack thought, he's jumping on the bandwagon.

'Yeah, he talked to my girlfriend, she's one of the maids here. He offered her money.'

Jack raised an eyebrow. 'What for?'

'I dunno, he gave her about fifty quid as far as I can remember.'

Jack took his wallet out.

'Not here,' the young man said. He edged Jack forward and round the side of the steps, out of sight of the main doors.

'How much?' Jack asked.

'Twenty,' the bellboy replied.

Jack took a note out of his wallet and held it. 'Make it worth my while.'

'This bloke came and asked Dilly if she'd check on a room, to see if there was a couple in there. They'd just checked in so she went up and knocked and opened the door. They were, you know, at it, so she apologised and ran down again. He gave her fifty quid, or it might have been a hundred...'

'Don't push it,' Jack warned. 'Description?'

'What?'

'Did she describe the bloke or the couple?'

'I dunno.'

'No fee then. You're making this all up.' Jack went to walk off and the young man said, 'No, wait! All right; she said the bloke was posh, didn't look like a journalist, more like a bank manager. And he drove a snazzy car.'

'What sort of car?' Jack asked.

'A red Porsche.'

Marcus, Jack thought. He said, 'And the couple? Names? Did he ask Dilly to check the register?'

The young man nodded, but said nothing. Jack took out another note and added it to the one he already held. 'He hung around and when they'd gone Dilly checked the payment on the computer – told reception she thought they might have had something from the mini-bar and not owned up.'

'Any idea at all of the names?'

'Nah, don't remember.'

'Did this bloke ever come back? Did he ask Dilly to keep an eye out for the couple, anything like that?'

'Don't know.'

Jack handed over forty pounds. 'Thanks,' he said. He glanced up at the hotel, then said, 'I don't suppose...' But he didn't finish his sentence because the bellboy had gone.

Sarah glanced at her watch as she heard a car come up the drive. It was a black Mercedes soft-top, it had a CD blasting out of the stereo and the roof was down. It stopped, the music cut off and Sarah waited, suddenly nervous. The door went and she crossed the hall to answer it.

'Hello.'

Sandra stood with her arm round an embarrassed Jamie. She was nut brown, bottle blonde and wafer thin. She stared at Sarah, looked her up and down, then smiled, but not at all warmly. Looks her age, Sarah thought nastily. She said, 'Hi, I'm Sarah Greg, a friend of Jack's. I'm sorry but he's been held up in London on a job and I said I'd get over here to meet Jamie. He won't be long, he should be back after supper.' Sarah looked at Jamie. He had shrugged off his mother's affectionate embrace and now stared hard at the ground. Rory appeared behind Sarah and said, 'Hi, Jamie. How come you've got two Machokes? I've got Machop and I could swop you Machoke for Haunter if you like. You've got Gastly but you haven't got Haunter. It's got sixty hit points'

Jamie looked up.

'OK. Have you got two Haunters then?'

Sarah stood aside as he went into the house after Rory and Sandra called, 'Jamie darling, aren't you going to say goodbye to Mummy?'

'Bye!' he shouted from upstairs and Sandra smiled tightly.

'Would you like to come in?' Sarah asked.

'Oh no, no thank you, I must get going. Tell Jack I'll be back on Friday to collect him.' She turned and headed for the car and as she climbed in Sarah thought, cellulite on the upper thighs;

462

ood. Sandra waved, the engine started, the music blared and Sarah went inside. She glanced own at her pink dress and high-heeled sandals nd smiled. It may only have been on for fifty econds but it was more than worth it.

oz took the call from Jack and told Lucie xactly what he'd said. Lucie looked wretched nd Roz didn't know what to say.

'Andrew's talking to a lawyer this evening,' she ffered. 'You never know, what Jack said could be ight, the investigation by the DTI might not ome to anything...' But Lucie didn't even seem ⊃ hear her. She stared blankly at the wall and ℓoz left her to it.

t took Jack a good deal longer to get back from ⅃ondon than it had taken him to get there. 'ictoria Station was closed due to a bomb scare ⊃ he sat in a cafe nearby drinking horrible coffee nd waiting for it to reopen again. It did this at ⁚ven, he got the seven-forty-five train to Gat- ʳick and was home by nine. When he got to the ʰottage he found Sarah in the kitchen, all dressed ℘, with her notes, her diary and her phone bill ut on the kitchen table in front of her. The boys ʳere in bed, sharing Jamie's room, but a long way ff sleep.

'Hi. You look nice.'

'What? This old thing?' Even as she said it ;arah knew it didn't wash. She blushed and, ℩eeting Jack's eye, said, 'OK, the truth is I got ʳessed up to meet Sandra. I couldn't let her see ℩e in scruffy shorts and a tee-shirt.'

Jack pulled out a chair. 'I bet she was pea-green by the time she left.'

'I'm not sure. She's tough competition.'

'Not for you, Sarah.' He said it so casually that she almost missed it; almost. He reached for her phone bill. 'What's this?'

'I've been doing some thinking,' Sarah said 'and some checking.'

'And?'

'I'm not sure, but look at this. Marcus always phoned me on his mobile, but look, I was checking my phone bill for any clues and I found number I didn't recognise, here. It's Marcus' office. I rang it to check, which means that obviously phoned him once. I then had a look through my notebook which, I might add, I had to go home for, but it did mean that Rory could get his Pokemon cards so the boys were quite happy. When I looked back over my notes I saw that the date I called him was around the time of the Sarasota deal. I'm pretty sure that I must have rung him for some query and it'll be on his office line.'

'And taped,' Jack said.

'I don't know exactly what this means but...'

'I'd hazard a guess that it probably doesn't mean anything, but it might be useful, Sarah.'

'How?'

Jack stood up. 'Let me go and see the boys, you open some wine and then we'll sit down and talk about it.' He headed for the door, then stopped and turned. He took two paces back to the table and kissed her mouth for the second time that day.

'Oh, I...'

He pulled back. 'Yes?'

She blushed. 'Nothing,' she murmured.

Jack stood straight. 'No, it's not nothing, Sarah,' he said. 'It's something, it's definitely something.' Then he turned and left the room.

Lucie pulled into a parking space directly outside her house, something that had almost never happened before. It had taken her two hours to get home from Sussex – she had left Chadwick Farm on impulse, creeping away without telling anyone – but she wasn't tired; she was too strung-out to be tired. She parked Alex's car, climbed out and looked up at her house. She hated it; she hated it because it had meant to be so much and had amounted to so little. It was chic, glossy and expensive and empty of any warmth or comfort. It wasn't a home, it was a place she slept in, a place she was unhappy in. It was a house and she would put it on the market as soon as she could.

She glanced at her watch and went inside. She didn't turn on any lights; she didn't need to. She knew exactly what she was doing and she could do it in the half-light of twilight, in the shadow of falling darkness. She smiled as she took the extension lead out of the cupboard in the kitchen. It was appropriate, this light; it was the odd light caught just between the end of the day and the beginning of the night. It was something and nothing, it was like her life. She checked that the extension lead worked and then took it into the bedroom. Marcus was at work; she knew that because his briefcase had gone and he'd tried on a couple of suits, seeing which one went best with his tan. He must have gone in to check what was going down in the office. He must have needed to see if the DTI had contacted him. She shook her head. They could contact him all they liked after tonight; he wouldn't be answering any questions.

Lucie plugged the extension lead into the socket next to her bed and then took her hair-dryer out of the drawer and plugged it into the extension lead. She turned it on, blew cool air over her face and neck for a few moments, then stood and checked she could throw it into the bath from outside the bathroom. She could; she was ready. She switched everything off, rolled the extension lead up and carefully placed the hair-dryer behind her bedside table. When Marcus got home after a day in the City he always took a bath; it helped him relax. Marcus would be home soon and then she would be free of him. She left the bedroom and went upstairs to the guest suite; there she sat on a chair in the dark and waited for him to come in.

Janie called Roz as soon as Andrew had put the phone down to the lawyer and had briefly explained to her what he'd said. She rang Sarah first but there was no reply, so then she called Roz.

'Andrew has just spoken to a lawyer and he is pretty certain that they won't be able to put together enough of a case to prosecute,' she said. 'Apparently there's no evidence, apart from circumstantial, and these cases are incredibly difficult to try.' Janie took a breath. 'Roz? Roz?'

But Roz couldn't answer. She handed the phone to Graham and collapsed into a chair, covering her face with her hands. Graham spoke at length to Janie, then to Andrew and, finally satisfied with what they had to say, hung up. He turned to Roz, saw her and went across the room to kneel in front of her. He gently pulled her hands away from her face and kissed them. 'It's all right, love,' he said gently, 'there's no need to cry, it's going to be all right...' She was his strength, his rock; she coped with things in a way that filled him with awe. 'It's all right, Roz love, honestly, Andrew is sure it's going to be all right.' But everyone needs to be looked after at some point, even the strong and the capable, and Graham knew that Roz had reached that point. He lifted her to her feet and, as Roz continued to weep, led her upstairs and into the bedroom. There he helped her into bed and lay down beside her, holding her close and stroking her hair. He would tell Lucie in a while – he would see to supper and get them all a stiff drink. But for now he would love his wife and help to ease away the heavy responsibility that she bore.

Sarah put her spoon and fork down neatly in the centre of her plate and said, 'That was the best spaghetti and tomato sauce I have ever had.'

Jack said, 'It was linguini and the sauce was supposed to have had mushrooms and bacon in it.'

'Was it?'

He smiled. 'Yes. Never mind, you obviously

enjoyed it.'

'Gosh, did it show? Was I that greedy?'

'No, but you've got it on your chin.'

'Have I?' Sarah swiped at her chin with her napkin.

Jack leant forward. 'Come here.' She tilted her chin upwards and gently he touched it with the tip of his napkin. 'There.'

'Thanks.'

He didn't move back but stayed close to her, their faces almost touching. 'Sarah?'

Sarah held her breath, her stomach did a back flip and, without thinking, she reached forward and eased his mouth on to her own.

It took him a few moments to register the kiss then he kissed her back. 'Sarah, I...' She pressed her finger to his lips and stood up, moving back a pace to lean against the work surface. One of the straps of her dress had fallen down and as Jack stood in front of her he kissed her bare shoulder and licked the skin. 'Spaghetti sauce,' he murmured, 'how did it get there?'

Sarah smiled and closed her eyes. Jack moved his lips across from her shoulder to her neck and kissed to the edge of her dress. She slipped the other strap down and gently eased the dress to her waist. 'My God,' Jack whispered, 'you are so lovely.' He moved his hands up her thighs under her dress and put his mouth on to her breast. Sarah gasped. She eased her legs apart and reached down to touch Jack. She kissed the top of his bent head, murmuring his name, and then the phone rang.

'Shit...' Jack stopped and looked up. Sarah

moved but he said, 'No, leave it, it can't be anything...' He looked at her, at her worried face, then said, 'Don't move, I'll answer it and be right back.'

Sarah glanced down at her naked breasts. 'I'm hardly going anywhere like this, am I?'

Jack hurried to answer the phone and threw a smile back at her, fastening his trousers as he went. Sarah stood where she was and waited. She waited for several minutes, then crept to the door to see what was going on. She heard the murmur of Jack deep in conversation, felt a stab of irritation and pulled her dress up, slipping her arms back into the straps. A few minutes more and he came back into the kitchen.

'What's up?'

'That was Graham. Apparently Lucie has gone off, just left with out telling anyone.'

'So?'

Jack frowned. 'She left a note for Janie.'

'So?'

'It says... "I know you loved him; sorry, sorry, sorry."'

Jack looked at Sarah. 'Oh shit,' she said.

'Exactly.'

Chapter Twenty-four

It was late when Marcus got in; he had been for a drink with a colleague and had gone on for a meal. He didn't know where Lucie was but he wasn't worried. Personnel had confirmed this afternoon that the DTI had looked at him and passed him over as not involved in Lucie's case. He was home and dry and if Lucie didn't want to play it his way then that was up to her.

He went straight into the bedroom and undressed. He felt hot and dirty; the City in the summer always made him feel like that. Then he ran a bath. He went into the living area naked, and slipped a CD into the player – they had speakers in the bathroom – and turned the volume up high. It was Elgar, slow and soothing. Back in the bathroom Marcus had a shave, then dimmed the lights and sprinkled some lavender oil into the bath water. It was a ritual he had most nights he was home and he stuck to it with precision. It was a ritual Lucie knew only too well.

When Marcus slipped into the bath, Lucie came down and headed towards the bedroom. She didn't make a sound. She saw his suit and shirt discarded on the floor, just as she had been discarded without any care or consideration, and she hated him. She hated the house, she hated her life but above all of that she hated Marcus.

470

She heard him humming to the music and she hated him with every living fibre in her body. She reached for the extension lead, pulled it to the door of the bathroom and switched the hairdryer on to low. Her heart was beating so fast that the vein on her neck was pulsing. She held her breath. One throw, just one throw into the water and the current would electrocute him. One step forward, one lunge through the door and one throw. He would never get out, it would send the voltage right through his body and fry his brain. She took a pace forward.

The phone rang.

Springing back, Lucie held her breath but the phone bleeped only twice and then went immediately on to answerphone. She switched off the dryer and heard Janie's voice.

'Lucie, please, please call me. I've got some news, some good news – please, please call me now Lucie, don't do anything silly, please, just pick up the phone if you're there or call me please...' The line went dead and Lucie pressed herself back against the wall. She caught a sob in the back of her throat and closed her eyes. Oh God, oh dear God, what was she doing? How had she come to this? She dropped to her knees and hugged her arms round her body 'I could have killed him,' she whispered, 'I nearly killed him...' The tears came uncontrollably and she had to bite back the sobs that rose in her chest. Trembling, she got to her feet and, leaving the hairdryer on the floor, made her way out of the bedroom, then out of the house. In the street she finally let herself cry. She stumbled to Alex's car, climbed in and bent double with the pain in her heart. She had lost everything, but much, much worse than that was the fact that for a few moments back there she had almost lost herself.

Janie looked at Sarah and said, 'I don't know if I can do it, Sarah. I'm sorry, I don't think I can agree.'

Roz lit a cigarette. 'Whether you agree or not, Janie, I think we should do it. If we don't then the bastard gets off scot free – doesn't he? Are you happy with that? Because I'm bloody well not.'

Janie rubbed her hands wearily over her face. 'Sarah? Are you sure you want to go through with it? Do you honestly think it will work?'

Sarah was pacing the floor. As soon as they had heard from Lucie, she had called a meeting. It was after midnight, but none of them seemed to realise the time or the fatigue that showed on all of their faces. They were at a point where nothing mattered except getting it straight. They also needed to talk. Talking was the only way forward. She stopped and turned.

'Jack seems to think it'll work and I trust him. Apart from which, let's face it, what have we got to lose?'

'But what if it does incriminate him; it'll presumably incriminate us as well?' Janie said.

'How can it do that? Who will ever know apart from us?'

'And if you don't call his bluff?' Janie asked. 'Will you go through with the threat?'

Sarah shrugged. He deserved it, by God he did, but where it would lead and to whom she didn't know and couldn't take the chance.

'Maybe.'

Janie shook her head. 'No,' she said, 'there must be another way. Perhaps if we talk to him, reason with him?'

'I think,' Roz said, getting to her feet, 'that we are all beyond reason at this point. I want revenge and I'm sure Sarah does too.' She yawned and stretched. 'I've got to get home, Sarah; I'm sorry but it's all catching up with me and I'm shattered.' She came across and kissed Sarah. 'I'm with you on this one. Do it, Sarah love, and do it tomorrow.' Sarah looked at Janie.

Janie closed her eyes for a moment. She didn't know about revenge, or about evening up the score; she just knew about pain and people getting hurt.

'No one will get hurt,' Sarah said, as if reading her mind.

Janie opened her eyes and returned Sarah's gaze. 'OK,' she said, 'I'm with you as well.'

Sarah let out a breath. 'Good.' But she didn't smile at all, her face was set in grim determination. 'I'll go and tell Jack. We'll need to get things sorted.' She headed out of the kitchen towards Jack's sitting room, then stopped and glanced over her shoulder.

'Tomorrow? We're agreed it's tomorrow?'

Janie nodded and Roz said, 'Yes, tomorrow. We do it while there's still the fire in us.'

It was decided. As Sarah had said, what did they have to lose?

Chapter Twenty-five

Jack woke Sarah up with a cup of tea. She had slept in his spare room – she hadn't wanted to, but she hadn't had the courage to say so. She sat up and rubbed her eyes and he said, 'We need to go over everything one last time, Sarah. Is that OK? Are you up to it?'

'Yes, that's fine. How're Jamie and Rory?'

'They're watching CBBC. They seem to be the best of friends.'

Sarah smiled. At least something has gone right, she thought, but she didn't say it. 'Right,' she said, 'I'll get up then.'

'There's a clean towel in the bathroom for you and I'll put the toast on.' He hovered by the door and Sarah willed him to say what he had to say. 'After today, Sarah,' he began.

'Yes?'

He coughed. 'I mean, once we get through it all, would you, erm, I mean, can we...'

She looked at him. 'Go to bed? Yes we can, Jack.'

He took a pace back and stared, then suddenly smiled. 'Oh, gosh, I was going to ask you if we could have dinner, but going to bed is fine.'

Sarah screamed and dived under the duvet. 'Oh God, oh God, this is so embarrassing, this is so awful ... I can't believe I said that, I...'

Jack came across and lifted a corner of the

474

duvet, looking under it at her. 'Just joking,' he said. 'Of course I was going to ask if we could...' He paused. 'Actually, I was going to say "cement our relationship", but going to bed is much more direct. It's what I meant anyway.' He dropped the duvet and walked out of the room. When Sarah emerged she was smiling.

Janie arrived with Katie at eight-thirty sharp to look after Rory and Jamie. Sarah and Jack were ready, the equipment was packed and Sarah was perfectly rehearsed. Jack spoke quietly to Janie while Sarah got the kids some drinks.

'As soon as you get my call, drive to the nearest phone box, ring the police and ask to be put through to CID. Tell them you think you can help with a road accident and say you saw a silver Mercedes – give the registration number, I've written it down there for you – purposely drive into a 2CV. Give the time and date, both are written down here too, and say you don't wish to be identified. OK? They'll trace the call but it'll be a public phone so you should be safe. Then get back here and be ready to go when we arrive.'

'Right.'

Jack smiled. 'And don't worry about it, OK?'

'OK.'

'What time will Roz be here?'

'As soon as she can. She's bringing Mel to help Graham with the kids.' Janie looked at him. 'You really think this is the right thing to do?'

Jack touched her arm. 'Yes, I do, but you don't have to come if you don't want to, Janie. I'm sure the others will understand.'

Janie shook her head. 'I do have to come,' she answered, 'they need my support. And besides, I started this so I should finish it, right?'

Jack nodded. 'Right.' He turned as Sarah came into the hall. 'OK, Sarah, let's go!' He opened the door for her and they left. Janie stood alone in the hall and watched them go. Everyone should get what they deserve, she thought, but boy, they rarely did.

Stan Gamley parked his car in the short-term car park at Gatwick airport as he always did and climbed out. A woman came across to him as he did so and said, 'Excuse me, sir, but I'm from the airport authority and I wonder if you could spare me a short amount of your time?'

Gamley shook his head. 'Sorry, love, I've got a plane to catch.'

'It's just five minutes and we're giving away free parking for up to five days in this car park as a reward. It's five minutes at the most, really.'

Gamley sighed. 'Will the free parking do for now? I don't know if I'll be back for a while.'

'I can give you a voucher for parking today and over the weekend. It's a saving of thirty pounds, sir.'

'All right, go on then.'

The woman smiled. 'Great! Thank you. If you wouldn't mind stepping towards the lifts, sir, the light's better there.'

Gamley went with the woman to the lift area and as soon as he moved off Jack crouched down at the back of Gamley's car and picked the lock on the boot. He raised it just high enough to get his hands inside and saw the combination lock on Gamley's case.

'Shit,' he muttered. He tried the catch anyway. It opened; Gamley hadn't locked it yet. Gently, Jack prised the lid off the suitcase just enough to see inside. Clothes. He dug his hands in and came across something smooth. He pulled. A wadge of money – fifty-pound notes, all neatly rolled – came out.

He smiled. 'Gotcha.' He pushed the case shut, clicked the boot down and crawled five cars along. Then he stood and went towards the lifts.

'I'll give you this,' the woman said to Gamley. She filled in a slip of paper. 'You can take this to the airport authority desk inside the terminal with your ticket and get your free parking.'

Gamley took the voucher and stuffed it into his pocket. 'That's all I do, is it?'

'Yes, sir, that's all.' She smiled, but Gamley had walked off. 'Thank you for your time, sir,' she called after him. 'Have a nice flight.'

Gamley collected his case from his car and headed towards departures. Jack, already inside the terminal, had just made his call to Customs and Excise. He stood out of view of the BA Channel Islands desk and watched as Gamley went to check in. Two Customs officials appeared before he'd even shown his ticket and asked him to accompany them to an interview room. Gamley protested but they insisted. One picked up his case and Jack smiled. He took out his phone and called Janie. 'Ring the police, Janie,' he said. 'One down, two to go.'

As he made his way back to his car, the woman

with the clipboard was waiting for him. 'Bloody nice work, Sarah,' he said. 'The case was stuffed with cash and Gamley is history.' He took her hand. 'Janie is calling the police as we speak, so hopefully that's Redfern taken care of.' He unlocked the car. 'Now that little bastard Marcus.' They both climbed in. 'Let's give him what he deserves.'

Bill Redfern was in a meeting when one of the secretaries knocked and put her head round the door. It was a high-level discussion on future development in West Sussex and he was just about to present his brief to the chairman and chief executive when she appeared. He had to stop mid-way through the opening lines of his presentation.

'Mr Redfern?' she said. 'I'm sorry to interrupt, but we've got someone from Crawley CID here and he'd like to talk to you.'

Redfern blinked, then frowned. 'Can't it wait? I'm just about to start my–'

'I think you should see to it, Bill,' the chief executive said. 'The presentation can wait.'

Redfern nodded and shuffled his papers back into his file. He left the meeting room and outside in the corridor met with two uniformed officers along with two men from CID.

'Mr William Redfern?'

'Yes.'

'I wonder if you'd be good enough to accompany us down to the station, sir. We are making enquiries into a road traffic accident on the seventeenth of July and we believe you might be able to help us with those enquiries.'

'I'm afraid I'm in the middle of a meeting and I shan't be finished until...' He broke off and glanced at the blank, cold face of the CID officer. Beyond him, through the plate-glass window, he saw a swarm of officers closing in on his car, parked, as always, just to the left of the chief executive's Jag. He closed his eyes for a moment, then he said, 'I'll just get my jacket.'

Marcus was more than surprised when he was told that Sarah Greg, Roz Betts and Janie Leighton were in reception. He hurried down hoping that they weren't there to make a scene.

'Ladies, good morning.'

'Hello, Marcus,' Janie said coolly. 'We need to talk, is there somewhere we can go?' He looked momentarily confused as he took in all three faces. Women united; it unnerved him. 'Oh, yes, erm...' He looked behind him at the girl on reception. 'Is there a meeting room free at all?' he asked.

She checked her book, then said, 'Meeting room three.'

'This way please...' Marcus opened the door for them and led the way up to the first floor where all the meeting rooms were. Once inside, he turned and said, 'I'm sorry for all this mess, I really am. If there's anything I can do to help, then please, let me know.'

'You could start by telling the truth,' Roz said.

'I'm sorry?' Marcus frowned. 'I don't understand, I...'

'Oh for God's sake, Marcus!' Janie snapped.

'Stop it, will you? This is me, Janie, your sister, remember? You can't bullshit me any longer, Marcus, I know what happened. We all know what happened, that it was you...' And despite her steely determination not to get upset, Janie had to stop and bite back the tears.

'Janie, this is ludicrous! What are you saying? Why on earth would I do something like that, why would I...'

Sarah interrupted him and said, 'You were the one who set this whole thing up, Marcus. You used Janie, Roz and me to further your own ends. We're not stupid, at least not any more. You pretended friendship, fed me information, so-called tips from Alex which were in fact all your own recommendations, given on the back of knowledge that you gleaned from Lucie, illegal knowledge, price-sensitive knowledge...'

Marcus stood shaking his head. 'I simply can't believe this!' He looked at Janie. 'Who told you this? Was it Lucie?'

Janie looked away.

'I thought so! You would rather believe a woman who deceived me, a woman who was sleeping with someone else, fucking around in her lunch hour, lying, cheating...' He spat the last two words out so vehemently that Janie jerked round to look at him. 'You would rather believe that slut than me, your own brother. How could you, Janie? For Christ's sake get a life!'

Janie took a sharp breath in and Sarah stepped forward. 'You knew about Lucie's affair, you've known about it for months and this was your revenge, your own clever little nemesis, wasn't it,

Marcus? Well, it didn't work, it didn't succeed. We know what you've been doing and we're going to talk to the DTI about it.'

Marcus suddenly laughed. He leant forward towards Sarah. 'And I thought you had at least a modicum of intelligence, Sarah. I mean, I never thought you were very bright, but this is truly pathetic. How will you talk to the DTI? What will you say? You have proof of this ridiculous accusation, do you?'

Sarah clenched her fist. The temptation to hit him was so strong that she had to force her arm against her side.

'Yes, I have proof, Marcus. On my phone bill I have a call that I made to your office. I made a few notes before I called, look...' Sarah opened her notebook. 'It was at the time of the Sarasota deal and I rang to ask you what the chances were of Sarasota being taken over. You said, and I've written it down, you said, "a very strong chance, upwards of ninety per cent".' She showed him her notes. 'There's no way you'd make that sort of comment if you didn't actually know that the company was going to be taken over and, like you say, I'm not very bright so I'd have to write everything down. The call will have been taped, Marcus, and I have the number in my pocket for Janice Stimpson's direct line. She's the woman at the Stock Exchange who started the investigation.'

Marcus was very still. Sarah took her phone bill out and showed it to him. 'Recognise the number?' she said. 'It's even got the date there.' He took the bill and stared at it. 'All I have to do is ring Ms Stimpson and ask her to check your calls.'

Marcus screwed the phone bill up into a ball and stuffed it into his pocket. 'This is rubbish. I never said that, I wouldn't be that stupid.'

'No? Well, even the clever ones make mistakes, Marcus, we all do.'

He stepped back. 'You're lying, Sarah, the DTI will have checked my tapes. This is fantasy, you're making it all up...'

Sarah shook her head and smiled. Thinking about it later, she didn't know how she'd managed that piece of acting, but she smiled and said, 'I might be, but are you prepared to take the risk? If you're completely innocent you will be. Let's ring her now. If you think the DTI has already heard your phone tapes, then let's call Janice Stimpson and check.'

Suddenly Marcus took another pace back and felt for the table behind him. He gripped it and Sarah could see that his knuckles were white. He turned to Janie.

'Give me a minute with Sarah,' he said. 'Please?'

Janie glanced at Roz and they moved towards the door. 'We'll be right outside, Sarah,' Roz said. 'Shout if you need anything.'

They closed the door and Marcus looked at Sarah. 'What d'you want, Sarah?' he asked. 'Money? Presumably, seeing as you're so clever, you already know that they won't be prosecuting you. In fact, I'm amazed it got as far as it did. They can't pin anything on you or anyone else. It's all speculation; there's no proof.'

'They can pin something on you, Marcus,' Sarah said.

'How much?' Marcus asked. 'How much do you want?'

'It's not about money, Marcus. I want you to tell me the truth to start with and then we'll negotiate.'

'The truth? What do you need with the truth?'

She looked at him. 'It would help, that's all.'

Marcus sat down. He dropped his head in his hands and stayed like that for some time. It was a relief; to finally be able to talk was a relief and when he looked up Sarah could see that on his face. 'The truth is that I did it to frighten Lucie. I did it to get back at her, to make her hurt in the way that I hurt. I did it to get that little bastard she'd been putting out to.' He returned her stare. 'Revenge. Plain and simple. I did it to get my own back.' He shook his head. 'I knew they couldn't get the investment club and I was pretty sure they couldn't get Lucie. I wouldn't have been sorry to see Mr Stanton hung though, smug fuckwit.'

Sarah pulled out a chair and sat down as well. She thought she would feel angry, upset, even tearful, but all she felt was pity. Marcus had lost it; he was pathetic. She was glad now that Jack had insisted on the microphone, on taping it all. It reassured her to know that she had a witness to all this.

Marcus said, 'So what do you want, Sarah?'

And Sarah said, 'I want your time, Marcus, and your skill and your expertise.' She faced him. 'I want you to do something that isn't for you, something that's for someone else.' She sighed. 'Though God knows if you'll manage it. Personally, I don't hold out much hope.'

Janie and Roz were waiting for Sarah out in the corridor and when she left the meeting room they turned to look at her.

Roz raised an eyebrow and Sarah shrugged. They stood in silence for a few moments, then, linking arms, together they walked towards the lifts.

'Is it over?' Janie asked.

'Yes, in one way,' Sarah answered. She took a deep breath and let it out slowly. She shook her head. 'And in another,' she said, 'it's only just beginning.'

DECEMBER

Chapter Twenty-six

Sarah put the phone down and underlined the note on the pad, then she shouted up the stairs and opened the front door. Jack appeared at the top of the stairs tying his tie and Rory was right behind him.

'Come on,' Sarah said, 'we're going to be late if you don't get a move on.'

Jack came down, two stairs at a time, and grabbed his blazer off the back of the chair in the kitchen.

'Who was on the phone?' he asked.

'It was an order for six Christmas terracotta urns. I said you'd suggest the plants and that they started at sixty-five pounds each.' Rory came down and Sarah said, 'You look great, Rory. Have you got your microphone aid?'

He smiled and patted the belt round his waist under his sweater.

'I also said you'd ring back this afternoon,' Sarah went on. 'They're for a party and she wants them next week.'

Jack came into the hall and kissed Sarah on the forehead. 'Thanks, SG.' He then looked at Rory 'All wired up?'

'Yup.'

Jack ruffled his hair. 'Top man. Where's Jamie?'

'Here.'

'You look smart. Good boy! Let's go then.'

Sarah led them out of the cottage and glanced behind her at the house that was now her home. She smiled. She had an awful lot to smile about.

Roz was driving, Graham was combing his hair in the passenger seat, Kitty was fighting with Oliver in the back and Justin was singing loudly as they pulled out of the drive of Chadwick Farm. Miraculously, they were on time.

'Stop a minute, love,' Graham said. 'The Gordens are up the road.'

Roz ground her teeth. 'Graham, we haven't got time.'

'Just slow down and I'll wind the window down.' He looked at her. 'Come on, love, all's well that ends well.'

Roz slowed and Graham wound the window down. When the deal with Glover Homes had fallen through, Graham had made the Gordens a good offer for their land but they wouldn't sell. It had enraged Roz, she'd thought it was petty and mean, but Graham was sanguine about the whole affair. He knew the Gordens didn't want the farm on their doorstep and besides, after buying the Major a drink in the pub, he had secured the promise of first refusal should the Gordens ever want to move.

'Good morning,' Graham called to the Major as they passed by. 'A lovely cold crisp one, isn't it?'

Cecil Gorden turned. 'Hello there, family Betts. Yes, it's a glorious morning. How about coming over for a drink later, just before lunch?'

Surprised by the invitation, Roz turned and

Daphne waved. Graham glanced at her. 'We'd love to,' he said. 'What about midday?'

'Perfect,' the Major declared and finally Roz smiled.

'See you later then,' Graham said. Roz waved and they drove off. As he wound the window up, Roz said, 'Wonders will never cease.' And Graham smiled. 'If you'll let them,' he replied.

Janie hung back by the front door while Katie and Andrew waited in the car. She glanced across at them and Andrew pointed to his watch.

'Tell Mummy we're going to be late if she doesn't hurry up,' he said to Katie, but just as she was climbing out of the car the post van pulled up and Janie slammed the front door shut, taking the mail from the postman.

She climbed into the car, looked through the letters and found the one she had been waiting for. She glanced at Andrew 'Open it,' he said. She nodded but still held the envelope, too frightened of what it might or might not contain to open it. Andrew took it from her. 'Shall I do it?'

'Yes.'

He ripped it open and pulled out the letter. He read, then without looking at Janie said, '"Dear Janie and Andrew, it is with great pleasure that I am writing to inform you that you have been accepted on to our foster programme and I will be in contact soon to arrange an initial meeting with our foster team."' He looked at Janie. 'It goes on...' He stopped, then reached over to hug her.

'What's the matter, Mummy?' Katie asked. 'Why are you crying?'

Janie pulled away from Andrew, took a handkerchief out of her bag and blew her nose. 'I'm crying because I'm happy, darling,' she said. She looked over her shoulder and smiled. 'We've had a letter from the social services to say that we can foster a child.'

'Wow,' Katie said.

'My sentiments exactly,' Andrew added.

The church was packed for the Ledworth House Christmas service. It was an annual occasion; the choir sang, the boys read and the headmaster spoke about the year for the school. It was on the last day of term and this morning, Saturday, December the thirteenth, Sarah sat in the front pew next to Jack and Jamie, Roz and all the Betts family and Janie, Andrew and Katie. Rory sat with the rest of the boys down at the front, ready to sing and nervously awaiting his reading.

They sang the first carol and then the headmaster stood up to speak. He took the lectern and Janie squeezed Andrew's hand.

'It is with great pleasure that I welcome you all here this morning for our Christmas service,' he began. 'But it is with particular warmth that I welcome our guests, the Betts family and the Leighton family, all of whom have been instrumental in setting up, for the first time in the history of Ledworth House, a trust fund, a substantial sum...'

'Half of his bonus,' Sarah whispered to Jack.

'Donated by Mr Marcus Todd, one of the City's top analysts, and invested in the stock market under his own expert management. The interest

490

from this fund will pay for two assisted places in the school for the coming academic year.' There was a round of applause and Sarah caught Roz's eye. She winked.

Later, outside the church, Sarah, Roz and Janie stood together, as they had stood many months earlier outside school.

'There'll be no trips to London to catch up on the latest fashions,' Roz warned. 'No turning up to school looking as if you've just had your hair done...'

Sarah threw a look at Roz that warned her she was going too far; things had changed between all of them but old rivalries die hard. 'I mean,' Roz said, 'that life with toddlers is very different.'

'Good,' Janie replied. 'Different I can handle, it's staying the same that frightens me.'

Sarah squeezed her arm. 'Well, I think it's great. Good on you, Janie, and good on Andrew too. Have you any idea when you'll start fostering?'

'No, lots of hoops to jump through first.'

'Talking of jumping through hoops,' Roz said, 'to coin a phrase, Janie.' They all smiled. 'How's Marcus? I notice he declined the invitation to come today.'

'He's all right,' Janie said. 'Happier, I think, than he was.' She frowned. How could she not defend him; despite everything he was her brother. 'Actually, he's done a good job on the fund, he's increased it by two hundred per cent.'

Roz almost quipped, legally? But she held her tongue; for once she held her tongue and just smiled.

Jack joined the women and took Sarah's hand. 'Shall we decamp for coffee?'

'Good idea.'

'Heard from Lucie?' he asked Janie as they walked off towards the cars. Janie nodded. She didn't want to talk about the past. She now had a future and she resented all this remembrance. She said, 'Lucie is in Africa at the moment, working for Oxfam. She sent me a letter the other day. She's...' What could Janie say? Lucie was bitter and angry and full of recriminations. It wasn't a letter, more a diatribe on Marcus, but she didn't say any of that; pride wouldn't let her. 'She's fine,' Janie finished. There are some things, she thought, that you never get past, some things that almost destroy you and she knew that she was thinking about herself as much as Lucie. But she had got past it – in a way – and she had not been destroyed. She was lucky. They had all been lucky. The dream catcher, she realised, wasn't about catching dreams, but making sense of them.

The publishers hope that this book has given you enjoyable reading. Large Print Books are especially designed to be as easy to see and hold as possible. If you wish a complete list of our books please ask at your local library or write directly to:

Magna Large Print Books
Magna House, Long Preston,
Skipton, North Yorkshire.
BD23 4ND

This Large Print Book for the partially sighted, who cannot read normal print, is published under the auspices of

THE ULVERSCROFT FOUNDATION